COPPE

A Novel About the Copper Country Labor Strike in 1913

Donna Searight Simons

Empire Publishing
Macomb, Michigan
https://sites.google.com/site/copperempire

Published by
Empire Publishing
Macomb, Michigan
https://sites.google.com/site/copperempire/

ISBN 10: 1482656698
ISBN 13: 9781482656695

Printed in the United States of America.

ACKNOWLEDGEMENTS

I would like to thank the following people for their contributions to this novel:

Carol Searight, for her tireless editing expertise over many years and for believing in the book.

Frank Searight, for his editorial assistance and for introducing me to the Keweenaw in the first place.

Janet Searight, for her unfailing support in my dreams.

Ron Simons, for his love and support.

Donna Winters, for her advice on writing and publishing a novel.

Jim Floriani, for his technical assistance and support. Also, for allowing the use of the song titled, "Thirty First Level Blues". His father, the late Vladimir "Lado" Floriani, wrote the melody and first verse when he worked in the Calumet & Hecla mine, Ahmeek #3, in 1936. Jim wrote the last two verses and added them to the song during the 1970's.

And to the late John "Cousin Jack" Foster — his love and enthusiasm for the Keweenaw were a true inspiration.

Chapter 1

December 24, 1913
Red Jacket, Michigan

Marie Weyburn reattached a fallen Christmas bow to the paneling, thankful that the women's auxiliary agreed with her suggestion to host the party at Italian Hall. She wanted this occasion to be extra special, especially in the midst of a five-month labor strike. Many of the children and their parents were already upstairs, enjoying the merry festivities.

Her fingers straightened the velvety ribbon with precision as if Mrs. Claus herself would be one of the four hundred guests expected. She stepped back for a moment and admired her work. Red bows with green centers stretched along the paneling to the top of the staircase.

Satisfied with her work, Marie lifted the sides of her dress—just enough so the hem didn't touch the steps—and headed for the auditorium. She couldn't help her outstretched hand that wanted to primp the bows once again, but Richard, her sixteen-year-old son, stopped her as he flew down the stairs like an avalanche, nearly pinning his mother against the wall.

He called out, "Back in half an hour, Ma."

"Hold on, Mister." Marie pounded the stairs all the way down to the landing. Her tone was a motherly scold. "You're supposed to perform your Christmas play soon for the children, so just where do you think you're headed?"

Richard swept his arms toward the door to emphasize his need for escape. "Ma, it's so noisy upstairs. I need to sort out some things before the play."

She had never understood her creative son. "No. Go back upstairs."

"Ma, I'll be back in a few minutes."

Marie sighed at his plea. "You have five minutes."

Richard's lips pecked her on the cheek. "Thanks, Ma," he said and yanked the door open for a brief escape. A gust of chilly air hit Marie's face when Richard shut the door.

Marie mentally rehearsed all of the tasks that still needed to be completed. She bent her fingers one at a time as if reviewing a checklist. *I'll take the cookies out of the oven soon, and then set out another punch bowl. . .* She was so lost in thought that she was startled when a hand gripped her shoulder.

Marie jumped. "Oh, Paul." She held a hand to her glistened cheek while the ends of her full lips curled into a frown. "You gave me a start."

"I'm leaving for awhile. Probably head to Vairo's." Paul said.

"What? And miss Richard's play?"

"I'm not in the Christmas spirit this year, Marie."

Marie huffed her disapproval. Vairo's saloon was next door, just feet away from where she and Paul stood. Paul was drinking too much lately, but what could she really do to stop her husband?

"When his play begins, why don't you thump a broomstick on the floor a few times?" Paul compromised. "Since I'll be at Vairo's, I'll hear your signal and know to come upstairs."

"I'll try to remember that, Paul." She found it difficult to hide the sarcasm.

He gently reached for her elbow. "Marie," he said in his most loving tone, "you did a tremendous job here. The children are having a wonderful time upstairs."

Marie curtly nodded. "Thank you, Paul." Her words sounded forced. "I wanted this to be a Christmas party to remember."

2

She felt the tickle of Paul's moustache when he leaned to kiss her, but Marie turned away. "Pick us up at 5 o'clock."

"All right, Marie."

* * *

Paul Weyburn could have entered Vairo's from the side door that connected Italian Hall and the saloon, but he needed fresh air. He stepped outside of Italian Hall, leaving his coat unbuttoned, since it was unusually warm for Michigan's Upper Peninsula during the Christmas season. In fact, only tiny patches of snow were pocketed on street corners, resembling an unfinished painting.

He walked across the street and leaned against a lamppost, facing Italian Hall. Paul lazily stared at the two-story building and tried to forget about Marie and the labor strike. Beneath the building sign "Societa Mutua Beneficenza Italiana" was the auditorium that occupied the entire second floor. Housed underneath were Vairo's and the Great Atlantic and Pacific Tea Company.

Paul watched Marie's rounded figure perched under Italian Hall's arched entrance, ushering children inside. She scowled at him, and then shut the door. Could he ever set things right again with their 21-year marriage?

He decided it was time for a drink. Before Paul could cross the street, though, a parade of men marched along Seventh Street in front of Paul. The vocal band of strikers each held a sign as they picketed and chanted, "Two man drill, two man drill!" as if the town of Red Jacket would comprehend. Most of the townspeople would have understood, but it was Christmas Eve, so the strikers' bitter shouts fell on deaf ears. Paul sighed, tired of the five-month-old strike. It would have to end soon.

As the strikers passed by, one of the men motioned to Paul to join their demonstration, but he shook his head as he watched the remaining protesters disappear around the corner.

Paul was relieved to avoid picketing duty. He planted his body against the lamppost once again, this time watching a huddle of eight men and women gather in front of the alley next to Italian Hall. He listened to the group sing, "O Come All Ye Faithful", their harmonic voices growing stronger with the refrain. An elderly man stood in front of the group, swinging his frail, bony arms as if he were conducting a symphony. When they finished their song, Paul applauded and smiled at the animated conductor. While he wasn't in the Christmas spirit, the song made him feel somewhat better.

Paul called out "Merry Christmas" to the carolers, and then walked across the street. He entered Vairo's and found the saloon dark with men sitting in groups at tables. Most of the regulars were at home or enjoying the party upstairs. As he walked past a row of moose heads displayed above the mantle, he was about to select a stool next to a lone customer sitting at the bar when he stopped himself. It was Cece.

Cece's head turned and his eyes blazed a steely gray. No doubt, the two men were still enemies.

Paul chose a stool at the opposite end of the bar, as far away as possible from his former best friend. While he waited for the bartender to appear, he snuck a peek at Cece's scraggly salt and pepper beard. The burly miner looked even more unkempt than usual.

The stale air of cigars made Paul wince and he almost wished that he had joined his family upstairs. But he needed a drink.

The portly bartender finally approached the counter. Paul motioned to him. "Brandy for me, please." He snapped his suspenders into place and noticed the looseness. None of his clothes seemed to fit anymore with all the weight he had lost. He appeared frail, as if he had never spent his life working in a copper mine. On the other hand, Cece's Paul Bunyon-type build told most everyone he was a miner. Cece was hunched over the counter, staring into an empty shot glass.

4

Paul strained to listen to the cheery hum of voices one floor above and hoped to hear Marie's broomstick soon, but felt the air crackle with tension from Cece instead. The bartender handed Paul his brandy, looked at the ceiling and commented in a thick Italian accent, "Glad to-a hear some-a happiness up-a-tere. I tink it balance outta rough time you strikers have, don't you tink?"

Paul nodded and sipped the liquor. It had been months ago when he and the other miners had jobs and the means to provide for their families. Now, his house was falling apart from disrepair, there was little food to live on, and the miners' hope for settling the long strike had diminished.

And he had lost his best friend.

Cece slapped the counter with his gigantic hand. "Another forty-rod for me."

"Coming right-a up, Ce Ce." The bartender set aside his wet rag and poured the liquor into the shot glass Cece held.

"Not Ce Ce," he growled. "The name is Cece." Muttering under his breath, "It rhymes with peace, which I haven't had in five months."

The bartender laughed as he stored a bottle of liquor underneath the cabinet. "I was-a only joking, but I-a heard someone say your name was-a Ce Ce."

Cece emptied the shot glass, exhaling loudly. Paul hated the silent treatment Cece was giving him, so he concentrated on the clapping and cheering that rang from above at Italian Hall, the revelry so loud that it could be heard through the saloon ceiling. Even the subdued men had to smile.

"Wish I could go upstairs for a piece of cake. Getting around to meal time," said Cece, patting his large, round stomach for effect.

The bartender tucked his chin into cupped hands. "Just-a climb ta stairs and-a grab some-ting to eat."

"Anti-strikers ain't welcome up there," Cece retorted.

5

Paul looked at his former friend and noticed his cold stare. "Don't start, Cece." He matched the gruff man's stare, just waiting for him to initiate an argument. Cece, however, remained silent.

The bartender interrupted, easing the tension. "Anotor drink?" Paul waved his hand, dismissing the bartender's offer.

Suddenly, the ceiling seemed to jump.

The bartender squinted. "What's-a going on up-a tere?"

"It's just Marie," said Paul. "I told her to thump a broomstick on the floor when Richard's play begins."

Cece shook his head and glanced at the jiggling lamp above. "Too crowded upstairs."

Then, the men heard distant cries. "Fuoco!" "Palo!"

The bartender pointed to the ceiling. "Did you-a hear somebody a-yell 'fire'?"

"C'è un fuoco di sopra!"

"Tämä rakennus on tulessa!"

"Fire!"

At that moment, the men heard feet pounding down the stairs next door to them. Paul got off the stool and ran through the adjoining side door of the saloon and stood in the Italian Hall vestibule. Fire. The cry had been unmistakable. He went to the stairs and what he saw made goose pimples rise from his pale skin. Men and women, but mostly children, were piled on top of one another at the stairwell.

Paul shouted, "What's going on?"

Screams of children and their mothers and fathers wrenched the air.

Voices cried out even louder in broken English. "Fire!"

"Help us!"

"In God's name, get us out!"

Paul desperately wanted to provide assistance. He saw a little girl sandwiched between other bodies. He yanked on a little girl's hand, but couldn't free her. In the meantime, the pile of bodies grew higher as people threw themselves on top of each other, frantic to escape the building. "Stop. You can't get out this way. Go back inside!" he shouted. The desperate cries continued.

"What's-a going on, Paul?" yelled the bartender, his eyes practically bulging out of its sockets.

"Run to the firehouse and get help," Paul ordered, and then he tried tugging at another arm, but to no avail. Bodies were packed like sardines. Children's screams for help began to fade. People gasped for air, and then only muffled cries could be heard. The entangled bodies were quickly being asphyxiated. It was no use. Paul couldn't free anybody from the bottom of the stairs. He somehow had to get to the top.

He ran from the vestibule. Outside, masses of people had gathered on the street, sidewalk and around the building. Paul knew there was no other entrance to Italian Hall. He had to get to the fire escape at the side of the building – in the alley.

Paul yelled at the crowd, "Move!" He used his body to muscle people away until he reached the narrow alley. Toward the back, he saw a throng of partiers running down the fire escape stairs.

"Save my boy!" a woman screamed. Paul looked up to the second story. A young mother banged her fist against the glass. Her attempts to escape, however, seemed futile.

Finally, the young mother gripped a chair and rammed it against the pane. Crack. The window, incredibly, resisted the blow.

"Keep trying!" Paul yelled up to the woman.

The mother struck repeatedly until the glass shattered. Small shards flew down, some of them nicking Paul's face. She began to lower her son from the window. "Catch him!" she cried, then let go of her child.

The tot landed square in Paul's arms and he clutched the screaming child to his broad chest.

"Help is on the way," cried an elderly man. Paul instantly recognized him as the bony-armed conductor of the carolers and shoved the toddler into the old man's arms.

"Take him," Paul cried out, "I have to save my family!" Paul tried to move closer to the fire escape, but it was no use. The panicked masses pushed him away from the alley. He ended up again in front of Italian Hall.

Fire engine sirens blared their alarms through screams of terrified onlookers.

Paul tried to shove his way between people to reach the arched entrance, but he couldn't get through the crowd. "Marie," he cried, "kids. I'll save you!"

Chapter 2

Paul Weyburn adjusted the sides of his mining cap, careful not to touch the flame emitting from the carbide lamp attached on top. As he walked along the drift, a flickering shadow on the cave wall reminded him of a moving picture show until he looked closer and saw that it was only himself. The light beam danced around the copper crevices as if something important were going to happen.

It was a special day, after all. Paul was sure he was getting promoted.

Warm, dusty air clogged his nasal passages, reminding Paul to return to work. While he plodded along Copper Empire's 31st level with only limited vision from his lamp, Paul thought about the miners' complaints that grew with each day and knew he would have to speak with Peterman about more than just his promotion.

He could almost hear the miners' stern voices again from earlier that morning.

"Paul, when's Peterman gonna give us more money?"

"Why do we have to work with that widowmaker?"

"Can we work in pairs again? I'm scared for my life down here."

"Are we ever gonna get a third shift?"

"When is Peterman gonna hire a new trammer?"

"We need more help down here!"

The ear-splitting hammering sounds from the drills nudged Paul back to work. With each step he took through the blackness of the drift, the squeals of drill bits chewing through the rock became louder. Finally, he came upon his best friend's bulky shadow. Cecil McAllister's frame shook with the vibration of a 150-pound drill penetrating the rock wall.

Paul stayed a safe distance behind and watched Cece use the one-man drill — nicknamed widowmaker by the miners — to carve out the last hole. Supported by tall steel posts, the drill was powered by air compression and was difficult to handle — it was used by only the most experienced men.

The machine drilled deep into the copper-laden rock at a steep angle, creating a blanket of dust on Cece. Finally, when Cece finished the chore, he coughed up phlegm, and then gave a labored sigh. He took a rag from his pant pocket and wiped sweat off his forehead. It was always too warm on the 31st level.

Cece turned around. His carbide lamp shined on Paul's face. "Made eight holes today," said Cece. "Hard to believe we used to do only half that."

Paul nodded, carefully setting down his blasting supplies. "Miners are expected to do more these days."

"When are Peterman's demands going to end?"

Instead of answering the question, Paul said, "I'm getting ready to blast. I'll see you outside."

But Cece wouldn't give up. "Shoot, Paul. You get the same pay as all of us, even though you're more than a miner. You're the mining captain too, even if Peterman won't call you one. Things have gotta change."

"It's honest work, Cece. It keeps my family fed and a generous roof over our heads." Paul was referring to the boarding home that he and his wife operated a few miles away from Red Jacket. Cece was one of many boarders who resided with them.

"Plain as this copper piece, you should be called a mining captain and be paid like one," said Cece, tossing a nugget against the wall.

10

Paul warmly patted his friend's back. "Peterman told me Copper Empire didn't make enough profit to warrant paying a captain's wage."

Cece tilted his head, aiming the light from the carbide beam at Paul's face. "Speaking of the devil, have you heard from Peterman?"

Paul turned away from the light. "No."

"This catacomb's been buzzin' since sunup."

"Yeah, I know. Just today some have asked me about a raise. . ."

"Oh, bull, Paul. You know the real talk. You gotta find out now if Peterman is gonna jump you to engineer."

Paul shrugged. "I can wait a while longer."

"I can't," Cece blurted out. "When you become the engineer, it'll be safer down here."

"I'll certainly do my best as engineer, if I'm promoted."

"Some fool miners even been taking bets." Cece humphed. "Day shift bettin' the late shift."

"What are they wagering?"

"Loser works the winner's Saturday shift for a month."

Paul laughed out loud. "What are my odds, Cece?"

"Day shift's bettin' you're the new engineer."

Paul tapped Cece's back again and chuckled. "I'm flattered this shift has such faith in me."

"Even Lowell would be proud of you."

Paul frowned. He hadn't heard his father's name mentioned in years.

Cece cleared his throat a couple of times. "So go talk to Peterman. Ain't you curious?"

Paul fibbed. "Whatever happens is fine."

"Bull, Paul. You gotta be the new engineer. We need help down here."

Paul sighed. "I've got to finish this job first. Anyway, my first priority when I speak with him is to encourage safer working conditions down here."

Cece snorted. "Peterman don't have the brains of a peacock. Might as well skip the other talk and just get your promotion."

"The mine will still be here tomorrow, even if I'm not promoted. Why are you so concerned?"

Cece grumbled, "Working more Saturdays if you don't get promoted."

Paul chuckled. Cece grunted as he lifted the drill off the post, and then laboriously walked away with the machine. Paul watched Cece's shadow on the mine wall get smaller and smaller, and then disappear altogether. He picked up his blasting supplies, and then shined his carbide lamp on the eight holes Cece had just drilled. Paul inserted the dynamite into each hole and arranged the blasting caps.

With the explosives in place, he wiped the sweat from his forehead, and then lit everything. "Fire in the hole," Paul yelled to warn anyone in earshot of the impending explosion. While the detonating fuse neared its target, he dashed around the corner and waited.

Boom! The sound of shattering rock thundered throughout the drift. "One," Paul counted out loud while he thought about his father. When was the last time he saw Lowell? Why did Cece mention him? Three more blasts pounded his ears. Paul figured he hadn't seen his father since early '92.

As he silently counted out the remaining explosions, he thought about his father and remembered the advice given many years ago. Lowell Weyburn's baritone voice had ordered him to return to the Michigan Mining School, a college located in nearby Houghton, to become an engineer. *No, Paul* rationalized, *I wouldn't be married to Marie or have my four children if I had heeded all my father's wishes.* On the other hand, he wouldn't be estranged from his head-strong father if only he had found a way to compromise. And he'd be a respected engineer, instead of an overworked miner with little worth to the company.

Paul crept around the corner when he was satisfied everything had detonated properly, and then made his way through the tunnels. He walked around the first bend of the drift, the twists of the tunnel leading him right and left, left and right. Soon he would hold a position of importance within Copper Empire, Paul thought optimistically. And maybe his father would even speak to him again.

Suddenly, a dark-haired, teen-aged boy bumped into him. "Mr. Peterman will be likin' a word with you, Mr. Weyburn," the boy said.

*   *   *

Sam Huston rode inside the Lake Superior Limited train, his skinny frame sprawled across two hard seats that jumped in harmony with the coach's wheels upon the steel rails. Worn out from the northbound journey to Red Jacket, his eyelids struggled to stay open. He managed to lift open one eye and was glad that he did, because the rolling, tree-lined hills of Michigan's Upper Peninsula passed by his window.

As the train wound around sharp curves, Sam raised himself to a sitting position and scooted closer to the soot-dotted window. More alert, he drew in his breath at the panoramic views of Lake Superior, the water sparkling as if it had been sprinkled with sapphires. The view was almost worth the price of leaving South Carolina. Almost.

"Deed you hefe a good sleep?" a female voice asked, interrupting Sam's thoughts.

Sam spun around to find Mrs. Karlsson, the kindly Swedish woman he had conversed with since Detroit. Her pudgy hand offered a pastry.

"Here, Meester Huston. For you."

"Ma'am, I appreciate it," Sam said, trying to wave away Mrs. Karlsson's generous offer. He remembered how an attendant had sold food between the aisle hours ago. "But we'll be arrivin' in Red Jacket soon. I'll find my supper there."

Mrs. Karlsson's jaw was set as solid as the train seats' uncomfortable wooden backing. She grabbed Sam's clenched fist, forced it open, and then stuffed the clothed offering into his palm. She leaned close so only he could hear her words.

"Meester Huston, pleese take this. It is my onlee way to repay yur kindness. I vish you luck een this Copper Country." Mrs. Karlsson patted him on the shoulder, and then crossed back to her seat, her puffy skirt swishing against the aisle.

Sam nodded and smiled. He had met Mrs. Karlsson only two days ago. She and her three children had looked impoverished, so he had dug into his coat pocket and retrieved coins so she could buy food. Sam's Southern hospitality extended to everyone, especially when it came to women traveling without their husbands.

He glanced across the aisle and caught Mrs. Karlsson's watchful eye. Better eat the pastry, lest he hurt the woman's feelings. He bit into the crusty, golden-covered mound and was pleased to taste a meat filling with potatoes and carrots. He polished off the remainder and stuffed the cloth into his traveling bag.

Playful sounds of youngsters turned Sam's head from the window. It was difficult to concentrate with childish prattle buzzing around his ears; nevertheless, he thought about his mission in Michigan's Upper Peninsula: to begin a new life for himself. It wouldn't be easy.

Sam looked about the train and marveled once again how it was mostly full with immigrant women and children anticipating a long-awaited reunion with husbands and fathers who already resided in Red Jacket. He had learned from broken pieces of conversations with some of the passengers that they had eagerly left their home countries of Austria, Finland, Croatia, England and Ireland in hopes of improving their lives.

An uneasiness settled in Sam's stomach. He was a foreigner, too. Maybe not from another country, but a newcomer from Charleston would likely turn some heads at the train depot when they heard his Southern accent.

Suddenly, something whacked the side of Sam's head. As he rubbed his chestnut brown hair, he turned around to see what hit him. A young boy picked up his red ball and tried scuttling away.

Sam laughed out loud, "It's all right. No need for alarm."

As luck would have it though, the boy's mother had turned her gaze from the window just in time to witness the mishap and grabbed her son's arm to reprimand him in her Irish brogue. "Mind yer manners."

"That's okay, ma'am," said Sam as he stretched his skinny arms and legs. His two-piece brown and black-checked wool suit was rumpled from the long train ride. "I love kids," he said. "What's yer name, little fella?"

The child looked at his mother for approval to talk to the man with the funny accent, but he didn't get any. "Cum alon," the mother said as she tugged on her son's arm. "Oi don wan you blatherin' wi strangers."

A sharp pain of loneliness struck Sam's heart. He closed his eyes ever so tightly and pictured his life in South Carolina — a life he had left just a week ago. His cousin, Clarkston Huston the third, had told him fantastic tales of a wild empire full of copper and wealth in Michigan's Upper Peninsula. It would be a stark change from his roots in the Deep South. Sam could still remember what his kin and friends had to say before his departure.

"Sam, ya can't live up North. You'll become an outsider."

"Minin'? Sam, have ya gone crazy? Ya want to work in the mines?"

"They have winter nine months outta the year."

"I need a change," Sam had told them.

"Yer goin' to be mighty lonely, Sam."

"The Yanks'll never welcome you."

"Yeah. And what would Millie think?"

Sam mercifully slipped into a daydream and remembered a time, not so long ago, when he had felt at peace and in control of his future. He recalled his small house with the parcel of land directly behind. It had been a typical day in Charleston with the hot sun beaming down on his back as he toiled away at his cotton farm. Sam put his basket down for a moment, stood up and stretched his aching arms. He glanced at the back of his house and noticed the door swinging open. His beloved Millie stepped outside and glanced at him with a radiant smile that could take the gloom out of anyone's day.

"Supper's almost ready," Millie yelled as she wiped her hands on her apron. "It's gonna be extra special tonight. Roast chicken and green beans."

Sam walked away from his crop and toward his one true love, careful not to touch her because of sweat dripping from his body. He gently kissed her on the cheek and stepped back. "Now don't ya work too hard just to feed this growin' belly," he warned, pointing at his flat stomach.

Millie smiled at his joke, turned on her heels and stepped to the house. She looked back to Sam for a moment and blew him a kiss.

Sam was certain he would never care for another woman as he did for Millie. . .

16

The train's whistle blew, shaking Sam out of his daydream. He looked out the window, and then slid the panel upward for a better view. The train was almost at the Calumet Station.   With his elbow, he leaned on the wooden ledge and watched horse carriages and a streetcar and even a motor vehicle maneuver about the town making deliveries or moving people from here to there. Sam watched the bustling people on the street, hustling in and out of stores, tending to business with shop owners, stopping for a drink at one of the town's numerous saloons, or waiting for a friend arriving on the train.

The locomotive stopped and immediately began to yield its cargo, pulling Sam into his new reality. He took his turn at the end of the jostling line, the aisle so crowded that passengers pushed to move it along.   Some of them bounded off the train in a rush and stepped off the platform to greet familiar faces and reunite with loved ones they perhaps had not seen in months or years. Others moved about more leisurely, looking for anyone familiar. Still others seemed not to know anyone or anything and had the open-eyed look of strangers.

Sam wasn't in any hurry. He allowed Mrs. Karlsson and her kin to depart the train ahead of him. Sam waved goodbye to them, glad that he knew at least one family in such a strange town. With his tattered bag, Sam stepped off the locomotive and momentarily wished he'd never left Charleston. It had been a fool idea, just like his friends had said.

"C'mon Sam," he mumbled to himself. "This is the change ya wanted. Now walk proud."

Traveling bag in hand, Sam strolled into town. With a cheery smile, he tipped his hat to a couple of women walking toward him. "Afternoon, ladies. A mighty perty day, ain't it?"

The women gave Sam a curt nod and continued walking. Sam shrugged off the cool reception. With a forced spring in his step and a toothy grin, he continued his investigation of the land of copper that was supposedly filled with such great promise. Suddenly, Sam stumbled backward when a series of muffled explosions shook the ground beneath his feet. He lost his bag and hat to the dusty ground.

A portly man wearing an apron bounded off the saloon's porch to help Sam reacquaint himself. "You must be new around here," the man said, handing the bag back to him.

"What in tarnation was that?" asked Sam.

"It's only a blast from the mines."

Sam chuckled heartily. "I shoulda known that," he said. "I was told to expect a region that sounds like a war zone."

"If you can't handle it," the pudgy man said, slapping a dusty hat back on Sam's head, "Get on that train and go back to wherever you came from."

Chapter 3

Paul left the shafthouse along with a crowd of miners who flocked to him like iron shavings to a magnet. They were eager to remind him of the poor working conditions and unfulfilled promises of pay raises, along with their hopes that Paul would be promoted to engineer.

It wasn't easy to shoo the men away. No matter which direction Paul turned, he bumped against a dusty mining jacket or a dirty pair of overalls. He usually enjoyed the miners' company, but this time he first wanted to hear Peterman's news. "If you'll excuse me, men, I need to meet with Mr. Peterman to discuss our labor issues. So go home and get a good supper. You'll find out the results tomorrow."

"Good luck, Paul."

"Yeah. We believe in you, Paul."

Paul managed to break away from the noisy farewells. To reach his boss, he only needed to walk next door to the red sandstone building. It had an expansive window pane directly in the center, dressed in brown linen curtains that looked as drab as a boring Sunday church sermon.

He formed a fist to knock on the door, but stopped when he noticed Peterman through the parted curtains. Mr. William Peterman sat in an oversized chair that threatened to swallow him, zipping through his dollar bills as if a greedy fly was likely to swoop down and carry some of it away. A tailored jacket hung neatly on a peg behind him, and his shirt sleeves were rolled up to his elbows, allowing him to work more efficiently.

Paul knew from years of experience to let his boss count money first, so he chose a nearby boulder to lean against. He admired the fiery red Keweenaw sunset while observing miners heading for home. Paul's jaw muscles tightened when he watched an elderly co-worker, too old to be toiling in the mines, making his way slowly along the road. The handle of an empty lunch pail dangled on his bony, wrinkled hand, swinging back and forth like a pendulum. Paul thought it a poignant example of what needed to be changed at Copper Empire.

In stark contrast, a young man passed the bony old miner in the opposite direction. He walked so fast that he kicked up dust behind him, causing the elderly man to stop and wheeze. The young stranger paid no mind and continued his frenzied pace toward Peterman's office. Paul thought there was something familiar about the boy, although he was sure he hadn't met him before. Nevertheless, Paul rose from the boulder and nodded at the young stranger.

"Are you here to see Mr. Peterman?" Paul asked.

The young man smirked. "You first."

Paul rapped on Peterman's door, then let himself in and closed the door, leaving the young man outside. He whipped off his mining hat before saying a word.

"Excuse me, Mr. Peterman."

"What?" Peterman asked, counting the last of his currency. "Oh, yes, Paul. What is it?"

"Pardon me, Mr. Peterman," Paul said, walking toward the mahogany roll-top desk where his boss sat. "One of the drill boys said that you wanted to see me."

"Yes, yes," his boss said. He stood up and walked to the window, snapping his fingers and motioning to the stranger outside.

The young man opened the door and walked to the general manager's side.

"I trust you are in high spirits today Paul," Peterman began, accompanied by phony laughter, "for I'd like to introduce my nephew, Russell Ubel." He affectionately put his arm around the young man's shoulders, like a father to a son.

"I just stepped off of the streetcar," Russell said with a boyish grin. "I'm now a graduate from the Michigan College of

Mines." This was the same college that Paul's father, Lowell, had demanded he attend when Paul was a teenager. At that time, it was known as the Michigan Mining School. Paul briefly attended that college for a semester, then disobeyed Lowell and dropped out for good.

Peterman said, "I've hired Russell to be Copper Empire's newest engineer."

A dull thud settled in Paul's stomach. How could his boss choose an inexperienced young man like Russell over his years of knowledge and respect for the copper mines?

Only two weeks ago, Copper Empire's last engineer had started and quit his job the same day. It was then that Paul confronted Peterman and asked to be considered for the vacant engineering job. Peterman had promised to consider it, and even wired Paul's credentials to the Board last week. Paul was sure he would get the job, and even tricked himself into believing that whatever happened was fine.

But Paul did care about losing the promotion. A mix of emotions, ranging from disappointment to anger, raged in Paul's mind. He had been a loyal and faithful Copper Empire employee for 13 years. He had never missed a day of work, and he always performed more duties than was required of a miner without extra pay. Since Copper Empire engineers usually quit their employment within just a few months, due to the poor working conditions as well as unsuccessfully dealing with Peterman's deceitful ways, Paul figured he would eventually be promoted to engineer, even without a college degree, as long as he worked hard, minded his own business, and didn't pester Peterman too much. He also figured, once he became engineer, that he could help solve some of Copper Empire's problems. He'd make conditions safer by demanding new equipment and more men. He'd also insist that the workers receive raises. Happy men are productive men, Paul reasoned, and labor and management would both win.

Paul knew that would never happen now. If Peterman's young, inexperienced nephew was anything like Peterman, the mine would probably become more dangerous to work in, and a raise in pay would be out of the question. His father was right. He should have gone to college. He failed the men, but worst of all, he failed Marie and the kids. What would they think when they found out that a kid beat him to the engineering job?

Paul remembered his manners and stuck his hand out toward Russell, promising himself to confront his boss later in private. "I'm Paul Weyburn."

Russell accepted the handshake. "I understand you were being considered for my position. I trust there are no hard feelings?"

Paul struggled to make his voice sound sincere. "Welcome to Copper Empire." He attempted to shake the boy's hand but was met with such a limp grip that he quickly let go and took a few seconds to study the new engineer. The ruddy cheeks on Russell made him look no older than Paul's oldest son. Scaling back the years even further was Russell's short build.

Peterman inspected the cuffs on his sleeve. "Paul is an expert in the mines, Russell," he said with confidence. "In fact, his grandfather was a mine owner in these parts many years ago."

Russell raised an eyebrow. "You don't say?"

"Yes," Paul said. "Flint Weyburn was highly respected in his time."

Russell cocked his head. "I dare say you should have inherited his copper mine?"

"I believe that's none of your affair," Paul said, trying not to scowl.

A gutsy chuckle escaped Peterman's throat. "Yes, yes. Mind your manners, Russell." He leaned close to his nephew's ear to tell him something private. Peterman lowered his voice, but Paul still heard every word. "Paul's father inherited most of the estate," said Peterman, chuckling, as if he had just revealed the world's best kept secret.

Paul clenched his fists to stifle his anger, but it wasn't working.

The obnoxious reign of words spewed from his boss's mouth like an eruption from a volcano. "This is even more interesting," he said, drawing his nephew closer to him. "Paul's father and I were roommates at Harvard," he said, squeezing Russell's shoulders. Peterman turned and looked directly at Paul. "How is he?" he asked. "I haven't seen Lowell since my last return to Boston in say, well over two years now."

Paul snapped, "My father and I do not correspond."

Peterman let go of his grip from Russell's shoulders, as if he were let down that Paul didn't take the bait to spar with him. "Oh, of course. I had quite forgotten."

Paul turned to Russell. "I'd like to discuss some things with your uncle. Please excuse us."

A grin formed on Russell's fresh features. "Of course. It will indeed be a pleasure working with you, Paul." Before Russell exited the office, he lifted a thick book from the bookshelf to take with him.

When he was finally alone with Peterman, Paul gripped the edge of Peterman's desk, leaned closer, and looked at his boss squarely. "Sir, with all due respect, I believe I was most qualified to be promoted to engineer."

"Your qualifications are remarkable," said Peterman, taking his seat, as if to use the desk in front of him as a shield. "Nevertheless, Russell possesses a college education — something that you lack."

Paul's voice deepened. "Not all mining engineers have degrees. You told me so only last week, Mr. Peterman, I have the expertise that Copper Empire needs."

Peterman's thin eyebrows inched together so that they almost connected. "That may be. However, I've selected the new engineer and I expect you to give him your full cooperation."

"Copper Empire employees deserve better. Those men wanted me to become engineer."

"Is that so?" Peterman asked, his eyes clouding over.

"I've worked in a mine half of my life and trained trammers, timbermen and miners. I know every aspect to mining, including engineering. I've also performed mining captain duties without the occupational title or extra pay."

His boss tried to laugh, but it sounded more like a nervous giggle. "Paul, I already explained this to you. While Copper Empire does not have the means to reimburse you for extra job duties, I have allowed you to choose whatever shift you wanted to work."

"In the meantime, other miners, trammers and timberman were promised raises —"

"I never made such a promise," he snapped. "I said that raises would depend on production —"

But Paul cut in, "Copper Empire always meets its monthly and yearly production goals."

"And depending on the Board's approval," Peterman finished. "The Board refused my recommendation to raise wages."

"Yet they agreed to raise your salary and give generous dividends to the stockholders."

Peterman held up a hand to stop him. "Enough, Paul. This conversation is over. Get out of my office."

"Not yet," said Paul, slamming his mining hat on the desk, causing a stack of dollar bills to scatter over the desk top. "I promised the men I'd ask you about the one-man drill."

"What about it?"

"It's too dangerous operating the drill alone. We need to go back to the two-man drill."

"Nonsense. Mines throughout the Keweenaw use the one-man drill exclusively."

"It seems to me the one-man drill scaled back on jobs and made mining cheaper and more dangerous."

Peterman raised his voice. "The one-man drill is here to stay."

"Do you know what they call that new contraption?"

"I don't care."

"Widow-maker, Mr. Peterman. Wives losing their husbands, children losing their fathers."

Peterman leapt from his chair. "We've never had a miner killed here because of that drill. Tell the men they either work the drill alone or they'll be replaced."

Paul grabbed his mining hat from the desk and moved toward the door. "Would you have me replaced, too?"

"Out of respect for your father, no. Good day."

"My father and I haven't spoken in years. You don't need to do any favors for him."

"I'll see you in the morning."

Paul let the door slam behind him as he walked out.

*   *   *

Marie Weyburn gripped the hoe to clear a final dirt path. Her efforts were rewarded with long imprints in the stubborn earth. Best of all, the red-streaked sky that jutted from the Keweenaw horizon told her it was time to finish gardening for the day.

Her round face glowed with energy, but when she glanced at Nancy working the next row over, she saw her oldest daughter drenched in sweat and her shoulders slumped. Murky circles outlined the sides of Nancy's thin underarms.

Marie sighed. The labor was too much for Nancy. She inspected her own thick, weathered hands for a moment, turning them inside and out. Rough callouses marred her palms.

Nancy's tiny body was too small for even the narrow blue skirt she wore; the front of her outfit was concealed by a large apron for protection in the field that dwarfed the young woman. Marie peeked at her own garment that covered her extra poundage and wished she had Nancy's dainty stature. However, what Marie lacked in an hourglass figure she made up for in physical strength.

Even Nancy noticed the difference when she looked up. "Ma, you're twenty years older than me," she sighed, "and yet you've managed to plant twice as many seeds as I have today. Where do you get your energy?" Nancy's limp arms tried to carve out topsoil, but the hoe barely made a crack in the hard ground.

Marie straightened and balanced her weight with the hoe in her right hand. "From God," she said, and jokingly added, "the Lord ordained that I'd be working this garden and running a boarding house someday, so He gave me a husband and four children to raise to build up my strength."

"I'm serious, Ma," said Nancy. "Doesn't running the boarding house, digging out here, and raising a family make life dreadful for you sometimes?"

Marie chuckled, and then wiped the sweat off her face with the back of her hand. "Sure it does," she said. She smoothed some wrinkles in her brown linen skirt and continued, "In fact, for the past few days I've had nightmares about coming out to these fields and finding the potatoes already mashed."

"Ma!"

From the twist of Nancy's mouth, Marie saw the doubt that lurked inside her daughter. She was about to address Nancy's concerns more seriously when she heard distant squeals. Marie straightened her torso for a better look across the field, straining her eyes to see through the dusk. Jeanie and Joey, her youngest children, were approaching the house. Behind her children she recognized Roberto, their Italian friend. They were yards away from the boarding house, playing tag. Despite the distance, she heard all of their shouts.

"Ha, ha. I beat both of you," Jeanie snickered, brushing red strands of strawberry blonde hair from her face.

"You-a win," said Roberto with a slight Italian accent, breathing heavily. His skinny hand pushed a worn pair of spectacles closer to his face.

"No she didn't," said Joey. Marie noticed her son pushing the tip of his cap close to his eyes, as if he were ashamed to lose a game of tag to his big sister.

"You're just sore because you lost," said Jeanie.

"I let you win," Joey retorted.

Marie was about to stop the argument between her two youngest, but Jeanie and Joey stopped on their own accord when they finally noticed her. They ran to reach their mother with the exuberance that always seems to come in a burst after a long day at school.

Joey shouted behind him, "Come on, Roberto." The boy drew in a deep breath, and then released energy by sprinting after them.

"Ma. Ma," cried Jeanie and Joey.

Marie turned to Nancy. "Lord, they're louder than two pigs in a bathtub." Nancy laughed.

"Hey, kids," Marie yelled, "how was your day?"

Jeanie answered her mother with a beaming smile. She untied a bow at the back of her head to free her wavy locks. "Great, Ma. School's almost out for the summer."

Joey spoke next. "Yeah, we don't got no homework tonight." He pulled his brown, felt cap downward so it hid his eyes.

Marie mimicked Joey's poor use of the English language. "Don't got no homework?"

Joey carefully nodded.

Marie gave a pointed look. "Well, if you don't not start getting some homework," she mocked, "I'll see that the school finds someone that can teach you proper grammar."

Everyone seemed to have forgotten Roberto, so Nancy put an arm around his shoulders. The eight year-old boy cuddled close to Nancy, looking upon her like an older sister.

"Did you learn anything new in school today, Roberto?" Nancy asked.

The boy's thin, red lips parted into a smile. "Yes. Did-ya know tat we live in-a Upper Peninsula?" he said excitedly. Marie noticed that the boy's accent sounded less Italian during the short year the boy lived in America.

Roberto's eyes seemed to pop out with all the knowledge he had gained in school. "And-a Red Jacket almost became-a capital of Michigan?"

Marie chuckled. "Well I'll be." She ruffled the boy's black, matted hair, and then turned to her son, Joey. She pulled up the tip of her son's cap so she could look into his hazel eyes. "May I ask why you and Jeanie are so late coming home? You should have been here a couple of hours ago."

Jeanie rolled her eyes at her mother, revealing a light blue shade as well as annoyance. "We just went frogging at the creek with our friends."

Marie gripped her youngest daughter's chin firmly. "Young lady, I asked your brother a question. From now on, you will let your brother speak and you will also remember to treat me with respect."

Jeanie shamefully cast a glance toward the ground. "Sorry, Ma."

The matron turned her attention to her oldest daughter. "Nancy, you've put in a hard day's work. Now I want all of you to go inside."

"But, Ma—"Nancy protested.

"I'll be along in a minute or two."

Nancy sighed. "Thanks, Ma. Come along, kids."

Jeanie and Joey ran to the boarding home, but Roberto was content to grab onto Nancy's hand.

Marie called out to Roberto, "Stay with us for supper."

Roberto jumped up and down. "Tanks, Mrs. a-Weyburn."

Marie wiped black strands of hair from her face with a proud smile as she watched her children and their friend walk up the porch steps. She sighed and rubbed moist hands on her dress, grabbed the hoe, and resumed her work. Suddenly, Marie heard one of her children stomp on the top plank of the porch.

"Ma," Jeanie called out. Marie stopped working and looked at her. The young girl lifted her hand to cover her mouth in an effort to carry her voice across the field. With her other hand she pointed to the dirt path. "Someone's coming our way."

Marie turned around to find a stranger walking the pathway toward the house. The man wore a dirty brown hat and carried an equally filthy carpet bag. Was it another drifter begging for a free meal?

Chapter 4

"Ma'am, please don't be startled," said the stranger. He smiled and tipped his felt hat.

Marie listened to the man's Southern drawl. That, coupled with the dirty clothes he wore, led her to distrust him on sight.

"Townspeople were right about yer landmark," he continued, looking at the red water pump behind him. "They told me it would stand out."

Marie set down the hoe and clapped her hands to rid them of dirt. "What can I do for you?" she asked, but had a feeling that all he wanted was a meal. "Wait," she said, holding her hand up to stop his response. She turned toward the boarding home and raised her voice. "Jeanie, go tell your sister to set another place."

"Yes, Ma."

"That's a fine garden ya have there, ma'am," he said, admiring the rows of neatly planted seeds. "This place reminds me of home. My farm was about the same size of yer property."

"Look here mister," Marie said and picked up the hoe as if it were a weapon. "I suppose we have enough to feed you tonight, but you're not staying for more than a few hours, so don't talk my ear off." She used the hoe as a walking stick and headed for the shed door at the side of the boarding house.

"Ma'am, I think ya mighta misunderstood," he tried to explain.

Marie scrunched her nose, not only because of the stale odor exuding from the man, but because she was unsure what to think about him. This man was too friendly. Was he a traveling salesman or a vagrant? Either way, she would have Paul get rid of him after supper.

"What part of your speech didn't I understand?" she asked and set the hoe next to a rusted wheelbarrow. Marie placed a hand on the arch of her back and stretched, giving herself time to scrutinize the man with the strange, drawn-out accent.

"I heard tell that ya run a boardin' home."

"From who?" she asked, hearing her spine snap back into place.

"A bartender at Vairo's."

Marie didn't respond, so he resumed speaking. "Ma'am, I'm an honorable gentleman from South Carolina. I just stepped off the Lake Superior Limited train that operates on the Duluth, South Shore, and Atlantic railway. I'm aimin' to stay in a homey place like this. The name's Sam Huston," he said.

"I'm Mrs. Weyburn," she said and jerked the sides of her skirt to sidestep a muddy patch in the shed. As soon as Sam exited behind her, Marie shut the door and walked the spacious grounds, leaving him to scramble to keep in step. "But I thought all you wanted was a free meal."

"No, ma'am," Sam insisted. "I'm here for room and board and I aim to pay ya what's fair."

"I only take those with references," Marie warned him as they drew closer to the two-story mansion. She looked behind to find Sam scanning the white picket fence and evergreen trees that surrounded several acres of land. The carpet bag he was lugging had him walking lopsided and he panted to keep up with her pace.

"I apologize, Mrs. Weyburn, but I have no references from these here parts. Leastways, not right now. I just arrived from Charleston and wanted to stay in a place that could help me get to know others. . .like this here boardin' home."

Marie stopped just short of the columned porch and faced Sam Houston. She noticed something in his eyes that

31

grew distant, and the dusty smile he tried to form betrayed a deep set loneliness. She had seen it before.

"All right," she said with hesitation. "You may stay here for the week—on a trial basis." She extended a hand that invited him inside her home. "After you."

"Oh no, Mrs. Weyburn. Ladies first, I insist."

Marie nodded at his polite manner and she couldn't help but wonder if he was married. All of her boarders were single gentlemen. She lifted the heavy material of her dress again so she could ascend the white-painted steps, passing the hyacinths and tulips that bordered the porch.

But Sam hadn't reached the steps yet. He gulped for air, trying to catch his breath. "Sure is a purty palace," he said and pointed to the gabled rooftops. A turret adorned the right peak, its tip decorated with a prized copper nugget, shaped like a miner's ax.

"My husband's grandfather had this house built thirty-five years ago."

Sam whistled. "Looks to me like it was made for a rich mine owner."

"It was," she said, the corners of her mouth pulled down.

"Sorry, ma'am," said Sam. "I'm talkin' too much again."

"You're too nosy," she said, letting herself in the front door where she was immediately pounced on by the family dog. "Down, T-bone," Marie commanded. The black Labrador obeyed, panting as if he had just been out for a run.

"Friendly thing, ain't he?" Sam said, about to set his carpet bag on the marble floor.

"Oh no you don't, Mister," said Marie, motioning with her hand. "I keep a clean house and you'll not set that indecent piece of luggage down until I show you to your room."

Sam obeyed. He gripped the bag with both hands to make sure he didn't accidentally drop it.

Marie bent down to pet the dog's black fur. "You sure are a bundle of energy," she said to the dog, as if he understood her every word. T-bone was set to jump on Sam, but she steered the dog toward the kitchen.

"I'll show you to your room," she said to Sam. "Wash up, and you may join us for a nice supper."

"Thank ya, ma'am. I'm mighty obliged to ya. I—" Sam was about to ramble on again, but Marie snatched his bag from his hands and headed for the staircase.

Sam leaped to the robust woman to retrieve his luggage. "Please, ma'am, I'll carry my bag."

Marie shrugged her shoulders, then climbed the winding staircase. "Where did you say you were from, Mr. Huston?" They made their way up the spacious, snake-like staircase. She ran her right hand across the sleek mahogany banister, carved with designs of boats and ships, both big and small.

"Oh, please, call me Sam. And may I call you by your Christian name?"

"No, you may not," Marie retorted.

They reached the second floor and passed by closed doors. She stopped at the end of the corridor, opened the door, and pointed inside. "There's your room. You'll share it this week with another boarder."

Sam's face lit up like a candle. "Ma'am, you've been too generous. I appreciate yer hospitality." He stepped inside, apparently grateful for even the smallest bedroom in the boarding home.

Marie leaned her hip against the ledge. "I presume you want to work in the copper mines?"

Sam's head bobbed like a restless cork in water. "I'm a hard worker, too. In fact, last year my cotton crop was so plentiful, I was able to save plenty of coins for this move here North. And I tell ya what, ma'am—"

But Marie covered her ears. "Take a breath, Mr. Huston, and let me speak for a moment."

Sam's mouth pinned itself shut.

Marie raised her fist and pounded it downward, as if striking a gavel. "There's no cursing, drinking, carousing with women and if I so much as catch you smoking a pipe inside this home," she said, shaking her fist, "the door is downstairs and I'll throw you out."

"Yes, ma'am."

Marie held out her olive-skinned hand to collect money. "That'll be five dollars right now, Mr. Huston."

"Of course, ma'am," he said, fumbling in his pockets for the money. Sam retrieved some papers and bits of beef jerky that he put on a table, but no currency. Marie drummed her fingers on the wall, each sound threatening him with immediate eviction.

Sam tried to chuckle, but it sounded more like a nervous cackle. He reached into his carpet bag and finally had enough coins to hand to the matron.

Marie was about to slam the door but stopped herself. "I'll speak to my husband about work at Copper Empire."

"Copper Empire?"

"It's a mine," Marie snapped with an emphasis on the last word. "My husband and the boarders here are miners."

Sam reached for Marie's hand and gave it a vigorous shake. "Thank ya, ma'am, ya won't be sorry."

*   *   *

Sam Huston unbuckled his faded carpet bag inside the bedroom he hoped to call home one day—that is, if Mrs. Weyburn could ever accept or tolerate him. As he patted his rumbling stomach, he wondered why the plucky woman was so

34

harsh with him. Back home, he had treated strangers like they were his kin.

He dropped his hands from the travel-worn sack and studied his living quarters, whistling softly. The room was unlike anything he had ever lived in. The dark wood paneling reminded him of Michigan's forests that were in close proximity. The two double beds in the room were covered with white, woolen blankets designed with small black and red stripes. As he ran his hand along the prickly warmth of the blanket, he heard children shouting and laughing near the grounds below.

It was dusk, and he strained to see through the spotless window pane. Children were chasing T-bone near Mrs. Weyburn's vegetable garden. Sam was willing to wager that the outspoken landlady would be angry if she knew how close her gardening work was about to be trampled upon.

"Hey there." Sam yelled, lifting the window. "Yer ma will have a fit if she finds ya in her garden," he said, assuming that all three children were Weyburns.

Jeanie held firmly onto her hips and scrunched her mouth into a pout. "Ma wanted us out of the kitchen," she said, then switched to lean her weight to the other side. "Who do you think you are anyway?"

"Mr. Sam Huston from Charleston, South Carolina," he said confidently. Satisfied when the children edged away from the garden, he yanked the window shut and moved toward a cherry bureau tucked away in the corner. Beneath the bureau's oval mirror were two smaller pull-out drawers, one on each side. Sam opened one and discovered combs of various sizes. He decided that his roommate must be a finicky sort. Wouldn't one comb be enough for anyone?

He pulled out more drawers for inspection. Glad to find two unoccupied, Sam began to unpack his bulging bag. He extracted a picture of Millie and placed it on top of the dresser.

"Well, Millie," he said out loud to himself, "I made it North safe 'n sound. I know you'd be proud of me."

Sam traced his fingers on the frame. His gaze seemed to pierce the picture, as if he and Millie were truly looking at one another.

"I have the feelin' I'll be chattin' with ya lots 'round here," he said, "it might be awhile before these Northerners accept me." Sam chuckled out loud. "It might be even longer for me to accept them." Growing serious, he continued his monologue. "Just ya remember, Millie, it don't matter where I am. North or South I'll love ya always." He kissed the treasured photograph, and then stashed it into one of the empty drawers.

"Supper in fifteen minutes, Mr. Huston," called out a voice from the hallway. Sam already recognized the husky voice.

"I'll be there, Mrs. Weyburn," Sam said.

As he continued unpacking, the door creaked opened and Sam figured that she was conducting a surprise inspection on him. Instead, a slender man peeked inside the bedroom, his eyes popped open like a mouse that was caught emerging from a hole. He entered the room, straightened his tie and cleared his throat. Sam wasted no time introducing himself.

"Hi. The name's Sam Huston."

"Good evening, Mr. Huston," said the startled stranger, still looking somewhat perplexed. "I am Arthur Cooper, but everyone addresses me as Artie." As the two shook hands Artie continued, "I presume you are the surprise Marie mentioned to me?"

"I'm boardin' here for the week," said Sam.

"Is that a fact? It appears you will be residing here for a longer duration." Artie motioned to the carpet bag. "You have already unpacked most of your belongings, have you not, Mr. Huston?"

36

Sam chuckled. "I s'pose I'm hopin' to make this my new home. And I'd prefer if ya call me by my Christian name."

Artie crossed his arms close to his chest as if to protect himself. "Certainly. And you may address me as Artie."

Artie's dark blond hair was slicked perfectly back, while Sam's own strands were messy after the long journey. He figured he better run a comb through it before supper.

"Your accent is unusual," said Artie, emphasizing each syllable. "Where are you from originally?"

"I'm from Charleston, South Carolina," Sam continued. "A pure bred Southerner."

Artie raised his eyebrows, almost to the tip of his widow's peak. "I assumed that when you said you were from South Carolina."

"Oh, I'm delighted to have a friendly roommate," said Sam, laughing easily. He closed a dresser drawer. "Sharin' livin' quarters'll be so much easier."

Artie's lips pursed and his jaw clenched. "Yes, I suppose that is true." He took a seat at an organized oak desk, and then straightened a sheaf of papers next to a brass inkwell.

Sam faced his intense roommate. "Anythin' wrong?"

Artie chuckled, relaxing his facial muscles for a moment. "Pardon? It is nothing, really." He still looked pensive and shrugged his shoulders. "Actually, I am concerned about several matters. I apologize for the troubled appearance. I found today quite challenging."

"When I'm not constantly talkin', I'm actually a good listener," Sam offered.

"That may be, however —" began Artie.

"C'mon now," cajoled Sam. "What's upsettin' ya?"

Artie loosened his tie and leaned against the high-backed chair. "I want to be a respected journalist, then marry Nancy and take her away from this mining town."

"Who's Nancy?"

"She is Paul and Marie Weyburn's oldest daughter," said Artie. "You shall be introduced to her at supper. Anyhow, she deserves better than to reside in an unrefined mining town."

"My advice, from a Southerner to a Northerner, is to stick it out. Keep workin' hard at what ya love to do, and someday ya might just be the editor for Harper's Weekly," said Sam.

"I prefer the Detroit News," Artie blurted out. "Besides, there is something else that concerns me."

"I'm still listenin'," Sam said.

Artie folded his hands neatly on his lap. "I am a self-employed writer. I only earn a wage when a newspaper has a need for my articles. Lately, however, the newspapers do not seem interested in my writings. For instance, today the Gazette editor rejected my article about a possible copper mining strike."

"A strike!" Sam exclaimed. "I came here, all the way from South Carolina, in the hopes of gettin a minin' job."

Would he have to pack up and go home before he had a chance to begin a new life?

Chapter 5

"I do not believe there is much cause for concern of a strike," Artie said, rising from his chair. "I have heard various rumors, but nothing concrete."

"Phew." Sam swept a hand over his brow. "I was afeared I came all the way up here for nothin'."

Artie slid his chair carefully under the desk. "You must understand Mr. Huston—"

"Call me Sam." He rummaged through his carpet bag, found a comb, and ran it through his unkempt hair.

"Sam, the life of a copper miner is difficult. It should never be pursued without serious consideration."

"I should get downstairs," Sam said, throwing his comb on the bureau, not wanting to think through Artie's warning. "I wouldn't want to upset Mrs. Weyburn."

"Has she been cross with you?"

"She hasn't takin' kindly to my presence yet," Sam said. "How long did it take for her to warm up to ya?"

"Approximately one hour. After I unpacked my belongings, I offered to tidy up the parlor." Artie stared at the bureau.

"What's wrong?" Sam asked.

"That is not where your comb belongs. If we are to be roommates, you must keep this room immaculate at all times."

Sam sighed, picked up the comb, and put it inside an empty drawer. "Time for supper."

He and Artie walked down the stairs, across the marble floor and into the dining room. Sam whistled, this time inaudibly, not wanting to draw undue attention to himself. The gold-plated paintings that hung on all four walls made him think he had just slipped into an art gallery instead of a dining area.

Artie tapped Sam's shoulder three times and explained, "The paintings you see are of Paul's father and grandparents. They were wealthy mine owners long ago when they built this house." Indeed, each canvas depicted a man, his wife and a little boy who wore the fashions of a bygone time period.

If Mr. Weyburn's grandparents had been wealthy, why was he just a copper miner? Why did he have to work at all if he had already inherited the mansion? Sam's mind was swimming with questions, but he decided not to ask any of them so soon. The last thing he wanted to do was to offend Mrs. Weyburn.

Just then, a troop of boarders entered the room, passed by Sam and Artie, and seated themselves around a dining table that could equal King Arthur's round table, only this table was rectangular.

Artie tapped Sam's shoulder three times again. "Eighteen boarders reside in this house. All are miners with the exception of you and me," he said in a whisper. "Some of them work with Paul at Copper Empire."

Sam nodded, observing the grand place settings. The mahogany table was the perfect backdrop for the silver dining ware placed before each chair. His mouth opened, amazed at the fine possessions the Weyburns owned, but when his eyes met Mrs. Weyburn's glare, he snapped his lips shut. Sam guessed that the man with the moustache sitting next to Mrs. Weyburn was her husband. He stood up and walked toward Sam.

"My wife told me about you," the man said, shaking Sam's hand. "I'm Paul Weyburn."

"Delighted to meet ya. Sam Huston's the name."

"Please sit next to me," Paul said.

Sam followed his landlord and took a seat next to him, across from Mrs. Weyburn's watchful eye. The Weyburn couple had the contrast that Abraham Lincoln had shared with Mary Todd. Paul was lanky and as tall as the former president, while Mrs. Weyburn's short, round figure matched that of Lincoln's wife.

"Mr. Huston?"

"Oh, please call me Sam."

"Sam, I'd like you to meet Cecil McAllister." Paul pointed to a man seated on the other side of Mrs. Weyburn.

Sam grinned. "Do they call ya Ce Ce for short?"

But Cece greeted him with a puffy gray beard and moustache that bordered around a frown, furrowed brows and a cold stare. "That's a sissy name. My name is Cece, and don't you forget it."

When everyone was seated, Paul remained standing at the head of the table. "Sam, I'll introduce everyone else during dinner."

Sam nodded and grinned.

"Before we begin the meal," Paul called out, motioning to Sam, "I'd like to introduce Mr. Sam Huston. He is sharing Artie's room for the week. Welcome to our boarding home, Sam."

Paul bowed his head and closed his eyes. "Lord, we thank you for this meal. We are also grateful for our jobs, though we pray for safer working conditions. Amen."

After Paul was seated, the hungry household passed around platters of food. Pasties were the main dish being served, and Sam's mouth watered in anticipation, even though he had already eaten the same meal on the train. No matter, since he had already acquired a taste for the dish. He sliced through the thick pastry crust with his fork and found an aromatic blend of chopped meat, potatoes, carrots, and onions inside. He speared a small portion onto his fork, but before he could pop it into his mouth, he heard many voices speaking at the same time.

"Paul, tell us the good news."

"We've been waiting the whole day to hear it."

"Yeah. You're the new engineer."

"Let's toast Paul."

Mrs. Weyburn nudged her husband. Paul nodded and stood up.

"I want all of you to know," Paul said, looking specifically at his boarders, "that I didn't get the promotion to engineer."

Silence swept across the room. The boarders and the Weyburn children stopped eating, apparently surprised by Paul's announcement.

"Who's gonna be engineer?" barked out Cece.

"His name is Russell Ubel," said Paul, taking his seat once again.

The boarders griped to one another about the news. With so many people talking at once, Sam couldn't make out what anyone was saying except for those sitting right next to him.

"Don't know any Russell 'round here," said Cece.

Mrs. Weyburn asked, "Is he from another mine?"

"No," Paul said, "he's Peterman's nephew, fresh out of college."

Cece pounded his fist on the table as if giving an order. "You know more about mining than that whippersnapper. We'll only be in more danger now."

During supper, the boarders continued gabbing and complaining to one another about the new engineer. Sam felt like he was eavesdropping. He hardly knew anyone seated at the table. He felt as if he was listening to private conversations

42

that were none of his business. But, he decided, it was his business to know the happenings at Copper Empire — if he was to work there soon. He had thought he wanted to work in the copper mines, but listening to the boarders gripe wasn't making him confident about his decision to move up North. Sam interrupted their complaints, raising his voice so he could be heard. "But I was goin' to get me a job copper minin'."

Paul dabbed his mouth with a napkin. "Marie already told me, but I'm not sure I can help you."

"Can I go to Copper Empire with ya tomorrow?" asked Sam. "That's all I'm askin'. Just a chance."

"Of course you're welcome to walk with us to the mine," said Paul, his voice strong and affirming. "Be ready at seven a.m."

"Much appreciated." Sam gulped a mouthful of pasty. He decided to change the subject. After all, the loss of Paul's promotion and the hiring of a new engineer wouldn't get resolved tonight. Sam cleared his throat. "Mrs. Weyburn, this is a better meal than I had on the train."

One of her eyebrows slanted as if the dark brown line was about to fall and strike her cheek. "And what is that supposed to mean, Mr. Huston?"

Sam wiped his mouth with a napkin as if to clean it out with soap. "Ma'am, please forgive me. What I meant to say was that I already ate a pasty on the train, but these pasties are far superior."

"You can thank Nancy for the pasty." Mrs. Weyburn nodded once toward her daughter.

"Sam, you haven't met my family or the others yet. Why don't I name off everyone who lives here?" Paul offered. While Sam ate his supper, the patriarch introduced his family and each of the boarders.

Sam instantly liked Paul because he seemed to genuinely care about people, even taking the time to say a kind word

43

about each person as they were introduced. But how would he ever remember the names of all the boarders? They seemed to get along with the Weyburns, as if they were blood members of the family. Sam wondered what each of the boarders did to gain Mrs. Weyburn's approval.

As it was, the boarders seemed apathetic to Sam's presence. The men talked and ate amongst themselves and didn't bring Sam into their conversation. He knew it would take patience and trust to break into their circle.

At least the Weyburn children tried to make him feel more welcome. All four of them took turns asking Sam questions throughout supper to get to know him better. He noticed the dainty way Nancy conducted herself, so different from her forthright mother.

"Nancy, please pour me more tea," said Artie.

Mrs. Weyburn spoke up, the edge in her voice pronounced. "The tea pot is only steps away, Artie."

But Nancy sprang from her chair. "It's all right, Ma." She took Artie's cup to refill it.

It made sense that Artie would choose to court a docile woman like Nancy, since he came across as a superior, domineering sort. Artie was precise about every move he made, from the way he dabbed a napkin to his lips twice after a few bites of food, to lifting his cup of tea with a pinky in the air. Sam decided Artie would probably be a highfalutin roommate.

Further table conversation revealed that Nancy was the oldest Weyburn child. Richard was second oldest and had another year before finishing his education. His manner and looks were quite different from his older sister's. Richard's build was similar to his father's, but shared the dark hair and skin color of his mother, as well as an outspoken personality.

Jeanie was the next Weyburn child at eleven years old. Precocious, she seemed every bit of Nancy's twenty years. Joey was the youngest and either looked up to Jeanie or fought with her. Either way, it appeared that Jeanie and Joey were closest to each other.

Sam liked the Weyburn children and wanted to get to know them better. "So ya work in the garden with yer ma?"

"For now I do," Nancy said and blushed.

"Are ya plannin' on doin' somethin' else soon?" asked Sam. He noticed a secret smile between Artie and Nancy.

"They're gonna get hitched someday," said Jeanie. Sam chuckled at her comment. Jeanie was a natural know-it-all.

An irresistible member at the table was Roberto, the Italian friend of Joey and Jeanie. He was a small boy with wire-framed spectacles who seemed perfectly content to dine with the Weyburns instead of his own family. He was the first to clean his plate. Roberto took a long drink from his cup, sighed loudly, then tugged on Nancy sleeve. "Don't-a get married. I want you to-a stay here always." The child's mouth was outlined in milk and he looked like a mischievous elf. Nancy kissed Roberto's forehead. "I'm flattered, Roberto."

Artie cleared his throat. "Nancy will need to move forward and our marriage one day will be a part of that transition."

Sam stifled a chuckle. He noticed that Mrs. Weyburn's eyebrow slanted once again.

"She needs a legitimate marriage proposal first," Mrs. Weyburn quipped.

Artie said nothing more.

"How about ya, Richard?" Sam asked. "Are ya plannin' anythin'?"

"Yeah," Joey said. "He's gonna get hitched to Sally Jane." Everybody at the dinner table laughed.

"So ya got yerself a lady, huh?" asked Sam.

Richard hastily took a drink from his cup, then put his cup down and blurted out, "Yes, but I'm not getting married anytime soon." Sam was sorry that he had asked, because he caught Richard's harsh glance at his younger brother. Joey's freckled face looked down shamefully at his plate.

"After I finish school, I'm planning on joining the theater," said Richard, his smile exposing dimpled cheeks.

Paul chided his son for his choice of occupation, apparently unhappy with his whimsical nature. "We'll discuss that later, Richard."

"Pa, we've talked and talked about the theater," said Richard, who threw his napkin on the plate. "I'll do what I want with my life."

Paul raised his voice. "I won't tolerate disrespectful behavior from you." His fist thudded on the table, making his plate jump.

"Yes, sir," Richard responded.

Sam put down his fork. He had not expected to see Paul show anger with anyone.

Mrs. Weyburn wasn't happy either with the father-son exchange. "Like your pa said, we'll discuss it later."

Sam watched the boarders seated at the table, and it gave him some insight into what mining was like. The boarders were a rough-looking bunch, probably in their twenties with wrinkles, cuts and bruises and a few gray beards sprinkled about the table. Copper mining had aged these men in looks and spirit.

Cece was the oldest and crudest boarder of the lot. Mostly, he crammed food into his mouth and chewed with his mouth open, sometimes making a comment that caused morsels of food to spit out. What Cece lacked for in table manners he made up for in boldness.

"What are you doing here anyway?" Cece demanded of Sam.

Sam had already helped himself to a second pasty, and a portion of it stuck in Sam's throat. He swallowed before he had a chance to choke. It would be difficult to get along with the gruff copper miner, but he figured he could get along with just about anyone if he set his mind to it.

"Cece." Paul held up his hand as if he had the power to prevent further insults spewing from Cece's mouth. He then asked the question in a more polite way. "Sam, what made you decide to visit Red Jacket?"

"Oh, I'm not visitin'. I'm plannin' on stayin' awhile…maybe a long while."

"You're only staying in this house for the week," Mrs. Weyburn coldly reminded him.

Sam chewed the last bite of his pasty. He swallowed hard and wanted to protest, but felt Artie elbowing him in the ribs to keep quiet. He obeyed at once.

"What are you planning for work?" Cece sneered.

"Like I already said, I wanna try out copper minin'. Back in Charleston there was lots of talk about opportunities up yonder," said Sam.

"My papa works in the mines, Mr.-a Huston," said Roberto. The child wiped a milky stain from his mouth with the back of his hand.

"Well how 'bout that," Sam said. "You plan to be a copper miner, too?"

"Yep, Mr.-a Huston," Roberto said. "Just as a-soon as I'm outta school."

But Cece put down his cup and shook his fork as he talked to Sam. "You'll work sunup to sundown for beans."

Sam sensed trouble again. *Best to get off the mining topic,* Sam thought. "May I help ya clear the dishes, Mrs. Weyburn?" He thought that the matron might be grateful for his offer to help, but instead her lip curled with distaste.

47

"I suppose so," said Marie, the distrust in her voice more pronounced than ever. "Children, enough chow time. If you have any homework, get to it. Richard, consider that a personal invitation."

"Yes, Ma."

*   *   *

Nancy walked outside of the boarding home, joining Artie, her father, and Cece, along with other boarders, on the porch. She loved the extensive, wrap-around portico, feeling that it was a wonderful way to simply relax after supper. As it was, the boarders had already settled themselves on velvet, upholstered rocking chairs that were scattered this way and that, mostly to smoke a pipe and discuss their plans for the following day.

She sat on the edge of a white-painted railing, looking out into the darkness, the evergreens silhouetted underneath a full moon, listening to the familiar sounds of crickets close by.

Nearby, along the walkway, Cece leaned his massive frame against a columned beam, drawing in the mild night air. Nancy mimicked his action, inhaling deeply. The smells of her mother's hyacinths brought her a sense of comfort. The familiar aroma was home.

Cece dug into his pocket to retrieve his pipe. He stuffed some tobacco inside and lit up. He inhaled deeply, and then opened his mouth to allow the addictive substance an escape. Nancy sighed. The evening routine had begun.

"Don't know, Paul," Cece commented as smoke rings filtered near Paul and Artie. "Part of me says to quit Copper Empire. Maybe I can find work again at Calumet & Hecla." He was referring to the largest copper mining company in Red Jacket.

She watched her father's reaction. Nancy was proud of her father's strength, but worried now that he wouldn't be the new engineer at Copper Empire. Mr. Peterman's demands on her father might prove to be too much one day. Certainly, some of the boarders were unhappy working at Copper Empire. Even though her father was a respected leader, she feared many of them would just leave the Keweenaw area for good, forcing her family to sell the boarding home. Her pa didn't earn enough as a miner to keep the mansion as a one-family home.

Ever since she was old enough to remember, her parents had welcomed boarders into their 12-bedroom home and collected rent in order to keep the mansion's title in their ownership. Cece was their first boarder, and the only miner, at that time, allowed to reside with them. Many years ago, her ma would only allow church members and school teachers to board with them. A few years ago her pa's pay shrunk, as all miners' pay did. Reluctantly, her ma had to allow miners to board because they earned more money than school teachers and, therefore, could afford to pay more rent. Eventually, the family had to pair up and share bedrooms in order to collect more rent money to meet expenses.

Nancy knew her Grandfather Lowell was a wealthy man who lived in the Boston area, but didn't know why he was estranged from her father. She had never met her grandfather and wondered if she ever would. While she often pondered what the mansion would be like to live in without all the boarders her parents took in, she thought perhaps the place would be lonely without them.

Nancy understood why her pa had to put up with Peterman's nasty ways. The pay was low, but the job was steady and kept food on the table and provided shelter for her and the boarders. Her father wouldn't want to go from copper mine to copper mine in the hopes of finding a better man to work for. Rumor had it that most mining bosses were likened to dictators from foreign lands.

"The mines aren't hiring many workers these days," said Paul. He waved the smoke away from his nose. "I don't even know if Peterman will hire Sam Huston."

Artie spoke, placing his hands firmly on his lap. "And apparently hiring less than experienced engineers." He finally noticed Nancy's quiet presence and smiled at her. Nancy grinned. She knew Artie wanted her to join him on the porch swing that looked more like a love seat.

"You must pardon me for saying, sir, but the situation does not appear encouraging," Artie said, continuing the conversation with her father.

"We'll have to make the best of it," Paul said. "I let Peterman know that I disagreed with his choice. Why, Russell is only a few years older than Richard."

"He won't know nothing about mining," said Cece who set his pipe aside for a moment and abruptly changed the subject. "What do you think of that Southerner?"

"He's likeable," said Paul. "It's really too early for me to tell for certain, though."

"I think Sam Huston's a gentleman," said Nancy.

Artie said, "He was quite understanding with me earlier today." Her beau straightened his tie, and then smoothed his hair back. A hair out of place just wouldn't do.

"I think the guy's strange," blurted out Cece. "Don't trust him."

"Don't you think you're being too dramatic?" Paul asked. "Let's give the poor fellow a chance."

"He ain't normal," Cece said. "Talks too much and his lips are always parted too widely in a weird smile—"

"Would you prefer that he look at you cross-eyed?" asked Artie. "Let us extend to him the benefit of our doubt. Since he is seeking employment in the copper mines, you will have an excellent opportunity to know him better."

"Good grief," said Cece sarcastically. "Only thing Peterman can hire him for is a drill boy."

"Cece," exclaimed the others.

Cece's cheeks lifted. He crammed the pipe in his mouth. Nancy thought perhaps he did so to suppress a grin.

Just then Nancy heard a dish shatter. She was standing next to an open window and inwardly groaned. Her intuition told her Sam had broken the dish. Sure enough, she overheard her mother's scold. "Mr. Huston, I've had quite enough for one evening."

Everyone, except for Paul and Nancy, chuckled at Marie's declaration. "Johnny Reb won't last out the week," Cece said.

Nancy reached around her shoulders for her shawl. "I think I'll join you for a swing, Artie." The other men took their cue to leave so she and her beau could be alone.

"I'm turning in," said Cece. "Beat tonight."

Paul agreed with his friend, "We sure put in a hard day, Cece. I think I'll join Marie for a cup of coffee before I go to bed, though."

Nancy received a warm hug from her father. She felt his strong hands encircle her back. She always felt secure near him.

"Goodnight," Nancy said.

"Don't stay up too late, honey," Paul suggested, tugging at her shawl to make sure it draped snug about her shoulders.

"I won't," she promised.

Paul, Cece and the remaining boarders retreated into the house, the door squeaking shut after them.

Nancy and Artie sat on a porch swing and said nothing for a few minutes. As the swing cradled back and forth, the rhythmic creak sounded as though a mouse was pleading for help. She interrupted the silence by asking, "Why are you so pensive tonight?"

"I was considering our future in Detroit," said Artie.

"Why don't you go there and find out for yourself?"

Artie put an arm around her shoulders and smiled. "Someday, Nancy. Someday we shall do just that."

Nancy faced her beau. "But why not now? What are you waiting for?"

"Darling, we cannot leave Red Jacket for Detroit without prospects for employment."

"The two of us can get married soon," said Nancy, thoughtfully, as she smoothed the wrinkles in her dress. "Then we could move to Detroit where there's plenty of opportunity."

Artie laughed condescendingly. "Oh, Nancy. I simply do not know where you get your puerile ideas. We would become indigent in no time."

Nancy's eyes smarted with tears, but she did her best not to show hurt feelings. Her beau never seemed to understand her sensitive nature. But the tears threatened to release, so she wiggled free from Artie's arm. "Goodnight," she announced abruptly and stood up.

"What is the matter with you?"

Nancy shrugged. "I'm just a little tired is all."

Artie snorted. "Perhaps it would be best for you to turn in."

Nancy entered the house and slammed the door shut.

Chapter 6

Paul awoke at the sound of his wife's yawn. He stayed in bed a few more moments, watching the lacy curtains flap in rhythm against the window pane. A cool breeze swept into the bedroom that perked his senses along with the smell of morning coffee.

"'Morning honey," he said, finally pulling back the cozy Mackinaw blanket.

"Did I wake you? I'm sorry," Marie said, her voice even deeper than usual. She cleared her throat. Dark brown curls dangled across her face, hiding her eyes. Using both hands, she swept her long tresses away.

"But I depend on your yawning to wake me up," Paul said, smiling. He walked to an overfilled closet and began rummaging through shirts and overalls.

Marie approached her husband from behind and gave him a bear hug. "I'm so sorry you didn't get the promotion."

Paul sighed. "Marie, I was counting on that promotion for the extra money, not to mention making Copper Empire a safer place in which to work. How am I going to pay for Richard's college tuition?"

Marie whispered, "We'll manage."

Paul broke away from Marie's embrace. "I'm getting nowhere at Copper Empire. I'm a miner, just like I've been for 20 years. I make even less money now than I did back then."

Marie asked, "What would happen if you left? At least you're the boss —"

Paul interrupted, "Unofficially —"

"Yes, unofficially, but you're the captain underground. Those men need you to stay. You know what would happen if you quit? Another mine would take advantage of your skills, but this time, you wouldn't be the boss. You would have to deal with a captain who would bully you into longer hours with even less pay. What if he forced you to do your job faster? I don't want you to have an accident. I'm certainly not prepared to be a widow —"

Paul interjected, "Okay Marie, I'll try to make things work."

"Do you think Mr. Huston has a chance of being employed there?" Marie asked, pretending as if the previous conversation never transpired, while putting on her favorite brown dress. The frock was roomy and comfortable, even for her plump size.

"Maybe," Paul said, fastening the metal clip to uphold his overalls, "but you might scare him away from Red Jacket altogether with your stern manner."

"I manage this boarding home the best I know how." She tiptoed over the cool, hardwood floor to reach Paul, and then stood on tip toes to plant a kiss on his cheek. "I want only decent folk here." Marie hastily wrapped her hair in a bun and scurried out of the bedroom calling back, "I can smell the bacon. Nancy's almost done with breakfast."

Paul followed, touching her arm. "Marie, go easy on Sam. He doesn't know a soul around here."

"I know, Paul. But I'm still unsure of that man. He broke one of my dishes last night. He's fortunate I didn't ask him to pay for it." Marie broke away from his hold and left the room.

"Marie —" he called out. But she was already gone.

*   *   *

Paul took his place at the head of the dining table that was crowded with boarders. With the exception of Artie and Sam, the other boarders wore overalls. The furniture and dining ware seemed far too grand for a boarding home full of copper miners.

Paul went out of his way to greet Sam first before taking a seat. He gripped the Southerner's shoulder and said, "Sam, I trust that you slept well your first night here?"

"Slept like a baby," Sam said, too loudly for the early part of morning, and inhaled deeply, smelling the aroma of biscuits. "I'm as hungry as a babe, too."

"And you almost sound like one," grumbled Cece.

Paul nudged Cece in the ribs, but Sam ignored the insult. Sam lifted a red and white checkered napkin from his plate and crammed it inside his shirt.

"Richard, please say grace," Paul asked his son. The teen folded his hands close to his dark hairline and began to speak. Paul listened to the voice that was so similar to his own timbre.

Richard prayed, "Lord, we thank you for this food. We also thank you for bringing to us Mr. Sam Huston from South Carolina and we hope he'll feel welcome as long as he stays here. Amen."

Paul smiled, glad that his son was thoughtful enough to mention Sam. Indeed, Sam's face lit up as if he had just been told he was the greatest person to ever reside in Red Jacket.

"Mr. Huston—I mean, Sam—," said Marie, "Would you like a cup of coffee?"

"No, thank ya, ma'am, but I'm delighted that yer callin' me by my Christian name."

"As long as you remain under this roof, Sam is what I'll call you," Marie promised.

Paul grinned at his wife.

Breakfast was usually the quietest meal, but this morning boarders were vocal about having to work with the new engineer at Copper Empire. It was as if the supper conversation from the night before had never ended. Cece smacked his lips while eating breakfast. "You should've been engineer, Paul." The boarders agreed and said, "Here, here."

Paul swallowed a bite of his eggs. "I thought we already spoke of this yesterday."

"You've worked so hard, you deserved the promotion," said Marie, ignoring her husband's comment.

"There's nothing that can be done about it now," Paul said. "All of us need to give Russell our support."

"I say we give him trouble," said Cece.

"You said it, Cece," a boarder called out from across the table. "We'll let Mr. Russell Ubel know who the real boss is."

"You'll do no such thing," Paul said, meeting the stare of each one of his boarders. "Besides, creating tension won't help," added Paul.

"Won't hurt none neither," said Cece.

"I want safer working conditions for all of us," Paul reminded the miners. "And what better way to ensure our safety than to help Russell learn the best methods in copper mining?"

"S'pose," said Cece.

Paul hoped that was the end of it, but knew his boarders and miners were as loyal to him as a dog was to his master. Russell Ubel would have a tough time gaining their trust.

"I'm sure glad I won't be working in any copper mine," said Richard. He lifted his glass of milk to clink with Nancy's cup of tea. "Here's to working at the Calumet Theatre."

"What?" asked Marie.

Richard puffed out his chest and straightened the collars of his shirt. "Ma, Pa, you didn't want to listen to me yesterday. But I got myself an ushering job at Calumet Theatre. After that, I'll become an actor, then a playwright, then who knows?"

56

"You sound very sure of yourself, son," said Paul. "But you'll be working with me at Copper Empire for the summer."

"Huh?" asked Richard. Jeanie and Joey snickered, as only younger siblings could.

"You need to learn a trade. Copper mining has been in our family for three generations. I want you to learn how to manage a copper mine someday."

"Pa, I'm not interested."

"Aw," screeched Jeanie, "you're in trouble now, Richard."

"That's enough young lady," said Paul. He dropped his napkin on the plate. "Richard, my decision is final."

His son slapped both hands on the table, causing some biscuit crumbs to fall to the floor. "But Pa, can't I keep my ushering job until summer begins?"

Paul took a sip of his coffee, and then shook his head.

Richard stood up. "Pa, I don't want the hardships you always have to face. I want to work at what I love to do and that happens to be acting and writing for the stage."

Paul tried to steady his temper, but with little success. "Richard, remove yourself from this table, get your books and go to school."

Richard gulped.

"Now!"

Richard grabbed his books and left the home in haste.

"Don't blame the kid," Cece blurted out.

"Paul, please reconsider," pleaded Marie. "If you're not even sure Peterman will hire Sam today, how can you be sure he'll hire Richard after school lets out?"

Cece talked with his mouth full of food. "Too dangerous in the mine. Let the kid be an usher."

57

"What harm would there be in it?" asked Marie. "Let Richard usher until he has a job offer from Copper Empire."

Paul looked at his plate and declared in a cool, deep tone, "I'm the man of the house and I'll decide what's best for our son."

Marie turned to Jeanie and Joey and told them to get ready for school. When they left the dining room, Marie picked up dishes and thudded away to the kitchen.

With the mealtime winding down, T-bone romped into the dining area until he planted himself at the head of the table. His long, black tail wagged back and forth and a tongue panted happily for scraps.

Paul took some deep breaths to regain control. Everyone at the table was silent, making him uncomfortable. He knew Artie would take the dog's presence as time to leave for work, and Paul hoped everyone else would leave soon, too. Both Artie and T-bone adhered to strict schedules; T-bone with his meals and Artie with his responsibilities. Sure enough, Artie took the last sip of his coffee, and then placed it on the saucer with precision. He neatly folded a newspaper and excused himself. "I must be going to the newspaper office. I shall see all of you again tonight."

"Goodbye, Artie," said Nancy.

Artie swung around as if he just remembered something. "Nancy, could you see to it that my pin-striped suit is pressed today? I have an important meeting tomorrow with the editor and wish to look my best."

"But I'll be in the garden most of the day," Nancy said. Artie tapped his foot on the floor, apparently waiting for Nancy to change her mind. She thought a moment, and then said, "I'll try to make time for your suit."

Marie hustled back into the dining room, her voice growing testy. "Artie, your suit will be cleaned and pressed when it's always done, on Mondays." Artie scowled, and then left the room.

Nancy followed after her beau saying, "I'll walk you to the path."

Marie cleared more dishes. As Paul put a forkful of food into his mouth, she took his plate away. Paul swallowed hard. "Marie, I wasn't finished—"

"Oh yes you are. You're the man of the house, so you'll decide what's best for Richard. Well, I'm the woman of the house and I'll decide what's best for the kitchen and dining room."

Cece chewed and chewed, trying to stifle a chuckle. Sam began to whistle a fast tune, sounding like a cross between "I Wish I was in Dixie" and "I've Been Working on the Railroad".

Paul sighed. "Marie, I'm sorry I said what I did. If you want to let Richard be an usher, then I'll allow it. I can't fight you and Peterman on the same day."

Marie returned Paul's plate of food.

Cece glared at Sam and his whistling. The Southerner's whistling soon died down. "Ya don't like my song?" Sam asked with an impish expression.

Rolling up his napkin, Cece threw it on his plate. "Don't know it, don't like it and don't want it. You should have stayed in Charleston where you belong."

"That's enough," said Paul. Cece shrugged his broad shoulders, the quarrel finished.

The boarders dropped their napkins and got up from their chairs, tipping their hats politely to Marie as they headed outdoors to the mines.

Cece rummaged through his pockets for a clean handkerchief. He found one with greasy spots on it, and stuffed it back into his pocket. "Come on, Paul," he said. "We'll be the last ones if we don't hurry."

"I agree," said Paul. "In fact, I'd like to be there a little early, if possible."

Sam placed his soiled napkin on his plate and stood up, looking like a lost boy about to start his first day of school. Cece offered to Sam, "You can walk with us, I guess."

Paul snatched the remaining food on his plate with his fork and popped it into his mouth. He slapped Cece's back proudly while the Southerner nodded his thanks. Paul only hoped that Sam would be able to secure employment at Copper Empire. He hated to think that Sam had traveled over a thousand miles, only to have to go back. But what was Sam's real purpose for moving to Red Jacket? There had to be another reason, other than just needing a job. Paul couldn't put his finger on it. Not yet.

*   *   *

Flanked by Paul and Cece, Sam arrived at Copper Empire. "Hells bells," he said out loud, reacting to the unusual structure before him. The building—Sam estimated it had to be over a hundred feet tall—was a geometric complexity with a roof that sloped at a steep angle. "I've never seen the like," said Sam.

"That's the shafthouse," said Paul.

Cece's beefy hand opened the door; Sam and Paul stepped in behind. Once inside, Sam tried to absorb his surroundings. Miners were seated on benches, three to a row. Then, he heard a clatter, like hailstones, overhead.

"Is that copper I'm hearin'?"

"Sure is," Paul said, pointing overhead. "The copper rock is unloading into the hopper in the rockhouse."

"Investors must make a fortune off that copper," muttered Sam, mostly to himself. Paul gripped his shoulder.

"In all fairness, it's been risky for some of the investors," Paul said, still looking overhead, as if he could see through the plank ceiling to the copper. "Only a few companies have paid any sizeable dividends to speak of. Calumet & Hecla is one of them. Copper Empire is another." Paul nudged him, and then pointed ahead. "That's William Peterman, the general manager."

Peterman was positioned near the benches. A young man was standing beside him, arms folded, staring at Sam.

"Say, Paul," Sam said and took a step forward, "those benches over there look like they're on some kind of track system—"

But Paul interrupted. "In case you're wondering," he said, "the man next to Mr. Peterman is his nephew, Russell Ubel. He's the new engineer I spoke about at home."

Sam felt a rush of excitement at the prospect of working in a copper mine and rubbed his hands together. "Shall I introduce myself to the boss?"

"No," Paul said, tucking his shirt neatly inside his overalls. "Let me speak to him first."

Paul walked toward the platform where Peterman stood with Russell. Sam was grateful to have a little time to observe more of the shafthouse. He was curious about the rows of benches on the platform and why men were sitting on it. Even more strange was the angle of the seats. It seemed to match the angle of an opening pointed to the underground. Surely they wouldn't think of taking men underneath the earth. Sam thought miners did their job by walking through horizontal tunnels. In the meantime, Paul's rapid gestures and Peterman's finger pointing worried Sam. Paul just had to get him a job.

Sam glanced at the floor and, despite the noise and activity about him, quickly thought of a prayer. As he muttered the comforting words, several pairs of mining boots scurried across Sam's narrowed vision. He looked up. Young boys carried equipment, rushing in and out of the shafthouse. The sweat that rolled down their faces revealed the difficulty of their job. The boys should have been learning the three R's. It didn't seem fair. At least Sam had a fair amount of schooling.

Minutes passed and Sam hoped that Paul had good news for him. But somehow the men were no longer at the platform. Sam turned around, wondering where they could be, when his stare met Peterman's. The general manager was inches from his face. He squinted and left his mouth open, while Russell looked on, arms folded tightly against his chest.

"Paul, perhaps we need to speak in private again?" asked Peterman.

"Please sir, if you'll give him a chance," said Paul, "perhaps even one week. If he doesn't perform to your satisfaction, you can hire the school boys you wanted."

Sam took this as his cue to make himself known. He stuck out his hand. "I'm Mr. Sam Huston from Charleston, South Carolina."

Peterman clasped Sam's hand. "How do you do?"

Grinning, Sam shook his hand eagerly. "I do fine, just fine. I'm new here, though and aimin' to work in the mine."

Russell dutifully stepped forward to introduce himself to the newcomer. "And I am Russell Ubel. I'm new here, as well."

Peterman placed a finger on his chin for a moment. "You have no mining experience."

"Right ya are," Sam said.

"I'm afraid I can't use you. I'm set to hire a couple of boys to assist the trammers."

"Let me do it," Sam said. "I'm strong and can do the work. Those boys belong in school."

Peterman kept a finger on his chin. Sam figured his words had offended him, but when he believed in something, he felt he had to say it. Peterman's face softened as he belted out a laugh. "You said quite plainly that you have no mining experience."

Russell leaned his hand on Peterman's shoulder. "Give it a try, Uncle," he chuckled. "It might prove amusing."

The boss cocked his head. "I suppose you're right, Russell." He tipped his bowler hat and said, "You'll get two dollars a day, six shifts a week." Russell held onto his suspenders as if they were in danger of falling off, and then walked behind his uncle, leaving the shafthouse.

Sam waited a beat, and then whistled. "That was close. Thanks fer yer help, Paul."

"I don't think I was much help at all."

After Paul gave Sam a hat, jacket and gloves, they were ready to work. Cece stepped onto the platform and reached the closest empty seat on one of the benches. He planted his hefty frame and exhaled swiftly.

Paul nudged Sam. "Let's get on the man-car."

Sam pointed upward, "Ya mean on that thing?" The man-car looked like a nightmare amusement ride from a state fair.

Paul smiled. "Sam, welcome to Copper Empire."

Sam's legs shook, and when he stepped forward, he thought his knees would buckle. He climbed into the man-car and sat next to Cece. More men stepped inside, and Sam felt squeezed, with no elbow room. When the man-car was fully loaded, Paul reached over and jerked the bell cord.

The man-car descended along the tracks. Sam ducked his head close to his knees to avoid contact with the rough ceiling. He tried to listen to Paul's description of the man-car's operation, but he was distracted at the click of the car's wheels over the rails that sounded like teeth gnashing in hell. He was able to glean some of Paul's words though, such as the explanation of an unseen operator in the steam hoist building, located behind the shafthouse, releasing the brakes from a huge cable drum.

He inched his head up and saw that they were descending into a dark hole. The vehicle lowered into the bowels of the mine. With each downward jolt, Sam felt the air becoming warmer. The breeze blew his hair back, whipping it into disarray.

The man-car stopped at intervals. Sam couldn't see much in the shadowy darkness, but he perceived the man-car's heavy burden lighten every time they briefly stopped. He watched the flicker of carbide lamps exit the man-car as miners got off at their work level. Despite the increased temperature, he shivered.

When the car ground to a halt again, Sam lurched. He felt the cable that was connected to the man-car stretch and then recoil backwards up to the proper position at the work level. He wondered if he would last his first day as a trammer, already detesting the foreign conditions.

The man-car lowered once more and Sam felt Paul's nudge. "We're almost there," Paul said. "Hang on."

The transport sank into its final stop. Sam stood to exit, allowing himself to breathe normally again at last. He extracted a handkerchief from his pocket and mopped his sweaty forehead, struggling to adjust to the darkness. "Golly. It's black out yonder."

"What did you expect? Chandeliers on every level?" shot Cece.

Paul shined his carbide lamp on Sam's unlit lamp. He showed Sam how the lamp worked. There were two parts. The top part stored water and the bottom stored carbide. Paul explained that when the water and carbide mixed, gas forms. Using a flint striker, the lamp lit, and then he put the hat on Sam's head. "This should help."

It didn't help much. Just a nickel size light in front of him was all Sam could see.

Cece already began walking into the tunnel. "See you at the grass."

"What do ya mean?" asked Sam.

Paul chuckled. "It means he'll meet us outside when our shift is done. Careful now, we're going to head to our location."

Sam wasted no time finding trouble. He had only walked a few steps when he cried out, "Ow. What in tarnation is that?" He banged his knee on a huge, black, steel cart.

"That's a tram car," Paul said.

Sam rubbed his bruised knee. Despite his carbide lamp providing little illumination, he did his best to follow Paul. Sam's body smacked into walls and he tripped numerous times on the rocky terrain, but he was determined to succeed. He kept his head level, trying not to bump, trip or fall again while following Paul across the passage.

"It's blacker than midnight down yonder," Sam said.

Paul pointed at Sam's mining hat. "That's why you need your mining hat. The carbide lamp is your only source of light down here."

"Sure don't help much." Sam thought he could see better with half an eye barely open above ground than he could with both eyes wide open and a lamp shining below.

"Don't worry. You'll get used to the darkness." Paul stopped, and then turned toward the wall. "We can't always use the man-car to go up or down a level. We'll have to climb." He snatched the sides of a ladder, and then began his ascent.

Sam copied all of Paul's movements, but the ladder felt unsteady. With each step the ladder creaked and moved. Sam didn't dare look up or down, but it didn't really matter since he couldn't see a darn thing anyway.

"Watch out," Paul cried out. "This rung is broken." Just in time, Sam lifted his feet over a tattered step.

"Another matter I'll have to speak with Peterman about," muttered Paul. They finally reached the job site.

Sam coughed harder. "How can yer sniffer work with all this dust?" The novice trammer coughed several times.

"It won't be like this everyday, Sam, just on the days following when I blast."

"Ya must-a blasted here just a short time ago." He coughed even more.

Paul nodded. "Yesterday. The dust'll settle soon."

Sam continued coughing.

"Sam, are you okay?"

"Yeah, just hard catchin' my breath. Do miners ever die of suffocation?"

"Mining is dangerous work, Sam. We've had too many accidents lately. But you don't need to worry about suffocating. Cleaner air is pumped in," Paul's voice drifted off, "although lately those pumps have been in disrepair, too."

"If ya don't mind, maybe we can sit for a spell?"

"Sure, Sam."

Both men sat down on the rock floor of the mine. Their carbide lights shone on the dust particles floating in the light like snowflakes.

Sam was grateful he could take a few minutes to catch his breath and adjust to his surroundings. The area in front of him looked like a steep rock hill. Paul explained to him it was called a stope. Paul took the time describing to Sam the mucking process. It would be Sam's job as a trammer to lift, carry, shovel or roll the blown rock from the stope into the tram car, depending on the size of the rock. Once the tram was loaded, Sam had to push the tram—which was on rails—to the shaft, where he would then dump the tram contents into the skip to be hauled to the surface. Paul warned him that tramming required extreme physical exertion, so he needed to be strong. Sam actually welcomed the opportunity. He wanted to push his body to exhaustion. It might help take his mind off of Millie, after all.

He also had a chance to learn more about Paul. Paul told Sam how he and Cece first became a mining team in '91. They contracted with Calumet and Hecla to shaft-sink, drift, and stope (Sam didn't know what all of that meant but was sure he'd learn soon) and made good money. That period of time was known as the "golden years" for miners. Paul and Cece entered into contracts with the mine, so they were their own bosses, and Paul was so confident of his future that he left the Michigan Mining School after one semester to remain partners with Cece. Soon after, he married Marie and started a family. Life was good for Paul. As the years went on, Calumet and Hecla had to dig deeper for copper, so Paul and Cece had to contract for less money and work even harder.

Sam learned that Copper Empire opened at the turn of the century, and that Peterman had lured Paul and Cece away from C&H. Since Copper Empire was new, Paul and Cece didn't have to dig far down for copper. They worked less hard for a decent wage.

A couple of years ago, Copper Empire stopped hiring contractors. Instead, Peterman paid miners for their time, not their skills. All of the mines in the area eventually did the same thing, so Paul and the rest of the miners had no choice but to accept the pay cut.

At the same time, since Paul had the most knowledge of mining, Peterman suggested to Paul that he take on the duties of mining captain, without the extra pay or job title, in return for Paul's choice in working shift. Paul even performed engineering duties, up until Peterman's nephew was hired yesterday. Sam thought that was a shame. The way Paul spoke, Sam knew he was a mining expert, and should have been promoted. He hoped working for someone as inexperienced as Russell wouldn't turn out too badly.

"I guess I've been doing every aspect of mining for over twenty years," Paul finished.

"But ya didn't finish college?" asked Sam.

"No, but I was lucky to even have the chance to attend college. Many of my friends had to quit school when they were only ten years old."

"That's a shame, Paul. I stayed in school until I was fifteen or so."

"I'm afraid, Sam, it doesn't always work like that here."

"Might as well start working." Sam got back on his feet, lifted a piece of blasted rock and let it drop inside the tram. He heard drills operating at a distance, perhaps a hundred feet below and raised his voice. "How old were those young fellers outside carryin' those parts?"

"Around fifteen or so. They run errands for miners."

Sam dumped another chunk of copper in the tram. "They had to quit school?"

"Yes. Their fathers work here. That's how the boys got their jobs."

"Is it like that in every mine?" asked Sam.

"Actually, no. The other mines usually won't hire anyone younger than eighteen. It's just too dangerous down here for kids."

Sam shot back, "Then why does Copper Empire have kids working here?"

"Because Peterman saves money hiring youngsters. He doesn't mind taking the risk. And, fathers want their sons to work here. They need all of the extra money they can get."

"But, why? I'll be making a whole two dollars a day here. If I work twenty-four shifts a month, why, I'll be earnin' close to fifty dollars a month. That's more than I ever made back home."

"Sam, you forgot to deduct mining clothes and equipment."

Sam touched his mining hat. "I have to pay for this?"

"Yes. And the jacket. And the gloves. And the tools."

Sam grinned very slowly. "Yer pullin' my leg, ain't ya?"

"Nope. And don't forget to deduct for medical expenses."

"I won't be needin' medical treatment. I've always been healthy."

"That doesn't matter," said Paul. "The chances are you'll be needing a doctor. Accidents, even death, is a possibility around here."

Sam wondered, if mining was so dangerous and costly, why would Paul want his son Richard working here in the summer? Sam didn't dare ask. He didn't want to risk angering Paul. He really wanted to reside at the boarding home longer than the one-week trial Marie permitted.

While Sam continued loading, Paul asked, "Sam, if you don't mind my curiosity, why did you decide to move to the North?"

Sam shrugged. "I needed a change."

"Farming cotton not interesting enough?"

"I suppose not. Hey, Paul-"

"Sh."

"What?"

"Sh."

Sam heard footsteps. Someone was coming. "What's wrong, Paul?" he asked. He shone his carbide lamp in the noisy direction when Cece emerged from the darkness.

"Another accident," Cece said. "Gotta come with me, Paul."

"Oh, no," were the only words Paul could mutter softly.

Chapter 7

"Who's hurt?" yelled Paul, in a deepened voice that reflected his outrage. Not waiting for an answer, he shot up from the ground and ran along the tunnel behind Cece.

"Wait for me," Sam cried. He lagged behind Paul and Cece, taking careful steps across the tunnel and down the ladder. Once he reached the ground, he tried to match Paul's footsteps, but couldn't compete next to the miner's twenty years experience negotiating the terrain of a copper mine. The soles of Sam's shoes tore when he ran through a floor of sharp rocks, and he told himself to purchase mining boots the first chance he got. In the meantime, it was all he could do to keep balanced along the uneven ground with only a glimmer of his carbide lamp to lead the way. No wonder he kept losing his footing.

Suddenly, Sam stumbled and fell. "Can't hardly see nothin'," he shouted to himself. Luckily, he found his lamp still shining. He knew he was closer to the accident scene when he heard a loud commotion of voices, all trying to get in the last word. He got up and followed the alarming sounds that led him to men crowding around an injured miner.

Paul pushed several of the miners away. "Get back. Give the man some room." The miners obeyed him immediately, dispersing to the uneven walls of the mine.

Sam felt goose bumps rise from his forearms. Why did someone have to get hurt on his first day at Copper Empire? His heart beat rapidly from fear of the unknown while drops of water tumbled from the rock ceiling and cooled his flushed forehead. He hoped the man wasn't injured too badly.

Paul bent to his knees and leaned over the hurt, moaning miner. "You'll be all right, Jackson." He raised the ends of his shirt that was tucked inside his overalls, and then ripped the bottom portion. Paul took the strip and placed it around the miner's arm, acting as a sling.

"Leg's hurt, too," Jackson sputtered, pointing to the left one. "I think it's broken."

"Let's get him to the hospital," shouted a miner.

A Finnish miner waved his hands wildly at the group. "Dis proofs we don't worrk alone. We should worrk wit udder people."

Paul stood and held both hands up. "I already discussed this with Peterman yesterday. I'm afraid there is nothing else that can be done as long as Peterman is in charge. All of you must work alone, or lose your jobs. Now, let's get Jackson out of here." He knelt to the ground once again to mend Jackson.

"What happened?" Sam asked.

Cece backed up next to Sam. He whispered, "Fell off the ladder."

"What?"

Cece shined his carbide lamp on the mangled ladder and raised his voice. "Look over there," he said with a huff.

Sure enough, several rungs of the ladder had been torn away. Jackson was lucky since he had gotten more than halfway down before the ladder gave way. Any closer to the top and the injured miner might have broken his neck.

Jackson touched his broken leg, talking incoherently. He seemed to move in and out of consciousness. Sam could almost feel the man's misery. He aimed his light and was relieved to see a couple of men bearing a stretcher.

Paul saw the men, too, and shouted, "Quick. He needs his arm and leg tended to right away."

Cece followed behind the men and said, "I'll help carry him to the grass." He and another miner lifted the injured man onto the litter.

"Gently now," said Paul. He covered a sheet over the victim. Cece steadied the carrier, and then disappeared into the darkness with the others on the rescue team.

A young miner stepped forward into a carbide light beam. "We're not safe down here. What if something happens to one of us while we're working alone and there's nobody to hear us?"

"Yeah," cried another miner. "Our equipment is old, some of it broken."

"Who found Jackson?" asked Sam.

The Finn stepped forward. "I forget I left tools back dere so I went back and saw Jackson."

"Why can't miners pair up?" asked Sam.

Paul shrugged. "Mining companies in this region have turned to the one-man drill to save money. I've tried talking to Peterman, but he won't listen to reason."

A dark-haired Croatian spoke up. "Vee poot our life at reesk for vat? Ve do not eefen get pay rase."

"And we never will," said an older miner, stroking his beard. "If we're hurt, someone else will take our job. Maybe we should join the Western Federation, Paul."

"What's that?" asked Sam.

"A mining union," one miner cried out.

Sharp comments sprang from the huddle, both favorable and protesting the idea of joining the union.

"All right men," Paul said, indicating to the miners to stop talking. "Return to your work stations."

The miners and trammers respected their leader's request, breaking off into groups and heading back to their jobs, leaving only Paul and Sam at the accident scene. "I suppose you're lost, so I'll walk you back to the tram," said Paul.

"I can get back all right. Already had my first tumble," Sam said reassuringly. "Paul?"

"Yes?"

"I didn't believe ya when ya said I'd be needin' medical attention. Miners get hurt a lot, don't they?"

Sam's carbide light shined on Paul's face. He didn't like what he saw. Deep circles were woven under the mining captain's eyes, making him appear older than he really was. "Now that we have the one-man drill, we don't work in teams anymore. More accidents are bound to happen," said Paul.

"And Peterman won't listen?"

Paul shook his head. "I've been thinking though, maybe I can talk some sense into Russell."

* * *

Paul squatted to refill the wood-burning stove, placing logs in the contraption to warm the boarding house. The evening had turned quite chilly. He shut the stove door, and then straightened himself to watch Sam, Cece, Artie and other boarders mingle in the parlor. They quietly conversed with one another, read or played a friendly game of cards on the rosewood game table. His wife allowed no rough play, gambling or liquor. Marie's rules were respected and adhered to always. Even without the rules, Paul knew their boarders were quiet and private, and therefore respectful of his property.

"I wonder where Richard is?" Paul asked of anyone in the room.

Marie pulled a lace curtain away from the window and looked out. "He was supposed to be home from the theater a half hour ago." She let the curtain fall to its original position, and then shrugged her shoulders. "Ever since he's been courting that Sally Jane, there's no telling when he'll come home."

"I'll put a stop to that," Paul promised. He frowned upon Richard's choice in girls to court, especially Sally Jane.

No matter how many years Paul spent living in the mansion, he would never overcome the immenseness of the parlor. It stretched across the west wing of the house. Walnut settees with emerald green embroidered pillows were placed against the corners of the parlor. On either side of the settees were matching arm chairs. A Victrola rested on a Renaissance-period credenza, patterned in walnut burlwood with glass doors. The music box was ready to be cranked for a tune. Sam sat on the chair closest to the Victrola, but he looked too tired to even listen to music. Paul understood the tuckered-out feeling. When he began working the mines twenty years ago, he thought he would never adjust to the back-breaking labor and the uncomfortable underground conditions. Paul heard Sam's coughing fits and decided to pour him a cup of tea, which was accepted gratefully.

"I sure hope Jackson'll be alright. It ain't right for someone to get hurt on my first day at work," Sam tried to joke as he coughed. Then, he blew on his tea to cool it down.

"Shoot. What happened to Jackson ain't so unusual," said Cece. He stomped his boot to the floor. "Would you quit that infernal coughing and wheezing?"

"Cece—" Paul warned.

"I know, I know—" Cece said, holding up his hand as if to surrender. "Not another word."

Paul wondered if Sam would be able to withstand Cece's brusque manner. That is, if Marie allowed him to stay long term in the boarding home. Cece really wasn't such a bad guy once people got to know him. He met Cece on his very first day of school thirty-five years ago. They were both six years old and were arguing over who broke Cece's pencil. Cece formed a fist, but Paul shoved him to ground and ended the fight before it even started. Grandfather Flint had taught Paul the tricks of winning school yard brawls.

Strangely enough, Paul felt his Grandfather Flint had been more of a father than Lowell ever was. And now that Paul had been estranged from him for over twenty years, he wondered if they could ever reconcile. . .and what his father would think of the current copper mining problems.

After their boyhood confrontation, Cece never bullied him again and the two eventually became best friends when Paul understood that Cece picked fights only because he felt intellectually inferior to the other children. When Marie's family moved from Copper Harbor to Red Jacket four years later, the three became inseparable.

That still left Sam to deal with Cece. Paul had considered talking with Cece in private about his rudeness, but decided it would be best to allow Sam the chance to fit in on his own terms.

Sam stared at Cece, his jaw clenched with unusual anger. Instead of responding to Cece, he resumed sipping his tea. Then, he put his hand in one of his pant pockets and withdrew a handkerchief for another round of coughing.

"Good grief, Cece," Marie said, glaring at him. "Sam just started working in a copper mine, and that takes some getting used to. You're just upset over other things."

Paul's heart warmed at the sound of his wife coming to Sam's defense. She was slowly letting her guard down. Maybe Sam would be able to stay permanently after all.

Sam appeared to feel more at home. He unraveled a soiled rag revealing a bone which he handed to the dog. T-bone snatched it away from the Southerner, hungrily gnawing at the remains.

In the meantime, Marie's hands were actively knitting a red scarf. The needles weaved and bobbed dark green patterns that looked like Christmas trees, giving the wrap some holiday character. She put her knitting on her lap for a moment. "Paul, did you ever speak to Mr. Peterman about the miners working in pairs again?"

Paul planted himself on a settee and said, "I have, but he's determined to cut labor costs. Besides, all copper mines now require men to drill alone."

"More profits and accidents at the same time," said Cece.

Joey dashed into the room in his tweed knickers and skidded next to Sam. "I made this choo-choo train, Sam. Wanna come play with me?"

Sam's eyelids had almost drooped to a close, yet they sprang to life again at the child's voice. "I'd really like to see yer train. Maybe in the mornin'?"

Defeated, Joey frowned and slumped his shoulders. T-bone pranced along the marble floor, making tiny clicking noises like keys meeting paper bound in a typewriter. The canine finally reached Joey to receive some much needed attention.

Marie walked over to her son and put her arm around the child's shoulders as he petted the friendly dog. "Joey, Sam's too tired to play with you."

"I know," the boy said, understanding as only a child would. He continued stroking T-bone's black head.

Marie gave Joey a hug, pulling him close to her puffed sleeves. "Anyway, it's your bed time, young man. Jeanie's been asleep for half an hour already."

"But Ma—"

Marie gave him a stern look. "Say goodnight and I'll tuck you in."

Joey looked around at everyone. "'Night," he said, with more than a hint of disappointment in his voice.

Suddenly, an eerie choking noise filled the parlor. It was coming from the dog. "Ma," Joey cried, "what's wrong with T-bone?"

Paul leaped from the settee and dashed across the parlor to the dog who finally vomited the bone and his dinner from earlier that day. In no time at all, T-bone was breathing normally again, panting and wagging his tail like a happy dog.

"He's fine," said Paul, trying to calm down Joey.

"How did T-bone get this tiny chicken bone?" cried Marie, pointing at the bone and vomit on the floor.

Sam slithered his exhausted body off the settee and went to the dog, startled from T-bone's mishap. "I saved the bone from my supper, just for him."

Marie turned Joey around and pushed him out of the parlor. "Run along. I'll be upstairs in a minute." When the boy left, Marie faced Sam. "Mr. Huston, until you move out at the end of this week, you are to ask me first before feeding that dog another scrap. T-bone can't be trusted with small bones."

Sam stuttered a bit. "Yes, ma'am, I'm sorry. I—"

"Look at this mess," Marie said, pointing again at the vomit. She turned around and thundered out of the room.

Paul called out after his wife. "Marie, Sam didn't mean any harm—"

But Marie wouldn't listen. Several miners, quietly chuckling, announced their own farewell, retiring to their rooms. Even Cece laughed at T-bone's mishap—or was it from Marie's anger toward Sam? Paul could count on his fingers the number of times Cece exhibited mirth in four decades.

Paul put a hand on Sam's shoulder. "I'm sorry, Sam. Marie just needs a good night's sleep. She'll get over it by the morning." He was about to say more, but noticed Richard trying to sneak by the parlor and up the winding staircase.

"Richard, come here please."

Richard shut his eyes for a moment, sighed, and then retraced his steps to join the others in the parlor.

"Sorry I'm late, Pa."

"Where were you?" Paul asked, hearing the edge in his voice. He tried to soften his tone. "We were worried, son."

Richard stood in front of his father. "I had to escort Sally Jane home from the theater."

"Didn't you attend the play with Sally Jane and her parents?"

"Her parents were at the play, but they went somewhere else after the last curtain call."

Paul leaned forward. "Sally Jane's parents may not care that the two of you are courting this late at night, but I do."

"But Pa," Richard said, his hand punching a pillow, "The other fellas take a moonlight walk with their girls, too and —"

Paul gripped Richard's shoulder. "If I can't trust you with a girl, how can I permit you to work evenings at the theater?" He frowned at his happy-go-lucky son.

"Oh, Pa, I promise to get my school work and chores done everyday. And I'll be too busy to court Sally Jane if I'm working at the theater. Please let me usher."

"Can I trust you to fulfill your responsibilities?" Paul asked.

"Yes, sir."

Paul decided, if he let Richard usher, it might help keep him away from Sally Jane, a girl that Paul rather disliked. "All right, then, you may usher until this summer."

Richard smiled and jogged up the stairs to escape further lecturing.

Sam slumped back in a chair. "I'm as good as gone by the end of the week. Do any of ya know of other boardin' homes around here?"

Cece laughed and suggested, "You can try Caleb's downtown."

Paul stared at Cece for a discomforting minute, and then turned to Sam. "Caleb's is a house of prostitution, but I'm sure there are other decent places to live."

Artie sat in the rocking chair opposite Sam, intensely reading the daily paper. With each rocking motion in the outdated piece of furniture, the chair let out an annoying squeak. Artie never seemed to be able to relax, always dressed in a stuffy, double-breasted coat with a silk neck tie. Artie threw the newspaper he was reading on the floor. "I do not believe it."

"What's wrong?" asked Nancy who had been sitting quietly on the settee next to him.

"Those journalists. Those irresponsible, groveling reporters. Just who do they think they are?"

"Calm down," said Paul, lying on another settee. He looked at the ceiling, as if Artie were up there instead of across the room. He softened his tone for effect. "What did you read that's so terrible?"

"There is an article about the impending strike with the Western Federation of Miners. The story is biased, as if it were written by a mine owner himself."

Sam grabbed his handkerchief for more coughing. "How's that?"

"To begin with," said Artie, "they assert that miners are demanding more compensation in return for less labor. Furthermore, it mentions that one way they would reduce production is requiring the use of two men for the drill."

"But I thought that was necessary," Sam croaked.

"It is," Paul said. Sitting himself upright, he continued, "Far too many people have been hurt because of that machine."

"The miners are certainly aware of the deplorable working conditions," said Artie. "I am not concerned about them. Red Jacket citizens may grasp the wrong idea about miners. The miners certainly do not have rapacious requests. At the very least, when I write, I attempt to report both views."

Nancy finished cleaning T-bone's vomit from the floor. She left the room for a moment, and then returned, having discarded the rag. She stood next to Artie and put an arm around his shoulders. "Don't worry," she said, "I'm sure we'll see another angle of the story sometime soon."

Artie handed her the newspaper. "Nancy, put this on the coffee table."

"Of course, Artie."

Paul looked around his group of family and friends. "It's rumored that workers at the Quincy will sign with the Western Federation of Miners."

Cece frowned and slapped his leg. "They might have Copper Empire going on strike, too." T-bone wanted more affection, so he chose to snuggle next to Cece. Paul watched with amusement when the hefty miner, who rarely touched T-bone, unconsciously stroked the pet's fur, an action which comforted both parties.

"Our unit will meet with the Federation in a few weeks," Paul reminded him. "We'll take a vote then whether or not to join."

Lowering his handkerchief from his mouth, Sam croaked, "Maybe the Federation could help."

"Dream on, Southern boy," growled Cece. He finally realized he was petting a dog and brushed his hand away from the black Labrador. "If I didn't have my mining job, I'd starve to death. I quit school when I was eleven. Ain't trained to do nothing else except mine." The angry man continued his soliloquy. "Now I'm not going to let some greenhorn tell me what he thinks is right or wrong."

Paul cleared his throat several times to capture Cece's attention. When Cece looked at him, Paul shook his head, warning his friend not to start a fight.

Cece took a deep breath. "Already know it's wrong. But I'm not gonna do nothing to risk my job." The hefty man took an embroidered pillow, placed it behind his head, and closed his eyes. He took long, slow breaths, trying to relax.

"Nancy, I have forgotten something else," said Artie. "Retrieve the paper again." Nancy shot up from the settee to do his bidding. Artie nodded his thanks and looked at the newspaper again. "The Federation has signed over one thousand members throughout the Keweenaw region."

Cece's eyelids snapped open again. He leaned forward with his chin resting on his hands. "Nothing but trouble."

Chapter 8

Paul lifted his mining jacket that hung on a rusted hook and threw the bulky garment over his broad shoulders. The dryhouse was crowded with miners who were gathering their mining gear to head down into the shaft. The men didn't get paid until they reached their workplace, so they were anxious to get to the shafthouse with all due haste.

Across from him, Paul studied Sam. The Southerner lifted his mining cap as if it were as heavy as a skip loaded with copper, then placed it on his head. Paul winced, knowing Sam's body ached all over. Over the past couple of weeks, Sam had struggled to adjust to a trammer's back-breaking work.

Paul admired Sam's ability not to give up. His perseverance had landed him a permanent job at Copper Empire, and maybe even a place to live in the Weyburn boarding home. Although Marie remained undecided about Sam's boarding status, she had cooled off enough about T-bone's choking incident to put him on a week-to-week trial basis.

Paul rested his foot on the bench. "You look worn, Sam."

Sam grinned. "Don't ya worry about me, I'm as fit as a fiddle."

"You're doing well here," Paul said, gently patting the Southerner's back, "but I know it takes time to adjust."

Paul had wondered, ever since he first met Sam, what motivation possessed him not to pack his bags and return to South Carolina. Paul had asked him more than once why he came North, but Sam's answers were always evasive.

An accident had occurred every day at Copper Empire since Sam began his trammer job, though the Southerner was certainly not to blame. Most of the victims had only suffered minor cuts and scrapes. However, a few days before, part of a hanging wall fell on two hapless miners, and they died instantly. Paul thanked God it hadn't happened on his shift. He knew the hanging wall needed better support, but Russell had disagreed. In fact, Russell stubbornly refused to consider any of Paul's suggestions.

Despite the dangerous conditions, Sam managed to lighten the mood on the 31st level with his carefree spirit and jovial manner. The miners, with the exception of Cece, were beginning to accept Sam as one of them, like a brother. It was the only way miners and timbermen and trammers could work in the dark, thousands of feet below the surface, and feel relatively safe.

"I'm not coughin' near what I did yesterday." Sam withdrew a handkerchief from his pocket, waving the worn rag like a patriotic veteran. He stuffed it back into his pocket. "I'm ready for the man-car whenever you are."

"I'd like to speak with Peterman first," said Paul, choosing his next words with care. "You go on down, but don't let on to the men where I am."

"Why not?"

"I'm going to try and persuade Peterman to allow repairs, but I don't want to raise the men's hopes unnecessarily. I'll be along soon."

"You can count on me," said Sam, walking out of the dryhouse.

Paul crammed one arm, then the other into his mining jacket's sleeves, then smoothed some loose strands of his sandy-brown hair. Anything but a professional look wouldn't do when approaching his boss.

When he thought of Peterman, all Paul could do was let out a sigh. He wasn't any closer to a promotion now than when he had begun working there. After the engineer's job had gone to Russell, he knew he would never stand a chance of moving up the ranks. Peterman was a Boston man and had grown up in a wealthy family, much like Paul. The only difference was that Peterman had never lost his social status or money because of the woman he married. It was just like Peterman to look on those without a formal education or substantial wealth as though they were beneath him.

Just when Paul craved his childhood years of fancy clothes and horses, he remembered his vivacious wife, their children, and knew he had made the right decision to marry against his father's wishes. Lowell Weyburn was the problematic one for disinheriting him because Marie came from the working poor.

Paul brushed aside his father's estrangement and remembered his purpose for the morning: to confront his boss. As Paul strode out of the dryhouse, miners greeted him as they did each day.

"'Mornin', boss."

"'Comin' with us on the man-car?"

"Good morning men," said Paul. "I'll be along shortly."

"Right," said one of the miners. "We'll see you down there."

Paul felt the cool air of an Upper Peninsula spring when he left the dryhouse. It would be another month before any real warmth permeated throughout the Keweenaw region. Nevertheless, the crisp breeze was a vast improvement from the winter when Red Jacket residents sometimes were forced to endure temperatures of twenty degrees below zero.

"Pa!" shouted a female voice. Paul recognized it as Nancy's childlike, trusting tone. She pinched one side of her dress so that the end wouldn't drag on the ground and ran to him, carrying a lunch pail. "You forgot your dinner," she said and handed him the pail. "This should fill you up in a few hours."

"Thanks, honey," Paul said with a smile. "I would have had to beg Cece to share his meal with me if you hadn't come."

"Well, well, who do we have visiting here?" It was Russell, wearing a smirk that could have spelled out the word arrogance.

Paul just didn't like Peterman's nephew, though he had tried. Russell was sneaky and always seemed to appear out of nowhere, spying and snooping on everyone. Both Russell and Sam had begun their respective jobs two weeks ago, but Sam always outperformed Russell. Sam needed the job and went out of his way to go beyond the call of duty. Even after Paul sent the men home each day, Sam grunted and pushed the tram further so the copper might reach the skip in time to be processed that day. Sam earned every penny of his wages. Russell, on the other hand, deserved to be fired. During his short period of employment, Russell's finest deed was to take a stopwatch into the mine and bully the men into drilling and blasting faster to increase production. Paul had tried to talk him out of it, but Russell insisted that timing the miners was the latest technique being taught in colleges. Russell seemed quite sure that Paul's practical work experience didn't count for much in comparison to his academic knowledge.

Nancy's eyes were cast downward as she waited for Paul to introduce the two.

Paul cleared his throat, striving for a polite tone: "Russell, this is my oldest daughter, Nancy."

Russell deftly lifted Nancy's pale-skinned hand and kissed it softly. "Miss Nancy," he said, "the pleasure is indeed mine."

"Nancy, this is Russell Ubel, Mr. Peterman's nephew," said Paul.

Nancy blushed and stammered. "I, ah, I've heard about you. You're from the Michigan College of Mines."

"I am, indeed I am," said Russell, tugging on his bow tie at both ends. "And what a pleasure it is to work with your father."

Nancy looked down again. "Well, I must be going."

But Russell stepped forward. "I overheard some of the bachelor miners saying they pay you to do their wash."

Nancy nodded. "Yes, I do."

Russell lowered his voice, and Paul couldn't be sure if he was flirting with Nancy or just showing off. "Would you have the means to wash my clothes as well? I can pay what you ask."

"Can you stop by Sunday evening?" Nancy asked. "That's when I gather all the clothes to wash."

"Hee, hee, hee," Russell snickered. "I can do better than that." He lifted his hand to his mouth as if to prevent any more sinister outbursts and said, "With your permission, may I stop by after your church service? I'll give you my basket of clothes as well as an invitation to escort you to dine anywhere you choose."

Paul tapped his foot on the ground, his patience almost gone.

Nancy blushed again. "Mr. Ubel, I'm flattered, but I already have a beau."

Russell waved his hand as if to dismiss his prior suggestion. "No matter. I'll arrive at your home Sunday evening, then."

"Goodbye," Nancy said, with a smile spread from cheek to cheek. "Oh, bye Pa," she said, as if forgetting Paul was there.

"See you tonight, honey." Paul was about to walk to Peterman's office, but Russell stopped him.

"Paul, aren't you going to the shafthouse?"

"I have business with your uncle," Paul said, not missing a beat. Thankfully, Russell shrugged his shoulders and took off in the other direction to the shafthouse, not giving him trouble. Paul knew he had to respect Russell as his superior, but it was difficult. Not only did Russell show up late and leave the mine early, but when he did manage to show up for work, he seemed to take pleasure in holding a stopwatch and timing workers.

They were bringing up more copper, but the miners were paying a price with accidents. How much more would it take to make Russell realize it wasn't worth the extra copper?

If only Russell would take Paul's advice and treat the miners as human beings. Paul couldn't decide who was worse: the uncle or nephew. Both were cut from the same cloth, both hailed from Boston's classiest section of town. As Paul reached the manager's office and knocked on the door, he decided Russell was far worse. Russell was interested in his daughter.

"Come in," said Peterman.

Paul entered, keeping his mining cap at his side, like a soldier's sword. "Sir, I'm here to discuss our worsening work conditions."

Peterman lit a stogy. "We already discussed this days ago—"

But Paul finished his boss' sentence. "Right after Jackson's accident, I know." He drew closer to the mahogany desk. "Mr. Peterman, the conditions on the 31st level warrant substantial repair."

"Come again?" asked Peterman, taking off his spectacles.

"Ladders need replacing, timber needs to be installed and the men need to work in pairs again."

Peterman slammed his ledger shut. "Paul, that is quite enough. I've already assigned Russell to inspect that level. He has assured me everything is in working order. And, unfortunately, my answer is no in regards to working in pairs." He puffed on his stogy a few more times. "I don't have to explain that to you again."

"Russell is too busy timing the miners to notice necessary repairs."

"Is that so?" snorted Peterman.

"Sir, if you'll come with me to the 31st level, I can show you. As you know, we've had numerous accidents ever since Russell began two weeks ago."

"You're not suggesting that Russell is incompetent?"

"Yes, sir, I am. He can't read blueprints. He's useless surveying the underground. He doesn't know which lode to leave behind —"

"I don't believe you, Paul. He's a college graduate." Peterman blew smoke at Paul's face.

"And every morning, since his first day here, he's had blood shot eyes."

Peterman put his stogy down. "The boy is new. He's had to learn quite a bit in a short time. He's tired."

"Yes, Mr. Peterman, he's tired, but not from overwork. I've heard that he spends a lot of time at Caleb's."

Peterman stood up and glared at Paul. "Just rumors, Paul. But I'll tell you something factual." Peterman raised his voice ever higher. "Russell has proposed that we no longer need a mining captain, official or unofficial, as you may be."

"Why is that?" Paul asked, gritting his teeth.

"He said he can perform engineering and captain duties at the same time. Naturally, I've disagreed with him. Russell can't survey the area if he's too busy supervising the miners. Besides, the men like and respect you."

"Maybe because I have more experience than your nephew?"

Peterman took a seat again. "Back down, Paul, or you'll find yourself just a miner again."

Paul slammed his mining cap on his boss' desk. "You need me sir, or you would have fired me long ago. However, I'm putting the needs of my men over my own. If your nephew doesn't start addressing safety issues, I'll tell the newspapers and I'll telegraph the Board. All of Red Jacket will know how dangerous this mine is. You'll never hear the end of my complaints until you address them." Paul swiped his mining cap and headed for the door, but Peterman stopped him.

"Wait just a moment," said Peterman. Paul didn't so much as flinch, so the manager continued. "If the miners increase production by ten percent, I'll match their efforts with a pay increase. And, I'll see to it that repairs are made, if they're really necessary."

"How much of a raise and when would repair work begin?" asked Paul. He tried to calm down, but his heart beat a rapid pace.

"If production is increased by July, fifteen cents per week, plus repairs."

"No deal."

Peterman snapped open his ledger book and scanned a column with his finger. "Very well, twenty-five cents. It's my final offer." A pinched look showed on his boss's face, as if someone were squeezing his cheeks.

"And the repairs?"

"I'll put you and Russell in charge of compiling a list of needed repairs. I'll contact the Board, though it'll take some doing to convince them."

"Then talk nicely to the Board, Mr. Peterman. Good day." Paul left the office for the shafthouse. He entered the building, climbed into the skip, hung onto its edge and signaled to be lowered. The man-car only made several trips per day down the shaft, so if he missed his ride, he had to use the skip. It was uncomfortable, but at least it would get him to his location. The hot air only made his flushed face more heated as he plummeted beneath the surface. When the skip stopped briefly at the 31st level, he hopped out, and then almost ran into Sam.

"Hi there," Sam said, giving the tram one last push. "Look at all this copper we're bringin' up."

Paul shined his hat on the tram filled with rock. "At least that's one thing Peterman will be happy about."

"Did yer talk amount to anythin'?"

"I need to keep the details to myself for now. All I can do is keep monitoring conditions down here and making recommendations to Russell," said Paul. All of a sudden, he heard hob-nailed boots pounding over a floor of rocks. Whoever it was, he was in a hurry.

"Paul, you gotta get rid of Russell," shouted Cece, appearing from the darkness. He slammed his mining cap against the tram. "That boy is wet behind the ears and he's drowning us with his stupidity."

Paul gave Cece a concerned slap on the back. "What happened?"

"It's that stopwatch of his," said Cece. "No wonder we've been having all these accidents. If I don't watch out, I'll end up like Matthew and die from a sleeper."

"What's a sleeper?" asked Sam.

"Dynamite that doesn't detonate with the other charges, but explodes when the miner approaches the blast site," said Paul.

"What seems to be the problem, gentlemen?" Russell asked, stepping into the circle.

"Nobody likes to be timed while doing their job," said Paul. "A miner's work requires concentration."

"Are you suggesting something?" asked Russell.

"Yeah," said Cece. "Maybe he's saying that the longer you're here the more scrapes we'll get into."

"You're talking to a superior," said Russell. "Watch your tone."

"Use that stop watch if you must," said Paul, "but we need safer working conditions. Your uncle has agreed."

Russell threw his stopwatch up and down in the air, as if playing catch. "I agree with you, Paul. Copper Empire will only lose money with accidents. It decreases production."

"Couldn't have that now, could we?" snapped Cece.

Paul looked at Cece and Sam. "Both of you get back to work."

Russell clicked the stopwatch. "Now."

Cece retrieved his mining cap from the ground and grumbled as he walked away.

"I'll start filling up another tram after Cece blasts," Sam called as he followed Cece.

When all was clear, Paul stepped closer to Russell. "What business did you have telling your uncle that a mining captain was no longer needed?"

"Touchy, aren't we Paul?" Russell clicked the stopwatch on and off as if it were a game.

Paul's hand, like magic, shot out and grabbed the annoying time piece. "I've been the mining captain down here a long time. These men are like brothers to me."

"Correction, you were the unofficial mining captain. Frankly, we no longer need you to fill that role."

"Your uncle wants me to continue in that rank."

"Only to stop the miners from—"but Russell cut himself off, as if he said too much.

"Russell, what is it?" asked Paul.

"Let me re-phrase. Ever since I began employment here two weeks ago, I've heard rumors about miners joining a certain Western Federation."

With a hand, Paul motioned for Russell to continue.

"My uncle will fire anyone who joins up with that union. You best tell your so-called mining brothers to stay away from that socialist organization."

Paul grabbed the young man by the collar. "Don't ever threaten me again."

Russell broke away from Paul's grasp and disappeared into the darkness.

Chapter 9

Nancy carried a basket of clothes to the back of the mansion to prepare for tomorrow's wash. All members of her household had left a half hour ago to attend a social at Italian Hall, leaving her and T-bone alone in the house.

While struggling to stack heavy baskets, she heard the gongs of the grandfather clock in the parlor. It was already seven o'clock and she was late. Nancy still had to get dressed and curl her hair before joining her family. The first dance would have already begun by this time and she would need to hurry to the hall before Artie found another dance partner.

She walked to the foyer to retrieve the last basket when T-bone began barking. Nancy groaned. She hoped it wasn't another miner seeking her laundry services. The wash already took her days to complete and always left her tired. When she stepped onto the porch, she saw Russell Ubel jump out of his Model T automobile.

Her heart skipped a beat. It was flattering to have a young man like Russell pay attention to her, even though she had a beau. Nancy wondered why her pa had taken such a dislike to Russell—perhaps her father's judgment had been clouded because he had desperately wanted the engineer's job.

Nancy was drawn to Russell's self-confident nature, a quality she felt sorely lacking in herself. She found him strangely attractive, especially his high cheek bones that well contrasted his short stature.

"Inside, T-bone," Nancy said and pushed the dog's black hide into the house. T-bone put his nose to the screen door and growled.

Russell lifted his basket of clothes with ease and hopped the steps that led to the columned porch. "Just like I promised, Miss Nancy," he said, placing the load before her. He stuck a hand in his pocket and she noticed Russell was every bit as skinny as his uncle.

"Indeed," Nancy said with a smile. "And I hope it's the last—I mean—oh I'm sorry," she said, struggling to find the right words to speak. "What I mean to say is that I'm up to my ears in laundry."

Russell shook his head as if he sympathized with her burdens. "Miss Nancy, I'm indebted to your service. I wish you'd allow me the pleasure of escorting you to dine in town sometime." Before she could protest he said, "I remember you have a beau."

Nancy looked at the basket of clothes. It was easier than meeting his intense stare. "I shall have to think about it, Mr. Ubel." She shyly glanced at him again.

Russell tipped his hat. "Perhaps next Sunday? After church service?" He stared at her.

Nancy shrugged, feeling uncomfortable with the silence.

"It's awfully quiet around here," Russell said, "has your family retired for the evening?"

"No. Everyone is at Italian Hall attending a dance."

"Aren't you going?"

"Yes, of course. Artie, my beau, is waiting for me there."

"Why isn't he escorting you himself?"

Nancy blinked rapidly.

"Ah, so you're alone?" Russell stepped closer.

Nancy took a step back and her heart pounded. But Russell wouldn't stop. The gray flecks in his eyes looked evil and gone was his pleasant, polite manner.

"Since your beau couldn't escort you to the dance, I'd like to take his place." Russell reached for her hand and grabbed it. Nancy stayed rooted to the porch. She didn't know what to do. No gentleman had ever been so bold with her before. Nancy was sure her thudding heart was louder than T-bone's growls coming from inside the house. She tried to take her hand away, but he tightened his grip, and then yanked her body toward his.

Suddenly, Russell forced his mouth onto hers and kissed her hard. With her free hand, she pushed on his chest, attempting to free herself, but Russell was too strong. He finally let her go, walked backward down the steps and laughed. Nancy clamped a hand over her mouth, her eyes watering with humiliating tears.

Russell deepened his voice. "Now don't start spreading stories of that stolen kiss, Miss Nancy," he said, wagging a finger at her. "I'm afraid if your father found out, he'd be angry, and then he'd pick a fight. He might just offend me, and then I'd have to fire him. You wouldn't want your father to lose his job."

Nancy screamed, "Get out of here, Mr. Ubel."

Russell took a step forward. "Come again?" he asked.

Adrenaline shot through Nancy's veins. "You are trespassing." Despite the tears that continued to pour over her cheeks, she managed to inflect authoritative coldness into her next words. "Turn around and leave, or I'll contact the sheriff."

But Russell didn't budge. He slowly smiled.

Nancy's body shook from head to toe as the seconds crept by.

Russell charged the steps again. "I want more than just a kiss this time."

Nancy's heart pounded and fluttered, terrified that he would follow through on his desires. She wanted to scream, but her voice box was paralyzed and T-bone's barking would have drowned the sound anyway. She grasped the doorknob from behind and yanked it open. T-bone jumped outside and landed on Russell's chest, pushing him down the porch steps. Russell beat the dog with his fists, but it was no use. T-bone snarled and barked and bit the engineer several times.

Russell hollered, jumped up from the ground and tried to escape, but T-bone clamped his razor-sharp teeth into his ankle and wrestled with it as if it were a bone. When T-bone finally let go, Russell leaped into his automobile and sped away.

Nancy sobbed and ran into the house.

*   *   *

Sam passed through Italian Hall's arched entrance and jogged up the stairs. When he reached the top step, he was reminded of his tardiness when he saw that the dance had already begun. Sam walked several steps and stopped in front of the auditorium. Tables were set up throughout the room with men, women and children dressed in their Sunday best. He knew that a few of the male attendees were actually representatives of the Western Federation and had arranged the dance as a way to encourage miners into joining their mining union.

He pulled down on his navy blue bowtie and walked backward on the floor, trying to take in the full effect of the affair. He liked the yellow crepe paper that streamed around the auditorium. It reminded him of sunny, spring days in South Carolina.

"Sam, be careful," yelled Mrs. Weyburn.

Sam halted, and then turned around to see what the problem was. One more step and he would have tumbled down the staircase. "Whew," he exclaimed. "Mrs. Weyburn, I'm sure glad you were watchin'."

Mrs. Weyburn placed a hand on her hip, her other hand leaning on a white parasol. "We've been waiting for you. Even Nancy arrived a few minutes ago and she was the last one to leave the house."

"I wanted to have a look-see around town and chat with some of the town folk before I came here," Sam lied. Actually, he had been trying to find another place to reside. Mrs. Weyburn had refused to commit to him a more permanent place in her home, so he needed to prepare for alternate lodging.

Almost all of the chairs were occupied, and the noisy room of adults and their children grew more boisterous with each passing minute. Sam felt a tug on his coat and looked down to see who the culprit was.

"Hi-a, Mr.-a Huston," said Roberto, pulling up his oversized knickers.

Sam tousled the boy's hair, genuinely pleased to see the boy. "Roberto, do an old man a favor and just call me Sam."

Roberto scrunched his forehead, trying to figure out something. "Mr.-a Sam, how old-a are you?"

Sam chuckled. "I'm thirty-three. Do ya think that's old?"

An impish smile spread across Roberto's face, emphasizing his thin, red lips. "Well, it's a-older than a-me!"

Sam laughed out loud. "Roberto, let's find a girl for ya to dance with," he said, pointing to the dance floor. "No doubt a lovely girl —"

"My papa's a-callin' me," interrupted Roberto, tugging Sam's coat again. "Bye, Mr.-a Sam." The boy dashed off to another table to join his family.

Sam waved goodbye to the boy, sniffed deeply and smiled. Cornbread. A favorite of his. At the buffet table, he picked up a plate and worked his way across the row of food. Nearby, Mrs. Weyburn was making herself useful by refilling the punchbowl as she talked to the women on either side of her. In spite of her extra weight, she looked attractive, especially with the dark brown ringlets at either side of her cherubic face. The rest of her hair was swept away to the back of her head, adorned with a turquoise hair clip to match her floor length skirt. Paul was a fortunate man.

At the sight of cornbread, Sam lifted two pieces for himself, and then grabbed a cup of punch to take back with him. The walk to the Weyburn table wasn't easy, however. He felt squeezed together by children who ran and shoved past him, one girl almost toppling over him. He lifted the plate and cup over his head to protect its contents.

"Oh, Sam," said Jeanie. Her rosy cheeks revealed her part in frolicking about the room. "I didn't see you."

Joey ran into his sister, nearly pushing her to the floor. "Hi, Sam. My pa's over there if you want to sit with him," he offered.

Several tables away, he saw Paul lift his hand in a friendly wave. Sam walked over and found an empty chair next to him. Paul seemed to be deep in discussion with Cece and a young red-haired man sitting across from him, so Sam sat himself down and began to eat. He looked at Cece once, then two more times in order to believe what he was seeing. Cece's hair was slicked back and his beard groomed. He even wore a clean, white shirt, though the sleeves were bunched to his elbows. Sam figured that was about as dressed up as Cece ever got.

Sam gave Cece a nudge. "Yer lookin' dapper this evenin'."

"Humph," Cece grunted, then rejoined the discussion with Paul.

Sam shrugged his shoulders. If Cece refused to converse with him, he might as well listen to Paul's conversation.

The red-haired man sipped his punch and appeared to be sulking. "I tell you, Paul, our unit should join up with the Federation." The man flipped open his jacket, took out a bottle of whiskey, poured some into his cup of punch, then stashed it back inside his jacket. He did it so quickly that Sam wondered if he was seeing things.

"Humph," Cece said again.

"I hear what you're saying, Henry," said Paul who leaned forward in his chair, his shirt sleeves almost touching chocolate cake crumbs that had settled on the table. "But if we choose to sign up with the union, there may be no turning back."

Henry wiped his red-stained lips with the back of his hand and scowled. "Meaning what?" The liquor was already turning the man's mood sour.

"We may have to go out on strike."

"That might not be such a bad thing." Henry tossed his napkin on the table and scooted his chair back. "See you later."

When Henry left the table, Cece leaned across the table so only Paul and Sam could hear. "We ain't striking, so don't even think about it."

"Now don't start anything, Cece," said Paul. He picked up crumbs from the table and set them on his plate. "You know Henry gets carried away."

"Isn't that Russell?" asked Cece, recognizing the engineer from across the room. "What's he doing here anyway?"

Russell looked as though he had just worked a twelve hour shift blasting rock in a copper mine instead of the engineer that he really was. Stains on his shirt and tears at the bottom of his pants encouraged a few partiers to point and stare at Russell's inappropriate attire. Something about Mr. Peterman's nephew didn't sit right with Sam, and it wasn't just his disheveled appearance. Russell's arms were crossed close to his chest and he seemed to be studying something. . .or someone.

Sam figured it out. Russell was watching Nancy. That had to be it.

Nancy and Artie were dancing to a ragtime waltz. The young woman looked particularly lovely in her pink, high-waist dress. As Artie took hold of her gloved hand for a twirl, he stopped her halfway through the turn. Sam cocked his head, unsure why Artie had interrupted their dance since the music hadn't stopped. Artie put his hands on Nancy's shoulders and applied pressure to align her posture perfectly. Nancy nodded and threw back her shoulders to demonstrate that she understood Artie's instructions. *Too bad Artie is such a demanding beau*, Sam thought. Before Artie could resume the waltz, Nancy pointed toward the middle of the floor, as if she preferred to be shielded within the circling dancers. Sam could have sworn that it had something to do with Russell.

"Artie could use a drink," said Cece, muttering mostly to himself. "I've never seen him have a good time. Always has to be the best."

Sam found himself agreeing with Cece, but didn't dare verbalize it. He was more surprised that neither Cece nor Paul noticed the fact that Russell had taken too keen of an interest in Nancy. For the time being, Sam decided to keep his comments to himself.

"It's Russell Ubel who I'm concerned about," said Paul, reading Sam's mind.

"Looks like he got into a fight with someone," noticed Cece.

Paul looked across the room, at Russell, and then shrugged his shoulders. "He must be here to find out if we're going to strike." Paul turned again to face Cece and Sam. "But he won't find out anything, because a final decision won't be made tonight." Paul sighed. "That boy is bad news for Copper Empire."

Cece rolled up his soiled napkin and tossed it at the center of table. "Why don't you give him what-for?"

"I already have," Paul said, and then chuckled. "Can't believe I took Russell by the collar last week and told him not to threaten me."

"Because of that stopwatch of his?" asked Sam.

"More than that." Paul took his hand away from the cup. "He told me that we're not to join up with the Federation."

Sam looked out to the dance floor again. He was glad that Artie had agreed to Nancy's wishes and took her into the center where other couples were crowded together and dancing, so they weren't quite so visible. Nancy still looked unhappy, her cheeks drawn and pale. It didn't help that Russell was on the other side of the room, staring at Nancy, seemingly memorizing every inch of her body. He hadn't even bothered to ask another young woman for a dance. No wonder Nancy looked as though she wanted to sink beneath the dance floor and run for home.

Henry returned to the table. He nudged Paul and said, "A Federation rep wants to discuss private matters with you — outside."

Paul scooted away from the table and said, "Excuse me, fellas, I'll be back soon."

Even with Paul gone, Sam didn't attempt to converse with Cece. When Cece wasn't looking at his food, he looked at the ceiling or the dance floor, but never at Sam. The silence between the two men was uncomfortable, so Sam observed Richard across the table talking to a girl, probably a classmate. It was obvious that Richard knew her well because they chattered on almost nonstop, not even pausing to eat. From listening to pieces of their conversation, Sam understood that Richard was talking to his girl about school and about how he would be graduating next year.

Richard suddenly noticed Sam. "Gosh, I'm sorry." His arm swept toward the Southerner. "This is Mr. Sam Huston, our new boarder. Sam, this is my girl, Sally Jane Armstrong."

"It's a pleasure, Miss," Sam said.

Sally Jane lowered her eyelids, and then lifted them up again. If the Keweenaw ever had a royal family, Sally Jane would have been one of its descendants. Her pretentious behavior didn't seem to faze Richard, however.

Sally Jane had already moved on to greet Cece. "Mr. McAllister, I never had a chance to wish you a good evening," she said, getting up from her seat. She lowered her torso down, then up, giving him a quick curtsey. It surprised Sam that she seemed to respect Cece.

But Cece wasn't taken in by the girl's charms. "Evenin'," he mumbled. He lifted a piece of chocolate cake and shoved it into his mouth without any tact.

Sally Jane took hold of Richard's arm. "I'd like to dance, Richard." It was more of an order than a request.

"Of course," Richard said, and then looked to those left at the table. "Please excuse us."

After Sally Jane and Richard went to the dance floor, Cece wiped his mouth with a napkin. "That is one hoity-toity gal." Cece wasn't attempting conversation with Sam, though.

To Sam's relief, he didn't have to endure the uneasy silence for long. Nancy and Artie left the dance floor and approached the table.

"Nancy, where is your mind tonight?" barked out Artie.

Nancy shrugged.

"Until you have settled down and your senses return, I shall have to seek another dance partner. You have committed too many dancing errors this evening." Artie walked away.

Sam cleared his throat. "Good evenin', Nancy."

Nancy looked up from the table, her eyes misty from Artie's criticism. "Good evening."

"Ya look lovely this evening." Sam meant it.

Nancy gulped. "Thank you, Sam."

"Is there somethin' wrong?"

Nancy shook her head and looked down again.

Sam knew her better than that, but didn't press further because, at that moment, a shrill command diverted his

102

attention. He turned to the cornmeal-littered dance floor where an elderly caller with a long, pointy, silver beard stepped up on stage, cupped gnarled hands over his mouth and yelled, "Choose your partners, ladies and gentleman. It's time for the quadrille!"

The crowd cheered and the band tuned their instruments. The toots of a horn and feathery notes of a flute blended in perfect harmony. The floor was crowded with eager couples.

Both men and women seemed to know exactly what to do. Four pairs lined themselves in a square. Artie found another young woman to dance with him, and led her to stand next to Richard and Sally Jane. Nancy stared at Artie and his new dance partner. She frowned and her head hung down.

Meanwhile, a woman who looked to be middle-aged grabbed Cece's arm. "Annabelle, no," Cece said.

"Get out of that chair and dance with me," cried Annabelle. Cece got up and followed her to the dance floor, shuffling his feet as if sentenced to the gallows.

Sam looked at Nancy again. He felt badly for her. Artie had treated her rudely, and he was fairly certain that Russell, even across the room, was making Nancy very uncomfortable. Fluttery feelings wavered in and out of his stomach, something he hadn't experienced in a while. He realized he cared for Nancy and wanted to make her happy. "Nancy, would ya do me the honor of tryin' the quadrille with me?"

Nancy's blue eyes lit up like a child. "Let's try, Sam." She clapped her hands together, her lace gloves muffling the sound.

Sam's throat squeezed tight. He hoped Nancy wouldn't misunderstand his intentions. Nobody could ever replace his Millie. . .

She stood up and smiled joyously, her cheeks turning rosy. Sam took her arm and led her to the dance floor next to Cece and Annabelle.

"Good lord," Cece muttered, rolling up his eyes. The hefty miner seemed to growl at Sam and he wondered why Cece disliked him so much.

Across from Nancy and Sam were Artie and his new dance partner. Artie leered at Sam, then leaned forward and said to Nancy, "I hope you recollect the quadrille steps so that you do not embarrass Sam."

"I'm honored Nancy's my partner," Sam said. "I'll need all the help I can get."

Circus-like music filled the room and the participants clapped together in unison, ready for the dance. Sam watched Richard bouncing up and down, clapping to the tune. Sam smiled to himself, admiring the boy's exuberant personality, just like his ma.

When Nancy nudged him, Sam was reminded to pay attention if he was to get through the dance. Nancy daintily clapped her gloved hands. Sam joined in, trying to clap with the beat. His natural clumsiness made the task hard. His hands always seemed to join together at the wrong time.

Over the loud clapping, Sam tried to explain to Nancy, "I really don't know how ta do this dance."

"Please don't worry," she called out. "I'll help you. First you bow to me."

Sam turned right to bow to Nancy. She, in turn, curtseyed, then whispered, "Bow to your corner."

Sam bended, but strangely enough, when he looked up again, he saw Nancy's pleated backside instead of her face. He felt a strong arm pull him in the opposite direction and found Cece's dance partner.

Annabelle yelled at him, "You're supposed to bow to your corner, not your partner." She curtseyed perfectly, but pursed her lips.

Sam obeyed, and then watched the others so he could perform the next move without a mistake. As expected, Artie executed the dance moves with precision. However, Sam was astonished that Cece was a graceful dancer. The burly miner had exact moves, keeping his right arm stiffly behind him like a gentleman should.

Sam breathed freely again when the men stepped back for the ladies. The women moved to the center, gracefully circling clockwise while touching their white-gloved hands in unison, then turned and glided counterclockwise. After finishing their routine, they returned to the square.

His heart sank when it was the men's turn. Nancy instructed Sam, "Now the men do the same thing that the women just did." Cece sprang first to the center and Artie and Richard glided perfectly to the middle to meet him. Sam gulped and followed. Cece tried to use his bulky frame to crowd him out, but Sam squeezed into the circle using his hip to push Cece away.

As the men rotated clockwise in a circle, Cece saluted his right arm far overhead, too high for Sam to reach. Richard and Artie stretched their arms and were barely able to meet Cece's hand. However, in order for Sam to reach their hands, he was forced to clumsily walk the circle on his toes. A cacophony of laughter rose from the audience. The faux pas caused Sam to feel even more self-conscious.

The men finished their circle, dropped their hands, and then turned smoothly around to circle counterclockwise. This time, Sam thought fast enough to play his own joke. He led the others into the next move. Instead of raising his hand to meet the others, he dropped his hands to his ankles. Richard laughed as he participated in Sam's joke, touching Sam's hand near the ankles. The other men, Cece and Artie, had no other choice but to follow Sam's move and awkwardly bend over, their rear ends in the air, as they circled. Sam laughed with the audience at his own prank. He made the best of an embarrassing situation.

When the routine was finished, Sam and the other men returned to the square to find the women laughing. Nancy touched Sam's arm.

"You're doing just fine, Sam."

Sam smiled. He convinced himself he would have fun during the rest of the dance, no matter what else Cece tried to do to distract him. The couples held each other's hands to form a circle and glide around. Sam tripped over his feet, but it didn't matter. He was having too much fun anyway. Sam and Nancy laughed throughout the dance until the music finally ended.

Cece scowled. "That was the worst dance ever."

Sam couldn't stop smiling. "It was still fun."

"Guess you were too busy picking cotton down South to get dance lessons," Cece growled.

Sam glared at him. "Guess yer father was too busy crammin' pasties in his mouth to teach ya manners."

Nancy put a hand over her mouth to suppress laughter and said, "Sam, thank you so much for the dance."

Sam stepped back as the music began again. Before he had a chance to ask Nancy to dance with him again, Artie grabbed Nancy's arm and called the dance steps out loud to Nancy as if she were a child, but the young woman endured the perfectionist behavior, at least until Russell walked away from the other side of the room and toward the dance floor. When Russell approached the couple, tears filled Nancy's eyes, leaving Sam no choice but to move closer to gauge the situation better. He thought Artie would deny Russell's request to dance with Nancy, but instead, he extended an arm to offer the young woman, all too willing to let Russell have the dance.

"No thank you, Mr. Ubel," Nancy said and reached for Artie's shoulder again. Russell grabbed her free hand and pulled her away from Artie.

"What is the meaning of this?" Artie asked.

"I just want to dance with Miss Nancy." Russell held her close and stepped heel to toe, but Nancy's feet remained still.

Sam marched out to the dance floor and broke up the couple with a firm hand on Russell's arm. "Ya heard the lady. She don't wanna dance with ya."

"Miss Nancy doesn't know what she wants," said Russell who backed away. "Isn't it past your bedtime, Sam? You have to be in the mine early tomorrow."

Sam pushed Russell away and yelled, "Ya heard me. Leave Nancy alone." Russell shoved Sam, and then the two men stared at one another. The band stopped playing music and the hall became as silent as a cemetery.

Russell inched close to Sam's face and whispered, "Mind your own business. I can make life in the mines very difficult for you." Russell grabbed Nancy's arm once again, but didn't get very far. Cece put his hand on Russell's shoulder, and then stepped on his foot. Russell grimaced.

"You're not wanted," Cece snarled. "Get outta here."

Russell limped to a nearby table, picked up his hat and headed towards the staircase.

Mrs. Weyburn approached the dance floor and put her arm around Nancy. By this time, people began talking and the band resumed their playing. "What's wrong? I was standing in the back of the room when Sam got between you and that gentleman."

"Ma'am, that ain't no gentleman. That was Peterman's nephew," Sam explained.

"Wouldn't take no for an answer," said Cece.

Nancy held a hand to her heart. "It's okay, Ma."

"All he wanted was to finish the dance with you," said Artie. He took her by the elbow and led her off the dance floor. "You embarrassed us in front of our friends."

"I'm sorry, Artie, but I just don't care for that man," Nancy said, this time a tear trickling down her cheek. She wiped it away with her hand.

Russell boldly approached them again. "Miss Nancy, I'll need to pick up my laundry tomorrow evening."

Cece walked to Russell, and with each advancing step, Russell retreated another step.

Sam called out, "Ya ain't welcome here or at the boarding home."

"You'll get your clothes back in the morning," Cece said.

"They need to be cleaned, starched and ironed," said Russell, his voice becoming weaker with each demand he uttered.

"You'll find them at the bottom of a mine pit if you don't get out of here," Cece yelled. Russell scampered down the steps.

Mrs. Weyburn drew her daughter in for a hug. "It's all right, Ma," Nancy repeated. "I'll do his laundry, return it to him, and then I won't have anything to do with him."

"No you won't." Cece blurted out. "I'll take the clothes to the mine tomorrow. But I'll let T-bone do his business on Russell's Skivvies first."

Mrs. Weyburn cleared her throat. "Thank you, Cece," she said, then looked directly at Sam. "I'm ashamed it took me this long, but I want you to know you're welcome to stay with us as long as you want." Her dark eyelashes opened wide. "Welcome to our family, Sam."

Sam's jaw dropped. "Mrs. Weyburn, I don't know what ta say. . . "

"Just call me by my Christian name."

"Thank ya Marie, I will."

Chapter 10

Nancy's knees ached after hours of kneeling in the vegetable garden. She finally stood up and straightened her back and took in the scenery around her, marveling at how July had already arrived. Summer was half over. The maples, birches and poplars all had a healthy shimmer that comes from the season's higher temperatures.

She resumed picking the pea pods. Her basket was close to overflowing when tears filled her eyes—a ritual she had come to know daily ever since Russell's attack on her weeks ago. Still as upset as if it had happened only moments ago, Nancy wanted to confide in someone about what had happened, but was afraid her pa would find out and confront Russell, then lose his job. Also, her own reputation was at stake. If word got around that Russell attempted to violate her and Artie found out, she would never receive a marriage proposal.

A tear threatened to release, but she held it back. She wondered why her beau hadn't prevented Russell from dancing with her at Italian Hall. Artie might have been eager to dance with another woman—he had been especially critical with her at the dance about maintaining perfect posture and performing the dance steps correctly. Nancy knew she was ruminating over something as silly as a dance, but decided she would need to practice some of the dances before the next social. Then Artie would be proud to have her on his arm.

That had to be it. If only she had put more effort into pleasing Artie, he would have proposed marriage to her by now. After two years of courtship, would he ever see her as adequate enough to become his wife?

Why couldn't Artie be more like Sam? Sure, Sam was homely, but in the two months that he resided at the boarding house, Nancy knew him to be kind and caring, as well as funny and talkative. Nothing like Artie. She tried to think of a future with Sam, but couldn't. Sam never attempted to court her, but how could he when she and Artie were a couple, and Artie was his roommate? Still, she enjoyed the time spent speaking with Sam, whether it was after supper on the porch or in the parlor. She wondered if it was really possible to have more than just a friendship with Sam.

A northeasterly wind picked up strength. She felt her blonde locks, tucked safely in a bun just hours before, suddenly begin to brush against her face. As she glanced at the sky, she found her spirits lifted simply watching the clouds race along the heavens. She tried to imagine the billowy pillows forming a bride and groom at the alter, but the image simply wouldn't form. Instead, her imagination created a picture of tall buildings and motor vehicles. Was that in her future?

As long as it didn't rain, she knew her duty was to pick peas. The ominous clouds would surely give way to rain at any moment, but Nancy returned to work, feeling pods to make sure they were filled before removing them. When her fingers detected flat ones, she paid closer attention to the crop and noticed that the lower leaves looked yellow and wilted. She knew what that meant — those peas would be useless.

"Ma, come here. Feel these."

Rising from the ground, Marie's knees cracked from the extra pounds she carried on her frame. She walked to her daughter and leaned over her shoulder.

"Hmm," she said. "No use wishing for something more. I'm just happy we collected what we did." Marie's face glistened. "Why don't you try that last patch over there? If we work a little harder, we can finish before the rain comes."

Nancy walked on her knees to the unharvested section, careful not to disturb the other vegetables. "That suits me just fine."

Marie knelt next to her daughter to assist in the effort. "Nancy, you look exhausted. Have you thought of earning money by doing something that doesn't require a lot of physical strength? Perhaps sewing?"

Nancy wiped her forehead with a dirty hand. "Don't be ridiculous, Ma. I wouldn't leave you here to garden by yourself."

"This work doesn't suit you. Why don't you at least give it some thought?"

But her mother's words only caused Nancy to work even harder. Barely out of her teens, her hands no longer had the smooth skin of a child. They had become calloused with years of gardening. Even her fingernails were worn down to the tips.

"I'm too tired to think right now," Nancy said with a sigh.

"Don't get discouraged," said Marie who looked up for a moment, streaks of dirt littering her face. "That's enough for now, honey. Why don't we go in?"

Nancy looked at the dark thunder clouds above. A storm would erupt at any time. "I like working hard, Ma. It keeps my mind off other things."

"You mean Artie?"

Nancy didn't answer. Actually, she meant both Artie and Sam, but she couldn't tell her mother yet of her feelings for Sam.

Warm droplets of rain began to fall, but Nancy stayed put. "Ma, it seems hopeless sometimes. I feel like I'll still be living here when I'm fifty years old and Artie will still be a boarder."

Marie chuckled. "Now that's what I call a long romance."

Nancy angrily threw pods in the hand-woven basket set between her and Marie. Her hair darkened as it got wet from the summer rain. "Why does he have to be so stubborn? Why can't Artie and I just get married and settle down?"

Marie placed her green harvest into the basket, slivers of rain pouring down her cheeks. "I don't know, Nancy. Maybe it isn't the right time. And maybe he's not the one for you."

She thought again of Sam, then pushed the image of him aside and thought back instead to her school years. She had never felt accepted by her peers, especially the other girls. Although attractive in an old-fashioned sort of way, she was quiet and unassuming. Consequently, most of the boys chose her more talkative and prettier counterparts as girlfriends and later on, as their wives. She felt overlooked and misunderstood and quickly took to Artie when the two met. He was the first male to show her any kind of attention. It didn't seem fair to her that the most honest and sincere girls were quite often the most ignored.

"Ma, there's no other suitors seeking to court me."

"So?"

"I don't wish to become an old maid."

Marie grunted. "That isn't a good enough reason to settle for Artie."

The rain poured down faster, with more urgency. Neither woman needed an invitation to retreat into the boarding home. Nancy stood, picked up her basket, and followed her mother toward the house; their long, wet dresses clinging to their legs. "If only Artie could see my finer qualities," Nancy said breathlessly, seeking shelter under the covered porch. "Then I'm sure he'd see the value in having me for a wife."

"You don't need to be anything different," said Marie, putting an arm around her shoulder. "Besides, women of your character are plenty valued."

Nancy held onto the porch column. The storm unleashed its fury around her. Bolts of lightning touched down as if punishing her for Russell's attack. Was it her fault for being nice to him in the first place? The storm sent shivers through her frail body. It was as if Mother Nature was shouting that her life would no longer be the same. She was ready for a change in her life, but could she afford to lose the dream of becoming Artie's wife?

*   *   *

Paul was impatiently waiting in the shafthouse. Earlier that morning, Peterman agreed to meet and discuss the ongoing safety problems in the mine. If Peterman refused to address the problems, as he had many times in the past, Paul imagined he would grasp Peterman's arm, shove him onto a skip, and force him underground so he could witness the concerns firsthand. Paul wasn't sure he could follow through on what he fancied, but he had to get his boss' attention.

It was fifteen minutes past the time Peterman had agreed to meet. Paul was about to the leave the shafthouse and look for him at his office when he saw a skip approaching the surface. A hand pulled the bell cord, and the skip stopped. Richard climbed out of the skip.

"Richard!" cried Paul.

"Hi, Pa." Richard lifted out a box that contained drill bits, pulled the bell cord again, and the skip rose to process its contents.

"What were you doing underground?" Several weeks ago, Paul had convinced his boss to employ Richard above ground, sorting copper rocks and poor rocks. Paul didn't want Richard or any boy working underground, considering the dangerous conditions.

"I didn't want to go down there, but one of the miners needed drill bits sharpened."

"It's too dangerous for you to work down there."

Richard shrugged his shoulders. "But, Russell ordered me to do so."

Paul despised Russell. He was nothing but trouble, and he deliberately sent Richard underground, just to antagonize Paul.

Paul softened his tone. He gripped his son's shoulder and explained to him, "Richard, you came up riding in a skip."

Richard explained, "Yes, sir. Russell told me to do that, too."

Paul expelled a large sigh. "That skip was full of rocks. Didn't Russell tell you to be careful? Didn't he tell you not to ride the skip unless it was empty?"

Richard shook his head. "I didn't realize I was doing anything wrong."

Paul patted Richard's shoulder. "I know. I know. Take the drill bits to the blacksmith. But don't take them back underground. I'll talk to Peterman about this. Your job is to assist surface operations, and that's it, understood?"

Richard nodded.

"I'll see you after the shift ends."

* * *

Paul left the shafthouse with all due haste, still fully clothed in his mining garb. He didn't even acknowledge the miners who passed by. He was on a mission, and he'd complete it while the sharp raindrops and fierce wind gusts blew on him. When he reached Peterman's office, he decided he wouldn't even knock on the door. He grabbed the handle, but the door was locked, so he pounded on the door with all of his might. No one answered, so he banged again.

"Mr. Peterman!" Paul yelled and knocked. He yanked his mining hat off and wiped away raindrops from his forehead. "Open this door now."

Paul hadn't decided whether or not to accept the invitation to the Western Federation meeting being held later that evening. He was inclined to believe that the Federation would force his unit to go on strike. On the other hand, labor conditions had worsened every day and he thought that a union might be able to help the miners.

As he leaned against the unanswered door, Paul closed his eyes. The rain smacked his face. He wanted to get away from the rain and go back into the mine, but it was urgent for him to meet with Peterman.

Suddenly, Paul heard a familiar voice in his ear.

"I don't think Uncle William is in there."

Paul's eyes snapped open. Sure enough, Russell stood beside him, holding an umbrella that shielded his well-combed hair from the rain.

"Tell me where he is," Paul demanded. He was sure he could smell the odor of residual alcohol from the forty-rod on the boy's breath.

Russell swayed a bit to the side, but kept his balance fairly well given the large amount of liquor he must have consumed. "Uncle William mentioned something about going into town this afternoon. Is there something I can help you with?"

"How dare you send my son underground. Both you and your uncle know I don't want him there," Paul yelled.

"Your son works for Copper Empire, and I told him to do a job. If he's unable to work, he'll be fired. Is there anything else?"

Paul decided he'd confront Peterman later about Richard's job. "A portion of the tunnel is going to cave in unless it's attended to immediately by our timbermen. I want your uncle to look at it."

Russell laughed. He reacted as if Paul was being melodramatic. "Really, Paul."

"There is nothing humorous about an insecure hanging wall," Paul shouted. "A miner could be killed if a rock broke loose."

"Surely you are exaggerating."

"Isn't it a bit early for you to make an appearance here?" Paul wasn't usually facetious, but felt he had taken enough abuse from Peterman and his arrogant nephew. While the miners worked under the most trying of conditions, Russell chose to frequent saloons and Caleb's. It fed the boy's lush appetite for booze and women, but left little time for engineering.

In one way, the miners had been relieved. For the past month, Russell only showed up to work in the late afternoon, and when he arrived, he didn't have the energy to ride the skip down and monitor workers with a stopwatch. The miners had been able to perform their jobs without the drawback of a mining dunce watching their job performance. On the other hand, safety at the mine had slid to its lowest point. Every week since spring, several miners had been injured due to improperly maintained equipment.

Moreover, in the last month Paul and Peterman's meetings had no longer been civil, but instead were filled with accusatory outbursts. Since production and profits had increased in the past weeks, Paul demanded that Peterman fulfill the promise he made back in May of raises and repairs. Instead, no raise had been forthcoming and Peterman continued to reject repair requests. Peterman reasoned the mine's good fortune was due to Russell's efficient management, so he didn't believe he had to fulfill his past promises. As long as the profits increased, Boston management was happy, stockholders were richer and Peterman chomped on more expensive European cigars. He didn't even seem to notice that Russell only came to the mine periodically.

With one hand holding an umbrella, Russell used his other to fish a watch out of his pocket and flip the cover open. "It's exactly half past five. Go back to the mine."

Paul slapped his mining cap back on his head and marched back to the shafthouse. He went inside and waited for the man-car to be positioned, then climbed aboard with the afternoon shift. Just before the car lowered into the mine, Russell closed his umbrella and hopped in. Steel wheels roared as they moved along the tracks into the mine, muffling Russell's voice.

"Did you hear me, Paul?" asked Russell.

Paul refused to answer. Instead, he listened as the man-car was being lowered. The squealing wheels sounded like mice pleading for the wheels to be greased. When the man-car finally reached their working level, Paul and Russell climbed out. With a flick of his thumb on the flint igniter, he lit the carbide lamp on his hat and walked through the drift, ignoring Russell's taunts.

"Who's singing?" Russell called out.

Paul heard the singing in the drift, too, but ignored Russell's question. The men walked further without speaking. They listened to the singing bouncing off the cave walls. Paul chuckled to himself. It sounded like Sam's voice.

The voice yodeled, "There is a copper underground, as pure as can be found, sometimes it's a mile below, a mine can be hot or cold."

The singing stopped momentarily, and then the voice sang, hanging on to the first word for at least 10 seconds, "Oh, the dangers there are several, death waits for you at any level."

The men neared the singer's location, and the singer drawled on, "I light up my gas lamp, go down into this slave camp, and I'm feelin' low as this 31st level hole."

Russell and Paul approached and shined their carbide lamps on Sam, who was sitting on the ground. He stopped singing and smiled. The carbide lamp showed sweat and dirt smeared across Sam's face.

"'Been waitin' for you, Paul."

117

"I'm not paying you to sing," Russell snapped. "Get to work."

Sam retorted, "I ain't workin' cause it ain't safe back there." Sam got up from the ground and grabbed Paul's arm. "Ya gotta get the men back there to stop working. The blastin' alone could cause an accident."

"Why are you so scared, little man?" Russell asked. Ironically, the engineer was no taller than Sam.

"My name is Sam Huston, not little man," Sam drawled. "The wall back there needs to be timbered."

"On the contrary. I checked it a few days ago. The wall is solid."

Sam ignored the engineer. "The men been complainin' all week about the cracks. Ya know it has to be fixed right now before somebody gets hurt, Paul."

Russell swayed on the ground. "I have an engineering degree, Mr. Huston. Surely that counts for something?"

Sam retorted, "Experience counts for more than book learnin'."

"I don't believe I like you're attitude," Russell said.

Paul grabbed Russell's arm. "And I don't like yours."

Russell brushed Paul's arm away. "Pardon me?"

Paul exclaimed, "It's not just the hanging wall back there. Did you notice the loose strands and rust on the cable? The cable needs to be replaced. It's worn out."

"Why have the men neglected the cable? Whose job is that?" asked Russell. "I'll write him up and report — "

"You'll do no such thing," Paul interrupted. "The men in charge of that job have been told by your uncle to delay replacing the cable."

"If that's the case, then I agree with my uncle."

118

But Paul didn't so much as flinch. "I've been around copper mines my whole life. And I'm telling you, it's getting much too dangerous to work here." He stepped closer to the engineer.

Even the darkness of the mine couldn't hide Russell's face being drained of all color. His arrogant smile turned into a frown. "If you're through, direct me to where you think the problem is."

"I'm comin' along, too," said Sam.

Paul led the journey, negotiating the barely visible tunnel with the aid of the dim light of his lamp. He was trying to think of his wife instead of all the problems. He breathed deeply to calm himself. Thank God for Marie. While his boots struck the damp ground, he thought of the violent thunderstorm at the surface that was pouring an ocean of rain from the sky. *One good thing about being in a mine*, he thought to himself, *the weather stays fairly constant underground, year round.*

"We're almost there," Paul said. "I can hear voices." Sure enough, they rounded a corner where Cece and other miners were standing at a stope and speaking loudly, each trying to out-talk the other. Every few seconds Cece would point to a place on the hanging wall and Paul knew that's where the worst of the danger was.

"Why aren't these men drilling?" asked Russell. "I never authorized a shut-down on this level."

"It's plain as rain—if you were ever here to do your job," Cece interjected, crossing his arms.

Paul smiled at Cece's insubordinate behavior. Leave it to Cece to give Russell what-for. Even as a child, Cece never had a problem telling the plain truth.

"Any decent engineer woulda had the timbermen down here already," said Sam.

"Don't use that tone with me," said Russell. He picked up a steel bar from the ground, and then walked to the stope,

119

wobbling on the rocks. He used the bar and rapped clumsily on the ceiling, as if struggling with a piñata. Some of the miners chuckled out loud. Cece snorted.

"That's enough," shouted Russell. The liquor had triggered his anger.

Paul closed his eyes, trying to keep his temper in check. Russell didn't have a clue how to check for wall weaknesses.

Russell ignored the taunts and picked up the long steel bar once again to swing wildly at the tunnel ceiling, but this time Cece came up from behind and grabbed the bar from him.

"What the—" Russell saw there was nothing between his hands anymore and spun around. "What do you think you're doing?"

"Are you inspecting the wall or trying out for the Red Jacket baseball team?" asked Cece. The miners roared their laughter.

"I'm your superior," said Russell. When he attempted to retrieve the bar, Cece held it away and towered over Russell, like a parent to a child.

"Where did ya learn about copper minin'?" called out one of the miners who held onto his stomach as he laughed.

"Any more outbursts like that and you'll be fired," hissed Russell, giving in to his anger. His carbide lamp shined on Cece's face. "If you're so clever, why don't you demonstrate?"

"No problem." Cece took the bar and rapped on the ceiling of the cave. The miners ducked and dove away from the rock cavity when debris fell.

Paul's heart skipped a beat. He recognized the hollow sound made by Cece's steel bar. The miners weren't laughing anymore.

Cece's husky voice could barely be heard when he uttered, "God almighty."

"I . . .uh. . .I'll get the timbermen to prop it up," said Russell in a softer voice.

"You'll do it now," Paul cried out.

Russell left and Paul said to the others, "Let's all go. It's too dangerous here. It's just as well, the shift is over anyway."

Russell led the way across the drift, with Paul close behind.

"This is your fault," Paul said when he finally caught up to Russell. "I've warned you and Mr. Peterman over and over again about these problems."

Russell pushed forward and tried to walk faster, but couldn't get away from Paul's physically fit pace. "I've detected the problem, Paul. No need to remind me."

"You mean I detected it," said Cece, charging ahead. "Get your facts straight. And while you're at it, go back to mining school."

"Listen to the miners," Sam called out. "Ya might learn a thing or two."

"Yeah!" shouted a miner. "You don't know nothing about copper or mining. Paul shoulda been the engineer, not you."

Russell pumped his arms from side to side, and then broke into a run toward the man-car. Some of the benches were already filled with miners, so Russell scrambled on the front bench and remained standing, as if he were going to make a speech. Paul groaned. He had hoped for a less hostile ride to the grass.

"You're all going to hear my side before we get to the shafthouse," shouted Russell. "Paul thinks he's smarter than me, but he's not. He's just a fake diamond pretending to be real. He acts like a king in that mansion of his, but he's really just a pauper."

"Give it a rest Russell," said Cece. "It's not like Uncle William is going to fire you or nothing."

But the forty-rod Russell had consumed earlier had worked its way through his system and made him meaner than all the mining bosses in the copper country put together. Russell raised his voice. "You're going to respect me, Paul. It's either my way, or you're fired. Now, you wouldn't want to lose that castle of yours? Your kingdom would crash faster than that hanging wall. And Princess Nancy. . .a pity I couldn't have my way with her before the social at Italian Hall."

The miners drew in their breath. Cece lunged toward Russell, but Paul held him back. The fight was his. Paul inched toward the man-car and felt as if the devil had ripped out his heart. He had never felt such revulsion for anyone before.

Russell continued, "Yes, Paul, I suppose Nancy never told you, but a few weeks ago I paid her a visit at your castle while you and your kin were dancing the night away. She's quite a woman. Almost as good looking as the ones I know at Caleb's."

Paul's fist struck Russell hard on the mouth. The young man fell on the bench, touching the wound, wiping away trickling blood. "It's over, Paul," he gurgled. "You hear me? You're fired."

Paul stepped forward to punch the engineer again, but Sam grabbed his arm.

"Don't make it worse," said Sam. "Let's get outta here."

Paul breathed heavily, trying to regain his composure. He held onto his skinned knuckles and looked toward the few miners who weren't yet on the man-car. "All right men, the show is over. Take your seats. Cece, if you don't mind, sit between me and that so-called engineer."

"Sure," said Cece who planted his hefty frame next to Russell, practically edging him off the bench. He looked right at him. "Now keep your trap shut."

Russell cowered in Cece's presence and moved as far to the edge of the bench as possible. He didn't dare utter another word.

Paul took his seat and pulled the bell cord, signaling the hoist operator at the surface. When the man-car lifted, Paul pondered how he would ever resolve these problems when he worked for an impossible, unreasonable boss and an engineer that probably attacked his daughter! That is, if he could convince Peterman to reverse Russell's decision and give him his job back. As the man-car stopped and started over and over again, picking up miners at other levels, he tried to think of bible verses, but nothing seemed to console him. Finally, up ahead, Paul saw glimmers of light that looked as sweet as a choir of angels singing in heaven. They were almost at the surface.

Suddenly, the man-car's wheels turned roughly and gave a preternatural squeal. The car lurched, and then swooped downward. The miners screamed for their lives. In an instant, the man-car jumped off the tracks, crashing against the shaft, hurling men into the air.

Chapter 11

Paul struggled to regain consciousness. He slowly opened his eyes and tried to remember what happened. When he regained his focus, he realized his torso was bent over the side of the man-car. He craned his neck and saw a miner lying with his eyes closed, mouth slightly ajar. Paul listened to the man's shallow breaths and then noticed his own breaths were short and rapid. He was thankful that his carbide lamp was still lit, illuminating the shaft. Paul took a shallow breath, then tried to breathe deeper, but his lungs burned. Someone's foot rested on his back which throbbed under the pressure. Other limbs were crammed against his abdomen. Paul's arms shook, but he managed to untangle various body parts away from himself. He took a breath and groaned. Almost at once, the other miners joined in with their misery.

A miner shouted, "Over here! Henry's hurt real bad." Paul tried to get up to help, but struggled to catch his breath. From every angle, the groans and cries of men reached his ears and he knew he was fortunate to still be alive.

Finally came Sam's welcome Southern drawl. "Paul, are ya alright?"

Paul groaned. He laboriously lifted his pained body and staggered to maintain his equilibrium. His chest felt like it was being squeezed by a dozen miners all at once.

Sam was fortunate that he escaped, having no injuries. He took hold of Paul's arm. "Easy now," he said.

"Thanks, Sam." Paul's balance wasn't steady, but it didn't help that the man-car was lodged diagonally in the shaft. He touched his ribs and winced.

"What happened?" Sam asked.

"Simple. The cable snapped and the car jumped the tracks."

Paul's temples throbbed from the accident, so he pressed his hands on either side to help clear his head. He had to act quickly to ensure every man's survival.

"Whew," Sam said while relighting his carbide lamp, "That was close. We coulda been killed."

Paul called out to the men, "I want anyone who can, get off the man-car now." He shouted like a drill sergeant, "Move. Hurry up!" until the men obeyed. When all capable miners crawled and limped out the man-car and into the drift, Paul turned to Sam. "Where's Cece?"

"I don't know. I thought he was sittin' next to ya."

Paul shouted once again, "We've got to act quickly. I want all of you to line up, get the injured off the car, and then I want you in groups to help carry the injured to the surface."

"Can't we wait for someone to fix the cable?" asked a miner.

Paul shook his head. "No. That will take too long."

"But the climb. . .it's gotta be five levels to the surface!"

"Look men, we've got no time to ponder options," said Paul. "Let's get these men to the hospital."

Sam joined Paul at the man-car and attended to the injured. Paul went to the first injured miner he saw and grasped under the man's armpits while Sam carried his legs, then handed him off to the miners on the ground. The miners obeyed Paul's order without another word. As each body was carried out, miners grouped and prepared to carry the injured up the ladders.

Minutes later, Paul shined his light across the man-car. All of the injured had been removed. He knew he didn't get to everybody, though. There had to be others. Where was Cece? He pointed his lamp along the shaft wall. Ahead of him lay a body wedged between the wall and the man-car. "Cece!" he cried out. Cece, however, didn't respond. Blood leaked from Cece's right eye and trickled down to his bushy beard. One of his legs looked mangled. Paul's insides froze. His buddy might be dead.

"C'mon," said Sam. "If we're goin' to save him, let's get him out." Two other miners lifted the front of the man-car away from the shaft wall, and Paul and Sam carefully but quickly carried Cece's body away. Paul and Sam reached the drift and laid Cece on the ground. Paul put his ear to Cece's heart. It was beating, albeit faintly. He looked above and thanked God that Cece was still alive, but didn't have more time to rejoice. He ran toward the shaft again.

Sam yelled, "Paul, we've gotta get outta here."

"I know," Paul shouted from the man-car. "But we're still missing some men. I won't be long. Rip a piece of your shirt and try to stop Cece's eye from bleeding."

Paul and the two miners continued their search. They climbed to the back, and when they lifted the rear portion of the man-car away, his breath caught in his throat as he found two bloody and mangled bodies underneath. It was pointless to even check for a heartbeat.

"Hurry, Paul!" Sam shouted. "Cece is as white as a ghost."

"I can't leave men down here if they're still alive." Paul ordered the other two miners to keep holding the man-car away from the wall so he could inspect the area. They lost their grip, and the man-car slid further. Paul climbed over the man-car and crawled on the tracks to look in front of the man-car. He saw a body lie contorted on the tracks. Paul inched over to reach it, and then rolled the body over to identify the man. When his lamp shined on the face, he found Russell's eyes were open. He had cuts and bruises and blood all over. Scanning the area one more time, he counted the survivors and injured. There were no other victims and Paul couldn't do any more for the dead, so he crawled back to the drift.

"How many, Paul?"

"Two are dead and Russell is barely alive," said Paul who pulled out rope from a tool box. "Tie this around Cece. Where are the others?"

"They're already takin' the injured and climbin' to the surface," said Sam.

"Let's get Cece up there, too."

"What 'bout Russell?"

"Leave him. Cece comes first."

With his own body aches and broken ribs, Paul rushed to the ladder to help pull, with Sam's assistance, while the other two miners stayed below to help lift Cece. When they reached the top of the level, he not only saw the miners from the accident, but was also met by a crowd of men who were descending the ladder from the fourth level.

"I heard what happened when I passed the others," said a miner with a thick, black moustache. He motioned to his group of men. "The engine operator sent us when the miniature showed the man-car stopped. Got down here as soon as we could."

"That cable should have been fixed weeks ago," cried out another miner. "I told Peterman —"

"We all told Peterman," interrupted Paul. "Never mind that. Two men are dead down there, Russell is close to death, and we have injured men who need help getting to the surface."

"God almighty," said the mustached man who looked at his group. "Men, let's help get everyone outta here."

*　*　*

"Pull, Sam. Pull!" yelled Paul as his aching muscles bulged from hauling Cece's massive body up the last level. Paul's shirt was drenched with sweat from exertion and injury. He was sure his ribs were harmed even worse from having to lift Cece up each level. And he felt dizzy, almost to the point of blacking out. But he had to save his best friend, so he labored on. Paul had noted, around the third level, that Cece had stirred and moaned a few times, but didn't seem fully awake.

Suddenly, Sam called out, "Whoa. I'm losin' the rope."

"What?" Paul asked. He and Sam were above, pulling for Cece's life on the rope while two other miners were behind for added strength. Paul's heart galloped. He had to admit the sweat from his hands was causing his hands to slip, too. Cece dangled in mid-air with only a rope holding his mid-section. Paul tried drying his hands one at a time on his pant leg.

All of a sudden, Cece mumbled.

"Cece, did you say something?" asked Paul. "Cece, I can't hear you, but we'll have you out soon."

"Trying to kill me?" rasped Cece in a weak voice.

"Thank God you're making sense now," Paul called out to his friend.

"What am I doing swinging in mid-air like a monkey?" asked Cece in a louder voice.

"Don't ya remember the accident?" asked Sam who started pulling on the rope again.

"Course I do. That durn car jumped the tracks and now my leg's broke."

"You've been out cold for hours," said Sam. "We've been pullin' ya up each level so we can get ya in a hospital."

"You're a clod," said Cece. "And you ain't strong enough to get me to the grass."

"I have more gumption than ya think," said Sam. He stopped pulling again. "My hands are so sweaty, I keep losin' my grip."

"Wipe 'em on your pants then, you nincompoop," yelled Cece.

"Try bein' grateful," Sam called out. "Ya might be dead if it weren't for Paul and me." Sam wiped his hands, one at a time, then gave the rope another mighty tug.

"Pull. Pull. Heave. Ho!" Paul cried out and groped the rope, lifting Cece's heavy body. Finally, they had Cece at the first level. Paul and Sam put Cece's body on the ground.

"We're almost at the shafthouse," Sam said.

"About time," Cece said. "I need a doctor."

Paul nodded. Breathlessly, he yelled up to the shafthouse, hoping somebody was there. "We need more help down here!"

"Pa, I'm on my way down to help," yelled Richard.

In a weaker voice, Paul sputtered out, "We need more men to help."

Richard hopped off the last ladder rung and ran to Paul, grabbing his arm. "Pa, you rest. I'll help get Cece up to the shafthouse."

Paul mopped his forehead and gasped. "Sam, Richard, can you help get Cece to the hos—"but couldn't finish his sentence. Paul lost consciousness in his son's arms.

*   *   *

Lowell Weyburn had stomped down the winding staircase, following Paul. "I forbid you to marry that girl!" he hollered. Paul turned around and looked at his father. Lowell's face was red and the veins in his neck were engorged. Paul thought it best not to respond right away; nevertheless, his fist clenched and he wasn't sure if he would be able to control his temper this time. Why did his father have to pick on Marie anyway? He wanted to marry the girl he loved since he was fourteen years old. His father joined him in the dining room and took a seat at the opposite end of the long table. Before he answered his father, Paul straightened his tie and threw back his shoulders. "I love Marie, Father."

A butler poured coffee into Lowell's cup. Lowell nodded at the butler, and then shook his head at his son. "I'll hear no more of this conversation. You will enroll again at the Michigan Mining School and cease this foolish talk."

Paul knew what he had to do. "No, Father."

Lowell looked up from his coffee. "Don't disobey me, Paul. I have worked and traveled and labored to give you opportunities few people on earth have."

"I'm going to marry Marie."

"Enough."

Paul spoke louder. "You can't stop me, father. It's my life!"

Lowell pounded his fist on the table. "You'll ruin your life. Do you hear me?"

Another voice, not in the dining room, sounded fuzzy to Paul. "Paul saved my life."

"Do you understand me?" Lowell yelled. "You'll destroy your life."

But again, a faint voice entered Paul's conscience. "Thanks to Paul, I'm alive."

Paul's eyes snapped open. His body still ached, but he was no longer in the mine or a teenager in a dream. Instead, he lay on a lumpy hospital bed. He sighed, wanting to forget the disturbing memory about his father. Paul tried to raise his head from the pillow, but weariness overtook him again, so he closed his eyes and listened to the rain pattering on the window as well as soft voices across the room.

"W-e-y. Hey Artie, come over here," Cece said. Paul assumed Artie walked over to Cece. Then he heard Cece say to someone else, "I'm giving an interview to Artie. Go away."

"Do I get an exclusive interview with you?" asked Artie.

"Sure, as long as you don't make me spell Weyburn for you," said Cece.

"Cece, you can't even spell Weyburn?"

"Sh. I quit school after the fifth grade. What do I need book learning for?"

Paul opened his eyes once again and struggled to lift a hand to his bruised face to determine the damage. He felt cuts all over his face. Nobody in the room realized he was awake. He felt woozy and wasn't sure if he was seeing things when he spotted a spider scurrying across the floor. Paul was amazed the creature could survive in such a sterile environment.

A hefty nurse spotted the spider at once. Paul recognized her as Annabelle, the woman who he heard had danced the quadrille with Cece at Italian Hall. She stomped across the room, her heavy shoes striking the clean tile with precision. The nurse lifted her leather shoe, pounded hard on the floor and killed the spider. She even threw it in the garbage without an ounce of squeamishness.

As Paul's eyesight sharpened, he watched nurses rush in and out of the spacious room, tending to the injured miners. The cots lined the room in a strict, orderly fashion. Several of the victims sat on the edge of the bed and others lay down, their feet protruding beyond its short length. Paul heard soft groans emitting from the injured, but all of them seemed to put up a brave front.

.It had happened so fast. One minute the men were seated on the man-car being lifted to the shafthouse, and the next minute they were racing against time to save lives. Two people were dead. Did Peterman know yet about Russell?

Annabelle bandaged Cece's lacerated eye, scolding him for not sitting still. Cece tried to brush her off with a wave of his hand. He was too busy being interviewed by Artie who stood in front of the injured miner, his fingers furiously writing on a small pad. Cece spoke in his usual short, quick grunts, telling of the accident and about Paul and Sam being heroes.

Paul certainly didn't feel like one. Why couldn't he have saved all the miners?

Annabelle finished patching Cece's eye and sharply fingered the cloth to ensure its security. Cece moaned, "Ow!"

But the strict nurse ignored his complaints. She stated in simple terms, "Your eye will be as good as new, Cece. But your leg is another story all together. You won't be able to work for six weeks."

Cece frowned. "I'd feel better if you'd just get away from me."

"You're welcome," Annabelle said in a snit. "A little appreciation would be good for the soul, you know." She walked to the door and held it slightly ajar to announce, "I'm permitting visitors in the room now. Keep your voices down out of respect for patients trying to rest in here." She put a pudgy finger to her lips saying, "Sh", as if she were talking to little children instead of grownups.

Sam entered the room and went to Cece's side, his clothes wet and matted to his skin from the heavy rain. "Well, nurse, is he goin' to make it?"

Annabelle sniffed, sounding more like a snort. "Give him a couple months and he'll look like his normal self again."

"Shoot. That don't matter. Cece was ugly to begin with," Sam joked.

"Ho, ho, ho. I knew you'd say something like that," Cece growled as he suspiciously touched the bandage. Then he stuck out his hand to the Southerner. "Thanks for getting me out. Mighta been wrong about you."

Sam accepted his hearty handshake. "I hope we're friends now."

Other visitors came in, shouting when they found their loved ones as if they had just found gold. Despite Annabelle's warnings to be quiet, wives and children squealed with delight and rushed to the patients' beside, thankful that their husbands and fathers lived through the ordeal.

Then Marie, Nancy, and Richard entered the room and rushed to Paul's side, barely escaping a fall on the wet floor, to greet him. Their clothes were drenched, as though they were wearing bathing suits instead of skirts and blouses.

"Oh, Paul, Richard just told me what happened —" cried Marie.

Paul put his arm around both wife and daughter. "Sh. I'm fine," he said.

"Pa, I'm just happy you're safe," said Nancy, throwing her arms around her father. Paul flinched from the pain but hugged her tightly. When he let go, Annabelle appeared at his side.

"So you decided to wake up?" Annabelle asked him. Instinctively, Paul knew not to take her brusque manner seriously.

"It was quite a nap I had," he admitted.

Annabelle grabbed a cloth and soaked it in a wash bowl, then tried to clean his dirty face.

"Let me," said Marie, reaching for the cloth, but the nurse snatched it away.

"Nonsense," Annabelle said, scrubbing Paul's face to a shine.

From across the room, Cece spoke. "Don't bother fighting with her," he said, explaining the nurse's aggressive behavior. "She won't listen to me neither."

"You're not worth listening to," Annabelle snapped, a sneer marking her face. Turning back to Paul, she said, "I hope you're not as stubborn as your friend over there."

Paul tried to grin, but cringed from the pain again. He touched his mid-section and felt tight bandages wrapped around snug to prevent further injury to his ribs. He would have to hold his laughter on the inside. When Annabelle finished, she set the cloth near the basin and left the room.

Cece announced to Paul from across the room, "I can't go back to work for awhile." With either hand he pointed at his bandaged eye and his leg in a cast. Cece almost seemed proud of his injuries.

Sam looked at Paul. "Ya should be proud of yer son. After ya passed out, Richard carried ya, without any help."

Richard smiled, as Paul patted his arm.

Marie continued the story, "Then he ran home to tell me what happened."

"I'm proud of you, son," said Paul.

Richard's eyes filled with tears. He gave his pa a bear hug. "I'm just thankful you're alive."

More families entered the crowded room, some wailing when they discovered that their loved one was dead. A young boy asked his mother, crying, "When is da cumin 'um?" The woman draped her arms around the boy. "Yer da is in 'eaven, now. 'Tis God's will," she explained in her Irish tongue.

Paul broke away from Richard's embrace, dangled his legs off the bed, and stood up.

"No, you shouldn't get up yet," Marie said, trying to hold him back.

But Paul slowly walked over to the woman. He gently touched her arm. "I'm sorry," said Paul. "Thomas was a good man."

Tears streamed down the woman's face. She nodded and said, "Thomas spoke 'ighly av yee."

Paul nodded and walked away, giving the widow privacy during her time of loss. With Marie's help, he lay on the bed again and looked out the window, trying to block out the sounds of mourning only feet away from him. Wondering why miners had to endure such a traumatic life, Paul watched the rain continue to pour.

Out of the corner of his eye, Paul watched Artie walk toward Nancy. From the journalist's stoic appearance, he knew Artie had something serious on his mind. Artie tapped Nancy on her sleeve and whispered in her ear. The young woman nodded, and then left the room with her beau. Paul drifted to a brief sleep; then, soon after, his boss entered the room. Peterman's shoes were caked in mud and his long, pointy umbrella dripped with raindrops. He walked with his head defiantly in the air, then slipped and practically fell to the ground. His arms flailed about, but he managed to regain stability and land squarely on his feet. If it wasn't for the recent tragedy, the miners may have let out a laugh. However, there was nothing funny about a mining accident that sent men to the hospital and others to their graves.

Peterman yanked his umbrella to a close. He and Paul looked at each other for a moment, surprised. The miners simultaneously voiced, "Sh" to their visitors.

"Mr. Peterman, I'm glad you're here," Paul said, trying to steady his voice. Marie helped her husband put on a clean shirt, guiding his arm into the crisp sleeve.

Peterman paced back and forth. "What happened? Where's Russell?" he asked as he pointed his umbrella at Paul. "Russell assured me there was no danger in the mine."

"Man-car hopped off the tracks," said Cece, delicately touching the bandage on his wounded eye.

Peterman's forehead furrowed. He took off his hat, causing the raindrops to drip profusely onto an already damp floor. Looking around the room, he asked again, "Where is my nephew? I tried to find him at the shafthouse, but—"

"Sir, he was on the man-car when it malfunctioned. He was thrown off," Paul said and heard the miners gasp.

Peterman's eyes widened. "What did you say?"

"Russell was thrown from the man-car. His life is in peril. I don't know if he'll survive."

The manager turned white and his lips quivered. "Russell—my nephew—might die?"

Sam spoke up. "Woulda never have happened if the cable been maintained."

Peterman took off his hat. Paul saw despair on his face, his eyes misting with a glassy stare. Then, his mood suddenly turned. "Which room is he in?"

"I don't know, Mr. Peterman. I don't even know if he's out of the mine yet."

Peterman yelled, "Did you leave him in the shaft?"

"Of course!" Paul cried out. "I had to see that the others got help."

"I've never heard of a man-car causing deaths. It's unbelievable. I'll go to the manufacturer of the car and—"

"Might as well blame yourself!" Cece shouted.

A miner said, "We all had to climb five levels to get above-ground."

Another miner added, "And we weren't going to use any more energy than necessary to lift two dead men and Russell."

"All right men," said Paul. "That's enough. Mr. Peterman has suffered a terrible shock."

Between gasps, Peterman uttered, "I've got to find Russell."

Marie walked toward Peterman. "Paul has been telling you of the dangers in your mine for a long time. If working conditions were safer, this tragedy would never have happened."

Peterman nodded his head calculatedly. "Of course. I took my nephew at his word. He told me everything was fine. Perhaps I made a tragic error. But may I suggest that you do

136

not comprehend the first thing about operating a mine?" He looked around the room full of injured miners. "None of you seem to understand the sacrifices I make to run a profitable enterprise. I answer to owners everyday about Copper Empire's profitability. They, in turn, have to answer to their shareholders."

Paul held onto his ribs with one hand and pointed at Peterman with the other. "But profitability at the expense of safety?"

Peterman shook his head, unable to speak. He pushed the point of his umbrella to the floor and looked down. "I just have to find Russell. What will my sister say when I tell her of this tragedy?" He placed his drenched hat back on his head and walked out of the examination room.

With Peterman out of earshot, the conversations began again. Cece and several other miners prepared to leave the hospital. Cece stepped down from the waiting table with Marie's help and used a crutch to limp around the room.

Sam pressed his face against the window, smudging the glass pane. The sky was still a dreary green color and the rain continued to pour. "So, who's next?" the Southerner thought out loud.

Paul glanced at Sam. "What?"

"Ya know what I mean," he said. "Who's the next person who's goin to get hurt...or killed?"

"Good question," said Marie.

"I hope to God this never happens again, Sam."

"I'm tellin' ya, Paul, some action needs to be taken now."

Cece hobbled over to his friends. "I'm ready to go home."

"Oh, Cece," Marie cried, clinging to his arm. "You look terrible. After the ordeal you went through today, I'll make your favorite dish."

Paul quickly looked at Sam and whispered, "What do you say you and me dine at the Central Restaurant?"

"Why? What's Marie fixin' for dinner?"

Paul mouthed, "Liver and onions."

"I'll follow ya, buddy."

"I'll see you back at the house later," Paul said to his wife.

"Oh, no you don't," cried out Marie. She grabbed onto his arm. "You're coming home with me."

Paul turned his wife around and leaned in close. "Marie, the broken ribs will heal, I'll be fine."

"But—"

Paul held a finger to her lips, and then kissed her. In a whisper he said, "I've got to take care of mining business first."

"How is Cece going to get home?"

"I'll figure out these durn crutches," said Cece, overhearing the conversation.

"Take the streetcar. Sam and I will return later," said Paul.

"Oh, all right. Come home as soon as you can," Marie said. She and Richard turned to help Cece use his crutches again and they left the room.

"What are ya thinkin'?" asked Sam.

Paul grabbed his jacket from the table. "Sam, you've been a good friend. I mean that. And I appreciate your support." He put his mining hat back on to offer at least minimal protection from the outdoor elements.

"We're goin' to the union meetin', aren't we, Paul?"

"Two men are dead, many more are injured and Peterman is walking around in a daze. You're right, Sam. We've got to take action."

"We're strikin'?" Sam asked as he pulled his jacket off, and then put it over his head to cover from the rain.

"It all depends what is said at the meeting."

Chapter 12

Nancy's arm was linked with Artie's. As they drew closer to the boarding house, she squeezed her arm against his, hoping to feel more secure after today's events, but it didn't help. Artie held an umbrella overhead that shielded them from the pouring rain, but some drops splashed on Nancy nonetheless. It wasn't a romantic walk. She had attempted conversation with him numerous times since they had left the hospital, but he only mumbled a few words at best. After they walked past the columned porch of the boarding home, Artie let down the umbrella and was ready to open the front door, but Nancy took his elbow to stop him.

"Is there something wrong?"

Artie brushed away her arm, opened the door without answering her and walked into the foyer. She followed him inside, hurt by his deed. She knew something was amiss. It wasn't like Artie to be so quiet during a walk, not ruminating or speculating about the story he was working on. Anything newsworthy usually set her beau to a verbose monologue about how impressed his editor would be with his proposed articles. Reporting on the mining accident surely would make a great story. Why was Artie silent about it?

T-bone was already competing for Nancy's attention, so she scratched the dog's ears, and then let him outside to run around the estate. By the time she returned to the foyer, Artie was pacing on the marble floor, five steps one way, then turning around to walk precisely five steps the other way. Nancy didn't bother prying into Artie's thoughts again. Instead, she went to the laundry baskets set near the staircase and began folding clothes for the miners' pickup the next day. As she folded a pair of overalls, Artie spoke.

"Nancy, I must leave Red Jacket."

His words startled Nancy so much that she dropped the overalls she was folding. "What? Where are you going? " she asked.

"I shall return to Chicago." Artie was born and raised there. "My father will assist me with stable employment." He rummaged through another basket and found a towel to dry himself off with.

"You're going to work at your father's store?" Nancy cried.

"Yes, until I find a permanent position with a newspaper."

"But you wanted to be a journalist in Detroit. And what about us? We'd never see one another."

"I am fully aware that marriage has been on your mind lately, perhaps because it has been on mine as well." Artie rubbed the towel against his shirt. "Reporting on this accident has enabled me to recognize the importance of achieving one's aspirations before it is too late to do so. I would wager that Cece never thought he could become anything more than just a copper miner. Well, I wish for more. I am a fine writer, yet I live on a wage comparable to that of a trammer. I shall never realize my dream to relocate to Detroit unless I preserve more of my earnings. "

"But you haven't even proposed to me," Nancy pleaded. "We're in this together. If we're going to be married someday, I can get a job to earn money for our future."

"No." Artie shook his head as if training a dog how to be obedient. "I will not allow a woman to perform man's work. You shall simply have to be patient until I am well established in Chicago. I should think two years will allow me ample savings." He decided that he was dry enough and tossed the damp towel on the floor, obviously expecting Nancy to pick it up.

Nancy couldn't move. She could only manage to stare at him. She whispered, "Wait just one minute." She cleared her throat and raised her voice. "I won't have you telling me what to do. I'm twenty years old and mature enough to make my own decisions." She had never rebelled against any man before. Suddenly, she realized what she'd said. A nervous twitch from her cheek made her uncomfortable. It fluttered like a butterfly's wings.

Artie picked up the towel he threw on the floor and neatly folded it. "Stop behaving in a ridiculous manner."

Nancy's eyes locked with Artie's. She was afraid to speak, because she didn't want the courtship to end. On the other hand, she didn't want to be treated like a child. Not knowing what to say, Artie tapped his shoe on the floor, apparently waiting for her to come to her senses.

She decided she had to speak the truth. She boldly raised her voice again, "I'm going to find outside employment, Artie. And I don't need your permission to do so."

"Please, none of your hysterics tonight," Artie said. He reached out towards her, speaking more gently. "Nancy, I care for you because you are quiet and supportive of me. You are generally a superb listener and heed my requests. That is what I desire one day in a wife." He let go of her hands, then shook a finger as if Nancy were three years old. "However, the confrontational behavior you are exhibiting is quite shocking."

"My behavior?" she asked in a hushed voice. Nancy pointed a finger at herself and repeated more loudly, "My behavior?" She stammered, deciding what to say next. She was hurt and angry. How much closer to perfection did she have to reach to please Artie? In a flash, she realized that no matter what she said or did, it would never be enough for him. Just like she had seen her father do a thousand times, she formed her hands into fists, ready to take on her beau. "I'll have you know that I take issue with your behavior as well."

Artie raised an eyebrow, then turned away and walked to the stairs.

"I'm not through, Arthur Cooper," Nancy yelled. Her boldness surprised herself. It's something her mother could do, but never she, until now. Her father had almost died in a mining accident today, and her beau wanted to leave her. She had tolerated more nonsense than any woman should be forced to experience in one day. When Artie climbed the stairs, she ran up the steps and grabbed his elbow. They were just steps away from the landing.

Artie jerked his elbow away. "What is the meaning of this?"

Nancy took a deep breath. "I'm speaking to you and would appreciate some courtesy."

Artie blinked, but said nothing.

"We've been courting for two years," Nancy said, fighting back the tears. "And I've tried to be everything you wanted. I gave you a sympathetic ear after you had a bad day at work. I've laughed with you at your stories about your childhood in Chicago. I stayed quiet when you asked me to and I've acted silly when you said I was too serious." Artie's lower lip trembled and Nancy knew he was furious with her, but she kept going. "But the social at Italian Hall was the last straw for tolerating your inconsiderate behavior. First, you disapproved of my dress, saying that the neckline was too high. Then you corrected my every dance move as if we were in a competition for a prize. But when you forced me to dance with Russell Ubel — Artie, that was too much for me to bear. You knew I didn't want to dance with him."

"You made a spectacle of yourself when you danced with my roommate," said Artie as he gripped the banister, "and I did my best to save your reputation." He sputtered when he spoke, saliva flying out of his mouth. "I learned about Russell's infatuation with you as well as the pleasure he had of kissing you. One of the miners told me in the hospital. You deceived me."

Nancy felt as if someone had punched her in the stomach. She was sick. It was bad enough that Russell had stolen a kiss and almost violated her, but to know that Artie blamed her for the incident? Tears flowed down her cheeks. "Russell kissed me. I—I didn't want him to." She began to hyperventilate. "I tried to stop him, but he attacked me. If T-bone hadn't knocked him to the ground—" Nancy sobbed, but Artie didn't even attempt to console her. When she regained composure she said, "Russell ran to his automobile and drove away before anything further happened. I was so ashamed—"

"And well you should be," Artie said, his distaste becoming more pronounced as his lip curled. "It is improper for a woman of your marital status to be unchaperoned. You are becoming more like your mother every day."

Nancy slapped his face. "How dare you? My mother is a respectable woman."

Artie grabbed her hand and Nancy tried to pull away. The two struggled on the stairs. Suddenly, the front door opened.

"Will that rain never stop?" Marie asked as she entered the boarding home with Cece and Richard. "What's going on?"

Cece burst through the foyer and hopped on one leg until he came to the stairs. He swung one of his crutches and hit Artie's side. "Get away from her," he roared.

Artie ran up the stairs, leaping every other step to escape Cece. "I shall move out within the hour."

Nancy ran down the steps and into her mother's arms.

*　*　*

Paul squeezed his way through the crowded vestibule, following Sam outside of Italian Hall. The darkness of the night was illuminated by a full moon. As he limped under the arched entrance and walked down the steps to the street, the warm rain pattered on his face. The humid air didn't daunt the celebration around him.

"Hooray for the Western Federation!" shouted a young miner.

A freckle-faced man yelled, "We'll bring the owners to their knees."

Red Jacket almost looked as if it were celebrating Independence Day, except the fireworks were missing. Miners poured out of Italian Hall like a host of bats emerging from a cave. Paul reached the flooded street and watched Sam warmly slapping the backs of men around him.

"We're on strike!" said Sam. He jumped with excitement.

Paul sloshed through the shallow river on the road and was quick to nudge him to a halt. "We might have a long fight ahead of us, Sam." Paul threw his mining jacket over his head, trying to keep somewhat dry.

"Don't matter. I'm gonna help the likes of ya git what's fair." Sam took off his jacket and mimicked Paul's method to keep dry.

"Why?"

"Huh?" asked Sam, peeking between the thick folds of his jacket.

"Sam, if we're on strike, you're out of a job," said Paul while he nodded his thanks to some miners who stopped by to congratulate him. "That alone should make you want to return to South Carolina."

But Sam grinned. "I moved out here for a reason. . .and now I know it's more than what I first planned."

It was Paul's turn to be confused. "Huh?"

"Now's not the time," said Sam. "Let's go home. I can't wait to tell the others about the strike."

"You go on," said Paul and nodded his head toward the man with an umbrella. "Look who's here." Peterman stood across the street from Italian Hall. The manager must have been standing there for some time, waiting for the Western Federation meeting to let out. The scowl on his face told Paul he already knew the miners were striking.

"No, I'll go with ya," said Sam.

Before Paul could protest, his boss had crossed the street and made his way to the two men. "Good evening," said Peterman. His eyes were bloodshot and Paul knew he had been drinking. Probably the same forty-rod that his nephew had downed earlier in the day.

Paul nodded. "Is there anything I can do to help?"

Peterman cast his eyes to the muddy ground. "I made arrangements for Russell to be transported back to Boston where he'll receive the best medical care for his extensive injuries. I sent a telegram to my sister. There's nothing more to be done."

Paul exchanged glances with Sam. Neither one had liked Russell. "Let's stand under the archway," Paul said, leading the way back to Italian Hall.

Once past the arched entrance and into the vestibule, Paul lowered his jacket.

Peterman sniffed. "I know the miners have voted to strike."

"We're demandin' better work conditions," said Sam.

Peterman held up his manicured hand. "Please let me finish. I understand why you're striking." He turned his skinny body to meet Paul's muscular build. "I should have done this years ago and I'm ashamed of making such a mistake. What I mean to say is, I'm offering you the engineer's job. You've earned it."

Paul felt pain from the broken ribs, but tried to breathe evenly. Finally, his dream came true to land the engineer's job.

Peterman, of course, didn't know that Russell had fired him right before the accident. But there was no need to tell him. Paul could make updates to the boarding home, buy Marie store-bought clothes, provide more meat on the dinner table. Paul shook his boss' hand. "Thank you, Mr. Peterman."

Peterman took his hand away and ran a hand over his worn face. "The cable should be repaired in a day or so, and then we can pull the damaged man-car to the surface to have it repaired. Calumet & Hecla have agreed to loan me a man-car until ours is fixed. I'll order our timbering crew to have the hanging wall re-enforced immediately."

Paul smiled. "That might make a difference, Mr. Peterman. Perhaps we can come to an agreement before our unit ever goes out on the picket line."

Peterman nodded, "Certainly."

"What promises can we make to the miners?" Paul asked with his head cocked. "A pay raise was promised months ago. Surely you intend to compensate them?"

Peterman shook his head. "I'm afraid not."

"But why?"

"Because the repairs will take money. Lots of it."

"How about a compromise?" Paul asked and held a forefinger to his lip. "You pay the miners the same wages, but drop their working hours to eight per day."

Peterman shook his head again. "The accident has set us back many days. I need all the manpower possible to catch up with the unfinished work."

"I suppose you wouldn't consider two men to a drill?" Paul snapped.

His boss continued to shake his head. "We need to stay efficient, Paul. No mine uses two men for a one-man job."

"What about safety? Can I have your word as a gentleman, that if I determine certain repairs are necessary, I'll have the authority to order the necessary supplies and assign the men?"

"All repairs must be approved by me," Peterman said. He opened his coat to withdraw a flask from which he took a drink. "However, you can assign the men work as you see fit."

"Mr. Peterman, I'm honored that you've promoted me to engineer, but how can I engineer in a mine with no workers? You haven't provided any incentive for the miners not to strike."

"I suspect, Paul, that a week without pay will send the men back into the mine."

"You underestimate the men."

Peterman raised his flask in the air as if to toast Paul's words. "I think you overestimate the union."

Paul's hands formed into fists. "Can't you see that's why you're in this fix tonight? I warned you for weeks about the cable and the hanging wall and problems using the one-man drill, but you never listened."

"That's enough," said Peterman, testily. "I do the best I can for you and your men. Those shareholders are merciless. They'd have me fired if I didn't return a regular profit for them. And they don't care how the money is made, as long as they get compensated for their investments." Peterman shut his eyes for a moment, and then took another gulp of the forty-rod. He lowered his voice. "You will begin engineering tomorrow, right Paul?"

Paul stared at the archway, as if Peterman weren't there.

"Don't let me down, Paul. The stockholders won't stand for any losses. They'll have my head."

Paul fixed his stare on Peterman, but said nothing.

"You must return to Copper Empire and convince the others to do so as well. I'll even increase your pay to what Russell was earning."

"Ya mean what Russell made, not earned," Sam interjected. "I don't wish ta speak ill of your nephew, but Russell never worked a hard day in his life."

"How dare you, Sam Huston!"

"Ya say ya have to turn profits? Ya shoulda thought about that before ya hired Russell."

"No, Mr. Peterman," said Paul, shaking his head.

"Maybe if yer sister hadn't spoiled yer nephew so much, he'd have had some common sense," said Sam.

Peterman held up a hand to mute Sam, then faced Paul. "What did you say?"

"No, I will not return to work, nor will I encourage others to go back to Copper Empire." Paul ticked his head, motioning to Sam that he was leaving. "Come along, Sam. We're on strike."

"Paul, you're making the biggest mistake of your life," Peterman called out. "How will you and the others survive without your pay?" He raised his voice to shout, "Flint Weyburn would hang his head in shame!"

"I doubt that!" Paul shouted behind him. He and Sam walked along the rain-drenched streets, using the full moon's light to lead the way home. Peterman's warning stayed with Paul, but when Sam whistled one of his strange tunes, a mishmash of "Johnny Comes Marching Home" and "Amazing Grace", he couldn't help but smile. He listened to the Southerner's interesting blend of songs and thought about how he would soon explain to his boarders what had occurred. His unit had joined the Western Federation of Miners, took a strike vote, and now was on strike. He was bewildered. Today's events didn't seem real.

Sam swung his arms back and forth, keeping rhythm with his whistled song. He finished as he and Paul reached the steps of the boarding home. Paul took the lead, ushering them beneath the gabled canopy. "Sam, let me do the explaining to the others."

Sam's face lit up, like a kerosene lamp. "Of course. I wouldn't have it any other way."

Paul slapped his thanks on the Southerner's back. T-bone was the first to greet the twosome with tongue and tail wagging. The dog tried to jump on his master, but Paul held his hand up. "Down, boy." T-bone obeyed instantly and sat with what looked to be a puzzled grin. Sam bent down to pet the black fur, but instead received a washing from the dog's wet tongue on his stubbled face.

Marie, dressed in her red, tattered bathrobe, joined the two men. The ankle-length robe had holes at the ends where T-bone had nipped his way through as a pup. "I thought I heard you two walk in," she said. Her rosy lips reached her husband's for a kiss. She gently took his arm. "I'm serving milk and coffee in the parlor. We're all having a hard time falling asleep."

Paul kissed his wife on her cheek. "That's perfect, honey. I have something I want to announce."

"Me too," she said. "Nancy and Artie had a spat, and Artie moved out a little while ago. He's going back to Chicago."

Sam took off his mining jacket, and then reached to hang it on a hook. "What a shame," he frowned. Paul wasn't certain if he was sincere, though.

"How's Nancy doing?" Paul asked.

Marie shrugged, and then asked, "How was your supper at the hotel?"

Sam was about to start spilling details, but Paul tapped his shoulder. "It's a surprise," Sam gulped. "Yer husband will explain."

T-bone pushed his way between the threesome to be the first to enter the parlor, his steps causing an echo on the marble floor. At the sight of Paul and Sam, some of the boarders muttered a pleasant greeting while the majority wanted some answers about the strike rumor.

As a dying fire sputtered in the fireplace, Sam passed by Cece to rest on the settee. "Why are you so happy?" Cece asked suspiciously. Sam simply shrugged his shoulders, accepting a cup of coffee from Marie.

One of the boarders rose from his seat, offering it to Paul. He gratefully accepted, then sprawled in the rocker with T-bone snuggling down at his feet.

"What happened?" Cece asked.

Paul took a deep breath, accepting a cold glass of milk from Marie, knowing he would suffer a fitful sleep if he dared to drink coffee. He fingered the cold, silver mug, hesitating. Carefully choosing his words, he said, "Listen up, men. Sam and I didn't go out to dinner. Some of us from Copper Empire, and others from smaller mines, went to the Federation meeting at Italian Hall."

The boarders nervously looked at each other. Cece sat forward on the settee, his steely look ready for the news.

"Two men died today. We're lucky to be alive and the accident could have been prevented." Paul said.

"And, as usual," Cece said, "Peterman will get away with this. Let's stop gabbing about it." He stood up and positioned the crutches under his arms. "I'm going to bed."

"Wait," Paul said, standing up. "You haven't heard me through."

Cece looked as if his good eye had popped out of his head. He sat back awkwardly on the dark green cushion.

Paul took a seat in the chair again, rocking back and forth. "Our unit agreed to join the Western Federation." The boarders nodded as if they had expected to hear the news. He folded his arms to his chest and looked squarely at Cece. "We're on strike."

Cece humphed. "Better tell Peterman."

"He already knows."

Sam piped in, "Peterman offered Paul the engineerin' job."

"What?" asked Marie.

Sam continued, "Marie, ya should be proud of yer husband. When Peterman refused to address pay and safety issues, Paul declared that we're all on strike."

Marie drew in her breath, her heavy chest rising like a tidal wave. "Paul," she said softly, "what will we do without money?"

"There will be some strike pay," Paul said.

"Yer a hero, Paul." With arms locked behind his head on a pillow, Sam said, "I don't know about the rest of ya, but I think what happened today was plain ludicrous. Accidents like that are bound to happen again unless we do somethin' 'bout it."

The boarders talked amongst themselves, trying to make sense of the decision to strike.

Sam pointed his finger to the other boarders. "When a friend gets hurt, I hurt, too. But we need the support of all miners to win this strike, not just a few."

Cece threw his hands out and sprang from the settee. "Paul...Sam...no," he exclaimed. He stood shakily on one leg. "I'm not gonna be a part of this. Gotta eat, you know."

"Sh," Marie exclaimed. "You'll wake the children."

Paul leaped from his seat to hand Cece his crutches. Cece positioned his walking aides and limped away. "I can't believe you—all of you," he said.

"Cece—"

The boarders got up from the chairs and settees to crowd around Paul, Cece and Sam. Even Marie put the coffee pot down to join her husband.

"I'm just a poor miner," Cece grumbled. "Just trying to drill 'n lift enough copper to keep me living. It's a harsh life, but it keeps food in my belly."

Silence blanketed the parlor. The boarders simply looked at one another and nodded their heads.

"Okay, Cece," said Sam. "Ya may for a short time lose yer security, but ya won't be alone. Yer goin' to have the support of all of us." Sam tapped on Cece's crutches. "Leastways ya can't work for another six weeks."

One of the boarders spoke up. "Some of us have our doubts, too."

"Yeah. Can we really win a strike?" asked another boarder.

"Well I'm all for it," said a boarder with graying hair at the temples. He nudged Cece and explained, "You can either join us and get support, or you can side with the mine owners and end up supporting 'em."

"Sam, why are you so fired up about striking?" asked Cece.

"Miners and trammers need ta make a decent livin' without puttin' their lives at daily risk."

Everyone looked to Paul for guidance, so he bowed his head for a moment, scratching his sandy brown hair. "Let's listen to the union organizer at the Palestra tomorrow morning. Cece, it might make you feel better about the decision I made."

A grunt escaped from Cece's lips. "I dunno, Paul."

Chapter 13

The Western Federation was holding their strike meeting in Red Jacket's sister town, Laurium. Cece and Sam stepped into the crowded, yet spacious auditorium, named the Palestra, which served as Laurium's ice rink in the winter time. "Over there," Paul pointed to the first row of seats. "Marie is saving us places to sit."

"God bless your wife," said Cece, limping with the aid of crutches. "I can't stand for long." All available seating was taken, which forced many attendees to stand if they wanted to hear what the Western Federation had to say.

The Palestra had also been home to Calumet's professional hockey team only years prior. But the mob of people weren't there for skating or a hockey game. Men, women and children were dressed in their Sunday best, many of them holding picket signs, waiting for the union organizer to speak.

"I thought you'd never come," said Marie who scooted across the bench to make room for the men. "I've been saving these seats for hours." She took a picket sign from her husband and held it up like a true patriot. Paul also held a picket sign despite suffering from the pain in his ribs from yesterday's accident.

Russell Ubel's mangled body was traveling to Boston and the miners had no place of employment. In his heart, Paul knew Red Jacket would never be the same again.

Paul didn't get much sleep the night before, but he wouldn't let Marie or the others know how worried he was about the strike. Despite his misgivings, he felt energized by the crowds of people that swarmed around him. The podium in the center of the rink was empty, and every now and again someone would point and wonder where the speaker was.

While Cece plopped himself on the bench and tossed his crutches to the floor, Paul looked at the other picket signs held up high. A miner proudly waved a sign that read, "Shorter hours, fair pay," while another one read, "we want a two-man drill." Several miners from the crowd approached Paul and thanked him for his selfless service at Copper Empire. Apparently word had spread quickly that Paul unselfishly declined the promotion to engineer in order to stand with his fellow miners to strike.

"What have we gotten ourselves into?" Cece shouted over the boisterous crowd. Perhaps he should have stayed at the boarding home with his injuries, but Paul had encouraged him to join the union rally in hopes that he would change his mind about the strike.

"Look," Paul said and indicated to a banner that hung near the podium. "Our town is supporting us." The ten foot-long banner proclaimed in huge red letters, "The Keweenaw Welcomes the Western Federation of Miners."

"Sh," said Sam who held a finger to his lips. "Let's listen to what the union leader has to say."

A team of bodyguards escorted a man who Paul guessed to be today's speaker. When the escorts drew closer to the podium, they stepped aside to allow the man access to the podium. He gripped the lectern and said in a strong voice, "Ladies and gentlemen, please quiet down." As the noise gradually softened to a reasonable level, the miners, one by one, dropped their picket signs.

"My name is Guy Miller, and I am on the executive board of the Western Federation," he said. The thousands of townspeople in attendance nodded their heads and poked one another to be quiet. They were ready to hear what this man had to say.

"For over fifty years," the leader belted out on the platform, "the copper miners of this community, as well as those in Montana and Arizona, have struggled for better working conditions. Unfortunately, things haven't improved."

"Got that right," Cece muttered.

"Most of us start off our day by coughing," Guy said, "a reminder of how rigorous working conditions were the day before." The miners responded with courteous applause. "Then, with mining equipment, which we, by the way, pay for," he informed the crowd, "we walk, often twenty minutes or more, without pay for that time, down to our work stations." Guy stopped to take a breath while hundreds of disgruntled miners shouted their agreement. He waited until the crowd calmed down, and then continued with his hands raised for dramatic effect. "For ten, eleven, even twelve long hours a day, six days a week, we continue this harsh routine. If we're lucky not to break our backs from lifting rocks, or suffocate from the dusty air, or die in some horrendous mining accident, we go home in the dark to our families that we rarely see."

Paul glanced at Sam, and then nodded his head.

"And you know what? The same thing is guaranteed to continue tomorrow."

The miners booed at Guy's prediction. Some even raised their signs in the air. The crowd began chanting, "Strike. Strike. Strike."

Guy raised his hand again to quiet the crowd. "After everything we go through, what do we get in return?" Silence enveloped the awe-struck miners. "Do we get any of the enormous profits the owners reap from the miners' labor?"

The audience collectively yelled, "No."

Guy chuckled. "Heck, forget about the profits. Do we ever see a raise in our pay?"

Again, the miners responded in the negative.

Guy chuckled again. "Wait...wait, forget the profits and a raise. Why don't we look at our neighbors in Detroit," he said, and then thought for a moment before shaking his head.

"No. Better still, why don't we have mine owners look at our neighbors in Detroit?" The miners, elated, picked up and waved their picket signs and cheered. Paul knew what was coming and apparently they did, too.

Guy hollered, "Henry Ford knows the value of hard workers. In only a month's time, he will be introducing the first automobile assembly line in Highland Park. There is speculation that by next year, the Ford Motor Company will pay workers double what they pay in this town."

The audience cheered, encouraging the speaker to continue.

"Can you imagine earning that much money in one day? Most of us barely make half of that, and I'm not even including money taken away for mining equipment, rent, and frequent trips to the doctor."

The audience was ecstatic. They cheered, "Strike. Strike!" Guy spoke again, but the volume of the miners' excitement drowned out his voice, as if they were cheering a matador as he teased a charging bull in the ring. Paul couldn't hear him and turned to Sam and Cece. They both shrugged. No one could hear the leader.

Guy held up both of his hands to quiet the enthusiastic masses. When the noise level dropped, he spoke again. "Fellow copper miners, we must band together. We must demand better working conditions." As the audience applauded, the leader continued. "We must demand a shorter work week so that we can get to know our families better. And, finally, we must demand better pay."

"How are ya gonna force the owners to go along?" Cece yelled.

"Thank you, sir, for asking that question," yelled Guy. "Take a look at that poor fellow with crutches," he said, waving a hand at Cece. "I'll wager he broke his leg from a mining accident."

"You wager right," shouted Cece. "I'll buy you a forty-rod at Vairo's." The crowd erupted into laughter and Sam and Paul proudly slapped Cece's back.

Guy laughed. "I just might take you up on that, sir. But back to what I came here for. Allow me to explain that we've already been more than fair. A couple of weeks ago, we wrote out demands and sent it to the owners. We asked that they respond before today. Ladies and gentlemen," the speaker slowly gazed over the crowd's eyes and lowered his voice, "we haven't had a single response. We have already asked, but that has not worked. It is now time to strike against the owners."

The miners waved their picket signs and shouted, "Strike. Strike. Strike."

Guy once again held up his hands to quiet them. "We must stop at nothing. When the owners offer you better working conditions but won't shorten the work week," he pounded the lectern for added effect, "we're going to strike back."

The audience roared, "Strike. Strike. Strike."

"And when the owners offer to shorten the work week but won't raise your pay, we'll continue to strike back."

Again, the miners collectively yelled, "Strike. Strike. Strike."

"No matter what the owners do to compromise, until all of our demands have been met, we will strike back!" Thunderous applause permeated the Palestra as Guy jumped off the platform, took his own picket sign, and walked out of the Palestra and onto the street with hundreds of strikers following him.

Paul believed the Red Jacket miners were united, but for how long?

*   *   *

158

The slanted roof of the shafthouse came into Sam's view as he walked toward Copper Empire. A sense of pride coarsed through him when he saw the slogans, "Two Man Drill" and "More Pay" plastered on signs carried by miners who marched in a long circle in front of the building. Though he missed his work as a trammer and had hoped a compromise would have been reached after two weeks of striking, he was proud that the miners remained united. His footsteps brought him closer to Cece who was propped up against a boulder, next to his crutches, exhibiting his trademark scowl.

"Hi Cece." Sam gave him a slap on his shoulder. "Peterman ain't budged yet?"

"What does it look like?" Cece grumbled. After a few moments he softened his tone. "They've been picketing for hours."

Straight ahead, dozens of miners circled and chanted their demands, "Two man, drill. Two man drill. Two man drill."

"Raise your voices," shouted Cece to the picketers. He pounded his fist at the sky as if fighting an enemy. "Let 'em know you mean business."

Sam was impressed that the miners indeed strengthened their shouts. Even that wasn't good enough for Cece, who was acting as their coach. "Louder," shouted Cece. "Like a one-man drill."

"Uh oh." Sam nudged Cece's arm. "Look what's comin'." A Model T automobile rounded the bend and headed straight toward them. He recognized Peterman as one of its passengers, holding onto his black top hat.

Cece scrambled from the rock, grabbed his crutches and hobbled to the picket line. "Let's go." The strikers saw the Model T as well, because the picket circle immediately straightened into one horizontal line, blocking the shafthouse.

"Don't let 'em through," Cece yelled at the men. The strikers intended to guard the entrance no matter what the cost.

Most continued to hold up their picket signs while others let it drop sideways so they could pound it with a fist, using it like a weapon.

Sam grabbed two picket signs next to the shafthouse and joined the line. "Let's stay tough, fellas." He offered a picket sign to Cece.

"What do you expect me to do with it?" Cece snapped. "I can't hold a sign when I'm on crutches."

"Then I'll hold one in each hand," Sam said, raising both slogans overhead.

"That oughta end the strike," Cece quipped.

The vehicle sputtered to a stop and Peterman stepped out of the vehicle, followed by a man carrying a tripod. Sam wondered what Peterman had in mind.

Cece was concerned as well. "Don't want no camera here." He gripped his crutches tighter, as if preparing for a fight. "Those newspaper men'll bend over to make mine owners happy."

Sam shrugged his shoulders. "Maybe a story in the paper won't be so bad. Leastways, the townspeople'll see us fightin' for better workin' conditions." Before Cece could retort, Sam stepped forward to address Peterman. "If yer here to stop the strike, plan on stayin' a long time." He tried to look tough through squinted eyes and a scowl. He had seen Cece tighten his facial muscles on many occasions and figured he could conjure up the same respect.

Peterman took off his hat and stepped toward the center, in front of the picket line. "Men, this is ludicrous." He held his hands open as if to offer the miners their heart's desire. "I appeal to your sense of logic. You can't win this strike and eventually you'll be replaced. Why not return to work now?"

Sam's face grew hot with frustration. "What are ya offerin'?"

"You may return to your jobs with no penalty."

"Are ya gonna raise our pay, cut our hours, make the mine safe?"

"I'll make the mine safer, but I can't guarantee your safety. You'll work the same number of hours and pay."

"No deal, Mr. Peterman." The miners booed and raised their signs. Just then, Sam noticed that Paul had joined the group. He was beginning to understand the frustrations Paul must have tolerated for years at Copper Empire. Peterman was so stubborn and so devoid of safety or business sense, that he was willing to risk the lives of miners to earn a profit.

"Mr. Peterman," Paul said. "I've already outlined our conditions for you."

An Irishman put down his sign and spoke up. "We've cum dis far an' we're stickin' together." He nudged a Cornishman who nodded. Sam was proud of the Irishman's words and for treating the Cornishman next to him like a friend. Sam knew that clashes between the myriad of cultures happened from time to time, so he was glad that the men put their heritage aside to remain united for one cause.

Peterman straightened his back, like one with an air of importance. "If need be, I will request that the National Guard remove all of you from this property." Governor Ferris had sent National Guard troops to the Keweenaw a couple of days after the strike began. The soldiers had set up their tents in Red Jacket, walking the streets with their rifles in hand. The soldiers were supposedly sent to establish law and order in Red Jacket. There had been clashes between strikers and mine managers since the strike's inception. Sam read about the fights in the newspapers, and even witnessed brawls at other mines. So far, thanks to Paul's leadership, the Copper Empire strikers were peaceful, but very active and vocal for the cause. Sam suspected the real reason the soldiers were sent was to guard mine property and help protect men who wanted to return to work.

"We haven't harmed you or your property, sir," said Paul, wiping his forehead with a handkerchief. "We only want you to hear us out."

"The lot of you needs to decide—are you going to be loyal to Copper Empire—or to the Western Federation?" Peterman folded his arms across his chest.

"We've got a family to feed," hollered one miner, "and our jobs are useless if we get hurt."

Peterman looked to the photographer next to him. "You may commence taking photographs," he said. The photographer eagerly set up his tripod.

"Fellas, line up and smile," Sam said.

"Have you lost your crackers?" Cece asked.

"Sam, if the townspeople see us picketing, they could end up opposing our cause and side with the mine owners," said Paul, who shifted his attention. "Mr. Peterman, let's talk. Let's compromise."

Peterman waved a finger. "Not good enough, Paul. I'm not negotiating. Not now or ever." He nudged the photographer. "I'm ready for those photographs."

Sam shrugged. "Let's just make the best of it."

"I'm not gonna." Cece hobbled forward. "Mr. Peterman, you'd be strikin' too if you struggled just to survive, while managers like you hoard their money. . .I mean, our money." The photographer set the camera on the tripod, which only infuriated Cece, so he threatened the photographer with a raised crutch. "Get outta here."

The photographer sighed. "I've got a job to do."

"You ain't taking our picture," Cece shouted.

Sam yelled, "Cece, stop!" But Cece swung his crutch as if it were a mallet, slapping the camera off the tripod, shattering the lens and just missing the photographer. Sam looked at Paul who had his eyes closed. A sinking feeling hit Sam's stomach as he was sure Cece's wild outburst would only hurt their cause more than ever.

* * *

When Sam arrived at the dining room, he took a seat at his usual spot at the table, next to the Weyburn children. One look at Cece told him that he was sorry for his actions with the photographer the day before. Cece's head was slumped into his cupped hands where he remained silent. For once, Sam didn't feel much like talking either. How he longed to return to Charleston for a delectable Southern meal again. While Marie said grace, Sam sat back in the chair and closed his eyes for a moment. He could almost smell the Southern fried chicken, mashed potatoes and hot biscuits. His mouth watered when he imagined the butter melting off the potatoes and dipping the rest of the meal into brown gravy. But when he opened his eyes, steam rose from a plate of plain potatoes. Next to that was a bowl of lettuce and other greens. Another meatless meal was being served since Paul and Marie had recently decided to ration their food, just as a precautionary measure, in case the strike lasted longer.

Two weeks into the strike, Sam and the other miners had remained upbeat until Cece's encounter with the photographer. Cece had to pay for the damaged camera and equipment with money he didn't have. Sam was forced to face the reality that the strike might last longer than just a few days. And he had been so sure that the owners would be on bended knees, begging their workers to return so that the mines would remain operating.

"Could you pass the potatoes, please?" asked Paul of his wife, breaking the silence at the supper table.

"Sure," smiled Marie as she gingerly passed a plate, "there's plenty if anyone else wants some."

"Ma, I'm still hungry," said Jeanie. "Can't we have some meat?"

163

"Yeah, Ma," said Joey.

Marie sighed. "Enough. We just said grace in which I reminded everyone to be grateful for the food we are eating."

"Your mother's right," said Paul.

"I'm a-grateful for tis food, Mr. and Mrs.-a Weyburn," said Roberto in his cute, childish voice. "If I was at-a home having-a supper, we'd-a only have spaghetti wit no meat."

Jeanie scrunched her nose. "What's spa-spa-ghetti?"

Roberto's thin lips formed a smile. "Its-a long strips of dough tat-a we call pasta. Ten my mama puts a tomatoes on it, just like-a sauce."

"Sounds like a scrumptious dish," said Sam who winked at the lad. "I might stop by yer home someday to try your mama's 'pagetti."

The children giggled at Sam's pronunciation.

"Spaghetti, Mr. Sam," said Roberto, holding a hand over his mouth to stifle more giggles.

Nancy dabbed a napkin over her lips, then put the cloth on the table and took a deep breath. "Ma, Pa, I'd like to find a job. With the strike, everything is uncertain, and I want to do my part to help the family."

Paul swallowed his food, and then answered her. "That's very mature of you, honey."

"I read the advertisements in the newspaper and I think I'll be able to be hired as a seamstress. I'll visit a few places tomorrow."

"That would be wonderful if you could find employment. Richard can stay in school and finally graduate next year," said Marie.

Richard gulped his food and waved his hand animatedly to protest. "Thanks, Nancy, but I should be the one looking for a full-time job. Maybe the theater can give me more hours to work."

"Absolutely not," said Paul, squishing the napkin in his hand into the shape of a fist. "While you live under my roof, you will attend school until you graduate."

"Our roof," Marie corrected. She put her fork down on the delicate China. "But I agree with your pa. You are not to leave school and that's that."

Richard winked at his sister and chewed his food. "I'm beholdin' to you, Sis. The last thing I wanted to do was quit school when I'm almost done." He ate a bite of his potatoes, and then turned serious. "I only work collecting tickets on the weekends, though. I'll see if the theater can hire me to clean the auditorium—at least until school begins, of course. Pa, is that okay with you?"

Marie turned to Paul. "We could use the extra money."

Paul put down his fork. "You may ask for extra work, if it's available. Be sure to thank the manager if he does offer you extra hours."

"Yes, sir," said Richard.

"I expect you to keep up with your studies, even while working extra hours. You need to be prepared to enter the Michigan College of Mines next year."

Richard shook his head. "I'm not going to college, Pa. It's enough for me to finish high school."

"As long as you live under this roof, you will go to school. Is that understood?"

"Yes, sir," Richard whispered. "But I'm not going to college."

Marie said, "Richard, working in the theater is a childish dream. You need to be practical."

"The theater is no place for a young, intelligent man like yourself. It's not a respectable profession, especially where actresses are concerned," said Paul.

"When I'm ready, I'll marry Sally Jane. I'm not interested in courting an actress."

"I'm relieved to hear that," said Marie.

Jeanie giggled, "I'm gonna tell Sally Jane next Sunday at church."

"Finish your dinner," Marie ordered.

"I hope your senses return and you change your mind soon. And that's all I want to hear about the theater tonight," said Paul.

"Yes, Pa."

Sam was puzzled by Paul's complexities. On the one hand, Sam admired the patriarch for his level headedness, courage and wisdom. But Sam saw another side to Paul, especially the longer the strike endured. Paul's alter ago revealed impatience and anger.

Marie handed the potato plate to Cece. "Want some more?"

Cece shook his head, put his fork down and slammed his fist on the table. "If I look at one more of those ugly, brown potatoes that look more like oversized peanuts, I swear—"

Marie slanted her eyebrow.

"—I swear to almighty God," Cece said and looked at Marie, "the very God you said grace to, that I'll go out there and destroy your garden."

Sam choked back laughter. He shared Cece's feelings. He, too, was plain tired of eating dry, tasteless food with little rib-sticking substance. However, he didn't dare laugh out loud. Marie's eyes turned black, furious over Cece's temperamental outburst.

"If you dare destroy my potato crop," Marie yelled at Cece, "I'll force you to pretend to be a man."

Cece looked up from his plate, grimacing like a ferocious bear.

"That's right, Cece," Marie continued. "You can take the shotgun and hunt for more food to feed this family—crutches and all."

"Are you saying I'm not a man?" Cece roared, missing the whole point.

Paul dropped his fork and held up his hands. "Okay, settle down. We've all been through a rough two weeks."

"I knew this strike wouldn't work," Cece groaned.

"At least we're not starving," said Nancy.

Cece's stomach growled.

"Paul," Marie asked quietly, finally regaining her composure, and diplomatically changing the subject, "How much did the union give you this week?"

"I haven't received anything yet, Marie."

"And you, Cece?" Marie asked.

"No strike pay yet," he said. "Can't pay this month's rent."

"I can't neither," Sam said. He put his fork down. "And I feel guilty 'bout that."

"Don't worry," Marie said. "We're not going to evict anyone."

"Fellas, I thought the strike would be done and over by now," Sam said and looked down at his finished plate. "But I was wrong and I never meant harm toward none of ya."

"Shoot Sam," Cece said, shrugging, "not your fault. It didn't help none neither about me brawling with that photographer."

Sam's eyes widened. That was the nicest thing Cece had ever said to him. "I 'preciate that, Cece."

"Some strikers are quarreling with their own neighbors," said Paul. "Imagine that. Folks who've lived next to each other for years are beating up one another."

"Even women are fixing for a fight," said Cece.

"How do ya mean?" asked Sam.

"The law won't tarnish women," Cece said. "So the lady folks are doing their own brawling around town. . .even flinging filth at their foes."

"Yuck!" said Jeanie.

"Cece, please watch what you tell the children," Marie requested.

"Today's newspaper won't be much help, either," said Richard.

"What?" the family and boarders asked.

Richard reached behind him, picked up the paper, and handed it over to his father. As Paul held up the newspaper, the family and boarders gasped. Sure enough, on the front page, the headlines read, "Strikers Attack Photographer".

Chapter 14

Peterman opened his office door. "Give this to Paul." He slapped a letter into Sam's palm.

Clutching the envelope, Sam tried to take a step forward, but the door was closing on him. "Mr. Peterman, we're expectin' ya at Italian Hall—"

The manager waved a hand. "I won't be attending," he said, nodding at the letter. "My explanation is in your hand. Good day." With that, Peterman slammed the door.

"Hell's bells," said Sam, his hand trembling, despite the letter's virtual weightlessness. "This can't be good news." He didn't waste anymore time and set off on foot to Italian Hall.

After seven weeks of striking, the miners ran out of patience and desperately wanted some sort of compromise so they could return to work. The Copper Empire employees, led by Paul, decided to attempt a settlement without the union's help. Paul had told Peterman that they would make reasonable concessions. Peterman, in turn, had agreed yesterday to attend today's meeting.

Sam thought about the meeting at Italian Hall, happening this very moment, discussing possible terms of settlement. He already knew the issues that Paul would concede on, because he had discussed it with the household during supper the night before. Paul explained that they would have to abandon their two-man drill demands because the one-man drill, most likely, was here to stay. Also, if Paul could get Peterman to offer him the engineer position again, he would try to implement inexpensive safety features. He also thought they should drop the issue of shorter working hours, since Paul had read somewhere that the Michigan legislature was working on a bill to shorten the work day to 8 hours state-wide. Paul had hoped that if Peterman saw the miners relenting on those issues that he would consider a pay raise, and then they would be enticed to return to work. Copper Empire had to be hurting financially since the labor stoppage, just like the strikers were. Returning to work would be mutually beneficial for owners and strikers alike. All Paul had to do was convince the other Copper Empire strikers to follow him, which Sam thought they would do.

Sam sighed. He sure missed eating good food and getting paid. When Peterman hadn't shown up at Italian Hall, Paul had sent Sam to find out why. Now that he carried the dreaded note, he wanted to run all the way back to South Carolina. He comforted himself with a memory of Millie, in their buggy, seated next to each other, as they went for a Sunday afternoon ride.

Millie had sat back in the seat and smiled. "I couldn't ask for a pertier day."

He loosened the reigns and glanced her way with a grin. "Just sit back and enjoy. We're takin' the country route."

She linked her arm with his, and they admired the cotton fields that lay on either side. The white glow from the fields almost looked like a winter wonderland. "Still," she said with a dreamy smile, "wouldn't it be excitin' to go a little faster? Maybe we'll see Fort Sumter if we hurry along." Sam snapped the reigns, signaling to the horses to trot faster. The two bodies were shoved against the buckboard. Millie was caught by surprise and held a hand to her heart. "Oh," she exclaimed. Once over the shock, they laughed together at his attempt for adventure.

Sam came out of his daydream and steered his walk onto Sixth Street. In Charleston he had heard of the northern autumn splendor; now he was experiencing and enjoying it. He and Nancy, that is. Ever since they had danced at the Italian Hall social last spring, Sam thought often of her. He accompanied the Weyburns to church every Sunday and, in fact, looked forward to Sundays when he would sit next to her in the pew. He would nod at the preacher's sermon and she would smile. When Artie moved out of the boarding home, Sam finally had worked up enough courage to ask Nancy to take an evening stroll with him. He was surprised that Nancy had agreed with such enthusiasm, since he wasn't working and couldn't afford to buy her flowers or a nice supper at the Central Restaurant. Nancy didn't seem to mind, however. For the past month they had taken walks in the crisp air of Red Jacket, admiring the once-green leaves that turned into vibrant colors of red and gold. If only he could get past his feelings for Millie, he might be contented with Nancy's companionship.

Poor Nancy hadn't gone courting since her separation from Artie, except for the walks they took together. Sam felt sorry for her because he believed she had developed into a mature young lady and couldn't understand the lack of interest on the part of eligible suitors in the area. It was almost as if the men were like crows, fighting over the flesh of dead animals along the road instead of stopping to notice a jewel. Moreover, Nancy wasn't having any luck securing employment. Each day she left the boarding home early to answer advertisements from the newspaper, but was rejected by potential employers every time. Lately, Sam detected the young woman's frustration, and she had even looked a bit depressed earlier that morning when she kept her gaze on the floor. Usually he could count on her for a cheerful smile and a twinkle in her blue eyes.

Marie didn't fare much better. During his stay at the boarding home, Sam had been accepted as one of the family, with Marie confiding in him from time to time. She worried that the strike might last through the winter, so she and Nancy worked hard to harvest what was left in the garden and store the goods in the cellar. Marie had vocalized her fears about the upcoming winter and how the family would struggle to endure the brutal snowy months.

Sam secretly considered returning to Charleston. He had never seen more than a couple of inches of snow in his entire life and wondered if he could bear the deep snows, bitter cold, and icy sleet – all without a job. In fact, he would have left Red Jacket by now, except he knew he would never see Nancy again. That, coupled with his own guilt about encouraging Paul and the others to strike in the first place. He was an honorable man.

Had it not been for his big mouth, he figured that Paul might have given in to Peterman's demands long ago. Sam had to see this strike through to conclusion.

What worried him the most was watching Paul's calm and contented disposition change to a darker and gloomier one. The union strike pay rarely came through, and when it did, it was too scant to cover expenses. Paul was too good of a Christian to evict anyone from the boarding home who couldn't pay rent, which only added to his troubles. That, and the boarding home needed repairs that Paul didn't have time or money for, especially the crack in the ceiling above the dining room table.

"Where have you been?" snapped Cece who grabbed the letter from Sam's hand.

Sam jumped at the sound of Cece's stern voice that seemed to have popped out of nowhere. "I tried to get Peterman to come with me, but—"

"Never mind," said Cece who held the letter up to the sunshine for a look-see. "Peterman wrote this? Why that lilly-livered skunk." Cece was ready to tear open the envelope.

"That's private mail." Sam grabbed the letter out of Cece's hand.

Cece grumbled. "Better get upstairs then. Those men getting jittery."

Sam walked beside Cece under Italian Hall's arched entrance and leaped two steps at a time to reach the top. Now that Cece's broken leg had mended, he was able to keep pace with Sam as they entered the auditorium. Some two hundred men sat on wooden chairs or stood around in tight knit groups, smoking their cigars.

Drifts of smoke stifled the area, so Sam waved a hand about his face to rid himself of the odor. He found Paul opening a window, and the closer Sam got to him, the more relieved he was when the pleasant breeze swept away the cigar smoke, breaking up stifling air in the room.

172

Sam tapped Paul on the shoulder. "He ain't comin'."

Paul turned around. "What? But it's imperative that we negotiate."

Sam handed over the letter. "I don't think it's good news."

Paul held the letter in his hand and stared at it. "Thanks, Sam. I'll call the meeting to order."

Sam took a seat in the front row while Paul stepped up the stairs to the wooden platform and cleared his throat so that the men would quiet down. But the men continued their loquacious endeavor, so Paul raised his voice. "Men, the break is over, so let's get started."

A good portion of the room quieted down, but apparently not quick enough for Cece. He cupped his hands over his mouth, drew in his breath, then let it all out in one sentence, "Everyone, shut your traps." Within seconds, it became silent.

Paul nodded his thanks to Cece. "I know we are all eager to return to our jobs." The men looked at each other and clapped at Paul's words. "I sent Sam to inquire about Peterman's absence," he said and gripped the lectern as if doing so would ease the bad news. "Apparently, he's chosen to write a letter instead."

"Peterman's a coward," shouted a miner.

"Read the note," yelled the excited men.

Paul ripped open the delicate envelope, sending tiny paper scraps to the floor. He glanced at the note, and then scrunched his face. Just as Sam suspected, it was bad news. Paul read aloud:

September 13, 1913

To the miners of Copper Empire:

You must educate yourselves concerning business affairs. Successful businessmen will not allow a group of workers to leave their job, protest job conditions – and then, at a later time, ask for their jobs back. Owners and managers regularly employ men who are willing to labor hard without imposing their radical beliefs. Your request for negotiation is denied. Doing so would be poor business practice and only recognize a socialist organization. For those miners who are interested in returning to work, they may do so, under the same work conditions. Of course, I will regretfully be forced to lower their pay to compensate for losses caused by the work stoppage.

I must warn the men who continue to strike: I fully intend to have Copper Empire operational soon. You will be permanently replaced by other men who are interested in and available for employment, even if I have to recruit them directly from Ellis Island. The choice is yours. I urge you to think through your decision.

Most Sincerely,

Mr. William Peterman
General Manager, Copper Empire

Paul stuffed the letter back into the torn envelope and took a deep breath. In the meantime, Sam looked at Cece's face that had turned pale.

"Are ya okay?" asked Sam.

"Yeah," said Cece. "Just hungry."

"What are we supposed to do now, Paul?" asked a striker. Others shouted their disapproval as well.

"Hold on now," said Paul, folding his hands behind his back and looking at the floor. "There has to be a solution."

Sam approached the podium, and then turned around to face the miners. "There's only one thing to do. We tried compromisin' without the union's help. Now it's time to really stick with the union."

Sam's declaration was met with mixed emotions. Some miners yelled, "Right, Sam." Others yelled, "Oh, no."

Paul relaxed his arms and lifted his head. "Sam's right."

"We've already tried that," said a miner.

"I know it's been seven weeks," said Sam who paced in front of the podium. "Shoot, sometimes it takes longer than that just to find a job."

The miners looked around the room. Some nodded, but others seemed unsure.

"This time, though, we need to pull together," Paul said and deepened his voice. "No matter what the owners say, or the townspeople say, or what the news reporters say, we must stick together."

A miner cried out, "Let's kill Peterman." Some of the miners applauded.

"That's stupid," piped in another miner. "We'd go to jail for murder."

"Then we'll have to beat the tar out of him so he'll have to crawl in order to move around."

"We'd still go to jail."

"Then let's get our wives to do it. They're handy with broomsticks."

"Yeah. The wives on my street attack men folk who try to go back to work."

Another miner chimed in, "Ain't that Big Annie something else?" He was referring to Annie Clemenc, a strong, young woman over six feet tall who towered over men. She led marches everyday in Red Jacket, using her brains and brawn to rebel against copper's paternalistic stronghold. She was revered in the striking community, but despised and feared by miners wishing to return to work. The strikers laughed as they traded stories about Big Annie's antics.

"Gentlemen," Paul called out, "no violence. If you want me to continue as your leader, you will follow my rules."

A miner said, "Paul, other strikers are beating up those traitors who are returning to work."

"It's working, Paul," said another miner. "Men are too scared to go back to work, so the mines can't operate."

When a few moments went by and Paul didn't respond, silence overcame the room with a sudden hush.

"Come on fellas," Sam shouted as if he were an evangelist. "Show some gumption. Let's beat these owners."

Paul glared at Sam. "Peacefully."

A striker jumped from his chair. "I'm not willin' to work for less pay. How's that goin' to help me and my family?"

Most of the miners cheered and clapped. Once again, the majority were in agreement. But for how long. . .

*   *   *

Nancy lifted the lace curtain that adorned her bedroom window and peeked outside. The autumn clouds shrouded acres of browning grass, fallen leaves and the bare vegetable garden. Holes dotted the brown earth after the harvest. Winter would come soon.

She enjoyed Sam's company, but she still thought frequently of Artie. She hadn't seen nor heard from Artie in two months. Her eyes teared up, but she sniffed and brushed them away. Artie was certainly stubborn. How dare he not even send her a letter telling her he reached Chicago safely? That was the least he could do. Was Artie punishing her just to prove that she couldn't live without him? Even if Artie returned to Red Jacket and they were to marry, Nancy wondered if she could tolerate marriage with such an unreasonable man.

Nancy returned to her desk and wrapped her legs around the chair's legs. She was answering her Cousin Molly Thornton's letter. She felt renewed energy flow through her. Finally, she had a chance to do something new rather than let life pass her by. As her hand furiously wrote on paper, she thought about Molly's invitation to join her in Detroit. Molly was seeking a divorce from her husband, so she asked Nancy to venture south where she would share a room with her in a boarding home. Nancy's mind began to zap like fire flies, full of ideas for her future. But with her excitement came apprehension. How could she even consider a temporary move to a large city like Detroit?

She opened a drawer and removed Molly's letter. The words on the page blurred before her. The decision she had to make was difficult. Molly's invitation to work with her as a switchboard operator in Detroit both tempted and terrified her. Nancy grasped her fountain pen tightly and attempted to convey her final thoughts on paper. She couldn't help but feel a little envious of Molly. Nancy wished for her cousin's outgoing, fiery temperament. Though Molly was several years older, the two had a close bond through correspondence. After Molly had married, she and her husband moved from Boston to Detroit for brighter job prospects, and Nancy seldom heard from her after the wedding. So, when she received a letter from Cousin Molly several days ago, she was overjoyed.

She refilled her pen with a glass eye dropper and realized that some of her ambition just might come to fruition. Satisfied with her decision, Nancy scribbled her name at the bottom of the note. She picked up the letter, scooted away from her desk, and headed out of her bedroom. She was on a mission.

Nancy quietly crept down the stairs, her fingers tracing the drawing of a ship on the banister. Slipping into a daydream, she imagined she was safely on a passenger liner, bound for an exotic locale. Independent and free, she finally had gained the self-confidence she had always wanted. Her brief fantasy ended when she reached the first floor. She sighed and wished she felt secure in real life.

177

She heard her parents' familiar voices. Now would be the best time to talk to them. Nancy tiptoed toward the dining room.

The soft voice of her father, like the whispering crackle of a dying fire, contrasted with the blunt, yet respectful tone of her mother. At a safe distance, she watched her parents discuss their meager finances at the dining room table. In between sips of coffee, Paul glanced sideways at the mural-sized painting. Nancy knew that her father must long for his earlier days of wealth. The depiction of his grandparents standing in front of their mansion told everyone that they had belonged to an elite class. For now, her father's pen pointed downward in an orderly fashion, and Nancy guessed that he was calculating the family's finances. Despite the fact that most everyone in the house worked at odd jobs, she wondered how much longer the work stoppage would continue before the men lost everything they had.

Marie drummed her fingers on the table, analyzing the figures on paper. Nancy's parents managed their money quite appropriately. They had skimped on food, clothing and home repairs. With letter in hand, she joined her parents and stood at the head of the table. "Ma, Pa. May I speak with you about something?"

Marie held a hand to her eyebrow as a way to remain alert. Nancy saw dark circles under her father's eyes, an indication that he had not been sleeping well lately.

"Can it wait a few minutes?" asked Marie. She removed her hand from her face to grasp the paper in front of her, as if trying to pound some sense onto the page. "Your Pa and I are trying to figure out a way to manage this budget."

"Well, I think I may be part of the solution," Nancy said. Like an Indian chief, she folded her arms reservedly.

Marie's eyes widened, her sleepiness vanished for the moment. "Have a seat," she said, pulling out a chair for her.

Nancy slowly took the seat offered and placed the letter on the mahogany table. She took a giant gulp and folded her hands together as if in prayer. "I received a letter from Cousin Molly."

"How are things for her in Detroit?" asked her father as he removed his glasses. He let the spectacles dangle in his hand, exposing the weariness under his eyes.

"Molly's husband left her two months ago," Nancy said, shifting her eyes from mother to father.

Marie asked, "Didn't he return?"

Nancy whispered, "They're divorcing."

"That rat," said Marie. She pounded a firm fist on the table. "I always knew he was no good for her. How has she been surviving without any family around her?"

Nancy took a deep breath, and then quickly spoke from pure inner resolve. "Not very well, Ma. But Molly says I can work with her as a switchboard operator." She focused on her mother, knowing her Pa would be difficult to convince.

Paul, however, didn't fall for the trap. He squared his chin and shook his head, knowing where the conversation would lead. "Never. . ."

"Pa," Nancy said, "I can bring in the extra money you need. It'll only be for a little while." She tried handing the envelope to her father, but he shooed the letter away.

Marie covered her husband's rough hand with her own, and then tried to speak in a gentle voice. The best she could do, however, was soften her determined tone. "Paul, listen to her."

Nancy rose defiantly from the table. Her chair screeched from the sudden push. "I need to get away from here. I'm tired of the strike."

"I think you want to leave because of Artie," Paul said, his gentle voice turning more tense.

"That, too," Nancy admitted as she paced the floor, "But Molly needs me now, and I've always wanted to live in a new town, and now I have the chance to see if I would really like it. And think of the extra money."

"You don't have to do that," her father said. "The strike will end soon."

"You don't know that, Paul," Marie pointed out, releasing his hand. "I know you don't want your little girl to go away, but I think it could be a tremendous opportunity for her."

Nancy shrugged her shoulders. "Maybe I'll be able to find you a job there, too."

Paul slammed his fist down on the table. Marie's eyebrows arched and Nancy's jaw dropped by her father's uncharacteristic anger. "I'll never move to another town!" he yelled.

"One step at a time, okay, you two?" Marie said. She held her strong hands up to protect both husband and daughter.

Nancy spoke again, her voice slightly quivering, "Pa, I promise if things don't work out in Detroit, I'll come back home. But remember, it's only temporary, until the strike is over."

Paul's hands trembled as he unraveled his fists. He looked up at the plasters of golden ivy on the ceiling, staring intently, to erase the anger from his eyes.

"Pa, please," said Nancy. She folded her hands tightly, the whites of her knuckles pleading to be understood. "I just don't feel I'm pulling my weight here. I think I can contribute more to this family if I get a desk job. Please, Pa, I'm scared to death, and I need your blessing."

"Paul, I do want Richard to finish school and he can't do that if he's forced to work a full-time job in the near future," said Marie.

Paul sprang from his seat. "I've always provided for this family," his voice deepened as if to accuse someone on the witness stand. "And I'm not going to let our daughter become head of this household." He spun around to look at Nancy. "Young lady, my answer is no!"

Chapter 15

Nancy and Sam sat down on wooden benches near the train tracks while Marie was inside the train depot, purchasing a one-way ticket to Detroit for Nancy. They admired the gorgeous ground that swirled batches of crisp, vibrant, colorful leaves. A chill in the air made Nancy shiver, but the autumn beauty made the wait outside worthwhile. Leaves spilled over the tracks, and she hoped those very tracks would one day lead her back home to those she cared about most.

She was deliberately defying her Pa's decision, and she worried about his predictable, turbulent reaction once he discovered Nancy left town, but she felt in her heart that things would mend once she was able to send money home. She had used almost all of her savings—money that she had earned doing miners' laundry—to purchase the train fare. She couldn't allow herself to fail in Detroit. She knew, once she arrived in Detroit, that she had to get a decent job and send as much money back to her pa as she possibly could. She just had to prove to her pa that she made the right decision to move to Southeast Michigan.

As the leaves rustled about her feet, Nancy thought about what the city of Detroit might be like. While she was both nervous and excited about her adventure to the big city, she couldn't help but already feel a little homesick. Red Jacket meant everything to her. She loved her mother for her outspokenness, her father for his strength. Jeanie and Joey, while they could be a pain at times, were usually cute youngsters to have around. Richard was growing more handsome by the day and seemed to have ambitions at Calumet Theatre. Cece had always been like an uncle to her. She had also grown quite fond of Sam with his humorous and friendly ways. She would miss them all, but was determined to help the family in their time of financial need.

Out of the silence, Sam blurted out, "I won't have nobody to take long walks with. I'll miss ya, truly, I will."

Nancy shyly smiled at him. "What a lovely thing to say, Sam."

"It's true. I lost my roommate, Artie, a couple of months back, and now yer leavin'."

Nancy felt it didn't hurt to have an extended separation from Artie. Her feelings were very mixed about her former beau. She secretly missed Artie, but there was a side to him she resented. She couldn't dismiss his lack of support at the social when Russell had wanted to dance with her, nor the bitter argument they had in the boarding home. She wanted so much to be cared for by a thoughtful, considerate man, yet he didn't seem to live up to either quality. Was Artie really worth all the fuss and bother? Nancy wanted to be thought of as an independent woman like her mother, rather than a docile woman she knew other wives to be. She wondered if she and Artie really had hope for a future together. Maybe not, but perhaps she and Sam did.

"If you don't mind, I'd rather not discuss Artie." The two remained silent for awhile until Nancy said, "I'll write to you if you promise to write back."

"Shoot, ain't much of a writer, like Artie is." Sam looked at Nancy. She was displeased to hear Artie's name again. "I'll try my best to write to ya."

"I'm glad. What shall I write to you about?"

"Anythin'. Just be sure to watch out for yourself and stay away from louses."

"Oh my goodness." Nancy shuddered. "I don't know what I'd do if I ever had to deal with a scoundrel like Russell Ubel again." She realized she said too much and put a hand to her mouth.

"Now don't ya worry. Russell is in Boston, far, far away from here. He can't hurt ya no more."

Nancy whispered, "How did you know he hurt me?"

Sam cleared his throat. "Right before the man-car accident, Russell suggested to yer father what he'd done, or tried to do."

"Oh, that's too horrible." Nancy looked down at the ground, ashamed.

"Don't ya worry, darlin'. Everybody knows yer a lady. If ya ever need to talk to someone about what he'd done to ya, ya can always talk to me."

Nancy nodded.

Marie broke the silence. "The train should be here soon." She handed the ticket to Nancy.

"I hope so, Ma. The longer I wait, the more jittery I become." Nancy turned to Sam. "Thank you for bringing the train schedule to me."

"I wanted to help ya, Nancy. Truth be told, it should be me lookin' for work in Detroit."

"Stop talking nonsense," said Marie. "You need to stay here and win the strike."

"That's right, Sam," said Nancy. "Sometimes, I think it's only because of your courage that Pa stays in the strike."

Sam muttered, "That's what I'm afeared of."

Nancy heard the faint sound of a train's horn blow, so she stood up from the bench. "The train's coming." Nancy gathered her belongings. "Ma, what are you going to tell Pa tonight? He doesn't know I'm leaving."

Marie's hands gripped Nancy's shoulders. "Don't worry about me or how your Pa will handle your going away. I think this experience will take you places you haven't even dreamed about."

The train's wheels squealed to a stop, pulling next to the station. Marie said to Nancy, "Don't forget us, and visit as often as you can."

Nancy nodded.

"I hope ya don't forget me," said Sam.

Nancy shook her head. "No, Sam, I could never forget you."

"All aboard!" the conductor yelled.

Passengers and families sprung from the benches. Nancy fought back the lump in her throat. The emotional knot was painful. She couldn't speak, so she threw her arms around her mother's thick neck and kissed her.

"Remember to send me a telegram when you get to Detroit," said Marie, caressing Nancy's fair-skinned cheek.

"Of course, Ma," Nancy whispered, her eyes watering. She looked at Sam and knew that she had to quickly put an end to the bittersweet farewell.

Sam extended his hand to Nancy. "Watch out for all those Detroit men who'll want to court ya," he teased. "Keep your chin up. I know what it's like to be a newcomer. Just give it time."

Marie took Nancy into her arms one more time. "Don't worry, Ma. I'll be fine. You'll see."

Marie nodded.

Nancy finally let go of her mother and stepped forward. She climbed aboard the train, and at the first empty seat she sat down, secured her hat in place, and then turned to look out the window. She waited for the longest time for the other passengers to arrive. Finally, when the last person boarded, the train's wheels were rolling and the whistle blew. Her loved ones were waving. She tugged down on the window. "I'll be back to visit soon. 'Bye Ma. 'Bye Sam," she said with misty eyes.

Marie and Sam waved and both replied, "Goodbye."

The train blew its last signal and departed from Red Jacket, chugging south. When Nancy's family was out of view, she rummaged through her handbag, snatched a handkerchief and dabbed away at the tears that had released down her face.

* * *

Paul and his family, along with Sam, left the Presbyterian church sanctuary. Usually, Paul found peace and relaxation attending the weekly Sunday service. Not this morning, though. Ever since Paul found out his eldest daughter had left Red Jacket—deliberately disobeying him—he was angry with his wife. Marie had told him about Nancy's departure later that evening. She had explained to him that the move was good for Nancy and would help with expenses during the strike. Paul had hollered at Marie, telling her she had no right to sneak Nancy on the train, and that he was the man of the house and would provide for his family. Marie had matched Paul's yelling by informing him that Nancy was her daughter too, and therefore could encourage her to do whatever endeavor she chose to accomplish. Marie had ended the quarrel abruptly by stomping upstairs to their bedroom, throwing a blanket and pillow at Paul, and forcing him to sleep in the parlor that night. Paul and Marie hadn't quarreled like that since they were first married. After a miserable night sleeping on the settee, Paul apologized to Marie in the morning for losing his temper. Officially, they were reconciled, but inwardly he felt somewhat betrayed by her. So, he had hoped his spirits would be lifted during today's sermon, but it didn't happen. He knew he had to find peace in his heart soon for what Marie did, because he needed her support during the strike.

"Pa, can't we have dinner first?" asked Jeanie.

"Yeah, I'm hungry," added Joey.

"That boring church sermon made me tired and hungry," Jeanie pouted.

"I'll fix you dinner once we finish helping your pa," said Marie.

"I found the church service refreshing," Richard said. He proudly straightened his tie.

Jeanie slapped his back. "You did not. You stared at Sally Jane the whole time."

Richard gave his younger sister a playful jab. "Snitch."

"Son," Paul began while he put an arm around his son's shoulders, "that piece of news isn't exactly going to make headlines in the newspapers."

"True, but we might make front page news after this afternoon," said Marie with a sigh.

Paul hoped his wife wasn't right, but with the strike and the rally they were about to attend, anything was possible. Sam, Paul and his clan walked down the church steps, then to Main Street. The women were dressed in white, frilly dresses while the men were in their black suits. They walked several blocks until they approached the rally for strikers and their families.

"Let's go to the front of the line," said Paul who guided his wife and family forward. "The union organizers are expecting me to lead the march today." The Weyburns and Sam passed by the regiment of men, women and children. At the front, they were handed picket signs.

When Paul was given the signal, he led the strikers and their families. "Forward!" he shouted and led the way along Main Street, bobbing his picket sign. Downtown Red Jacket looked like an army about to go into battle. "Two-man drill. Two man drill!" he shouted with the crowd.

"Pa, we're not miners, so why do we have to march?" Joey whined.

"Strikers need all the help we can git," said Sam. "Mine owners need to know that mamas and children support the cause."

"Where's Cece?" asked Jeanie.

Marie shouted over the boisterous crowd, "You know he doesn't attend church."

"I know that. But he's a striker," Jeanie complained. "He should be with us."

Paul raised his voice. "Cece will be along shortly."

It was late September and Paul was tired and growing bitter that Peterman and the other mine owners were doing everything possible to keep them from returning to work.

Sunday seemed to be a great opportunity for the strikers' voices to be heard. Red Jacket citizens had finished attending church services, just as the Weyburns had. With a well-dressed battalion of families walking and shouting for one cause, citizens watching along the sidewalks couldn't resist their curiosity.

Paul turned around and walked backwards on the street to give an encouraging smile to his family, Sam, and many strikers following him. Paul looked out into the distance and spotted Cece a block away. Paul waved at the burly man who weaved in and out of the crowd until he reached the front. "I'm glad you made it," said Paul. He put his arm around Cece's shoulders.

Cece humphed. "Let's get it over with."

Paul and Cece and the others walked past familiar stores and saloons and landmarks of Red Jacket. Paul glanced at the people on the sidewalks who once were friendly acquaintances, but now frowned and stared at him. The strike was certainly a spectacle, and the town newspapers didn't help when they portrayed the strikers as the town villains, but how else were they to win their fight?

Marie opened her mouth wide and expelled the next chant, "Safer conditions, better pay!" so loud that the people on the sidewalk heard her. The children were just as vocal. Richard, Jeanie and Joey shouted in unison, as if having a sibling rivalry instead of simply making a point.

Paul had thought about giving in to Peterman's demands numerous times over the many weeks they had been on strike, but he knew the men would lose everything they had worked so hard to achieve. Not only would they still be forced to work in dangerous conditions, but their pay would be lowered, according to Peterman's instruction. He had to continue the fight.

With Cece walking beside him, it was impossible to forget why they were striking. Cece turned around almost every minute to coach the picketers. "Louder!" shouted Cece. He shook his fist at the sky. "What is it we want?"

"Better working conditions!" the striking army yelled.

"What else?" Cece shouted.

"More pay," the strikers called out and jerked their picket signs high above their heads.

Red Jacket citizens stood on the sidewalks and whispered to one another. They certainly weren't persuaded to support the strikers by the rally. Even the strikers' wives and children who participated alongside husbands and fathers had done little to rouse community sympathy. Paul was disappointed by the lack of support from his neighbors. He bitterly wondered how they would appreciate working in a dangerous mine and struggle to feed their families, but figured that they just didn't care, as long as they weren't miners.

Then, Paul heard his name shouted and he looked in every direction, but couldn't find the caller.

"Paul Weyburn. Over here."

Paul looked ahead. It was Peterman calling to him. He stood on the sidewalk, motioning to come over. Paul lowered his sign and nudged Cece with it. "Peterman wants something," he said and pointed to the sidewalk.

"Humph," Cece grunted.

Paul shrugged and stepped out of the rally anyway and ran to get out of the strikers' way and onto the sidewalk. He approached Peterman, keeping a firm grip on his sign. Peterman pointed at an alley and raised his voice, "Let's speak over there, away from this disturbance." He patted his wife's hand. "Wait for me here."

Mrs. Peterman pouted, and then sighed. "Must I? My face will freckle if I remain in the sun too much longer." She whined further, "I'm getting a headache listening to this spectacle."

"Very well, dear." Peterman took his wife's hand, and Paul followed them into the alley.

Mrs. Peterman was many years younger than her husband. Not even thirty years old, she looked like a porcelain doll. Peterman spoiled his princess-wife, perhaps taking extra careful measures not to lose her. He had mistreated two wives already, and they both died young as a consequence. The third wife was much too la-di-da for Paul and his family, so he, gratefully, rarely saw her. Her attractiveness couldn't hide her shallowness, nor her annoying idiosyncrasy of smiling after finishing every sentence.

"Paul, you can't win this strike, you know that, don't you?"

Paul didn't answer Peterman.

"Paul, can't we settle this?"

"I thought we could," Paul retorted. "We waited for you to show up at Italian Hall." He raised his voice, "But you chose to write a letter to us instead, calling us socialists."

Mrs. Peterman answered, "Paul, the Western Federation is a union. Unions are run by socialists. You joined the Western Federation, so when my husband called you a socialist, he was speaking the truth." Mrs. Peterman flashed a grin.

Paul ignored her. "Mr. Peterman, we are going around in circles. The miners won't return to work until you negotiate."

"I'm offering you the engineering job," Peterman offered. "You should take the position as I don't intend to offer it to you again."

Paul shook his head. "I won't betray the miners."

"You're not betraying them Paul, you would be leading them back to employment. It's going to be a long, cold and hungry winter if the miners don't return to work now."

Paul shook his head again. "I can't recommend miners go back to the same unsafe conditions without a promise of change."

"Suit yourself, Paul. Copper Empire will open again very soon with new workers. You and the other miners will never work in the Keweenaw region again until you destroy your union cards."

"Paul, the union is despicable," Mrs. Peterman said and motioned with her parasol toward a steeple. "This is the Lord's Day and you and your kind are making a mockery of it." Her mouth curled up, and she managed to show her teeth.

Paul drew in his breath and remembered that the woman was no more outspoken than his own wife. "Ma'am, I apologize if you are offended by our demonstration. I only wish you understood our reasons—"

"There is no good reason for this," yelled Peterman, who lost his patience with Paul. He tapped his cane on the sidewalk. "Perhaps you and those thugs on the street should consider being grateful for the jobs you had in the mines."

"Amen to that." Mrs. Peterman pursed her lips, and then burst into a giggle.

"Ahh!" Peterman screamed. Something struck his cheek that caused it to bleed. Paul looked to the ground and saw a tin cup with blood marks on it. A second later, Peterman's top hat fell off. "What the—" but was interrupted by a couple of strikers' wives.

"That oughta' teach you mine managers not to snub us," a striker's wife yelled as she resumed her march on the street. She shook another tin cup at him.

"Our husbands deserve more than pennies and peanuts," screeched another striker's wife.

Paul left the alley and dashed to the street. "Please don't throw anything, ladies. We're conducting a peaceful rally."

"Hooligans. Why don't you take your demonstration to the mines, where it belongs," said Peterman who picked up his hat from the sidewalk and fixed it on his head once more.

Paul returned to the alley and sighed. "I'm sorry, Mr. Peterman, we would prefer to picket at the mines, but the mine owners got a court-ordered injunction. We aren't allowed to demonstrate at the mines."

"The injunction was right and proper and it should be extended throughout Red Jacket so that good citizens may walk the streets in peace."

His wife twirled her parasol. "Don't waste any more words on these socialists," she said. "They'll get their due one day." She smiled as she and her husband turned together and walked away.

"Lady, we already have our due," screamed a striker's wife. She shook a tin cup and threatened to throw it, but Paul dashed to the street again and held her back.

"Please ma'am, don't do that." Paul motioned to the rally on the street. "Go back to your husbands." Finally, the wives walked onward. He took a deep breath and thought about how close they had been to a brawl. He couldn't let that happen again. On the street were national guardsmen on horses, taking the right-of-way as they tried to force the rally's participants off the street and on to the sidewalk. Although Paul knew they were supposedly there to keep the peace, he had a sinking feeling they would only bring more trouble.

Crowds thickened along the sidewalks, and the strikers ventured further along the street. Unfortunately, the rally also grew more boisterous. Paul jogged on the sidewalk in order to rejoin his family at the front. Along the way, he witnessed several more of the strikers' wives throwing bottles and other sharp objects at the sidewalk and its audience. Paul groaned. Their reputation would only worsen with their poor behavior.

Then, Paul saw Richard's girl, Sally Jane, emerging from her father's general store. She pulled Richard out of the rally. His son gestured for her to return to the store, but Paul saw the girl's reaction. Sally Jane wanted her beau to stay away from the strikers and become more like her. Paul walked up to Richard and Sally Jane.

"Richard, I need you out here."

"Pa, this is important. I'll see you later." Richard walked into the store with Sally Jane.

"This strike is more important," Paul cried out. "Don't disobey me."

The strikers pushed Paul forward and away from the mercantile. Suddenly, in front of Paul, deputized citizens took billy clubs and swung into the crowd. Screams and cries sounded from women and children. For added measure, rifle shots were fired.

"No!" Paul screamed. He ran and shoved his way through the mass of people to reach his family at the front. When he finally arrived, he saw Jeanie lying on the ground, her leg bleeding.

Jeanie wailed, "I didn't do anything wrong, Pa."

Paul hugged her. "I know, I know, dear. I believe you."

Jeanie continued crying as Marie ripped the ends of her skirt to bandage the leg. His daughter reiterated, for the third time, how a deputy came to her and whipped his billy club.

"Honey, can you identify the man who did that to you?" Paul asked.

Jeanie sniffled, and then began crying again. "I don't know."

Paul hugged her once more. "It'll be all right. Go home and get something to eat." He looked at Marie. "I'll take care of this."

"Paul, no more demonstrations, at least not for the kids," said Marie.

"I agree," said Paul.

"But Paul," Sam argued, "the women and children are needed. Without 'em, we won't get support from the town."

"We will win or lose this strike without anymore help from my family. Is that understood?" Paul asked.

Cece and Sam glanced at each other, and then nodded.

"Marie, take the children home. I'll be along in awhile."

His wife put her arm around Jeanie. Joey supported his sister's other side so she could limp home with them.

"Cece, did you see what happened?" Paul asked.

"Can't swear to it, Paul, but thought I saw the sheriff's deputy club her."

"Then let's go visit the sheriff," said Paul.

"I tried to get him, Paul, but he ran away too fast."

"Those durn deputies," said Sam. The deputies were really miners and other citizens who were opposed to the strike. As a reward, the mine managers legally deputized them. As far as Paul was concerned, the deputies caused more harm than good in the community.

They broke away from the picketers and rioters. Sam and Cece followed Paul and walked a few blocks to the corner of Sixth and Elm streets. Red Jacket town hall was located in a building attached to Calumet Theatre. The men entered town hall and approached the sheriff, who was sitting in his chair, one leg crossed above his knee, and his hands against the back of his head.

The sheriff turned around to the back, where men were sitting on benches, locked up in jail. "Shut up in there, or I'll throw your wives in there with ya." When the jailed men were silent, the sheriff turned his body and faced Paul, Cece, and Sam.

Paul extended his hand. "I'm Paul Weyburn."

The sheriff didn't accept the handshake. "I know who ya are."

Paul dropped his hand and noticed another man walk over to the sheriff. Cece nudged Paul, indicating it might be the deputy who injured Jeanie. Paul said, "My daughter was clubbed during the demonstration. . .possibly by your deputy here."

The sheriff turned to his deputy and growled. "Know anything about this?"

The deputy leaned against his desk. "Yup, I sure do. A young brat spat in my hair and threw a bottle at my back."

"Ya don't seem hurt," said Sam.

"You ain't bleeding or nothing," said Cece.

"Well, the bottle didn't break any skin, but that little terror tried to hurt me."

"You're lying. I was with the girl," said Cece.

"She didn't have no bottle with her, Paul," said Sam.

"What direction were you traveling?" asked Paul.

"South, to stop you thugs."

"My daughter was walking north. Even if she had a bottle in her hand—which she didn't—she would have hit your face, not your back."

"Enough," cried the sheriff, standing up. "You strikers have been troublemakers since this strike started."

Paul pounded his fist. "I demand justice," he cried.

"What do you want to do about it? File a report against my deputy?"

"Just give 'em the papers to sign," Sam demanded.

The sheriff deepened his voice. "You rebels, beware. You're going to lose this strike, your job and your home if you don't stop your socialist activities. I suggest you turn around and walk out of here and forget what happened."

Paul lunged forward, but Cece and Sam held him back just before he reached the sheriff.

The sheriff yelled, "Get out of here right now." He pointed to the jail behind him. "Or I'll lock you up with the other troublemakers."

Cece and Sam grabbed Paul's arms and pushed him out of town hall.

When they were outside, Paul demanded, "Cece, let go of me. Why didn't you let me fight him?"

"Had no choice, Paul," said Cece who finally released his grip. "You were fixin' to have us thrown in jail."

Chapter 16

Autumn's final leaves crunched under Paul's feet as he escorted his wife and friends to the Calumet Theatre. The theater manager, Mr. Cuddihy, had given Richard tickets for tonight's performance as a reward for his ushering service—at least, that's what Richard had said. Paul, however, suspected another reason. Red Jacket was entering its fourth strike month, and its citizens were feeling the economic impact. Stores weren't selling as many goods as before. Saloons weren't as crowded as they once were. And the theater had to give away tickets in order to create the illusion that the house was as sold out as it had once been.

"I haven't enjoyed a night at Calumet Theatre in years," cried Marie, perhaps for the tenth time, to her husband. The illumination from a nearby lamppost allowed Paul to see the sparkle in her eyes.

Marie was correct. It had been a long while since Paul escorted her to Calumet Theatre. The theater first opened in 1900, and was built using surplus funds from the town's tax revenue. At that time, Paul was earning a decent wage, so he could afford to take Marie to a few performances every year. The main floor seats were much too expensive, but he was able to purchase comfortable seats in the first balcony.

Calumet Theatre was well-known across the country and attracted popular entertainers to perform there. A couple of years ago, the famous actress Sarah Bernhardt had performed at the theater and visited miners on her copper country tour. Around that time, Peterman had done away with the contracting system, and since Paul was no longer making the wages he used to, he couldn't afford to take Marie to see Miss Bernhardt perform. However, he had admired Miss Bernhardt's thoughtfulness for taking the time to meet with miners and, donned in mining garb, she courageously made the descent into a mine and watched the miners perform their duties. Paul didn't know what her motive was for visiting them, but he would never forget the beautiful thespian's apparent interest in the miners' lives.

The last time he and Marie patronized Calumet Theatre, they saw a play called "Wildfire" starring Lillian Russell, a lovely, voluptuous actress known for her clear operetta voice. Paul's heart pounded with rapture during her entire performance. When she took to the stage and stood underneath the proscenium arch, her well-padded figure glowed with the help of the incandescent lights that surrounded the curved masonry. Miss Russell had to have been around 50 years of age, Paul figured, and yet she seemed ageless. The white shirtwaist she wore enhanced an ample bosom, and her elegant white gloves were just long enough to cover her elbows. A plumed hat also rested on top of a bed of curly hair, which every woman envied. Thankfully, the hat did not hide her round, fair-skinned, beautiful face. Paul was sure that she was every man's dream, and for many weeks after that performance he would talk to Cece in the mine about her. Paul knew he would never meet Miss Russell, but his imagination was aroused enough just sitting a hundred feet away from her. He kept his infatuation a secret from Marie, though. She wouldn't like hearing about it, and Paul knew Marie would misunderstand his interest. His covert attraction for Miss Russell really meant nothing, because even if he had a chance to court her, he could never tolerate an actress's lifestyle. Furthermore, he knew Miss Russell was a suffragette, and even bolder than Marie could be. No, he didn't want to court or marry Miss Russell, he just enjoyed looking and listening to her.

Marie wasn't without her passions either, but, unlike Paul, she didn't keep hers private. Marie vocalized her boundless enthusiasm for only one actor—Richard Mansfield. In fact, she insisted on naming their first son after the actor. Initially, Paul was adamant that their son be named after his grandfather, Flint. Paul finally relented when he understood how important it was to her. Marie was convinced that if their son was named after Mansfield, he would grow up to be just as handsome and talented as he was.

Marie had followed Mansfield's career ever since she was a teenager and, one summer, traveled with her father to Detroit. Her father had treated her to a Mansfield play, and so her infatuation with the actor began. She would fawn over his picture in magazines and hoped to one day see him again. Paul would never forget the year he surprised Marie by taking her to see Mansfield perform in a Shakespearean play at Calumet Theatre. He couldn't remember which play it was—he didn't much care for Shakespeare—but he loved Marie and wanted to make her happy. That night, he enjoyed watching Marie watch Mansfield on stage. Her eyes followed his every move, and her mouth remained agape during his entire performance. Marie also didn't seem aware that Mansfield had aged, with wrinkles and a receding hairline. Paul supposed that, to Marie, Mansfield had aged little, just like Paul thought of Miss Russell.

"Cece, it's a perfect night for courtin'," teased Sam. "We shoulda left Paul and Marie alone."

"Why? I want to see the play. Don't know why we bother with the likes of you," said Cece. His heavy shoes struck the pavement loudly, almost like the sound of a horse clomping down a sidewalk.

"Cece," said Marie. "Sam was just being considerate."

Cece scowled. "Nobody can figure when I'm joking."

Paul bit his lip hard to prevent chuckling. Cece was right.

"Thank ya anyway, Marie," said Sam. "But I'm gettin' used to Cece's gruff ways. 'Sides, I have these here binoculars to make this trip to the theater worthwhile."

"Don't drop 'em on a copper owner," said Cece.

"What did you say?" asked Paul.

"Just like I said. We'll be on the second floor balcony looking down at the stage. Knowing Sam the way I do, he'll let those odd looking spectacles slip from his hand and knock out a copper owner cold."

Paul grumbled, "The strike being what it is, that might not be such a bad thing." He still had a bad taste in his mouth about the sheriff's deputy whacking his daughter's leg a while ago at the rally and discovering the sheriff would only work for justice for the mine owners. Lately it seemed that Paul fought many temptations to argue with people.

It was Marie's turn to do the nudging. "Really, Paul. You're beginning to sound like Cece."

"About time," Cece muttered.

Paul was the first to see the marquee's lights when they rounded the corner. He pointed ahead to the three-story, red sandstone structure. "We're here — even a few minutes to spare."

Marie grabbed onto his arm. "Look, Paul, it's our baby."

Sure enough, Richard stood at the top of the steps, behind the glowing marquee. Actually, had it not been for Marie, Richard would not be ushering this evening. After Richard had left the picketing, disobeying Paul and leaving with Sally Jane into the mercantile, Paul had punished Richard with extra house chores. He had demanded that Richard quit his theater job. Marie had pleaded for Paul to change his mind, since Richard's job was bringing home a few extra dollars. The family sure did need every last penny. So, Paul reluctantly reversed his decision, and Richard kept his job. Paul was very troubled, however, at Richard's ease at disobeying him. Before the strike, Paul never had much disciplinary trouble with any of his children. Lately, his relationship with Richard grew increasingly strained, and he shuddered at the thought that it was beginning to resemble his relationship with his father, Lowell.

Paul thought it was ironic that his own son aspired to be just as successful in theater as Mansfield had been. And he dreaded the thought. Paul worried about his son. What little he knew about the theater, he knew that actors lived no better than tramps. Paul wanted Richard to have a stable, easier life than he had. He needed to go to college. He wanted opportunities for Richard, the same as his father had wanted for himself years ago. He needed to be educated for a real job and live a respectable life.

Richard collected tickets from the patrons before they stepped past the theater's archway. The red velvet suit he wore seemed to match the flush on his cheeks. No doubt due to the excitement of working for Calumet Theatre.

"Ladies and gentlemen," Richard shouted, throwing back his head and rousing the crowd like a carousel barker. "If you'll be so kind as to step up and hand me your ticket, you'll gain entrance into this magnificent theater for a performance you'll never forget."

Well-to-do patrons snickered when they heard Richard's overzealous announcement, but most of the crowd grew even more excited as they circled and closed in on the front doors. Paul cocked his head, motioning to his group to head up the steps.

"Ma, Pa!" shouted Richard. The boy grinned. "I thought you'd never get here."

Paul lifted two tickets from his pocket and handed them over to his son. "Why the hurry?"

Marie leaned forward and kissed her son on his cheek. "He just wants to show us he can do the job."

Richard's grin never left his face. "That's right, Ma. This is going to be my life someday." He motioned to the blonde girl standing next to him. "Look who I brought with me." His gloved hand linked with Sally Jane's delicately laced one, embroidered with a heart in the center of her palm.

Sally Jane bowed her head to the Weyburn clan. "Good evening. I shall be enjoying the performance with all of you upstairs."

"On the third floor?" Paul asked.

Sally Jane pursed her lips into a forced smile. "My parents, of course, will be seated in the main auditorium, but I decided it was time to experience a play in the balcony."

"Let me have your ticket, then," Cece bluntly said, holding out his calloused palm.

"I have already exchanged my ticket with another patron," Sally Jane said, unable to hide a grimace.

"Why don't you run along with my parents?" Richard said, pushing Sally Jane toward Paul and Marie. "I'll meet you in the balcony after the performance begins."

"Very well," Sally Jane said, throwing her fur piece across her shoulder.

Cece slapped his ticket into Richard's palm. "There," he said, as if going to the dungeon, "remember I'm only doing this for you." Richard gave the ticket back to Cece. He also returned tickets to his Pa and said, "You can't get to your seats from the front entrance." Richard pointed away, "You have to use the stairs at the side entrance."

Marie cried out, "We've never had to use the side stairs before."

"We've never sat on the third floor, either," Paul stated.

"Sorry, Ma," Richard shrugged.

"We'll still have a good time," said Marie, smiling. She motioned with her head. "Come on. We've got a lot of stairs to climb."

"Humph," said Cece. "Look who's coming." Peterman and his wife were walking toward the theater.

"I have nothing to say to him," said Paul. "I wonder what else he wants to say to me."

"He and the Mrs. are always here to watch each new show," said Richard.

"Paul," Marie said, looking into his eyes. "Forget about him. Let's get to our seats."

Paul nodded and led the others to the side of the building. He didn't get a chance to begin climbing the stairs, though. Peterman stopped him.

"Paul, I was offended by your strike demonstration last Sunday," said Peterman.

Mrs. Peterman shook her head from side to side as if to belittle Paul and Marie. "Your labor strike is disgraceful," she sighed, then smiled. "And to think, they chose to rally the town on a day reserved for praising God."

Marie moved toward Mrs. Peterman. "You should be praising God. . .for your fine clothes, jewelry — and a mansion to live in."

Mrs. Peterman drew in her breath and clucked her tongue. She managed a smile, but took a step back, afraid of Marie.

Peterman's nostrils flared. "How dare you speak to my wife in that manner?" he snarled.

"Don't you take that tone with my wife," warned Paul.

Cece barked out, "You started it, Peterman."

"I was simply stating the truth, that a true Christian would not fight and demonstrate on the Sabbath."

"Is it Christian not to pay miners what's fair, and let 'em die in the mines?" Sam drawled.

Mrs. Peterman tugged on her husband's coat. "Let's find our seats, dear."

Paul guided his wife toward the side stairs, then looked back to watch the Petermans walk away. Peterman cried out, "Without a job, this will be the last play you ever see. I hope you peasants enjoy it."

Marie tightened her grip on his arm. "Come along, Paul. Pay them no mind."

Huffing up two flights of stairs, Paul and the others finally reached the balcony and took their seats on a hard bench with no backing. "It's better than nothing," Paul said and tried to smile at Marie. He didn't know how he would manage it, but one day he would treat her to one of the box seats on the main floor, at the side of the stage, with the white wicker chairs. She deserved the best. For now, they would make do with the complimentary seating arrangements.

Sam dropped his binoculars away from his eyes. "Look who's seated as if they were royalty."

Paul borrowed the binoculars and focused. Of course, the Petermans sat in the box seats.

"Hope those mine owners drive each other crazy down there with their highfalutin' ways," growled Cece, referring to the Petermans who sat in the best seats on the main floor. "They hate us strikers more than ever now."

"We're all tired over the strike," Paul held up a hand. "It's Richard's chance to shine, so let's enjoy this evening."

"Tired of the strike myself," said Cece, who squirmed on the bench to get comfortable. He had to keep shifting because of the woman who sat in front of him wore a long-feathered hat, blocking his view. "Might hafta do something about it."

"Like what?" asked Paul. "You can't force the owners to compromise."

"There's other ways," said Cece who tapped the woman's shoulder in front of him. "Lady, I can't see nothin' with that darn contraption on your head."

"Cece," Marie exclaimed, "remember your manners."

When the woman turned around, Paul recognized her as Nurse Annabelle. He groaned. A fight was brewing.

"You said it sister," said Annabelle who straightened her hat so it stood ever higher. "Cecil McAllister could use an etiquette lesson or two."

Cece raised his hand to protest, but Paul shook his head, hoping to stop any rude comments. "Nurse Annabelle, it's a pleasure to see you," said Paul who stood up and bowed toward the hefty woman. "Cece didn't mean any harm. He just wants to be able to view the play."

The nurse took off her hat and set it in front of her. "Now that you asked like a gentleman, I'd be happy to accommodate your request."

Cece grumbled.

Paul tried to relax as the band tuned their instruments to play the overture. With the labor strike in full swing, most of the miners had no means to pay for a performance at Calumet Theatre, so most of the people seated with them in the balcony were merchants or other laborers taking advantage of the theater's discounted ticket prices. Paul guessed that Calumet Theatre had only begun to realize the importance of the miners' past patronage. He looked down at the main floor and knew that the mine owners lived such a different life from the average copper miner and could never hope to understand the importance of having safe working conditions. Unfortunately, the owners only understood profits and dividends and knew that men, especially injured men, could easily be replaced. Thus, the strike would continue until the mine owners learned how to respect the miners or the miners became so desperate that they gave in to the owners' demands.

The lights dimmed throughout the auditorium. The audience began applauding as the curtain arose and an actor walked onstage.

Suddenly, Richard whispered into Paul's ear, and it made his hair and ears lift up. "Pa, you and Ma have to leave."

Paul's head snapped to face Richard. "What did you say?" Nearby folks frowned at the conversation, but he had no choice.

"Mr. Peterman complained to the manager about you and Ma." Annabelle turned around to shush his son, so Richard whispered into his father's ear. "Please, Pa, I don't want to be fired."

*　*　*

Sam took his turn at saying grace before the meal, but there were fewer things to be grateful about — and fewer people sitting around the table to listen to it. Following his short prayer, he drawled, "Amen". The hungry household quickly passed around the shepherd's pie, grateful to have something to eat. After Artie had left the boarding home in July, four more men had followed in September, moving south for greater opportunities. The most noticeable empty chair was the one where Nancy used to sit. He had received one letter from her since she left. It was a brief letter, describing how she had settled in the Detroit area and found a job. Sam wished she had written more. He had even hoped she would coyly suggest how she felt about him. However, she didn't do that. Maybe she would indicate her feelings for him in future letters. He surely did miss her.

He scooped a bite of pie onto his fork and ate a mixture of mashed potatoes, green peppers and tomatoes, enjoying the tasty treat. Sam leaned back in his chair and shivered. Despite wearing two thick wool sweaters, he was uncomfortably cold. He tried to feel better by reminding himself that they all had clothes on their backs and shelter at night.

T-bone was the only one who kept consistently warm with his ample black fur coat. The dog sat next to Sam and seemed to look at him with sad, droopy eyes. The Labrador longed for more than just meager scraps.

Sam wasn't the only one to remain silent during the evening meal. The entire Weyburn family and the remaining boarders were also solemn. With fewer people living at the boarding home, the dining table looked less cluttered, less alive. The only sounds in the dining hall were the passing of platters or boarders scraping their plates clean. The gloomy atmosphere made him uneasy, so he inwardly retreated to South Carolina. Sam used to feel so warm and secure in his daydreams. Lately though, he found the reverie mirroring his harsh reality.

This time, the mental scene carried Sam to his Southern home. He had been staring through his kitchen window. The field was full of cotton, ready to be harvested. Usually, by this time, he and his kin would help each other pick the cotton. But Sam couldn't perform his duties just now. He picked up a bowl and spoon and carried it into his bedroom. Millie was sleeping. He put the bowl down on a desk, and then sat on the edge of the bed.

Millie had finally woken up. She smiled at Sam who picked up the bowl and asked, "Are ya hungry?" He didn't wait for her answer. He had a spoonful of broth ready for her. She accepted the liquid in her mouth, and then sunk back in the pillow with a sigh.

"Why aren't ya outside, harvestin' with Clarkston and the others?" asked Millie.

Sam continued feeding her. "Dontcha worry, darlin', I'll get to the cotton in time. It's you that needs attendin' to right now."

Millie swallowed more broth. "But I'm worried about ya, Sam."

Sam tried chuckling, but a strange noise escaped from his throat instead. One of dread. "Let's just work at gettin' ya well and outta bed once again."

Millie said, "If I feel better tomorrow, I'll help ya and Clarkston with the pickin'. We've got a great crop this year, don't we?"

Sam answered, "The best we've ever had." He leaned forward to kiss Millie's cheek.

Cece nudged him back to reality. "Could you pass the salt?"

"Oh, of course, Cece," Sam said. He reached for the shaker. "I'm—"

"Don't apologize," said Cece. He grabbed the container from Sam's hand. "Almost getting used to your strange ways."

Sam sighed. He watched Paul staring off into space, as if in a trance, just like he was moments before. Sam waved a hand in front to snap him back to the table.

"I was just thinking," Paul said. "Nothing to worry about."

"'Been thinking myself," Cece said. "Might hafta cross the picket line and soon."

Paul didn't take Cece's warning seriously. Nevertheless, he leaned forward and said, "Don't do that, Cece."

Cece explained, "'Been friends more than thirty years. Only reason why I haven't crossed the picket line."

Paul gently spoke. "Peterman has to be hurting. He has to listen to us soon or Copper Empire will fold. Please, just—"

Suddenly, the front door opened and closed just as fast. The entire household looked at each other. The footsteps in the hallway grew louder and louder until the unknown guest stepped into the dining room.

It was Artie. He carried two suitcases, one at either side.

"Good evening," Artie hesitated, and then continued. "I trust I did not frighten anyone; however, I knew it was the dinner hour and did not want anyone to get up on my account." His eyes scanned the table—for Nancy was obviously on his mind.

Paul left his chair to welcome him. "Please come in, Artie."

But Marie grabbed her husband's arm. "Wait just a moment." She walked toward Artie, gesturing for him to leave the premises. "You have some nerve showing up here after the way you treated my daughter."

Artie took off his hat and held it over his heart. "I regret that, Marie." He nodded at Paul. "Please accept my apologies. I was frustrated and lost control of my temper. It won't happen again."

Marie was silent for a few moments, pursed her lips, and then said, "Very well," while helping Artie with his coat, "see that it doesn't." She placed his belongings on an empty chair. "Have a seat, Artie."

Artie scratched his head. "May I return to my original accommodations, as well?"

The boarders nudged one another, murmuring amongst themselves. Finally, suppertime seemed to be more warm and inviting. And alive.

Artie shrugged his shoulders. "My father found employment for me at the Chicago Tribune, but I was dismissed from the position last week."

Paul motioned to a chair across from him. "You'll fit right in this house. We're all unemployed."

Several miners at the table grunted their agreement.

Artie managed a smile, taking his usual seat beside Sam. He looked at the Southerner with curiosity. "I sincerely hope you do not mind having a roommate once again."

Sam gave one of his warmest smiles and grabbed Artie's shoulder with a grip that quickly turned into a hug. "I was gettin' lonely havin' that room all to myself."

Artie returned the hug, and then said, "Oh my goodness," as if he had forgotten something. He dug into his pant pocket, releasing two, crisp twenty dollar bills. "Here you are," he insisted, handing both bills to Marie. "This will be enough for two months of room and board, correct?"

Marie accepted the cash, stashing it into her apron pocket. "I can't deny that we can really use this. Thank you, Artie."

Artie accepted a roll on his plate, and then looked at everyone around the table. "May I inquire of Nancy's whereabouts?"

Joey licked milky remains that had settled around his lips. "She went to Detroit, just like you told her not to."

"Joey," warned Marie. "We don't need your negative comments."

Sam looked up just in time to see Jeanie smiling at her brother. She seemed pleased by her younger brother's rhetorical observation.

"It is quite all right," said Artie, holding up his hand, his skin still red from the bitter wind outside. "And I want all of you to know I intend to find employment beginning tomorrow morning."

"Why did you lose your other job?" Jeanie asked.

Marie reprimanded her. "That was a personal question, honey. Apologize at once."

Artie shook his head. "Please, Marie. I should explain." He quickly took a drink from his cup and set it on the table. "My editor warned me approximately one month ago that it was imperative I write articles describing the mine owners in the copper country and their financial losses." The journalist leaned back in his seat and continued, "I did not have a problem with the request. After all, it is the truth." He then leaned forward in his chair to face those seated with him at the table. "However, I attempted to write about the miners' struggles — their financial woes, their worries about losing their employment, homes, everything they have." Artie's eyes appeared fixed on his plate for a moment, then he looked up again. "I was told to discontinue writing those types of articles. My editor said that readers wouldn't sympathize with the strikers. The readers want the strike settled."

"We all want this strike to end," said Paul. "And nobody is hurting worse than the miners and their families."

210

"Precisely why I could not cease writing those articles," Artie agreed. "When my boss dismissed me, I packed everything I had and decided to return here." He looked to the family and boarders. "If I am to learn from this experience, I wish to be around those I care for and respect."

Marie handed him dessert. "I pray that you can find another job, Artie. So many miners have already left Red Jacket. Money is scarce in this town."

Artie took a small bite of his pie. "Paul, I understand the strikers have had trouble at the street rallies."

"Look at my leg, Artie." Jeanie swiped her plate away, lifted her leg and rested it on the table. She lifted her dress a bit to show the crusted-over scar on her leg.

"Jeanie," cried Marie. "Put your leg down and behave like a young lady."

Artie flinched as Jeanie slammed her leg down. "What happened?"

"A deputy swung his billy club at me."

"Is that a fact?" Artie looked at Sam. "I most certainly did not read about that story in the newspaper."

"That's 'cause the mine owners control the reportin' and justice in this here town," said Sam. "We were even booted out of Calumet Theatre last night 'cause Peterman didn't want us there."

Paul said quietly, "It would be helpful if you would write stories from the strikers' point of view."

"I shall certainly try. Paul, I recently read that the judge overturned the injunction against the strikers."

Paul's eyebrows rose. "If that's true, it's great news."

"What does it mean?" asked Marie.

"It means we can take the picketing off the streets and return the fight to Copper Empire."

"Yahoo!" cried Sam.

Chapter 17

Paul hopped in and out of footprints left by himself and the other strikers, circling the front of the Copper Empire shafthouse in the mid-November snow. His voice was deep and strong, just like the hardened white matter that had blanketed the Keweenaw in a blizzard the day before. "Two-man drill. Two man drill. Two-man drill!" he yelled as he bounced his wooden sign up and down, walking in a circle around and around with the strikers.

Over a month had passed since the court injunction against strikers picketing at the mines was lifted. The men had now been out of work for four months and suffered more with each unresolved day that passed. Paul had broken up more fights in the past month than he could count or remember, because of the men wanting to break the picket line, as well as Peterman bringing in new immigrants to take over their jobs. It was a wonder that an all-out war hadn't broken out at Copper Empire and throughout the copper country.

Paul felt a boom under his feet. Peterman had re-opened the mine in October, but had little to present to the shareholders. Copper Empire was using untrained European immigrants, and as a consequence, not much copper was being brought to the surface. Paul knew it was a fact since he didn't hear much activity in the shafthouse, and he had noticed earlier in the morning that the rail cars weren't full. The surface employees hadn't returned to work yet either, which meant that the copper brought up wasn't worth smelting. Moreover, Paul knew that many of these immigrants left Red Jacket after a brief stay, finding mining much too difficult to endure. Strikers and mine owners alike were losing the fight. Paul feared, however, that one day Copper Empire would be fully functional without them.

The miners were not united as they once were. They were tired and hungry and cold and angry. Many of the strikers would never cross the picket line no matter what hardship faced them. Their wives wanted them to keep fighting, but most of all, they wanted to keep their pride. Nevertheless, Paul had to convince a few men daily not to go back to work. Paul's pleas were mostly effective, but at least one man per week left the group to return to work, causing even more ire from the strikers. Paul had committed himself to conducting the strike peacefully. Keeping his promise was getting more difficult as the days were colder, cloudier and bleaker. If enough men defied the group and returned to work, copper would be brought up again, the strikers would never get their jobs back, and all of this misery would have been for nothing.

Paul trudged around the bend and passed Peterman's small office, wondering if he would ever step inside the structure again. A thick mound of snow swept downward from the roof, partially covering the company name above the door frame. His arms felt numb, but he couldn't decide if it was from the monotony of lifting a picket sign for so many months, or just the freezing weather. When he tried to move his arms for circulation, he felt a jab in his shoulder. Paul turned around and found Sam offering his canteen.

"I know ya forgot it today."

The two men left the circle. Paul switched the picket sign to his left hand and reached for the container with the other. "I appreciate it," he said, holding it to his lips as he drank. "Sometimes I forget the necessities." He handed the canteen back to Sam. Paul took a moment to study the circle. "Where's Cece?"

Sam shrugged his shoulders, and then nudged his way back into the circle to march.

Paul leaned his picket sign against the shafthouse. He desperately needed a break. He walked away from the noise and shafthouse and emerged into the forest. Each footstep in the knee-high snow drift required effort, so he used his arms as leverage to traverse the snowy area. Close to the creek, Paul wiped snow off a boulder and leaned his weary body against it. He stared for the longest time at the creek and thought about his father. Lowell had been right about many things. Paul should have obeyed him and gone to college. If he had, he would have been an engineer. Then he would have never dealt with the labor troubles. He and Marie could have settled into Flint's house as their own. They would have sent their children to the best schools and traveled the world. Paul snapped out of his daydreaming. That never would have happened because Lowell wouldn't have tolerated him marrying Marie or making any other decisions for himself.

Paul stared at the frozen creek ahead of him. Peaceful, icy drips plopped from evergreens and into the creek. At least something in the Keweenaw symbolized life. He stuffed his gloved hands into his coat pockets, trying to keep warm. Although he would never tell anyone this—not even Marie—he desired to go back into time, last summer, and undo his decisions. If he could, he never would have convinced Cece or the others to join the strike. He should have taken the engineering job when Peterman had offered it to him, the night his unit decided to strike. Peterman was right. He had overestimated the union. How could he undo everything that had been done? If he called off the strike, he'd feel like a failure. Still, he wished he could return to work. He missed the underground and the feeling of success every time they brought copper to the surface. He was so tired of the fighting, no money, a house in disrepair, and hunger. As he watched a lone blue jay perch on a branch hanging over the creek, Paul could feel his easygoing nature turn bitter and hardened. He couldn't stop the strike. He and the miners deserved better than what was happening.

Paul heard mumbling not too far away from where he stood. A tree obstructed his view, so he bent forward slightly. Ahead of him were two sets of footprints. Yards away, further along the creek, were Peterman and Cece. Paul sucked in a deep breath. Why would those two meet alone? Squinting from the sunshine, Paul watched the two while hidden behind the tree. He drew in his breath again when Peterman handed Cece a billy club and dollar bills. Cece nodded and they both walked away.

Paul turned away from the scene, fearing that Cece had just made a deal with the enemy. Suddenly he heard angry shouts, so he marched in and out of the footprints he created just a few minutes ago toward the shafthouse. Even at a distance, the scene looked disturbing. Cece had his back to the shafthouse along with three men who stood with Peterman. Apparently, Cece was guarding them from attack by holding his billyclub into the air.

"Cece. Put that club down," Paul screamed.

"I'm the law now, Paul."

"What did Peterman say to you?" Cold, angry vapors shot from Paul's mouth. He looked at Peterman, who stood next to Cece, with his arms crossed, smiling.

Cece stroked his beard. He looked at the snow, and then grunted.

"Answer me, Cece."

Cece put the billy club at his side. "I'm working for Peterman. One bad move out of ya and you'll get clubbed."

"Cece, we're in this strike together," cried Sam.

"Not me. No more."

"We all agreed to the strike," yelled Paul. "We agreed to stick together."

"It was rebel boy's idea to strike and you went along with it."

Paul's lip quivered. "We – all of us have scrimped on the necessities and sacrificed for months. How could you betray us?"

Cece looked at the snow again. "Don't wanna strike no more. Wanna work."

"Yer workin' fer a foe," cried Sam.

"I'm getting paid to protect the mine and anyone who wants to work in it."

Peterman took out dollar bills from his pocket. "Anyone else interested in these? I'm not negotiating with Paul." Peterman raised his voice. "Here's my offer. If you return to work today, I'll lower the shift to eight hours per day beginning January first."

"January?" shouted Sam. "Why not now?"

Peterman chuckled and shook his head. "I'd like to do just that."

Paul swept a gloved hand away from him as if to drive away Peterman's lame excuses. "Then why won't you?"

"Because the Western Federation would take credit for the compromise. The Federation needs to leave Red Jacket for good. Owners in Keweenaw County don't want to deal with those louses."

"Mr. Peterman, would ya put yer offer in writin' for us?" asked Sam.

"I don't believe that's necessary," said Peterman. "However, I will require that each of you surrender your union cards."

The three strikers, standing behind Cece, came forward and threw their red booklets in the snow.

"That union means nothin' for me," said one of the strikers who gave up his card so easily.

"Wait," Sam said and picked up the cards for safekeeping. "Don't give in to him. He wouldn't be out here if he wasn't hurtin'." Sam turned back to Peterman. "How 'bout the two man drill?" asked Sam. "If we accept yer proposal, we want to at least make sure we're safe down there."

Peterman wagged his finger at Sam. "I'm not negotiating with you."

Sam yelled at the three men. "C'mon fellas. Don't ya recall that terrible day in the mine when some of us were almost killed in the man-car? Peterman hasn't changed his ways. He won't even put his measly 8-hour-day promise in writin'. Do ya think he'll allow necessary repairs for our safety? If we return to work today, we could be killed tomorrow."

"None of the new workers I hired have had an accident since the day they started last month," Peterman said with a smile. "What more assurance do you need?"

"Mr. Peterman, there's no accidents because they're not producing copper," Paul shouted. The strikers raised their pickets and cried out, "Yeah!"

Peterman held up his arms to calm the men. "My proposal may not suit your every need, but it would get you back into the mine and money in your hands."

"Pay, for how long?" another striker ranted. "If I'm dead, I'm not worth nothin' to no one."

Sam tried to hand back the union cards to the three men who wanted to break the picket line. "Mr. Peterman will have to do better than that."

Cece took his billy club and slapped the cards off Sam's hand and into the snow. "Ya coulda broken my hand!" yelled Sam.

Paul walked up to Cece. "Put that thing down before you really hurt someone."

"We've had enough," said one of the strike breakers.

"The three of ya are double-crossers," Sam yelled. "We ain't holdin' out for the moon, just safer work conditions, less hours and more pay."

Cece's steely eyes locked on Sam. He held his billy club tight. "Back off, Johnny Reb, or more than your hand is comin' off."

"Cece, what's happening to you?" asked Paul.

"I want to work, pay for my room and board, eat a decent meal and order a forty-rod."

"The strike is more important than any of those things, Cece."

"If the three of you go back, nothin' will ever change," said a scarred miner who pointed to his face. "Each mark here has a life story of its own and I wouldn't have gotten any of them had it not been for working in a copper mine."

"Stop your yakking. One of those scars on your puss was earned at Vairo's," yelled Cece. He nodded to the men behind him. "Go on to work." The three men scurried into the shafthouse. "Give up, Paul. A real man would have gone back to work ages ago."

Paul stretched his arm back and formed a fist. "Put your club down and prove what a real man you are, Cece."

Paul and Cece stared at each other for the longest time. Finally, Cece put the billy club to his side.

"That's right, Mr. Deputy," said Peterman. His teeth gleamed in the sunlight. "Unnecessary violence is pointless." Peterman slapped Cece's back. "But make no mistake, Paul. Cece is in charge now." He closed his mouth, stared a few moments at Paul, and then entered his office.

Paul dropped his fist and began the picketing once again. "Two man drill. Two man drill!" The strikers re-joined the protest.

*   *   *

Paul walked into the parlor. While he threw a log into the stove and shut the tiny door, the boarding home's front

219

door opened and Artie walked into the boarding house, quickly shutting the door to prevent more cold air from ravaging the house, then walked into the parlor and sat down in a rocking chair.

Artie announced, "Good evening."

"Evenin'," said Sam, sitting at the end of a settee, cranking the Victrola.

Paul planted his lanky frame down on a settee, on the opposite side from Sam. The ragtime music began, and as he listened, he studied the parlor, once an active, social room that was often standing room only, now looking sparse and lonely. Several more of his boarders had moved out in October, so there was plenty of room – actually too much room for only three people – to lounge for the evening. He already missed the camaraderie of the boarders, who he felt were more like his family.

Sam broke the silence. "That was some day today."

Artie asked, "Did something important happen?"

"Not important, just disgustin'. Right, Paul?"

Paul's eyes had been closed and remained closed. He simply nodded.

"I hope we're not disturbin' ya, Paul. I'll shut off the music if ya want me to."

Paul waved a hand as if to shoo away a fly and murmured, "I don't mind, but I'm afraid I won't be much for company tonight."

"As I was sayin', I saw disgustin' behavior today. Cece switched sides on us."

Artie stopped rocking. "What do you mean?"

"Cece ain't strikin' no more. He's workin' for Peterman."

Artie responded, "I am simply flabbergasted. Paul, what is the meaning of this?"

Paul opened his eyes again. What little energy he had left today, he spent it by explaining to Artie about today's event, finishing with Cece's betrayal at the mine.

"My apologies, Paul. I am well aware that you and Cece have been friends ever since your childhood." Paul didn't respond, so Artie changed the subject. "I suppose I had a more productive day. I found employment."

Paul finally spoke, raising his eyebrows. "How did you arrange that?"

Artie smiled sheepishly, inspecting his perfectly clean fingernails. "It was your son who arranged it. I am presently a clerk at the general store. Richard convinced Sally Jane to have her father employ me."

Paul found himself chuckling quietly.

"I normally would not approve of obtaining employment in that manner," Artie continued. "However, I was desperate for any type of work. After all, Richard said that Sally Jane owed him a favor."

"As long as he stays in school," Paul said, "I don't care what arrangements he makes for other people."

"Miss Sally Jane is an unusual character. She is extraordinarily manipulative," said Artie. "I am certainly glad I have never been attracted to that type of woman."

Paul winced. Artie was just as clueless as his son when it came to women. Artie didn't even know the gem that Nancy really was, yet he found it easy to criticize Richard.

"That reminds me," said Sam, turning to face Paul. "I received a lovely letter from Nancy yesterday."

"You did?" asked Paul.

"A letter from Nancy?" asked Artie. "Why should she write you a letter?"

Sam explained, "Nancy and I have been writin' to each other for awhile," he shrugged. "As long as I respond, she keeps sendin' more letters."

"How dare you, Sam Houston?" Artie asked. "I find your behavior inappropriate."

"Why? We enjoyed each other's company when she lived here."

"She's my woman!" Artie yelled.

"Ya ain't courtin' her no more. And even if you were, so what? We can still write to each other."

"Sam, you are my roommate, and I trusted you."

Paul ordered, "Stop this, both of you. I can't take any more fighting today."

Artie stood up from the rocking chair. "I am not quarreling. I still think your behavior was inappropriate Sam, and it was only appropriate for me to tell you that."

Artie left the room as Marie's feet pounded the marble upon her entry into the parlor. She sat next to her husband. "Difficult day?" she asked, rubbing his back.

"You could say that." Paul, during dinner, had already explained what happened and didn't want to reiterate the fight between he and Cece.

Husband and wife looked into each other's eyes. Marie caressed his cheek, asking, "Tell me what's wrong, Paul."

Paul held her hand and answered softly, "You mean besides the endless strike, a house that's getting colder everyday, Cece becoming a deputy and betraying me, losing our boarders and our daughter living so far away?"

"Yes."

Paul let go of Marie's hand. "I confronted Peterman today. . .again."

"And?"

Paul rose from the seat, walking the room's perimeter. "Marie, Sam, I'm leading the men into a disaster." He paced the floor. "How are we going to keep from losing everything we have, Marie? Our boarders haven't paid rent in months."

Marie left the loveseat and hugged her husband. "We'll manage, Paul, we'll manage." Finally letting go from the long embrace, she looked at her husband with all seriousness. "Perhaps it's time you wrote to your father."

The suggestion riled Paul. "Marie, you know I can't do that. My father hasn't spoken to me in twenty years. Why would he want to talk to me now?"

They heard the front door open and slam shut. He looked at the hallway to locate the source of disruption. Surprisingly, it was Cece. Paul pointed at him and ordered, "You have just ten minutes to pack your belongings and move out."

Cece placed his hands on his hips and didn't waste words. "Sorry about the fight we had, Paul."

Sam jumped up from the settee. "Ya gotta be jokin', Cece. Sayin' sorry isn't enough for what ya did today."

"It's worked out for the best," Cece said. Paul remained silent, and for the first time in his life, Cece carried the conversation. "Since I'm working for that Peterman clod, I can keep my eyes and ears open for his dealings. Let you know if Peterman's got anything up his sleeve. That'll help strikers."

"Yer a foe," Sam declared.

Cece remained calm as he spoke to Paul. "Ain't a foe, Paul. We've known each other since we were lads. Shoot, Paul, you're my best friend. I only got the billy club so no one'll get hurt unless they start something."

Marie finally spoke. "I'm puzzled, Cece. You did switch sides, you are working, and you are accepting pay from Peterman."

"Right, Marie. Figured I could get paid and help the strikers at the same time." Cece turned to Paul. "I can spy for you and let you know if Peterman is planning anything dirty." Cece stroked his beard. "Hope I'm still your friend. Hope I can keep my room. Don't know where I'd live. Besides, you need my rent money to keep this boarding house running." Cece plunked down dollar bills into Marie's hand. "This'll cover what I owe you since summer."

"Thanks, Cece," said Marie. She looked at Paul. His mouth remained shut. "Cece stays, right?"

Paul stared at Cece for the longest time. Then, he nodded his head. Cece let out a loud sigh.

"Oh, Paul, you said this morning you need help getting snow off the roof. Let's do it now. 'Night, Marie." Cece ignored Sam. Sam left the parlor and jogged up the staircase.

"Good night," Marie whispered. They left her alone with the Victrola still playing ragtime.

*　*　*

As she lay in bed, Marie drew the Mackinaw blanket close to her chin. Her nose was damp and cold, and even underneath the wool covering, her body shivered. Listening to the howling wind outside, and staring through the window at the full moon, admiring how its brightness made the sky appear purple, she tried to drift off to sleep, but couldn't.

She heard Paul and Cece and other boarders on the roof top, shoveling off huge drifts of snow from the blizzard they had yesterday. Paul was giving an order to which Cece grunted. It sounded typical, yet Marie worried about those two. They had been best friends since childhood. Sure, they had spats in their younger years, but she had never seen Paul act so coldly toward Cece, as she had tonight.

Marie's teeth chattered. If she tried to keep still, maybe she wouldn't feel the cold draft. Only her eyes moved. The snow fell in clumps past the window, and then plunked down on the ground. She hoped Paul got the snow off the roof in time. The boarding home already had leaks in the dining room and one of the bedrooms.

It was almost Thanksgiving and they didn't have much to look forward to. Instead of the kids and boarders chatting about the fat turkey they would have and their plans for making ornaments for the Christmas tree they would cut down and put in the parlor, as they always did in past years, she only heard arguments. No one was happy anymore.

A tear fell down her cheek when she thought of Nancy, hoping that she was faring better in Detroit. She desperately missed her oldest daughter. With Nancy away, there was really nobody for Marie to talk with. The men picketed at Copper Empire or on the main streets every day, including Sundays. When they came home, they were tired and moody and sullen and hungry. Marie washed and cooked and cleaned alone without Nancy's help. Half of the boarders had moved out, but Marie was still exhausted doing all of the housework alone. During meals, Marie always tried to turn bitter union conversation to more pleasant talk, but the men weren't interested. They wanted their jobs back and the strike to be settled and they wanted mine owners to pay for all the misery they caused. It was going to be a long winter.

Even her husband wasn't the same man she had married. Paul had become withdrawn and had aged. For the first time, the two began having constant minor disagreements. Marie decided things couldn't get much worse, so based on the money that her eldest daughter had been sending, she knew in her heart that Nancy made a wise choice with her temporary move.

She despised thinking about her family being torn apart by the never-ending strike. She hated that six-letter word more than all the nasty four-letter words she had warned her children never to say. The word meant she and Paul could lose everything they had worked for over the years, especially their boarding home.

Despite her husband's objections, she thought maybe it was time to write her father-in-law a letter. Surely Lowell Weyburn wouldn't want them to lose the boarding home and have it fall into the hands of someone not a Weyburn. But how would she find her estranged father-in-law?

All attempts to keep warm were useless. Marie clapped her chilled hands, praying for the Lord to settle the strike soon. Her family must be whole once again.

Chapter 18

Marie opened a cupboard and extracted a mixing bowl in preparation for Thanksgiving. The vegetables were placed on the counter before her, all ready to be sliced.

T-bone panted and wagged his tail at her feet. The dog seemed to know that it was a holiday, one usually filled with mounds of food that awakened his taste buds. Marie empathized — how she wished they could all enjoy an abundant Thanksgiving meal. She stooped to stroke T-bone's coat, hoping he would forgive her for the meager meal he would receive tonight.

The day should have been a joyous one with family and friends gathering around for thanks. Alas, the effect of the strike outweighed any holiday. Marie was grateful to still own the boarding home, but she wanted her family complete. A noticeable gap was present in the household. Nancy's absence was the hardest for her to bear, but more boarders had also left for brighter prospects down South and out West. Marie missed them all terribly.

From her blue checkered apron, she removed a letter from her pocket. She had received the letter yesterday, and it was her third time reading it.

November 18, 1913

Dear Ma,

I hope all is well with you and Pa and everyone else. When I first arrived in Detroit a couple of months ago, Molly and I shared a room in a boarding house that would not have met your standards. I didn't want to write about it until now, because I didn't want to worry you. Ma, you have every reason to be proud of the boarding home you operate. I am sorry to say that the Detroit boarding house was uncomfortable to live in. Ma, please don't tell Pa this, but the woman who operated the house was intoxicated every day! Can you imagine? Our room was kept untidy. She burned a hole in my blouse while ironing. And I sure do miss your cooking, Ma.

As I wrote to you before, about two weeks after arriving in Detroit, Molly and I secured employment at the Ford Motor Company. In your last letter, you asked me if I ever met Mr. Henry Ford. Unfortunately, the answer is no. However, I am enjoying my occupation. Molly and I answer the switchboard. It's stressful employment at times, especially around noon as it's challenging to keep up with the incoming calls, but I'm becoming quite efficient at operating the board.

I've spent many sleepless nights thinking of you and Pa and the strike. One of my newest chums from work permits me to read her Mining Gazette that she receives about once a week. As of this writing, I know that the strike still hasn't been settled. I'm so sorry to hear that.

I am excited to tell you that Molly and I recently moved out of the Detroit boarding house. Aside from the dreadful living conditions, we were tired of taking the crowded street car ten miles to work. So, we rented a room at Hopkins' boarding house, located just a few blocks from work in Highland Park, several miles north of Detroit. You will be relieved to know that Mrs. Hopkins is a respectable widow who runs a fine boarding home.

Molly's divorce was finalized last week. Already, she is being courted by an editor for the Detroit News! Ma, have you heard from Artie? I sure haven't. I simply cannot believe that I haven't spoken to him in months. I am lonesome for you and Pa and the rest of the family, but I am adjusting well to my new environment. I'm saving money the best I can. I can only send ten dollars this time. I hope this helps you and Pa.

Please write back soon, Ma. I want to hear how everybody is doing.

All my love,

Nancy

Marie stuffed the letter back in her apron pocket. She picked up an onion from the counter and peeled the outer skin. Then she cleaned the vegetable in the sink. Marie had accumulated as many edibles as she could for Thanksgiving, but was still disappointed they couldn't procure a turkey for dinner. Artie had convinced his boss at the general store to donate yams and cranberries to add to the dismal feast in exchange for him volunteering to work the store counter all Thanksgiving afternoon.

She sliced and diced the onion. When fumes threatened to overtake her, she held a hand to her nose to halt the effect. Marie took that time to remind herself of a famous proverb that "This too, shall pass." The strike wouldn't last forever. She promised herself that, when it was over, she would prepare the largest turkey dinner—one that would surpass even Paul's wealthy childhood feasts. She began singing "Amazing Grace", which lifted her spirits for the time being.

Marie heard the front door open and shut and couldn't imagine who it was since the miners were out picketing. She heard a set of slow, heavy footsteps from the hallway when she called out, "Who's there?"

To her dismay, there was still no answer. She set down the onion and prepared to use the knife if she had to. When she saw who it was, her jaw dropped and the knife she was holding fell from her hands onto the counter. Marie decided she had finally seen everything.

Cece held a dead turkey, holding it from its legs, before Marie's eyes.

Marie's hands covered her mouth. "Cece—I don't believe it."

Pretending to be inconvenienced, Cece muttered, "Humph." He shrugged his massive shoulders, and then boldly said, "You told me to start behaving like a man. So I did." With that, he placed the plump turkey onto the counter.

Marie couldn't help her tears. "Cece, I believe this is the sweetest thing you have ever done." She kissed his rough-skinned cheek, and then worked at pulling feathers off of the turkey. She felt Cece's silent presence and looked up once more. Marie was in for a second surprise.

For the first time in the thirty years she had known him, Cece smiled so wide that his remaining teeth were exposed.

* * *

While eating his Thanksgiving meal, Paul turned sideways in his chair, lifted the lace curtain, and peered through the dining room window. A gentle snow fell from the sky, adding to the drifts that had formed earlier in the month. The snow wasn't falling hard enough, however, to cover hoof prints. The privileged few were enjoying sleigh rides across the Red Jacket landscape, many singing cheerful songs as they were pulled past the Weyburn boarding homestead, just outside of the picket fence.

Paul thought about the strike and his increasing discomfort at Cece's presence at the boarding home. Sure, it was nice to have a boarder who paid rent, but Paul suspected Cece wasn't as loyal to the strikers as he claimed to be. What if Cece was actually spying on him and the others, then told Peterman about their activities the next day? Paul let go of the lace curtain and turned to the dining table to eat the turkey that Cece had hunted earlier that morning.

A copper bowl sat in the direct center of the dining room table, almost as if it were a decoration piece, catching drops of icy water that had escaped from the roof and through the ceiling. Paul sighed. It was another repair that would have to be addressed when the strike ended. "Once again, Marie, you've outdone yourself," said Paul and smiled his appreciation. "This was a wonderful Thanksgiving dinner."

"It sure was Ma," Richard said. He continued to stuff cranberries into his mouth.

"Don't compliment me," said Marie, looking at Cece across the table. "Cece deserves most of the praise."

Cece looked up while he shoveled food in his mouth. "It was nothing."

"I didn't know Peterman gave you permission to stop guarding Copper Empire so that you could hunt for the turkey," said Paul with a twinge of sarcasm. Cece frowned.

"Do you own a gun?" asked Richard.

Cece wiped his mouth with a napkin and explained, "I don't, but your father does. He has several."

Joey appeared deep in thought and cocked his head to the side, looking at his father with skepticism. "Pa, can't you shoot Mr. Peterman? Wouldn't that end the strike?"

"No, son," Paul said. "We don't shoot people. We shoot game."

Joey drank from his glass and gulped loudly. "Oh."

Jeanie clucked her tongue and looked at her younger brother. "You're really dumb sometimes, you know that?"

Roberto tugged on Jeanie's blouse. "You should not-a say such a-ting about your-a brot-a."

Jeanie snapped, "Roberto, don't you ever have supper with your own family?"

Paul swallowed his food, and then leaned forward. "Jeanie, I am surprised at you," he said. "Hasn't it occurred to you that maybe Roberto's family is going through a more difficult time than we are?" He glanced at Roberto. Tears trickled down the boy's cheeks.

The boy backed away from the table, taking his glasses off to wipe away the tears. "I'm-a going home."

Marie draped her arm around the boy's shoulders. "Roberto, please stay," she coaxed, squeezing him into a bear hug. "You're a member of this family, too. Almost like a son to me."

Jeanie scooted back from the table. "I'm sorry. Really I am, Roberto. You can even have my dessert." She hugged Roberto. The boy wrapped his arms around Jeanie too, making up rather quickly.

Marie reprimanded her daughter with a tough scowl. "Jeanie, if I hear another inappropriate comment from you again, you will be punished."

"Yes, ma'am."

"Take your seat, then."

Cece didn't even wait another minute before displaying his special knack for inappropriately continuing the conversation after a heated argument. "'Sides," he said, referring to Joey's earlier comment about guns, "there are days I feel like doing more than just shooting turkey."

"Meaning what?" asked Paul.

"Nothing," Cece said and continued to chew his food. Everyone at the table looked up from their plate and glared at him. Not bothered by the silence, Cece dropped his fork on his plate and looked at Paul. "End the strike."

"He can't do that," said Sam.

Cece pointed at Sam's face. "Stay out of it, Southerner."

Marie shot up from her chair. "Enough, all of you. Thanksgiving is not going to be ruined over this strike. If you men need to talk business, do it while you're picketing." She began clearing dishes from the table.

Cece watched Marie walk into the kitchen. When he was satisfied she couldn't hear him, he whispered, "Heard of the Alliance?"

Paul nodded. He heard the gossip about the Citizens Alliance, formed recently by local businessmen. The Alliance members claimed it was created to stop striker violence. Paul suspected, though, their mission was more than that. Paul didn't condone striker violence, but he knew trouble emerged from both sides and that the Alliance really set out to rid Red Jacket of the union.

When he first found out about the Alliance, Paul tried to shrug it off and forget it. He was facing too many problems and couldn't deal with a new one. The Citizens Alliance claimed they were representing the citzens' well being and had no connection with the mine managers. Paul knew that claim was ludicrous. Yesterday, while picketing, he saw men with Alliance buttons on their coats enter Peterman's office.

Sam said, "The Alliance can't stop us."

Cece raised his voice louder than a whisper, "Oh yes they can, Reb. If the citizens want the union out of Red Jacket, then the Alliance will drive 'em out."

Marie pounded back into the dining room, collected more dishes and yelled out, "I thought I said I didn't want to hear any more of this strike. Take it outside and freeze in your britches if you must argue, just don't do it in my house." She thundered back to the kitchen again. No one spoke a word for a few minutes, and no one wanted to go outside to finish the argument.

Paul noticed in particular that Sam wasn't his usual self. "Sam, you've hardly said anything today."

"Don't remind him," said Cece. "I like it quiet 'round here."

"I was just thinkin' of my home in Charleston," Sam said, his words pained and slow.

Last week, when Paul had passed Sam's room, he glanced inside and saw him staring at a picture of a woman. When Sam realized Paul's presence, he put the picture face down on the dresser, and then curtly informed Paul that he needed his privacy. And that was that.

Marie returned to the dining room and said with a calm, deliberate voice, "I received a letter from Nancy."

"Is she love sick for Artie yet?" teased Richard with a mischievous grin.

"How do you know if she even mentioned him?" Marie asked, clearing away more dishes. "Women can get along just fine without men if they have to."

Paul was still eating, but tried to talk with a large mouthful of food. "So how's she doing?" he asked.

"She sounds very happy in Detroit. Actually, she's living a few miles north of Detroit in a city called Highland Park. Nancy's learning how to operate the Ford Motor Company switchboard," said Marie.

Richard shrugged his shoulders. "I think Artie's lonely."

Marie took a seat and sighed. "Richard, do you have time to write a short play?"

"I can always make time. Why?"

"The Women's Auxilliary met today. We've decided to have a Christmas party for strikers' children at Italian Hall. I've been put in charge of decoration and signs, but another lady was put in charge of entertainment, and she suggested a Christmas play. So, I told her my oldest son could do that."

Richard shrugged his shoulders. "Sure. I'll write it, act in it and direct it."

Sam ate another mouthful of turkey, gulped loudly, and then spoke to Richard. "Are ya nervous performin'?"

"Absolutely not. . .I. . .well. . .I'm going to be the greatest actor around someday," said Richard.

"Then it's settled," said Sam.

"Good," Marie said, pouring a cup of hot coffee for Paul.

The evening was finally winding down. Paul felt his wife's hand cover his own, so he knew the topic would turn serious again. Cece, Sam, the children and boarders politely excused themselves and left the dining area. When the last person left, Marie spoke. "The money Nancy sent us won't last long. We can't go on another month with no income."

Paul sipped the bitter coffee. "It's not our choice. The miners won't give up and neither can we."

Marie kept her mouth closed.

Paul wrapped his hands around the cup and took another drink. "Besides, we've made it this far."

"Perhaps Richard should quit school and find a job. He can finish school next year."

Paul shook his head. "Absolutely not, Marie."

"Darn it, Paul," she cried, striking the table with her fist. "We have to. It would only be temporary, until the strike is settled. Besides, Richard wants to help."

Paul shouted at her, spilling his coffee, "He's going to finish school, Marie. He didn't even begin his education until he was Joey's age. He's almost done. . .if he leaves now, he won't ever go back."

Marie remained silent.

Paul blurted out, "I think Cece needs to find another place to live."

"Excuse me, Paul?"

"You heard me," Paul said, his cup clamoring in the saucer.

"Besides Artie, he's our only paying boarder. Cece is also your best friend."

"Marie, I've known Sam about half a year and I trust him more than Cece. You heard him tonight, that crack about wanting to shoot more than turkeys."

"Paul, he'd never hurt any of us."

"He's a traitor."

"Sh," Marie cried. "I don't want Cece to hear you," she whispered.

"So what if he did? It's my house." Paul's chair legs squealed on the floor. He frowned as he got up, and then stomped out of the room.

Marie untied the apron from her waist and threw it on the table.

*   *   *

Marie placed an announcement near the general store. It irked her that she couldn't place it on the store's property because Sally Jane's parents were Citizens Alliance members and wanted nothing to do with miners or the strike. She put a nail directly over the advertisement and hammered, and with each blow, she thought of her recent fight with Paul, one of the rare outbursts the couple had since they were newlyweds. She stepped back to make sure she hung the poster straight. The sign read, "*Attention all WFA members and families. Bring your children to meet Santa Claus and unwrap a gift. Meet at Italian Hall on Christmas Eve at noon.*" Marie whistled the tune "Jingle Bells", glad that she was helping others even less fortunate than herself. People walking along the slick road stopped to read the announcement. Some wearing the white Citizens Alliance buttons jerked their chins up and walked away. Marie decided to remain cheerful during the holidays despite the disapproval of many in the town.

The wind picked up, whipping her scarf to the side of her face. Marie felt the cold sting of arctic air and decided to warm herself for a spell inside the store. She opened the door and stepped inside the well-stocked establishment, her eyes catching the rows of canned goods and knick knacks. She glanced at the counter and found that it was empty, so she crept down each aisle until she saw Artie.

Artie was sweeping the floor when he heard the footsteps and looked up. "Marie," he said, continuing to clean the floor. "What brings you into town?"

Marie placed one hand on her hip. "I've been posting advertisements around town and thought I would take a little break," she said. Her hands were still chilled, so she blew on them to warm them up. "I never get a chance to speak with you alone and there is something on my mind."

Artie stopped sweeping for a moment. "Anything I may assist you with?"

Marie dug into her coat pocket, producing a letter. She waved the cream-colored envelope in front of his stoic face. "I received this last week from Nancy. She asked about you."

Artie paused before asking, "How is she doing?"

"Why don't you write her yourself and find out?"

"No, ma'am. I will not quarrel with her again when I am right. Her place is not in Detroit."

"You're right, there's no sense arguing with you. I'll see you tonight," Marie snapped. She charged down the aisle, but felt a mental tug that pulled her back. She retraced her steps and found Artie again. His eyebrows arched at her mysterious return.

"Have you kept up with your writing?" she asked.

Artie smiled. "Amusing that you should inquire. I was going to dispense of an article I have been working on during my breaks."

"Why would you throw it out?" Marie asked.

"The newspaper rejects my articles — perhaps they are not exciting enough," he said, continuing his sweeping.

"May I have it?" asked Marie.

Artie shrugged his shoulders. "Certainly. I shall return momentarily." He walked to the back of the store, and then returned with papers. "This is an article about how justice was received by a Cornish man who was assaulted by Irish men. The sheriff who arrested the Irish men was actually Irish himself."

Marie grabbed the paper, folded the article and put it in her coat pocket. "Well, see you later Artie. You don't mind my taking this article with me?"

"No, ma'am. What do you intend to do with it?"

"Never you mind about that."

"Marie, when you correspond with Nancy, inform her that. . .I. . .said hello."

Marie nodded and left the store. When she got home, she had two letters to write: one to Nancy and the other to her father-in-law.

She could only pray that Lowell Weyburn wouldn't rip up her letter.

Chapter 19

Sam wrapped his coat collar snug to his neck, and then pulled out a handkerchief to wipe his wet, red nose. He shivered through the thick layer of clothing he wore as he walked the picket line. The slushy ground from the downpour of chilly rain made his boots wet and feet cold, but at least it was melting the snow. Marie had told him last night that the Keweenaw was experiencing an unusual warm spell, but Sam didn't feel warmer, only wetter.

Would he ever get used to the brutal northern winter when it had only just begun? Over and over again, he wished he could pack his belongings and return to Charleston, but he didn't dare. Sam couldn't let Paul down by walking away from the very fight he had encouraged in the first place. He surely did miss the hot sun though, beaming down on his weeping willow tree, the blue skies, green grass and warm ocean breezes.

Halfheartedly, Sam carried his picket sign and noticed the strikers were just as sullen as himself. They looked starved, chilled and downtrodden.

The picket circled past Peterman's office. And each time he got close enough to the manager's office, he'd glance at the front window. Inside, the curtains were open, and his curiosity was aroused. A young man, with his back to the window, was speaking with Peterman. It was a lengthy conversation as Sam figured he must have passed by the office a hundred times since the man first entered the office. There was something familiar about him. Sam was itching to find out who it was. He could have asked Paul about the young man, but didn't want to bother him today. Paul's mood had been sour all week.

As he passed by the shafthouse, he looked at Cece who stood in front of it, tapping his billyclub and keeping a watchful eye on the picket line. Cece called out to Sam, "Give up, you ain't winning."

Sam continued to walk the grounds, and then looked up at the sky to search for an appropriate answer. When he turned around the circle again, he met Cece's stare and said, "'Cain't give up now. Work conditions are still too dangerous and miners would hafta accept less pay."

Cece put his hands over his mouth to call out, "Less pay is better than nuthin'."

That comment gave life to Sam's picketing efforts again. He held up his sign and marched with a renewed spring to his step. The strikers had to win, no matter the cost. To fight the shivers, he allowed his thoughts to drift southward, hoping that just thinking about South Carolina would keep him warm. It proved just the opposite.

Sam had glared for a few minutes at the bare Christmas tree that stood in his hallway. He felt no urge to decorate it, though. He hadn't even wanted the darn thing, but cousin Clarkston had brought it to the house, thinking it would bring him Christmas cheer. Sam sighed and picked up a small gift that lay underneath the tree.

He had walked to his bedroom, put the gift on the bed, then took a cloth and sat at Millie's bedside, gently wiping her face. Her breathing was labored and her condition had deteriorated.

"Don't fuss over me," Millie said. She struggled to speak some more. "Open your gift," she whispered.

Sam put the cloth down and opened the present. It was a small, wood-framed picture of Millie. He smiled. "I love my Christmas gift, Millie. It's the best present you ever gave me."

Between labored breaths, Millie managed to ask, "Remember when that photograph was taken?"

Sam shook his head.

"Shortly after we married—" With each breath, Millie tried to speak, but couldn't.

Sam pressed a finger to her lips. "Don't try to talk," he said with a smile. "I'll do the talkin'."

Millie's mouth opened slightly, as if she were about to say something, but Sam snapped out of his dreaming when Cece tapped him forcefully on his shoulder.

"Sorry to interrupt your daydream," Cece sneered, "but look over there."

The picket line had scattered. The strikers mobbed the front of the shafthouse and thrust their bodies against the front door. Strikers yelled, "Traitor!"

"Oi'm eadin' back ter work, naw matter waat yer say," cried an Irish striker with a gaunt, pale face. "Git oyt av me way." He swiped at a striker who stood in front of the doorknob, but the other striker wouldn't budge from his space.

"You weer here yesterday wit us picketing," a Finnish striker cried out. "Weer suppost be fighting tis tawgeter."

Sam and Paul placed their bodies between the commotion. "We all want to work," Paul said, looking at the men, "but only under the right conditions. Please, join us again."

Cece barked, "Can't stop them."

"Cece, just let me speak."

"Let 'em through," warned Cece. He lowered his fingers to the billy club.

"I wasn't stopping them Cece — back off," Paul snapped.

Meanwhile, Peterman and the young man left the office and joined the commotion. Sam got a closer look at him. The young man had ugly, deep wounds on his face and neck, and Sam suspected the long, curly moustache covered a few more scars.

Peterman shook the Irishman's hand. "Welcome back to Copper Empire. I'll have to lower your wages to a dollar and a half a day, but one day soon I'll give you a raise."

Paul said to the Irishman, "Please, don't go back to work."

The Irishman ignored Paul and nodded at Peterman.

"Get your equipment, and you can start working now," said Peterman. "You'll find nothing has changed." Peterman slapped the young man on the back. "You'll even have the same boss—my esteemed nephew, Russell."

Sam's stomach cramped and his arms shook. Of course, behind the moustache and scars, the young man was indeed Russell Ubel. The evil eyes stared at Sam and Paul. Sam grabbed the Irishman. "Ya can't do this. Don'tcha remember what kind of a man Russell was in the mines?"

Russell yelled at Sam. "And what kind of a man are you? You and Paul left me in the mine to die."

"Ya should've died, instead of the other men who did."

Peterman turned to Russell. It was the first time Sam noticed both men wearing Citizens Alliance buttons on their coats. "Don't get excited, Russell."

Russell ignored his uncle and shouted, "I spent months in the hospital fighting for my life. My sweet mother wept at my bedside everyday, praying my life would be spared." Russell laughed out loud. "God listened to my mother. And God is condemning all of you strikers."

Russell's lip was quivering while his uncle patted his back. "Pay no mind to them," Peterman consoled. "Let them freeze out here, wondering when they'll get a decent meal again." Peterman turned to Cece. "Guard this place while we're gone." Cece clapped the billyclub against his hand while Peterman and Russell walked to the Model T, got inside, and then drove away.

Sam and the other strikers turned to Paul, "What are we gonna do now?"

Paul walked up to Cece. "You promised that you'd spy on Peterman for me."

Cece looked at the ground.

"You knew Russell returned from Boston, and you knew that Peterman was hiring him to engineer the mine again. How long did you know that information?"

Cece shrugged.

"Answer me!" Paul cried out. "Did you know this weeks ago, while you shared a Thanksgiving meal with my family?"

"Tried to warn you," Cece mumbled.

"You didn't say anything about Russell."

"I told you about the Citizens Alliance," Cece retorted.

"So what? That has nothing to do with Russell—"

Cece interrupted. "It does. Peterman, Russell and thousands of residents are a part of the Alliance."

"So it's true, what I've read in the newspaper. At least, according to the newspaper that prints the truth and doesn't always side with mine owners. The Alliance is run by mine managers."

"Mostly," said Cece. "They've got the power and they'll soon get rid of the union. If ya know what's good for you—all of you—throw away your union cards and picket signs and go back to work."

Sam tried to smooth things over. "Cece, be reasonable. Look how far we've come." He rested his picket sign against the shafthouse and stepped forward to persuade him. "We've been a team for five months. We have to fight for safer workin' conditions and fair pay. If we don't, generations of men followin' us will have to strike for the same things one day."

Cece faced Sam. "There's no ending this strike, because there's no beginning. Miners always had it rough and it won't never stop. Strike is only making it worse."

"Wrong, Cece. Ya made it worse by joinin' our foes."

"Least I'm getting paid."

243

"I tell ya, it's tainted money," Sam cried out.

"Wanna make something of it?" Cece covered the billy club with his hand, and with the other he tugged out his collar to show his deputy badge. "All of Red Jacket is tired of the striking and unions. We want it to end. Now, for the last time, I'm telling all of you to go back to work."

Sam heaved his arms on Cece's shoulders and pushed. Cece lifted his billy club, but before he could use it, Paul broke his vow of peace and punched his ex-friend square in his jaw. Cece plopped into the mud, the weapon flying away several feet.

Cece held a hand to his bleeding mouth and panted between words. "To. . .think. . .I called. . .you my best friend," he said, shaking his head. "Musta been crazy."

Paul held his bloodied fist, panting.

"Hit him again," a striker called out.

Paul stomped through the mud and Cece kneed his way through the icy slush, both men trying to get control of the club first. Simultaneously, they gripped the dangerous stick.

Paul yanked on one end, and Cece's body fell into the mud again, but he held onto the other end.

Sam cried out, "Grab his other arm." The strikers pinned Cece's free arm to the mud. Cece still wouldn't release the weapon, so Sam sat on his legs.

"Get off of me."

"Ya can't fight us all, Cece," said Sam.

With all of his might, Sam bit Cece's hand, forcing him to release the club. Paul picked up the club and was ready to strike Cece, but he just couldn't do it. He nodded to the men who had pinned Cece to the ground. "Let him go."

Cece stood up and hollered, "You'll never get away with this. The Citizens Alliance will take care of you."

Paul raised the club again, so Cece ran away from Paul, into the shafthouse, and slammed the door shut.

The strikers surrounded and cheered Paul.

*   *   *

Marie snuggled beneath the Mackinaw blanket. She sighed. It had been a laborious day, preparing for the Christmas party to be held at Italian Hall tomorrow afternoon. Then Cece had barged through the front door, yelling about his fight with Paul. He quickly packed a bag, left without saying goodbye, and slammed the front door. Later, during supper, Sam revealed more details about the huge fight. Paul didn't say much, though. Paul and Marie never even reconciled after their own fight at Thanksgiving. Paul had turned into a bitter man, and was drinking far more than he should. Marie knew the daily picketing took its toll, but why couldn't he manage to speak a kind word every now and then? He refused to say grace anymore, and she had to pester him to go to church. Paul was not the same man she married, and it frightened her.

Paul walked into the bedroom. He shut the door and climbed into bed without saying a word.

Marie said gently, "Do you want to to talk about what happened today?"

Paul barked out, "No."

"It'll be better tomorrow. I promise. How can a day like Christmas Eve go wrong?" When Paul didn't respond, Marie gave up having a conversation with him. "Goodnight, Paul." He didn't respond to that, either. Worries zapped around in her mind, but Marie finally closed her eyes and slept.

Suddenly, an hour later, Marie awoke and she tried to shake away the grogginess. She heard loud thuds coming from below at the front door. She scrambled out of bed and met up with Paul, who was already in the hallway, and they both ran down the stairs and to the foyer. Paul ordered Marie to go back into the bedroom, but she stayed with him anyway. Marie turned on the hallway light. Someone outside was trying to bust the door open. Paul put his body against the door. Marie, too, put her back to the door, trying to get leverage with her legs. Sam and Richard ran down the stairs.

"Who's tryin' to get in?" asked Sam.

"I don't know," Paul answered, out of breath. Sam relieved Marie by replacing her with his back to the door. "Richard, look out the window and tell me who it is."

Richard sprinted to the parlor. "It's a mob out there, Pa."

"Oh, no," Marie cried out.

"Richard, go to your bedroom and shut the door, and keep it shut," Paul demanded.

Instead of doing as his pa ordered, Richard ran to the back of the house.

Paul said, "We can't hold this door much longer." The door rattled as Paul and Sam used all the strength they had to keep it shut.

Suddenly, the door thrusted open, sending Paul and Sam to the ground. A dozen or so men came inside and toppled on them.

Marie screamed, "Get out of here!"

Sam yelled, "Yer trespassin'!"

"What are you going to do about it?" The man who spoke those words emerged from the darkness. It was Russell, with other men standing next to him. He grabbed Paul's arms, thrust them behind, and put handcuffs on them while the others invaded the parlor and overturned furniture. Another man put handcuffs on Sam as well.

"Both of you are arrested," said Russell.

"Fer what?" asked Sam. "We have rights."

"You had no right assaulting Cece. You're going to jail for what you did today," said Russell.

Two men in the parlor got on either side of the grandfather clock and tilted it.

Marie cried out, "Leave our property alone!"

Paul shouted, "You don't have a search warrant. You have no right invading my house!"

"The sheriff says we do," said Russell, lifting his collar and pointing at his deputy badge and Citizens Alliance buttons. "Didn't Cece warn you that the Alliance wouldn't let you get away with your antics?"

Richard ran to the door, this time armed, with T-bone barking behind him. At the same time, the other boarders and Artie ran down the stairs. T-bone ran to the men tilting the grandfather clock and jumped on an intruder. The man pushed the dog off, but T-bone bit the man's leg. There was a stalemate between the boarding house residents and the Citizens Alliance. Richard aimed the rifle at Russell. "Let my pa go." His hands were shaking.

The other men, all donning Citizens Alliance buttons, drew their pistols, pointing them at Richard. Russell stated, "Paul, if your son has any sense, which you don't, he better drop the rifle."

Paul said, "Son, put it down. I'll settle this matter with the judge."

"No, Pa. They'll kill you." Richard cocked the rifle, and T-bone continued his attack on the man in the parlor.

Russell yelled, "Your dog better stop attacking, or I'll have the men put a bullet in that beast's head."

Richard cried out, "No!"

Paul yelled to T-bone, "Heel. Stay."

T-bone stopped his attack, planted his body on the floor, wagged his tail, and panted.

247

"That darn dog attacked me once before," snarled Russell.

"Only because ya tried to harm Nancy," Sam cried out.

Russell shot back, "I almost had my way with her, if it weren't for this wretched animal."

"You've admitted to attempted rape," Paul yelled, writhing on the floor with handcuffs. "I'll go to the authorities and have them press charges."

Russell retorted, "You'll do no such thing." He turned to the other intruders. "Shoot the animal. I'm the law now."

Richard's hands, still trembling, aimed the rifle at no one in particular. "I'll shoot anyone who harms T-bone."

Russell laughed out loud until Richard pointed the rifle at him. In a deeper voice, Richard said, "Don't you ever harm my sister again."

Russell's lip quivered. "Shoot the boy."

Marie screamed, "Leave my son alone!"

"Drop the rifle," Paul ordered Richard.

"No, Pa."

The intruders cocked their guns and Paul yelled at Richard this time. "Do it now," Paul yelled.

His hands still shaking, Richard dropped the rifle to the floor.

Russell said, "Let's get them to jail." The Alliance members nodded, and then grabbed Paul and Sam off the floor.

"You Alliance cowards better pay Paul fer the damage you did to his home," said Sam.

Russell looked at Paul. "You can't afford this home anyway. Uncle William would be happy to buy this house so it won't burden you any longer."

"It'll never happen," said Paul.

Marie said something to Russell in a voice that sounded like a demon had invaded her body and took over her voice box. "If you harm Paul or Sam in any way, you'll wish you had died in the mine."

Russell shoved Paul and Sam out the door with the Citizens Alliance members following behind.

*   *   *

Paul and Sam were locked up in the Red Jacket jail. The cell was completely dark and very cold with Sam shivering on a stained, lumpy cot. His legs and arms were crossed, trying to keep a little warm, and his gaze through the darkness was fixed on the ceiling. After awhile, Sam's eyelids grew heavy and his eyes watered, but he couldn't sleep. He looked across at his cellmate.

Paul gripped onto the cell bars and pulled his body toward it, then rattled the steel columns. "Let us out!" he yelled.

"Shut up in there," the sheriff yelled from the front room.

"At least let me send a message to my wife."

"We'll contact her when we're ready," said the sheriff.

Paul softened his tone, "Sheriff, can you please light the stove back here?"

"Not necessary," the sheriff answered. "You and your partner can use the blanket I gave you."

Sam yelled back, "It looks like the rats 'been nibblin' on it. It's full of holes."

"Another word outta either of you two, and you'll be locked up for so long you won't remember how old you are when you finally get out," said the sheriff.

Sam began softly whistling "Silent Night." It comforted him a bit, and he figured it soothed Paul, too, because the yelling from both sides ceased.

When Sam finished whistling, Paul whispered, "Sam, it's going to be a long night."

"Looks like we're gonna be locked up through Christmas Eve and 'morn," Sam whispered back. "What a shame. We won't see Marie's Christmas decorations or Richard's play at Italian Hall tomorrow."

"We might be out of jail in the morning."

"Huh?" questioned Sam. "Are ya sure?"

"We'll see Judge O'Brien in a few hours, when the sun rises. Fortunately for us, the judge has sympathy for us strikers," said Paul.

"Is that so?"

"Judge O'Brien grew up in this area. His father died while mining. He seems to understand the strikers."

"I hope yer right. Paul, I'm very sorry."

"About what?" asked Paul.

"I'm sorry about them thugs invandin' yer house, I'm sorry Nancy's in Detroit, I'm sorry yer house is cold and we're survivin' on veggies. None of this woulda happened if I hadn't encouraged ya to strike."

"I don't blame you for anything that's happened." Paul banged the bars again. "Copper Empire was mismanaged. Men were getting hurt. I made the call to strike."

Sam sighed.

Paul let go of the bars. "Do you wish you were back in South Carolina?"

"I miss my kin at times."

Paul shook his head. "Why in heck did you come here in the first place?"

Sam didn't respond. Paul took a careful breath and said, "It's okay if you want to remain private. Sam, you're my friend, and Marie thinks highly of you, too." Paul chuckled.

"Remember the first evening at our boarding home? I thought Marie would have you packing your bag before you even had a chance to spend one night with us."

Sam sat up on the cot and blurted out, "Last spring, I lost a very special lady."

Paul stared at the darkness, listening to Sam.

Sam continued, "Millie, my wife, died after a short sickness."

Paul mumbled, "Well, this night has been full of surprises, hasn't it? You were married?"

"Happily, I might add," Sam beamed. "Met her when I was a young buck. When she died, I thought my life was over, too."

"So, what happened, Sam?"

"I didn't get outta bed fer a month. My kin pulled me outta bed one day and told me Millie wanted me to live. I couldn't stay in my house or Charleston. The trees, flowers, ocean, everything about Charleston made me think of her."

"That's why you came North?"

"Yep," Sam laughed. "And my cousin Clarkston told me of the opportunities up here."

Paul snorted. "Opportunities?"

"Ya know, it worked for awhile. Bein' around ya and Marie and the kids made me think I was part of a family once again."

"You are a part of the family."

"Thank ya kindly, Paul. You and Marie 'been real good to me. And how do I repay yer kindness? We're stuck in jail."

Paul turned around and leaned against the bars again. He lowered his voice. "Sam, we may not win this strike. If we don't, I still hope you stay with us."

"Don't say that, Paul. We've come such a long way."

"Sam, after Christmas, I'm going to hold an emergency meeting for the miners."

"Hope yer not goin' to end the strike," Sam said.

Paul sighed. "I heard that Calumet & Hecla has cash reserves of a million dollars. I bet Copper Empire has a gold mine of reserves to match. We're worth a raise, and we deserve to work in a safe environment. We're on the same side, Sam. But, families are hungry and cold and tired. My home was just invaded. And, I don't want other men to end up in jail. The Citizens Alliance is acting as if they're now the law. It's getting much too risky."

Paul and Sam heard a door, out in the sheriff's area, open and slam shut. The sheriff called out, "Cece, I'm glad you're here. Hope we didn't wake you up."

Cece yelled, "Of course you did."

Sam returned to his whistling of Southern tunes. He heard the sheriff ask Cece to sign papers. The sheriff also added, "Those troublemakers will be talking to the judge soon."

Sam whistled louder to drown out the sheriff's voice. The sounds escaping his lips were a cross between "Old Dan Tucker" and "The Yellow Rose of Texas".

Cece crossed over from the front room and opened the door that contained the jail, letting some light into Paul and Sam's cell. He yelled at Sam, "Quit whistling those infernal Southern songs. You're up North now."

Sam whistled the last note, drumming his fingers on his flat stomach. "I'm in jail now."

Cece looked like a bull about to charge its victim. His nostrils flared like fire brewing inside them. "It's your own fault, you Southern nincompoop." He gripped the bars from the outside, then yelled at Paul, "Your fault, too."

Paul didn't answer Cece's accusations.

Sam got up from the cot and walked over to the steel columns. "Yer a Northern scalawag."

"What?" Cece asked.

Sam's face was stoic. "Ya coulda stuck by us, but ya chose to help the mine owners, instead." His fingers laced tightly around a bar. He looked at Cece closely. "I'll tell ya one thing. Those owners don't care a lick about ya. They never will."

"At least I got a job."

"Correction. You've got a job with no friends and no decent place to live."

Cece threw a punch at Sam, but instead, smashed his fist into iron bars as the Southerner dodged.

The sheriff, from the front room, yelled, "Hey, what do you think you're doing in there?"

Cece and Paul's eyes locked for the longest time. Sam kept his body still. He tried not to blink or swallow. Finally, Cece crumpled the papers in his hands and walked out. "I'm dropping the charges," he yelled at the sheriff, then abruptly fled the building.

Chapter 20

Marie stepped onto the second floor of Italian Hall and into the auditorium. Walking to the center to get a better view of the children's party, she waved away red and green paper decorations that crawled over her face, proud of her efforts and that of the women's auxiliary. She was also grateful that Paul and Sam came home from jail earlier that morning.

People were snaked tightly around a buffet of food. Children and their parents picked up sugar cookies and lemon drops, placing them on their plate that they carried along the table. Some even accepted generous slices of chocolate cake. Their plates were filled, yet they managed to also pick up a cup of punch, and then steady themselves to find a place to sit.

Marie walked to the back and took the stairs to the wooden stage floor. "Ho, ho, ho! Have you been a good boy this year?" Marie turned to the side of the stage where Santa sat in front of the Christmas tree. Santa slapped his thigh and hugged Joey close. Her youngest son sank into Santa's lap, his legs dangling. Marie kicked a few stray balloons away on the stage while getting closer to Joey.

Jeanie cupped a hand over her mouth and yelled an emphatic, "No."

Marie tapped Jeanie on her shoulder and reprimanded her. Jeanie laughed anyway. She enjoyed teasing her brother. Besides, she didn't believe in Santa anymore.

Joey looked deep into Santa's eyes. "I tried to be good, honest."

But Santa only laughed, smoothing his thick, white beard down to its pointed end. "What would you like for Christmas, young man?"

Joey held a finger to his freckled chin and appeared deep in thought. Then, he leaned against Santa's chest and said, "Mister Santa Claus, I want this strike to be over."

"We all do," said a startlingly tall woman who stood next to them. Her round, dark face smiled at the boy.

Marie was glad that Big Annie, the fierce activist for the rights of miners, had asked her to help at the party. Big Annie's hand dug into a burlap sack to pull out a gift for the boy. "There you are," she said, handing the present to him. "Be proud your papa is a miner."

Joey beamed. "Oh, I am." He climbed off Santa's lap and sprinted for his mother. He looked over his shoulder and cried out, "Thanks."

Marie hugged her youngest son. She scanned the auditorium again and decided it was much too crowded and noisy, even for a Christmas party. Youngsters tripped over one another when they moved about the room, but they didn't seem to mind the congestion. Many adults, however, waved wrapping paper about their faces in an attempt to cool themselves.

"Mrs.-a Weyburn, look at-a my gift," cried Roberto. He blew on his shiny, new whistle.

With all the children who had already received their gifts and were using their whistles, Marie thought she would get a headache. "That's nice Roberto, but why don't you wait until you are outside to use it?"

Roberto nodded, but reached out into thin air for his whistle when Richard swiped it from his mouth. "Tat's-a my whistle."

"Really, Richard," Marie said, trying not to smile. "Stealing a whistle from a child."

Richard laughed, returned the whistle, and then squatted to meet the boy's eyes. "I could use your help, Roberto. I'm going to start my play on this very stage," he said, pointing toward the red curtain. "Once that curtain parts, the magic begins."

Roberto's chocolate-stained mouth dropped. "Wow. I've-a never seen-a play."

Drawing out a handkerchief from her apron, Marie reached out, lifted the boy's chin and cleaned the chocolate mess. Richard asked, "How would you like to be in my play?"

"What a wonderful idea," Marie said.

"Really?" Roberto asked. Marie wiped his mouth with the cloth. The boy continued. "Wha- would ha- do?"

"You'll be one of Santa's reindeer, of course."

Roberto's thin red lips parted into a genuine smile. He nudged Jeanie and Joey. "Did you-a hear that? I'm-a going to be in a-play."

"Come with me," Richard said, taking the boy's hand. Jeanie and Joey followed and they disappeared behind the curtain.

Marie walked to the side of the stage and down the stairs. She was glad everyone was having a grand time. However, a major part of her life was missing. In past years, on Christmas Eve, her family would go into the woods and Paul would cut down a pine tree. They would drag it back to the house where Paul and Cece would saw the trunk and fit it into the stand. The children would string popcorn and she and Nancy would make other decorations. Christmas just wasn't the same this year. Paul had been in jail, Cece was gone and over half the boarders had left. Moreover, the holidays wouldn't be complete without Nancy. Marie sighed. Perhaps next year things would be better.

"Merry Christmas, Ma."

Marie's head jerked to the side. Nancy stood at the doorway with a smile.

"Nancy." Marie grabbed her for a lengthy hug. When she finally let go, both mother and daughter laughed and cried at the same time. "What a nice surprise," Marie said. "When did you get here?"

Nancy wiped away a few tears. "I just got off the train a few minutes ago. I got your last letter, Ma. You wrote that the party would be today. I left my luggage at the station and came as fast as I could."

Marie hugged Nancy again. "I'm so happy you did." She released Nancy and stepped back to stare. Nancy wore her hair more loosely in a bun. She wasn't as thin as before. She seemed more filled out and mature. "How ever did you manage the train fare?"

"Mr. Ford gave us bonuses. With extra money, I just knew I had to return to Red Jacket for Christmas."

Marie embraced Nancy once again and leaned into her ear. "Now it really feels like Christmas." She took Nancy's arm. "Come along. Let's find a seat. Richard's performing a play."

"Oh, that's wonderful, Ma. Where's Pa?"

"He's next door, at Vairo's."

Marie and Nancy watched the stage where someone behind the curtain was poking at the fabric. Sam emerged from behind the curtain in a knee-length nightshirt and red-striped sleeping cap. Sam positioned himself toward center stage, holding onto a lighted candelabra. "Evenin' folks."

The crowd milled around the auditorium, but wouldn't stop talking.

Sam cleared his throat and spoke again, louder. "Evenin', folks." The din quieted to a murmur and then to silence. "The play will begin."

The audience clapped. Adults and children who were standing frantically found their seats, and the room quieted down.

Sam said, "This play is a parody of 'Twas the night before Christmas'. Do ya children know what a parody is?"

The children glanced at each other or shrugged their shoulders.

"This play is going to have fun with the story yer papa reads to ya Christmas Eve." Sam cleared his throat and began his coveted role in the play. "'Twas the night before Christmas and all through the house, the creatures were stirrin' includin' the mouse." Sam fidgeted with the curtain for a moment, and then pulled the velvety end across the bar, revealing the Christmas setting. The audience applauded.

Marie let out a hearty chuckle when Richard tripped onto the staged living room. The mouse costume she had made for him was too large, but the huge black circles attached to each ear made her son even more comical. Richard found an orange square that lay on a wooden rocking chair next to the Christmas tree. He grabbed the fictitious cheese, pantomimed a bite, and then scurried back to his imaginary hole.

Jeanie and Joey entered the living room, both carrying their own red stocking. They scrambled over to the fireplace to attach their wool stockings, topped off with a white, cottony stripe. Jeanie swooped down to bite a piece of popcorn from the string on the Christmas tree, which drew laughs from the audience.

Sam stood at the front end of the stage and continued narrating, "The stockin's were hung by the girls and boys, hopin' that Santa would stuff 'em with toys."

A teenage girl, playing the mother, walked into the room wearing a drab, brown dress that clung to her as if to beg for a more vibrant color. Her hands held a broom that she lifted threateningly over her head, chasing the kids to bed.

Sam continued, "The children were whisked by their mama off to bed."

The play mother said, "Now don't you dare leave," she waved a broom, shooing the children into the bedroom with her, "or I'll flatten your head!" The children in the audience laughed when the youngsters rushed into one bed, quickly crawling under the wrinkled covers.

Marie was enjoying her son's play, taking a moment to breathe deeply. Too bad Paul chose a bottle of liquor over watching his son's first attempt with theater. With the strike dragging on and on, she wondered if Paul would ever again be the man she once knew.

Nancy interjected, as if reading her mother's sad thoughts and attempting to dispel them. "Ma, Richard's play is wonderful. I'm so proud of him."

Marie wrapped an arm around her daughter's shoulder and resolved to watch the performance without dwelling on her problems. They even laughed when Roberto and other children galloped on cue, dressed in antler ears.

When the play ended, Nancy whispered to her mother, "I'm going to get something to drink." Marie nodded.

Marie walked to the stairs at the stage. Her intuition lured her into looking at the doors that led to the stairwell. A man stood there, looking out of place. His collar was up to his chin, and his cap was lowered almost to his eyes. Was that a white button on his coat? Non-union people weren't supposed to be at the party, but she recalled seeing at least five people, including Artie, who somehow had gotten past the people who checked for union cards at the stairwell. She didn't want to be pessimistic, but she kept her eyes on the mysterious man.

*   *   *

Nancy filled her glass with punch and took a sip. She leaned against the wall and watched the stage. Richard was leading the audience to sing, "Silent Night." Nancy was too embarrassed to join the audience with her unpracticed soprano, so she merely hummed along. Surprisingly, her brother's melodramatic hand motions on stage helped to create a soothing harmony throughout the auditorium

"Ya must be proud of your brother," said Sam.

Nancy jumped. The red and green link decorations were tickling her back, anyway. Without thinking, she hugged Sam. She accidentally spilled her drink on Sam while she embraced him and pulled away. "I'm sorry, Sam. How clumsy of me."

Sam touched the arm of Nancy's rose-colored, puffed sleeve. "That's all right. I'm delighted ya came back for Christmas."

"It's nice to see you again, Sam." Neither one spoke for a moment. Nancy was shy and found it much easier to write letters to Sam, telling her thoughts and feelings, rather than telling him to his face. "I enjoyed your Christmas narration, Sam. You managed to change out of your nightshirt quickly, didn't you?" The two laughed and watched Richard as he conducted the singing. When his elbow bumped against the Christmas tree, several pieces of tinsel fell from a branch. Undaunted, Richard held up a hand in the air as if telling his audience to wait a moment. He swiped a few popcorn kernels from a string that wrapped around the tree, and then tossed it into his mouth. Nancy and Sam laughed along with the audience.

Nancy gently nudged Sam. "Isn't that Artie over there?" Sam nodded, but even from the side, she recognized Artie's slicked-back hairstyle and perfectly tailored suit as he shook hands with Richard on the stage.

Nancy figured she had done much changing since she left Red Jacket. She proved she could move away, get a job and pay her own expenses without Artie's help. She was a responsible woman now.

Sam explained, "I suppose yer pa asked the union men to let Artie come to the party."

Nancy's eye involuntarily roamed to the edge of the stage. She couldn't help herself. She wanted to speak with Artie again.

Artie looked around the auditorium, looking for familiar eyes. Finally, his eyes locked on hers. Did he know how much she missed him? His face was expressionless. She couldn't tell if he missed her. Was he waiting for her to make the first move?

This is childish, Nancy thought. She broke their stare and her eyes wandered to the back of the stage where Santa Claus ripped off a white beard. Even Santa was tired of playing games.

"I'm goin' back to the stage to help Richard," said Sam. "Let's talk more later, okay?"

Nancy nodded, closed her eyes and inhaled the smell of fresh pine from the tree. It relaxed her. She briefly forgot her concerns. When she opened her eyes, Artie walked down the stage steps, brushed passed her and left the auditorium.

Then, Nancy's eyes locked onto evil eyeballs. She glanced away, and then looked again. It was a man with a dark coat, collar and a cap covering most of his face. He had a curly moustache and something was familiar about him. He had a white button on his coat, and when she looked at his eyes, she thought they were the same evil ones she saw many months ago. Was that Russell? Nancy was terrified at the thought.

"Fire!"

Nancy barely heard the muffled cry, but her breath drew in, anyway. She could have sworn it came from the mysterious man, and that same man ran out of the auditorium.

A woman screamed, "Fire, fire!" She grabbed her two children and began running across the auditorium floor. She brushed Nancy's shoulder as she exited the room and down the stairs.

Nancy looked to her left. Mothers, sons and daughters ran across the room, knocking down the refreshment table. Fruit punch spilled in pockets on the floor and the chocolate cake flew in the air, landing in a wasteful heap. The masses began stampeding past Nancy and through the only known exit door.

Nancy's eyes swept the stage, but her family was nowhere to be seen. Fathers, mothers, sons and daughters leaped from their chairs and ran. Nancy's view was obstructed. Some people jumped over or shoved aside chairs. The frightened crowd created a bottleneck at the door. Nevertheless, people muscled and pushed against Nancy's body to pass the door.

Nancy froze. The seconds passed more like hours. She witnessed nameless faces crying out for their loved ones, while youngsters whimpered for their mothers.

"Nancy, help-a me," she heard a boy cry out and recognized the shrill octave of Roberto's voice. "I can't find mamma." Roberto ducked and squeezed between people, reaching for Nancy's hand. Like planks of wood traveling downstream, they had to follow the crowd to the staircase.

Nancy's heart raced to a gallop. "Where's the fire?"

"I'm-a scared, Nancy."

"Hold tight to my hand, Roberto."

They passed the exit door and inched their way to the stairwell. A garbled cacophony of shrill commands came from every direction. Nancy didn't understand the foreign words and broken English, but she grasped their meaning. Fear. Terror. Death.

Nancy and Roberto's feet landed a few steps below, but then stopped. Nancy tried to escape the hot breath that brushed on her neck. "Move!" the woman behind her cried. However, they could go no further. Every inch of the step in front of her was covered with feet.

"We've got to get out of here!" the woman yelled again, this time digging her nails into Nancy's back.

Nancy screamed. Forcefully, she elbowed the woman behind her. The woman sobbed, but Nancy was too scared to care about anything except survival.

"We're not moving anymore!" a nameless face cried out.

"Don't worry, Roberto," said Nancy, breathlessly. "We'll be out of this building in a minute."

People screamed, "Step back!"

"Turn around!"

"Can't get out that way!"

Nancy yelled at Roberto, "We've got to turn around. We can't move forward because no one is getting out." Nancy turned and tried to shove her way past the woman behind her.

The woman said, "If we go back, we'll be burned alive. Stay put."

"Are we-a gonna die?" Roberto squeezed Nancy's hand.

Nancy squeezed back. "Let's hold on to each other."

The discordant voices of crying, confused people filled the stairwell. The screaming grew louder. Then people from behind shoved and pushed Nancy against the paneling. She groaned, her hip bruised by the impact. Several of her ma's Christmas bows fell down. The people who shoved Nancy rushed forward and filled the empty space she had occupied only a moment ago.

"Oh!" Nancy said with a grimace.

Nancy realized no one was holding her hand. She cried out, "Where are you Roberto?" She couldn't hear the boy's response.

More people pushed and squeezed against Nancy's body. Her ribs rested on the paneling. Nancy tried to scream, but felt the effort was too great. Facing the wall, she jerked her head sideways and saw the shadows of parents clutching their children by the hand, trying to move even an inch. The floorboards groaned under the weight of so many people. Icicles of fear coarsed through her veins. She had to get out of there. Her feet tried to obey her command to escape the building, but there was nowhere to go. Just below, a father took his child and threw the body below.

"Oh my Lord!" Nancy screamed. Other parents followed, throwing their children down the stairs, hoping they would escape. Nancy couldn't see it, but she imagined an ever-growing pile of bodies at the bottom of the stairs.

People yelled, "We can't get out!"

"We're trapped!"

"Go back!"

Another icy chill shuddered through Nancy's body. The crowd attempted to go in opposite directions: one crowd heading down, the others trying to retreat up to the auditorium. Nancy felt the pushes and pulls. Bodies in opposing directions squeezed against her. She felt suffocated and her mind screamed in fear.

Her chest constricted as those above and below pressed tighter against her. Her cheeks were as hot as a hellish, flaming inferno.

Darkness and suffocation overcame Nancy. She cried for air, but only managed a tiny squeak. She was stuck to the wall. Using what minute strength she had left, she pushed herself away from the wall and sucked in as much oxygen as was possible. She exhaled as her body was shoved up against the wall again. Her ribs cracked from the pressure. Deep breaths were no longer possible. Her vision blackened. She opened her mouth to scream, but nothing came out. Her thoughts called out for the God she had grown to praise and worship throughout her years.

Her body shook from chills while feeling hot at the same time, and it stiffened as if it were paralyzed. Suddenly, she felt the sensation of her body floating upward. Had heaven arrived at her door?

The shrill cries of only seconds ago muffled.

"What's going on in there?" called out a male voice.

Nancy thought, *it's Pa. He'll save me.* She opened her mouth, but her throat was constricted. She tried to pucker her lips to scream, "Pa," but still nothing came out. Her lungs heaved as she gasped for air—and received it. She tried moving her left foot, but it was pinned under something. Maybe a body?

Then, the cries diminished. Her father, from outside, demanded someone from the stairs answer him. But she couldn't respond. No one else did, either.

Only her mind was free to roam.

Chapter 21

Was it only his imagination, or did Sam hear a man shout 'fire'?

The doubts he had were gone instantly. He jumped off the stage. When he landed, he stood up and heard Richard yell, "Sam," but it was no use. Sam could not turn around or respond. The crowd pressed and pushed him toward the exit door.

Once he reached the middle of the auditorium, time slowed to a painful standstill, like a caterpillar trying to escape its cocoon. He was stuck in the throng of people. His face flushed scarlet. He lacked fresh air and space. He took baby steps along with the crowd, his shoes squishing jelly beans and other candies that were littered about, and he could only imagine how disarrayed the entire auditorium had become. He neared the stairwell, but couldn't see what was holding up the crowd at the exit doors.

"Move," the people shouted around him, each word pounding into Sam's eardrum like an African tribal dance. "Fire. Fire. Fire!"

Sam felt sweaty hands on his back, urging himself and others to go faster. But he couldn't go far. His nose was a mere inch behind the man in front of him. The dance was out of control. Sweat ran down Sam's face as he listened to the children scream, the women sob and the men bark out orders.

What was holding up everyone? Surely it wouldn't take long for partiers to run down the steps and out the building. When more precious seconds passed, Sam knew he was no closer to the stairwell and realized he would burn to death if he stayed put. Sam was quiet, his eyes darting across the room in search of anyone he knew. All he saw were nameless people forcing themselves through the exit, like a crowd trying to leave Calumet Theatre all at once, just as a play ended.

Millie. His mind raced back in time to Charleston when he had shared his wife's final moments. He had sat on their bed, intermittently caressing her pale cheek or holding her limp hand. Millie resembled a skeleton. She had lost so much weight and her skin was ghastly white.

Sam's eyes had filled with tears. He couldn't let Millie know how sad he was. He shifted his eyes to the table, next to the bed. Earlier that morning, Sam had picked a variety of colorful flowers from Millie's garden and set them in a vase. Sam had thought the flowers looked beautiful, but he still struggled to hold back his tears.

Millie had struggled for breath, laboring for her final words. "I love ya, Sam."

Sam sniffed. "I love ya, too, darlin'."

"Sam," Millie whispered, "promise me, you'll start a new life when I'm gone."

Sam had shook his head and tears rolled down his face. "I'll be joinin' ya soon, my love."

"I'll always be with ya in spirit, Sam, but you must go on without me. . ." Millie's monologue was interrupted with a final gasp of air, then the imperceptible hand of death.

Sam's chest had heaved with sobs that he finally released. He would never see his wife on earth again.

"Sam." His name, cried out, shook him back to reality. Sam clenched his fists. He had lost Millie and missed Nancy while she was in Detroit. He was determined not to lose another woman he cared for. He must find a way out.

"Sam!" he heard again. The brusque tone could only be from Marie. Sam stood on tiptoes until he saw Marie nudge and poke people around her, but no one would let her through. "Sam, I can't reach you."

Sam pushed against the tide of people. "Let me through." Like a madman trying to escape a sanitarium, Sam's arms flailed about to free himself from the crowd.

"Stop hurting me!" shouted the woman next to him. However, Sam had no time to behave like a gentleman. He shoved at no one in particular until he escaped to the other side of the crowd.

Marie grabbed his shoulders. "Sam, I can't find any of the children."

"I was with Richard only seconds ago, on the stage." They faced the stage, but no one was there.

"Sam, my kids are missing," cried Marie.

"I know. I know," said Sam. People were crowded from the exit door to the rear wall. The line was many feet thick. He looked around the auditorium. It was a disaster area. Torn wrapping paper lay on the floor, fruit punch glistened in pools and cookie crumbs littered the buffet and floors, with chairs strewn everywhere. Teenagers tripped over chairs and brushed Sam and Marie off their feet. They hit the ground hard, and Sam's elbow throbbed, but he lifted himself up and helped Marie.

Suddenly, Sam pointed upward. "I never noticed there was a balcony. Marie, can we reach the stage from there?"

"I don't know," cried Marie.

"It's either the balcony, or we have to fight all of those people in front of us. Let's try it."

Marie nodded. Sam walked fast and reached the door to the balcony. He opened it and took the stairs two at a time. When he turned around, Marie lagged far behind.

"Keep going, Sam, I'll catch up."

"No, I'm not leavin' ya." Sam jogged down a few stairs, took Marie's hand and helped her to the landing. Then, Sam and Marie entered the balcony and made their way across the long aisle, Marie huffing and puffing and following Sam as he cleared the way by kicking chairs away from their path.

"Sam."

He turned around. Marie stopped, catching her breath. She pointed down to the stage. "The children aren't there."

"Don't ya worry, Marie, we'll find them."

Marie sighed, took a deep breath, and then sobbed.

Sam put his arm around her. "Marie, I promise ya, we'll find yer children."

With tears still in her eyes, Marie nodded and followed Sam. They finally reached the other end of the balcony and ran down the stairs. Marie jerked Sam to the left. "This way," she cried. They walked along a corridor. Before she entered the women's restroom Marie pointed, "You look in the men's room."

Sam did just that, and before his very eyes, a man took a chair and rammed a window, shattering the glass.

"What are ya doin'?" yelled Sam.

The man grabbed his toddler, heading for the clearance.

"Dear Lord!" shouted Sam. He reached the man and tried to pry the boy out of his hands. "Are ya crazy?"

"Let me alone!" the man yelled, then elbowed Sam in his gut. Sam backed away and groaned.

Sam called out, "Joey, are ya in here?" He looked in all of the stalls, but no one was in the restroom except for the man and his toddler.

The man cried out, "Catch my son!" and dropped him out the window. Then, the man lifted himself to the window and jumped. Sam ran to the window. Red Jacket citizens below screamed and swarmed the area. Sam ran out of the rest area and met up with Marie.

"I didn't find anyone. How about you?"

Marie shook her head.

"The fire escape steps are just outside the window," said Sam. "The fire escape door should be near."

Marie pointed and said, "It's over there."

"Fine. Let's get yer kids and go down the fire escape." Sam pointed past her. "What's in that room?"

"It's the bar room."

"Come on, then." Sam took her hand and they walked to the end of the building.

Marie cried out to some of the miners, "Have any of you seen my children?"

"No, Marie," a miner called out.

She turned to Sam. "What are we to do?"

"Marie, there is no fire, so calm yourself down," the miner said.

"No fire?" Sam and Marie said in unison.

"Do you smell any smoke?"

Marie and Sam looked at one another. "Oh my Lord, why did everyone panic?" she asked.

"Let's get outta here," Sam said, taking Marie's arm. They left the room. He nudged his head. "What's down there?"

"The kitchen is beneath the stage."

"Let's go."

Sam and Marie ran down more steps and entered a dark, low-ceiling room. Tables and chairs were overturned and food and drink were strewn along the floor. Children were leaping onto a table next to the window and jumping out.

"Oh my Lord," cried Marie.

Sam nudged Marie and pointed. "Look."

Richard, Jeanie and Joey were at the far corner of the room.

Marie called out, "Thank God." She stumbled and tripped to reach and embrace all three children at the same moment. Jeanie and Joey cried along with their mother.

Sam touched Richard's arm and whispered, "Where's Nancy?"

"I—" Richard was interrupted by sirens. Everyone in the room was silent. At first the alarms were faint, and then they blared.

"Thank God, we're getting help now," cried Marie. She turned to Richard and shouted, "What about Nancy?"

Richard matched his mother's loud decibel. "I didn't know Nancy was here."

Marie turned pale.

"I've heard there's no fire, Ma, so there's nothing to worry about."

Marie's voice quivered. "I still don't know where your sister is."

"We're takin' no chances," said Sam, looking out a window. Just beneath the window was a shed and a group of men standing near it. "Marie, take the children and go out the window."

"Sam, I can't get out that way. Besides, I'm not leaving without Nancy."

"All right. Joey, you first." Sam lifted Joey, walked to the window and set him down on the ledge. "Now, on the counta three, ya push yerself off and land on the shed. Ya see those nice men below?"

"Yeah?"

"Yer gonna jump off the shed and into their arms. Got it?"

"Yeah, Sam."

"One, two, three, go!" Joey heaved his body down and thudded on the shed. Following Sam's orders, he jumped off the shed and a man caught him.

"Yer next, Jeanie." The girl retraced her brother's footsteps out of the window. Then it was Richard's turn.

"Ma, it'll be alright," Richard said, giving his mother's hand a squeeze. "Nancy may have already gone out the front door."

Marie's eyes teared up once more.

"What's wrong?" asked Richard.

Sam touched Richard's shoulder. He spoke louder, so Richard could hear him over the sirens. "There's a crowd packed on the stairwell. No one's getting out that way."

"Then I'm not leaving either. I'll find Nancy."

"No!" yelled Marie.

"Go on, Richard. Get outta here and go get the firemen," Sam said.

Richard shimmied out of the window, and then leaped from the shed, without help, to the ground.

"Richard," Marie yelled. Her son looked up to the window. "Go find your father. Do it now!"

*   *   *

Paul, stupefied, stood outside the inner Italian Hall door. In front of him was a mass of entangled bodies stuck in the stairwell. The pile of bodies was almost as tall as Paul's height. He grabbed a limp arm, trying to move at least one body, but his efforts were futile. Paul cried out, "If anyone can hear, answer me!" Sirens blared over his pleas, however. He turned around, squeezed between people, left the vestibule and waved at the firemen on the street. Their wagon came to an abrupt stop and the firemen leapt off the horse-drawn vehicle and ran up the steps, surrounded by masses of people who joined them from the streets.

"Where's the fire?" asked one fireman.

"I don't know," yelled Paul. "I haven't even seen smoke."

"I heard there was no fire," said a man on the street.

"There may not be," said Paul. "But there are people trapped in that stairwell." He pointed to the door.

"Why didn't you pull anyone out?" asked another fireman.

Paul yelled, "Because the bodies are stuck! We'll have to rescue people from the top."

The firemen looked at each other. "Let's find another way in."

One man cried out, "There are people jumping out of a window in the back. Go through Vairo's apartment and you'll see it."

"Get a ladder," one fireman called out, "We'll go to the back."

"I'll go with you," said Paul.

"We don't need anyone's help," said the fireman. Several deputized citizens stood at the front door.

One deputy said to Paul, "You aren't going with them. Let 'em do their job."

"Paul's going with the firemen and that's a fact," said a gruff voice.

Paul turned. It was Cece.

"Everyone, go back to the street," a deputy demanded, but was met with only cries from the people. Paul wouldn't move. The deputy looked right at him. "If you don't get away from this building, I won't hesitate to use my pistol." The deputy reached into his pocket, but before he could draw, Cece punched him. The deputy hit the wall and the crowd screamed.

Paul escaped with Cece following. He ran through Vairo's, then through the back apartment, knocking aside any person who got in his way. He shoved citizens away that were gawking at people jumping out of the back window.

"Pa!" Richard, Jeanie and Joey yelled out.

"Kids, I thought I lost all of you," Paul cried, hugging all of them. "Where's your Ma?"

Jeanie pointed up. "In the kitchen."

Joey said, "With Sam."

Richard added, "Pa, they can't find Nancy. Ma thinks she's at the stairwell."

"In the stairwell? Nancy? She's in Detroit, isn't she?"

Richard's tears ran freely and he shook his head. "I suppose she came back as a surprise, for Christmas."

"Oh, Lord," said Cece.

"Paul," Marie cried out from above. "Come quick."

Paul put his hands on the shed and pulled his body on top. "Marie, get some help. Is Sam there?"

Sam came to the window. "I'm right here." Paul jumped and grabbed Sam's hand. Marie helped Sam pull Paul through the window and into the kitchen.

Cece was already on top of the shed. "Sam. Help me up, too."

"You're the enemy." Paul put his hands on the window and slammed it shut.

Marie yelled, "Paul, no!"

Although Cece's voice was somewhat muffled, they still heard him shout, "Paul. Help me up!"

Sam put a hand on Paul's shoulder. "We have no time ta waste. We're gonna need Cece's help."

Marie pulled the window up, then turned to Paul. "Pull Cece in."

Paul nudged Sam, "Let's go to the stairwell."

Marie grabbed Paul's shirt. "Listen to me, Paul Flint Weyburn. I don't care that you hate each other. But my daughter may be dying in the stairwell," she wailed. "I want Nancy returned to me alive, this instant."

Cece shouted, "I'm going to help you. By God, I'll get Nancy out."

Marie shouted, "Oh, he'll darn well help you up, Cece." She pushed Paul to the window.

Cece jumped and Paul and Sam pulled him inside.

Paul said, "Marie, stay here. We won't be long."

Paul, Cece and Sam ran out of the kitchen, up the stairs and into the auditorium. "The crowd's gone," Sam said. "They were packed wall to wall just a few minutes ago." The three men ran, shoving chairs away and tripping over things that had fallen to the floor. They dashed past the main doors and down the stairwell. Paul choked on his own breath. He looked at a mass of tangled bodies. Other men were there, and they pried a little girl loose from the entanglement. She was in her best party frock. Her ribs looked sunken and her eyes were closed. Two men carried her away, crying.

"Look," Cece cried out, "there's Nancy." Nancy was on top of a four-foot high pile of corpses.

Sam, Paul and Cece ran up to the bodies. For the next hour, the men worked at detangling limbs that were intertwined with other bodies.

The crowd from below, outside, pointed and stared and screamed at the sight. Finally, the trio reached Nancy. Paul wrapped his arms around Nancy's upper torso, while Cece and

Sam gently pulled away other body parts that obstructed her release. Finally, Sam was able to free her caged limbs. Cece grabbed her lower torso, and he and Paul carried her away from the tangled nightmare, then back up the stairs and into the auditorium. They put her body down on a chair. Paul patted her cheeks, and then put his face next to hers. She was breathing, just barely.

The men who had taken the dead little girl away had returned. This time, they had just freed a little boy from the tangled mess and placed his body next to Nancy's.

Paul looked at the lad. The boy's mouth was faintly outlined with chocolate. His lips were blue and his face a ghastly white. Paul's breath caught in his throat.

Paul asked, "Is he dead?"

The men nodded.

"Oh, Lord," Paul cried out.

Sam called out, "What is it? Nancy?"

"It's Roberto. He's dead."

Chapter 22

Paul was slumped on a bench. He had briefly dozed off when a stretcher rushed past him. His eyes snapped open. The attendant shouted, "Coming through!" and wheeled away a motionless child. Another victim of Italian Hall. Marie had apparently napped, too. She lifted her head from Paul's shoulder.

Marie nudged him. "What's happening to Nancy?"

Paul squeezed his wife's shoulders. "She's in good hands, Marie." He heard a rigid clop-clop on the hospital's sanitized floors until Artie came into view.

"How is Nancy's health?"

Paul shook his head. "We've heard nothing."

Artie sat on the other side of Paul. "I have questioned numerous people about the Italian Hall incident. It appears many participants believe a Citizens Alliance member shouted fire deliberately to facilitate this tragedy."

Marie sat up. "Is that a fact?"

"I do not know of the Alliance's true involvement of this tragedy, if they were involved at all."

Marie looked at Paul. "What do you make of that?"

Paul sighed. "That possibility crossed my mind."

Marie's cry echoed in the hallway. "But why would anyone do such a horrible thing?"

"To put an end to the strike, once and for all," Paul said.

"I fear that may be true, Marie," Artie agreed. "I attempted to interview Alliance members, but thus far no one from that group will consent to an interview."

"Maybe they won't speak because they know who you live with?" asked Paul.

"Perhaps. Hopefully, when the latest edition of the Gazette is released today, we shall have more information."

Paul was about to offer comforting words to his wife when he heard a heavy pair of boots thudding across the hallway. It could only be from Cece. He stood in front of Paul. The man needed a bath and a shave.

"How is she?" Cece asked, crossing his arms to his chest.

"We don't know yet," said Paul.

The foursome became silent and the hallway was so quiet that one could hear a feather fall to the scrubbed floor. This never seemed to bother Cece, though. His gray eyes bore through Paul's.

Paul sat up straight on the hard bench. He wasn't sure if he wanted to save the friendship. Even if Cece did help save Nancy from a sure death in the stairwell, he had also helped mine owners who may have caused the Italian Hall tragedy. "What do you know about the Citizens Alliance involvement?"

"What?" Cece asked.

"The Citizens Alliance," Paul repeated, emphasizing each syllable as if talking to a three-year-old. "Artie tells me I'm not the only one who believes one of their thugs yelled 'fire' at the party."

Cece frowned, and his scraggily beard dipped lower than usual. "Don't know much about the Alliance."

Paul leaned forward and deepened his voice. "I'm sure you have underground information. You must have known the Citizens Alliance invaded my home last night."

"Of course, I knew they arrested you and Sam for the fight we had at the mine. Peterman and Russell wanted me to tell the judge you started the fight and that you're dangerous to the community, in order to put you in jail for awhile. I couldn't do it, so I dropped the charges. But, I don't know much more about that group. I swear, Paul. I'm not part of the Alliance, they wouldn't have me."

"Peterman must have said something to you."

"Never. He just gave me the billy club everyday and told me to protect the mine."

Marie rose from the bench. "Paul, I believe him. Cece didn't have anything to do with this."

"Saw Peterman a few minutes ago and gave him what-for. Never should have switched sides. Never should have guarded Copper Empire. Sorry about that. On your side now."

"What made you change your mind?"

"I hated guarding the mine. Knew it was wrong, too."

"Then why did you do it?" asked Marie.

"Scared, I s'pose. No money, no food, no one to take care of me in my old age."

"You were a part of our family. We would have taken care of you," said Marie.

Cece's lips quivered. "Miners are like my brothers and your family is my family." He looked down on the floor and was silent for a minute. Finally, he added, "Don't think that tragedy was an accident."

"Neither do I, Cece."

Artie read through his notes and said, "According to the sources I spoke with, they confirmed that someone – or a group of people – held the front door of Italian Hall closed to prevent anyone leaving."

"Trapping people in the stairwell," mumbled Cece.

Marie said, "All those children – "

Paul shook his head. "I was at the front door within seconds of the first cry of fire. No one held the door closed."

"Is that a fact? May I quote you?" asked Artie.

Paul nodded.

Cece's hands formed into fists, and he dramatically stated, "I swear, when I find out the scum who cried fire and murdered those children, I'll kill the person myself."

"If I can interrupt Douglas Fairbanks for a moment," said a sarcastic voice that was even more brusque than Marie's, "Nancy has two broken ribs and multiple bruises, but with some rest, she'll be fine." It was Annabelle, the nurse, announcing Nancy's prognosis.

Artie said, "This news is a tremendous relief."

"Thank you, Annabelle," said Marie.

The stout nurse's pudgy fingers wrote on some paper. Annabelle was silent, intent on filling out the hospital form to precision. She pounded the paper with her pencil to signify completion with her record-keeping, and then looked up to Marie. "You're welcome. Make sure you take Nancy straight home for rest."

Paul said, "Thank you, Annabelle." With that, she stomped away.

"Shall I remain with you and Marie?" asked Artie.

Paul shook his head. "No. You go on home, Artie. Sam is already there, watching the children. You have at least three more hours to catch some sleep." Paul turned to Cece and grinned, "Are you sure Annabelle isn't your long-lost cousin?"

"She ain't no cousin of mine," said Cece. He shuffled his feet, as if having trouble with his next words. "If it's alright with you, I aim to get my room back at your house." He awkwardly offered his hand to Paul. They shook hands.

Cece looked at Artie. "I'll walk home with you."

"That will be fine, Cece, but once we reach home, I insist you take a bath."

Paul and Marie chuckled as Cece and Artie walked away. Then, Paul commented, "It'll take me a long time before I'll trust Cece again."

Marie covered Paul's hand with hers. "I know."

*   *   *

Nancy's limp, battered frame shivered, so she leaned against her pa during the stroll from the street car to the Weyburn boarding home.   When they were close to the dwelling, her pale face lifted to see the home she was born and raised in. After three months of living so far away from home, a twinge of excitement ran through her when she saw the white columns and the miner's ax that adorned the turret.

The chilled morning air seeped to her skin and a medley of snowflakes flew by her face, some resting on her gaunt cheeks. Paul's firm hand guided her as Marie rushed ahead to the steps, her skirt swishing, opening the door to a panting dog. Nancy watched her mother raise her hand to tame T-bone in anticipation of the enthusiastic reception the overzealous pup would provide.

"Down T-bone," Marie sternly said. She stooped to pet the animal behind his ears so he would calm down. Sure enough, T-bone forgot about jumping and remained planted on the marble floor, his tail wagging happily between his hind legs. Satisfied that the dog was under control, she lifted her head to yell, "Merry Christmas kids. Your sister's home." Seconds later, pairs of feet ran along the marble stairway to reach the foyer.

It was Christmas. Nancy had clean forgotten. A wreath that hung on the door should have clued her in, but after her near-fatal experience at Italian Hall, she had forgotten her favorite holiday.

She found that even the few paces up the porch steps had left her feeling weak.   The loss of energy showed on her glistened cheeks and stray, ratty hairs acted as an adhesive against her perspiring face.

Marie's arm held the door open, allowing her and Paul to enter the home. As the door shut behind her, Nancy found herself the center of attention. She felt Richard, Jeanie and Joey wrap their arms around her slender frame. A painful groan escaped Nancy's lips from the intense hugs, but she didn't care.

Marie said, "Easy now," her eyebrow slanting in stern fashion. "She's been through a lot and needs her rest."

Nancy felt the arms of her brothers and sister squeeze even more tightly around shreds of her rose-colored dress. The pressure caused her to grimace again in pain.

"Never mind, Ma. I'm just thankful to be alive."

Joey struggled to catch his breath after his sudden crying spell. "Nancy, you're the best sister around."

Her blue eyes shimmering in tears, Nancy laughed and cupped the boy's face in her hands. "Thanks, Joey. But I would watch what you say around Jeanie."

Jeanie leaned against the bosom of her older sister. "Joey's right for once."

Richard grabbed a blanket that rested nearby and wrapped his older sister in the warm, brown cover-up. "You look cold, Nancy."

She drew the blanket close to her and shivered again. "I am."

Richard put an arm around his sister. "We couldn't do without you."

"Keep that blanket around you," said Paul. "We've hit some hard times around here."

Nancy nodded, her teeth chattering. "I know." She breathed deeply, turning around to fully take in the state of disrepair of the boarding home. The first thing she noticed was that she simply couldn't warm herself. In fact, it seemed just as cold inside as it was outdoors. Overhead, she saw the cracks in the ceiling and knew they were in part to blame. At her feet were scratches in the prized marble floor. If only Great-grandfather Flint could see the mansion he had built, he might do a flip-flop in his grave.

Even the scant Christmas decoration placed in the foyer couldn't bring the mansion to life again. Swirled around the stairway were red and green paper links that wrapped itself only half way up the railing. It hadn't occurred to her until that moment how fortunate she was to have a secure job waiting for her back in Highland Park.

Nancy knew she must look a sight. Black and blue bruises marked her face, a visible sign of the terrible ordeal she had survived.

Jeanie wiped away tears from her own eyes. "I was so worried about you, Nancy."

Joey's red cheeks quivered. "Yeah, some of our friends died in the stairwell."

"Roberto was one of them," Jeanie said quietly.

"I know," said Nancy, her eyes filling with tears.

Paul draped a strong arm around his daughter. "He's in heaven now," she said.

"A senseless accident," her father said, practically whispering. "There never was any fire in that building."

Nancy's eyes darkened. "I should go to Roberto's family."

Paul and Marie held onto their daughter. "Absolutely not, young lady," Marie said. "You need your rest."

"Ma, can we open our gifts now?" asked Joey, who pulled on his mother's skirt.

Marie lowered herself to kiss his forehead. "In awhile. I'm going to help your sister draw a bath."

"Good idea," Paul said. "Let's say we meet in the parlor in an hour."

"Hooray!" Jeanie said. She reached down to give T-bone a rub on his belly. "Now our family can be happy again, if only for today."

Nancy leaned against the railing, wiping her eyes. She turned to her mother. "Ma, I truly am a mess."

Marie snatched up the sides of her skirt to easily ascend the steps, placing an arm around her daughter's shoulder to assist her up the staircase.

"What you need is a nice, hot bath."

*   *   *

Clenching their older sister's hand, Jeanie and Joey gently pulled Nancy into the parlor, directing her to a rocking chair draped with a thick, wool Mackinaw blanket. Nancy eased herself into the comfortable rocker while her sister graciously draped the woolen material across her body.

"Thanks, Jeanie," said Nancy.

T-bone, of course, wanted some affection, but somehow sensed Nancy wasn't up to it. Nancy was surprised that the friendly Labrador chose to happily curl up next to her feet. The dog was satisfied just to be near her.

She closed her eyes for just a bit, realizing that her ma was right. A soapy, soothing bath had left her feeling safe, clean and sleepy. She heaved a huge sigh and lay against the chair's wooden backing, rocking away. The scent of sugar cookies pleased her olfactory sense, and she hoped her ma would bring a plate of freshly baked ones soon. As Nancy listened to the soft crackle of the fire, she dozed off.

When she opened her eyes, she found her entire family; Cece, Sam and several boarders had gathered around, facing the dour, four-foot Christmas tree. Strings of popcorn were laced around the pale branches of the tree, but she noticed that the pricey ornaments handed down from her Great-Grandfather Flint were absent this year. She thought that this was perhaps done deliberately, to remind her and the other family members that they were to do without until the strike was over. She remembered from Sam's letters that ten of the boarders had moved out because of the strike, and her heart twinged with sadness that the boarding home seemed almost empty, although eight other men still remained.

"What an amazing couple of days," she said in a low voice to herself. But her mother, pouring a cup of tea, heard her daughter's comment.

"Yes it has been," Marie said. Her mother was the first to notice that she had awakened. She leaned over and handed the hot drink to her daughter. While Nancy drank the steamy tea, her mother softly stroked her wavy blonde locks away from her face. "You were spared for a reason."

Nancy thought deeply, her mouth turned upward in doubt. "I wonder what God's plans are for me?"

Marie smiled, touching Nancy's golden hair. "Never you mind. It'll all be revealed in due time."

"Good morning, Nancy," said a familiar voice.

She blinked several times to make sure the person standing before her was real. It was Artie. He gave her a quick kiss on the cheek.

"Hi," Nancy said in return. Her heart pounded for a few moments. While living in Detroit, she had imagined that he would take her in his arms and apologize for his demeaning words that he had spoken many months ago. She felt let down.

Artie's lips parted to say something, but her father interrupted with a speech of his own.

"Attention, everyone," said Paul. He lifted his cup of coffee in the air, as if proposing a toast. His blue eyes sparkled. "As you can see, Nancy is here, awake and recovering." His comment drew laughs from the family and precious few boarders sharing his grateful moment.

The boarders called out a friendly, "Welcome back, Nancy."

Paul took a step back, causing his white shirt to brush the scrawny Christmas tree. "I just want to say that each one of you are important to Marie and I — you're all family."

A few of the boarders blinked away tears.

"We've been through a lot, but we made it this far," Paul said. "And we'll get through this strike together." He withdrew a handkerchief to wipe his eyes. "Most of all, I thank God for sparing my daughter yesterday."

Everyone held up their cups and said, "Amen."

Artie deliberately tipped his cup toward Nancy, as if saluting her.

Nancy grinned. Artie looked handsome. His moustache was neatly trimmed and matched in color to the short, blonde hair on his head. Pants firmly pressed, Artie appeared as smart as ever. But something bothered her. It was something that happened yesterday. Nancy wondered about it, and then remembered. Artie had been at the Christmas party yesterday. He had looked straight at her, but instead of welcoming her, he walked past her and left the party.

"Pardon me, everyone," Artie said, clearing his throat. "I would like to say something."

"Another toast?" grumbled Cece. "One was enough." The twinkle in Cece's eye gave away the fact that he was only joking. He lifted a mug to his wide mouth and downed the last of his coffee.

Nancy drew in her breath. What could Artie possibly want to announce to her family and boarders? She heard the crinkle of Joey unwrapping his gift, but Marie touched his arm softly and shook her head no. Her younger brother would have to wait a minute or two before opening his present.

"I must admit that I am not prepared for this moment," Artie said. He bent down on one knee and lifted Nancy's limp hand. "But this moment is long overdue. Would you do me the honor of becoming my wife?"

286

Startled, Nancy looked at Artie, then Sam. Her mouth hung open for a moment. It was the words she wanted to hear for so long. However, instead of her heart doing flip-flops with joy, she felt her blood rush in dread. She didn't understand why, but she couldn't accept his proposal. Not right now, anyway. She tried to force a smile, but locked eyes with her mother instead. Marie's thick eyebrows were knitted together and she looked pained, as if someone had just told her bad news.

"I'm speechless," Nancy said softly. Her family and boarders chuckled together, relieving some of the tension in the room. Sam wasn't laughing, though. He held onto his cup and saucer, waiting for her to answer.

Artie's hand shook and Nancy couldn't tell if it was out of anger or disappointment. "Would you be my wife, Nancy?" he asked again, this time his tone more firm.

Marie set her cup on the accompanying saucer and then rescued her daughter from answering. She wrapped her arms around Nancy's petite shoulders. "Artie, please give her some time. She's been through so much."

Nancy shut her eyes, grateful that her mother eased the situation a bit. When she opened them again, she looked into Artie's face, pained to see his cheeks color from embarrassment.

"Pardon me." He finally let go of her hand and left the parlor, his leather shoes striking the floor.

Nancy's eyes filled with tears, but she glanced at her father who nodded his head. She knew she had done the right thing.

Marie cleared her throat to change the subject and nudged her youngest child.

"Joey, now would be a great time to open your gift."

"Yes, Ma."

Chapter 23

The haunting toll of the church bell vibrated in Paul's ears as he labored down the Finnish church steps. His descent was slow and sure, careful not to step on an icy patch. It was his fourth church he attended in one morning, each hosting multiple funerals. There had been so many deaths just days ago, so many children who would never grow to adulthood.

Dark, puffy clouds clung to the early afternoon sky, as if they would forever resist the sun. More snowflakes fell. Red Jacket welcomed a few inches of the white matter, with snow covering the green and brown landscape. Paul pulled his coat collar close to shield the cold air.

The funerals filled him with much angst and sorrow. He couldn't forget the first one that morning. It had taken place at one of the Catholic churches. Poor little Roberto had lay still in his coffin, eyelids shut, arms crossed over his chest and his spectacles resting on his stomach. Roberto's mother and siblings had sat in the front row and wailed throughout the service. Roberto's father sat stoic and uttered not one word.

Paul's own children grieved. He had put his arm around Joey for the entire service. Richard, Sam, and Cece had sat together, eyes pinned on the coffin, but not reacting. Nancy sat next to Joey. Paul had told her not to attend, but despite her pain and soreness, she forced herself to the funeral. Marie and Jeanie had cried during the priest's gentle ramblings from the Bible. Nancy's lips quivered and tears loosened soon enough from her eyes, but she was controlled. Paul had figured her ribs would hurt too much if she sobbed.

Paul was supposed to attend other funerals with his family that morning, but he had told Marie, after Roberto's funeral, to take the children home and rest. Marie wouldn't hear of it. Instead, she and the children would join the spectators that lined Pine Street. Marie had explained that the only way she could pay her respects to the dead was to witness the two-mile funeral procession.

And so Paul shivered beneath his coat and slid here and there on the sidewalk to return to the Catholic church. There were several horse-drawn hearses parked near the church entrance. Sam and Cece, returning from other funerals, walked past the hearses and joined Paul.

Sam put his hand on Paul's shoulder. "How are ya holdin' up, friend?"

Paul tried to at least grin, but he couldn't even manage that. "I'm surviving. Cece, how about you?" Cece looked down and nodded. Roberto's father walked outside the church, carrying the boy's white coffin on his shoulder. Paul nudged Cece and Sam to join him.

"If you'll permit us," Paul said to Roberto's father, "we'll carry the casket with you in the procession."

Roberto's father nodded. Paul, Cece and Sam each grabbed an end and helped lower the casket to waist-level. They walked in front of the hearses, just behind the priest.

"Follow me," the priest said.

Paul held a tight grip on the casket handle in front, with Roberto's father on the other side. Cece and Sam handled the back of the casket. They followed the priest and other mourners on the street.

They stopped at the corner and waited for other hearses and caskets to pass by. Finally, there was a space available. The next procession participants were about twenty feet behind. The priest waved his arm, a signal for Paul and the rest to join the procession on Pine Street.

Paul was at the front, just behind the priest. Four hearses were a part of his group, and they were moving next to him. These special carriages were pulled by horses and controlled by a driver with a whip in hand and his bottom torso covered by a thick blanket, sitting on top of the carriage.

The men walked and carried in silence. Ahead of them, thousands of Red Jacket citizens, and perhaps those from other parts of the Keweenaw, had made their way to the city and lined themselves along either side of the street. They stared at Paul and the mass funeral that was unfolding.

Paul's steps kept in sync with the hearse in front of him. The glass carriage was ornate. Painted white, the top of the carriage had various ornaments and a cross in the center. Below, open curtains adorned the windows and behind that was a casket. Paul had thought, for just a moment, that the scene could have come from one of Grimm's fairy tales, perhaps Cinderella. Except, in a fairy tale, the carriages would drive lucky couples to a far away castle to attend a ball, while envious, impoverished citizens stood and stared as the carriages rode by them. But this was no fairy tale. The only occupants of these carriages were dead people, mourned by grieving citizens.

Paul jerked his head for a moment, looking behind him. A multitude of hearses and caskets had joined the procession. He looked ahead again. Paul could only guess his group was closer to the front than the back of the procession. "So many people," Paul whispered. He realized he was the first in his group to utter any words and he figured those might be the only words vocalized until they reached the cemetery. Paul heard sobs from the street spectators, the squeaking casket handle he held onto, and the horses' hoofs crunching the snow beneath.

Paul looked at one side of the street. Photographers were scattered throughout, setting up their tripods and mounting their cameras in order to capture the emotional scene before them. Artie had informed Paul earlier that day that the Italian Hall tragedy was the news of every major city in the country.

When Paul passed by a man who rotated a lever on a different type of camera, he wondered if it was to create a moving picture that would be displayed in a nickelodeon. Paul shuddered.

Cece panted, his cold vapors trailing up to Paul. Besides a few sneezes, Sam's presence next to Cece was hardly noticeable. Paul's sorrow and grief were too much to bear. He tried to find some solace in the gentle, lazy way that the snowflakes landed on his face. He swallowed the lump in his throat. He hadn't noticed it before, but Paul finally realized that iron miners from distant Negaunee and Ishpeming were marching alongside the caskets. The picket signs announced their unison with the copper strikers.

Despite throngs of people crowding both sides of the street, adults and children alike maintained a respectful air, keeping their voices soft and low. The group ahead began to hum, and then sing, "Rock of Ages". The street spectators and Paul's group joined in comforting unison.

A minister that Paul recognized from the Finnish church had stopped walking and waited for the priest in front of Paul to catch up to him. Then, they walked together. Paul overheard their conversation. The priest said quietly, almost in a whisper to the minister, "It was a terrible, terrible tragedy that struck our beautiful copper country — one that will long be remembered."

The minister replied in similar, soothing tones. "Eighty people lost. It's just unbelievable. Why, I believe a hundred years from now folks will still be talking about what happened here."

"I agree," said the priest. "But we'll get by." He gazed at the gloomy sky. "We're a tough breed of people, but we'll never forget what happened here."

Paul wasn't as confident that Red Jacket would recover. They passed another block where a newsboy held up the morning paper. A chill went through him when he read the headlines: "80 Perish in Christmas Eve Tragedy at Red Jacket; False Cry of 'Fire' the Cause." Paul sighed. Marie, Sam, as well as himself were all expected to testify tomorrow at the Italian Hall inquest. He could only hope that the miners' luck would turn around soon and that the coroner's inquest would implicate the guilty party and help end the labor strike for good.

Sam sneezed again, Cece was either still out of breath or stifling a cry and Paul didn't see the cemetery anywhere in sight. The funeral procession seemed endless. . . like trying to walk to the sun's horizon and never quite getting there.

*   *   *

Marie stood beneath the arched entrance of Italian Hall. Paul and Cece followed too close behind and bumped into her. She looked up at the gray, moody sky and muttered, "Lord, we could use your presence here today."

"Amen to that," muttered Cece.

Marie walked to the stairwell as she would a church sanctuary: quiet and respectful. It was cold and dark, just as it had been left on Christmas Eve. This time, however, she smelled fear and death.

The last time Marie was here, she had been straightening and primping the Christmas bows. She had worked so hard on the party decorations to bring joy to the strikers' families. Now the decorations were shredded and strewn along the steps. She bent down and retrieved the only bow to remain intact. A deep sigh escaped her lips.

Paul put his hand on her shoulder. "Easy, Marie."

Marie nodded. "I know, Paul. We must get through this inquest."

"We better get moving," said Cece who linked his arm into hers. "Inquest started by now."

Paul took Marie's other arm and they ascended the stairs. With each step, Marie said a silent prayer for all the children, men and women who lost their lives in that very stairwell. She also prayed that the inquest would shed light on the tragedy.

When Marie walked into the auditorium, she was surprised. It looked just as it did when she and Sam escaped it Christmas Eve. Chairs were kicked over and drinks and foodstuff left on the floor. Marie lifted herself up on her toes and whispered into Paul's ear. "You'd think they could clean this place up."

Paul whispered back, "Maybe they're trying to preserve it until everyone has testified." He lifted a chair from the floor and planted the legs on the ground, then motioned for Marie to sit.

She took her place and examined the area. Not many people were present, but the inquest wasn't open to the public, either. A dozen or so people sat in front of Marie, facing the stage. Presumably, everyone on the main floor was there because they were asked to testify. On the stage, it appeared like a formal court hearing with a panel of men seated on one side, behind a long table, and a lone chair on the other side of the stage facing them. It was rumored in newspapers that the chair would hold over 70 witnesses to the Italian Hall calamity.

A woman entered the stage and sat in the chair. Marie recognized the woman as Annie Clemenc. She remembered the last time she had seen Mrs. Clemenc – better known as "Big Annie". It was at the Christmas party, on that very stage. Joey had been sitting on Santa's lap while Big Annie assisted Santa handing out presents. Annie was known throughout Red Jacket to be aggressive and fearless during the strike, routinely confronting angry citizens, particularly men. This day, however, Marie sensed Big Annie's bravado was gone. In her Croatian accent, Big Annie proceeded to give details about where she was and who was around her at the time 'fire' was called out. Big Annie sounded forthright and her testimony honest.

Each panel member quizzed Big Annie mercilessly about the man who cried 'fire'. Big Annie testified she saw him, but could not recognize him. Marie knew, from the content and speed of their rapid-fire questions, that they did not believe Big Annie.

After a few minutes, they had finished with Big Annie. Cece took the chair next, although he couldn't testify to much of anything since most of the time he was in Vairo's bar.

Paul followed Cece, explaining that he, like Cece, had been at the bar at the time of the tragedy. Marie noticed the panel members bent forward, eyes squinting, hanging onto Paul's every word as he testified.

Chilling rumors of Citizen Alliance members deliberately holding the front Italian Hall doors shut during the tragedy had spread through newspapers and the town since the horrible event. Therefore, Marie knew Paul's testimony would be important. Paul informed the panel that when he left Vairo's bar and went to the Italian Hall doors to help rescue people, he did not see any Citizens Alliance members, or anyone else, holding the doors shut. In fact, Paul told the panel that he had easy access up until he entered the vestibule and stood outside the interior doors. After that, the panel had enough information and excused Paul from the chair.

Next, they called Marie.

After she sat down on a chair at the stage, a man from the panel asked, "Were you in Italian Hall on December 24th?"

"Yes, sir."

"Just tell us what you know about the trouble," the man said, his statement sounding as if he were the schoolmaster and Marie, the child in trouble. Marie sat erect in the chair, crossed her ankles and leaned forward. She wasn't going to let these men intimidate her. She plainly stated the facts.

"Where was that man?" sneered a juror.

"Which man?"

"The one you claimed cried 'fire'?"

"I'm not even sure if it was a man who cried 'fire'. I heard it, but I didn't see the person. My daughter, though, saw the man. His collar and cap were covering his face —"

A juror cried out, "You are out of order, Mrs. Weyburn. Do not tell us what your daughter saw."

"But she's not well enough to testify, sir. She almost died in the stairwell."

"We only want you to testify what you heard and saw, not your daughter."

The jury looked at each other. One lit his pipe, one looked at the ceiling, while others shrugged their shoulders. Finally, one member spoke. "Mrs. Weyburn, how many people attended the party?"

Marie's eyebrows slanted. "How should I know? I wasn't counting."

The man sighed. "Your best guess will do."

"The hall was full."

"But how many?"

"What difference does that make?" asked Marie.

"Mrs. Weyburn, we ask the questions and you are to answer. Did you see any man with a Citizens Alliance button on?"

"No, sir, but my daughter did. I thought I did, but he was too far away for me to see clearly."

The man scolded Marie, as if she were a child. "I am not going to remind you again, Mrs. Weyburn. Testify only to what you saw that day."

Marie blurted out, "After my son's play ended, I saw a suspicious looking man near the stage, so I watched him, but I couldn't find him when I looked away for a moment. So, I went to the bar room to find a union man to look after that check-in table, because I knew that strange man shouldn't have been there. I also saw several other non-union people. I know for a fact that people who shouldn't have been able to attend the party did so anyway."

A juror with a pipe drew in, blew out smoke, and then set his pipe down. "Just what are you suggesting?"

"There were union members assigned to check everyone's union cards at the check-in table. But since I saw non-union people, it's possible that any Citizens Alliance member could have gotten past the check-in and attended the party."

"Mrs. Weyburn, you are the only person, thus far, who has testified about that."

"I tell you, it's true," Marie cried out.

Another man, sitting next to the pipe puffer, waved the smoke away from his face. "Did you see any smoke or fire?"

"No, I didn't. When I heard the cry, I left the bar room to look for my children."

"Where did you find them?"

"Three of my children were in the kitchen."

"Various people who were in the kitchen have already testified they knew there wasn't any fire in the building. Didn't anyone in the kitchen tell you so?"

"Yes, there were rumors."

"Did you continue to panic?"

"Of course. You would, too, if you were stuck in a building full of screaming people who couldn't get out."

The men continued their inquiry. Each juror went out of his way to have a turn with her. When Marie finished answering a question, another juror would lob another question. Finally, the interrogation ended.

"That will be all, Mrs. Weyburn."

"Just one moment, sir. Have you questioned any Citizens Alliance member?"

The panel was incensed. The men either shuffled papers or yelled at Marie. "We ask the questions!" several jurors shouted.

"Well now I'm asking you a question," shouted Marie. "Am I to assume no Alliance members have testified?"

The panel was silent and stayed so for an uncomfortable moment. Marie continued. "For over a month, up until Christmas Eve, many people in this town displayed their Alliance buttons and shouted their objections to strikers that dared to picket or walk into town." Marie continued, lowering her voice into a terse grind. "Where are those people now?"

"You are dismissed, Mrs. Weyburn. I suggest you leave, before we contact the sheriff."

Paul ran up the stage stairs and grabbed her arm. "Come on Marie." He gently pulled her away, but Marie kept shouting. "Over fifty children died in that stairwell!" Paul and Marie walked down the stage steps, and then faced the stage. "Yesterday, we buried those children!"

A juryman ejected his pipe from his mouth. "I'll get the sheriff."

"Don't bother. We're leaving," said Paul.

Cece patted Marie's shoulder. "Atta girl, Marie."

Marie managed one more word before she left. Hand on hip, she faced the stage and screamed, "Cowards!"

Chapter 24

T-bone greeted Sam when he opened the boarding house door, but he didn't feel like petting the dog. Instead, he threw his coat on a hook, shook the snow from his head and entered the parlor with T-bone still nipping at his heels.

A stroll into town left him pondering about the events that bothered him most: the strike, the mass funeral, and Artie's proposal to Nancy. Sam couldn't do anything about the strike or funeral, and he wondered how much time he had before Nancy would finally accept Artie's proposal of marriage.

Everyone was seated around the fireplace—the remaining boarders, including Cece and Artie, and the entire Weyburn clan. Tall flames from the burning wood in the fireplace danced around and generated some needed heat in the room while adults held saucers and cups in their hands, staring at the fire.

Nancy and Marie were busy with needle and thread, patching overalls and shirts. Artie was reading a newspaper and Jeanie and Joey played with the jacks they had received from Santa, too absorbed to take notice of Sam. Paul, as usual, was the most observant of the bunch. "Hello, Sam," he said as he took a seat next to Marie, in front of the Christmas tree.

Sam scratched his head that was still damp from the snow. "I declare, this house is the toastiest since winter began."

Marie put her saucer and cup down on a table and nodded at her daughter. "You can thank Nancy for that."

Nancy smiled. "I used my bonus money to buy extra firewood. I thought this house could use it, even though I'm returning to Highland Park soon."

Sam chuckled. "It surely did."

"Hey Sis, I've been thinking of going with you," said Richard.

"What did you say?" asked Paul.

"I'm a man now, Pa. I can go to Detroit, get a job and help this family, just like Nancy."

Paul answered, "I never had a chance to tell you how proud I am that you defended this house, when the Citizens Alliance raided our home last week."

Richard smiled.

Paul looked at Marie, and then continued. "You're right. You are a young man now. I talked it over with your ma. You don't have to go to college, if you don't really want to go."

Richard hugged Paul. "Thanks for understanding, Pa."

Paul whispered in his ear. "I just want my children to be happy and alive. That's all."

After they broke away from their embrace, Paul took a drink, and then held a finger up to indicate his need to say something. "Richard, Nancy, it's not necessary for you to go to Detroit."

"But Molly sent me a telegram yesterday," Nancy said. She put her sewing down, stood up and put a hand on her ribs. She meant business. "If I don't return to work soon, I'll lose my job."

"Molly knows what happened to you at Italian Hall, doesn't she?" asked Marie.

"Sure she does, Ma. And she'll be here tomorrow morning. Molly is taking the train up here so I won't have to make the trip back to Detroit alone."

"That won't be necessary," Paul repeated. Jeanie and Joey stopped playing jacks. Even T-bone settled down on the floor. All eyes were on Paul. "I met with Peterman today."

"Why did ya do that?" asked Sam. His arm flailed and accidentally knocked down an ornament from the tree.

"After everything that has happened, I thought I should start a dialogue again with Peterman."

"Seventy-some people died because of those mine owners!" cried Sam.

"Sam—"started Paul.

"Paul, ya know the Citizens Alliance was behind the tragedy."

Paul nodded.

"Sam," said Nancy, softly. "I already told Ma and Pa that I think it was Russell who shouted fire."

"Are ya sure?"

"Pretty sure. He was covered up, but I saw his eyes. Ooh—those eyes. It was the same ones I saw when he attempted to harm me last spring."

"Paul, if Nancy is right, that makes it even worse. Ya can't negotiate with Peterman and his satanic nephew."

"If we return to work tomorrow and surrender our union cards, he'll only cut our pay by twenty percent."

"Yer jokin'." But Sam knew better. Paul's color was paler than usual. "They put us in jail just last week. Are ya sure Peterman would hire us again?"

Paul nodded. "Peterman's not happy with me, but he needs to rehire real miners to make Copper Empire fully operational once again." He gripped Sam's shoulder. "It's over Sam. We did our best."

"This fight ain't over." Sam scanned the room. "How do ya'll feel about this?"

The boarders yelled out, "I want to go back to work!"

"I'm starving!"

"We haven't worked since summer!"

Cece piped in, "Amen to that. When do we go back, Paul?"

"Tomorrow. January 1st. The start of a new year. We'll make it a better year, won't we, fellas?"

"Like fun we will!" shouted Sam. He turned from the parlor and fled up the staircase. He threw open his bedroom door and reached the dresser. With each drawer he opened, he grabbed items and threw them on the bed. Then, he began shoving his belongings into his luggage, all except one item. He gripped the edges of Millie's photograph and spoke aloud. "Millie, you'd be mighty upset if ya saw me now. I fought this strike with as much gumption as I got, just like ya did with yer illness." He put the photograph face down for a moment, and then turned the wooden frame over again to look at the image more intensely. "I used to be just like ya, never knew when to give up. Ya never stopped fightin' yer illness 'till ya died. But Millie, I've gotta quit. I wanna go home."

Sam's eyes watered, yet he continued to talk to the photograph. "I know what you'd say. 'No. It's never time to give up if ya really believe in what yer fightin' for.' What's the answer, Millie? What can I do for the miners? I helped get 'em into the strike. Oh, Millie, what can I do? Ya told me to go on livin', but even the woman I care for may marry another man soon."

Paul knocked on the open door, shaking Sam out of his monologue.

"Sam?" said Paul.

But the Southerner didn't answer. Instead, he continued staring at the photograph.

"Sam?" Paul called out again.

Sam gently placed the photograph in his overnight bag. He turned around and looked at Paul. He held back what tears he could. His anger was gone. "Seems like we have differin' opinions. My apologies for shoutin' in front of yer kids."

Paul took a seat next to Sam's rumpled clothes on the bed. "That's okay, Sam. I know you're upset."

"My outburst was about ya callin' off the strike. Copper miners deserve better workin' conditions and better pay."

"I believe that, too," said Paul. Then with a hushed and deliberate voice, he spoke again. "But we've been striking for over five months. Little Roberto's in heaven. Nancy's hurt. My house is falling apart. Sam, please understand, it has to end."

Sam leaned his elbow on the dresser, looking at Paul thoughtfully. "I cain't work for the twin devils again."

Paul nodded. "I don't want to work for Peterman or Russell, either. But, as Marie reminded me, 'Pride goeth before destruction, and a haughty spirit before a fall.'"

Sam's eyebrows pinched together.

Paul said, "You don't agree with Marie?"

Sam shook his head. "Not this time."

"What are you going to do, then?"

Sam quickly said, "I'm goin' home."

"Gonna go back to Charleston?" asked Cece, planting his burly frame near the doorway. "Have you gone loony?"

"No, I want to see sunshine again," Sam said. "I want to be happy again. I want to be near Millie."

"Who's Millie?" asked Cece.

Not answering Cece, Sam held out his hand to Paul. "I'll surely miss ya." Then, he offered his hand to Cece who accepted the handshake.

"It don't make sense, you leaving, when I'm getting used to having you around," said Cece.

Paul chuckled. "Why don't you sleep on it and decide in the morning? Have a good breakfast—"

Sam resumed packing. "My mind is made up. I'll be gone before sunup, even before Marie starts breakfast." Sam stopped packing for a moment and glanced at Paul. "I'll send ya the rent money I owe after I settle back in Charleston."

"I'm sorry your Northern experience is ending this way." Paul stuck out his hand to shake Sam's again. "I'll always value your friendship."

*   *   *

A mass of gray clouds hung in the sky as Paul and Cece somberly walked to Copper Empire. The miners congregated in front of Peterman's office window where Peterman sat at his desk, talking on the phone, with Russell sitting next to him.

Paul turned and stood in front of the miners to study them. The frigid air made their nervous breaths visible as it pulsed out of their noses and mouths. All of them carried their lunch pails, hungry to beg for work and receive pay again.

Paul stated quietly, "I'm sorry I couldn't do more for all of you."

One miner responded, "You did what you could." The miners nodded, apparently too tired and defeated to offer a differing opinion. Paul already missed Sam, who almost certainly would have had a more enthusiastic comment to make. He had hoped that Sam would reconsider leaving. True to his word, Sam didn't appear at the dining room to eat breakfast. Artie had confirmed that his former roommate had left so early in the morning that it was still dark outside. Paul sighed. His friend was probably already on the train, returning to a more hopeful life.

Paul glanced at the office and watched Peterman chat on the telephone, probably with a member of the Board. Paul looked above at the sign that read, "Copper Empire", as if to remind himself that he was waiting outside of the right mine. Almost half a year had passed since he had last mined for copper. The worst part of returning was knowing that he had to work for Russell again. Sam was right. He was the devil. He tried to harm Nancy, and he got away with it. Paul hated him.

With the cold air ripping through his mining jacket, Paul clenched his fists for added strength. He was ready to swallow his pride and return to work. What was taking Peterman so long?

Then, he watched a man with a long overcoat walk toward him. When the man was close enough, Paul recognized it was Artie.

"Hello," said Paul, his teeth chattering a bit. "What brings you here?"

Artie withdrew a small pad of paper and a pencil. "Marie informed me you would require my journalism services today."

Paul was confused. "She did? I wonder why she told you that?"

Artie furrowed his eyebrows, shaking his head. "You are terminating the strike, are you not?" He began writing, not waiting for an answer.

Paul's hands came together for a muffled clap. "Yes. We're just waiting for Peterman before we go back to work."

Artie stopped writing. "May I interview Mr. Peterman?"

"Sure," said Paul. "As soon as he finishes his telephone call."

Suddenly, Paul heard the office door open. He turned around to find Peterman leaving his office.

Russell and Peterman stood outside, with the latter stepping forward, using a slender finger to tip his hat to Paul. "Good morning. I hope everybody is eager to return to work. It has been a long time."

Paul nodded. "Why the long telephone call?"

Peterman shrugged. "I don't know. There are administrative rumors, but that won't affect us." He cleared his throat. "You will be happy to know that the Board has approved employing all of you again. However, as I already told Paul yesterday, there will be a twenty percent across the board wage cut."

"That's downright miserable," said Cece.

"Cece," said Peterman, with an edge to his voice. "You should be grateful, but if you are not, the least you can do is keep your antagonistic opinions to yourself."

Russell followed up and directed his comment to everyone, "If you can't be grateful for Copper Empire re-employing you after walking away from your job, you can leave now."

"Shut your trap, you man-child," said Cece.

"I'm going to make this clear for everybody," said Russell. "Uncle William put me in charge, so I'm your boss. Line up at the shafthouse, turn in your union cards and obey my orders. If you prefer to argue, you may return to the picket line and act like thugs."

"You're the thug—what you and the Citizens Alliance did to Paul's house," said Cece.

Russell interjected. "The Alliance and I busted the front door open and overturned some furniture. What I did to Paul's house, I did with the sheriff's blessing."

Paul turned to Artie. "Did you hear that? Our sheriff, who is supposed to be neutral, is a member of the Citizens Alliance—might make a good article."

Russell laughed. "All of the mine managers are members, Paul."

"Shut up, Russell," said Peterman. "Everyone, go to work." But no one moved.

"It doesn't matter if they know now, Uncle William. We're the law."

Paul snapped, "I could contact the governor—"

Russell replied, "You're naïve, Paul, if you think the governor can stop us."

Paul cut in, "I'm sure you've heard Clarence Darrow has taken an interest in the miners."

Russell laughed out loud. "That socialist lawyer isn't coming all the way to Red Jacket to sue me for home invasion."

Paul said slowly, "No, but he would gladly see you in court tried for murder."

Russell blinked. "Murder?"

"Nancy told me she's almost certain it was you who cried fire at Italian Hall."

Peterman raised an eyebrow. "Russell?"

"Where were you on Christmas Eve, around 4:30 pm?" Paul asked.

"Uncle William, pay no mind to his accusations."

"If it was you who did it—"Paul retorted.

"Prove it!"

Paul turned to Peterman. "Are you going to let him get away with it? Are you sure you want him to supervise and engineer this mine once again?"

Peterman looked unsure, but wouldn't answer.

"Hold it."

Only two words and Paul recognized the deep, authoritative voice as his wife's. Everyone turned around to look at Marie, wearing a bulky coat and a frown, followed by Sam.

Marie charged up to Peterman, carrying a letter in her hand. She threw the ripped white envelope directly into Peterman's palm. "Here," she said. "Read it."

The manager lifted the partially torn flap, withdrew the letter and read the correspondence.

Paul exclaimed, "Sam, what are you doing here?"

"Thought you were on a train going home," Cece barked.

Sam didn't answer, but he grinned.

Finally, Peterman dropped his hand by his side, dangling the letter before him.

Marie turned around to face the miners. "There has been a change in ownership," she said, spreading her hands outward to emphasize the miracle. "Mr. Peterman has been ordered to negotiate with all of you."

Peterman finally looked up, his features softening, although a noticeable twinge nervously stuck out on his left cheek.

"Uncle William, what's wrong?"

Peterman ignored his nephew. "Paul, I'm ready to listen to your demands."

The miners cheered, throwing their mining hats in the air. Paul turned around, lowering his hands to quiet the crowd. "Please, men. Let's get these negotiations over with." Satisfied that his men had quieted down, Paul stepped forward to the supervisor. "We ask for a seventy-five cent pay increase."

Peterman sighed. "I'm afraid that would close Copper Empire. I can grant a fifty-cent increase."

"Fine. We also want an eight hour work day."

"I will have to speak with the new owner, but I approve of your requests. The only concern I can't address is the two-man drill. In order to remain competitive, we have to work with the one-man drill."

Sam put his arm around Paul's shoulders. "We'll only go back to work if Paul is our new engineer."

Peterman hedged briefly, then nodded.

"Uncle William!" screamed Russell. "What about me?"

Peterman waved his hand and shook his head, indicating to Russell to shut up.

Paul scanned the miners' faces, and then said simply, "We'll return to work right now "

A resounding cheer filled the chilled air, miners grabbing on to one another for a bear hug. Tears streamed down their cheeks, laughter escaping their mouths. Their strike was over.

Peterman shook hands with Paul. "I must say, your family drives a hard bargain."

But Paul was confused. "Sir?"

Peterman turned to walk away, but he craned his neck for a moment, tipping his hat to Paul. "Good day to you."

"What's going to happen to me?" asked Russell.

"Find another job," Peterman walked away.

Cece tapped Russell's shoulder. Russell turned around and looked up at Cece's face. "Leave Red Jacket today and never come back again." Cece grabbed Russell's collar. "If I ever see you again, I'll throw you down the deepest mine pit. Your body will never be found and you'll be eaten by rats." Cece let go, then shoved him. Defeated, Russell walked away.

The miners cheered, slapping one another on the back.

Cece nudged his best friend. "Gotta wonder what was in the letter."

Paul twisted his head every which way, attempting to find his wife in the crowd, when he saw Nancy walking with a prominent-looking fellow accompanied by a photographer. Artie scribbled in his notepad when Nancy reached for his arm.

Nancy smiled. "I believe my mother told you to prepare yourself for a news story. This is your big chance." Nancy pointed to the man next to her. "This gentleman is an assistant editor for the Detroit News."

"Sir, I am Artie Cooper," he said, pumping the man's hand enthusiastically.

Nancy laughed. "He's also courting my cousin, Molly."

The editor said, "Mrs. Weyburn recently sent me an article that you wrote. I'm not guaranteeing anything, mind you, but I see a lot of promise in your writing, and so does the publisher. Please accept my offer of an apprenticeship with us in Detroit."

Artie looked at Nancy who bobbed her head affirmatively.

"Yes, sir. Absolutely, I accept."

Paul felt his daughter grab onto his arm. "Pa, isn't this wonderful? Artie's dream may come true after all."

Paul turned Nancy around so he could face the young woman he was so proud of. "And what about your dreams?"

Nancy shrugged her shoulders with a smile. "I haven't decided yet, Pa. One miracle at a time." She and Sam smiled at each other. "Artie told me this morning you were leaving for Charleston."

Sam lifted his hat and scratched his head. "Yer ma got me off the train after she got that telegram."

"You left without saying goodbye to me."

"Sorry about that. I would've written ya."

Nancy folded her arms and grinned.

"I'm here to stay. Wanna take a stroll with me, after work?"

Nancy nodded.

"Excuse me, but I have to speak with your ma," Paul said to his daughter. He tried to lift Marie and swing her around, but she was too heavy. Marie settled for a kiss instead.

Cece and Sam shook hands. Nudging Cece's arm, Sam said with a mischievous grin, "I'm gonna stick around Red Jacket a while longer."

Cece scowled, but with a twinkle in his eye, said, "I suppose one Southerner won't hurt the town." Sam shook his head, smiling.

Taking a quick break from his interviewing, Artie looked at Nancy, then twirled her around, unable to contain his excitement. "I really do love you, honey."

"I'm glad about the apprenticeship offer, Artie," said Nancy. "I really am. But our future together is uncertain. . .I'm going to need some time."

Artie gently touched Nancy's face. "After all the turmoil we have been through? I caution you not to throw our relationship away, Nancy."

Nancy touched her beau's cheek. "I haven't, but I've done a lot of growing up since the strike. I'm a different person."

"I—" Artie tried to explain.

Nancy put a finger to the journalist's lips. "I want to remain friends, Artie. That's all I can promise you right now."

Artie kissed her hand. "Very well, Nancy."

Sam interrupted them. "We all deserve a celebration, right Nancy?"

Nancy nodded.

"Too bad we don't have any food or drinks," said Sam.

"I'd drink to anything right now," said Cece.

"I'll propose a toast," Sam said. He whipped out his canteen bottle. "God bless America. . ."

Paul raised an eyebrow. He knew Sam would make a long-winded speech. The Weyburns, Artie and Cece all laughed. Sam, however, was getting very impatient. He was intent on concluding his speech, no matter how boring it would be.

Sam's face looked very serious. "Sh," he demanded. "Let me finish."

Everyone tried to quiet down.

Up went his canteen bottle. "To the success of Copper Empire. . ." Sam said.

Everyone grumbled, "Oh, no." The speech was never going to end.

Cece whispered to Paul, "What's gonna happen to all the other strikers at other mines?"

Paul shrugged. "I don't know, Cece. I hope the union can settle this strike for everyone soon." He sighed. "I can't solve everyone's problems, though. It's a miracle we settled." Paul faced the shafthouse and nudged Cece. "Let's go back to work."

"'Been waiting five months to go back to mining," said Cece.

A man in the distance walked toward Paul. As he got closer, he walked faster. Paul's heart began to flutter, then pound hard. Paul was curious, so he turned away from the shafthouse.

"Paul?" said Cece.

"Just a moment," replied Paul. His stomach tightened and his throat went dry. He tried to speak, but couldn't.

Cece asked, "Paul, what's wrong?" He shifted his gaze in the same direction as Paul's. Cece squinted, his mouth slightly open.

"What's wrong with all of ya?" asked Sam.

Cece nudged his best friend. "Good lord, Paul. Haven't seen him in twenty years. "

Sam yelled out, pointing at the man getting closer to the shafthouse. "Is he our new owner?"

"He sure is," Marie yelled. The miners clapped and cheered.

Sam approached Paul, asking, "Who's the new owner of Copper Empire?"

Paul managed to squeak out only two words. "My father."

THE END

About Donna Searight Simons

Donna's interest in the Keweenaw developed from her grandmother, Dorothy Carpenter Searight who was born and raised in Houghton, Michigan. Donna vacationed there many times during her childhood and adult years. In 1991, she met John "Cousin Jack" Foster, a local Keweenaw historian who told stories of copper mining and the tragic events that unfolded at Italian Hall. Donna was so intrigued by the local history that she began to write <u>Copper Empire</u>, a process that took more than two decades.

Donna has worked as an administrative secretary at Oakland University in Rochester, Michigan since 1994 and currently lives with her husband Ron in Macomb Township.

40395388R00180

Made in the USA
Charleston, SC
01 April 2015